Windproof
Beauty

Windproof Beauty

Roger Kirk

ROBERT HALE · LONDON

ISBN 978-0-7090-8702-1

Robert Hale Limited
Clerkenwell House
Clerkenwell Green
London EC1R 0HT

www.halebooks.com

2 4 6 8 10 9 7 5 3 1

For Isabelle, Iain and Rob

Typeset in 10/13pt Sabon
by Derek Doyle & Associates, Shaw Heath
Printed and bound in Great Britain
by Biddles Limited, King's Lynn

ONE

He was perilously close to the edge. Even on a calm day it would have been inadvisable. Today, in a gale, with the wind horribly violent and unpredictable, leaning out on tiptoe to try to see down the cliff face was downright foolhardy. He wasn't unaware of the risk though. Buffeted yet again, he stepped back smartly and turned away, almost tripping in the rough grass.

With his back to the wind he blew his nose and resumed the cautious exploration of his broken tooth. He'd been prodding it since Sleaford where his lift bought him breakfast. His tongue was sore. It had been embarrassing, having to spit everything into his hand in the crowded café. There, within his soggy, partly masticated bacon sandwich were fragments of amalgam and a shard of tooth, the latter an unlovely thing stained by years of tea and cigarettes.

He wondered, not for the first time, why it was that any unfamiliar cavity in your mouth felt the size of a gravel pit. Fortunately it didn't hurt much, Kathy's aspirins seemed to be doing the trick. He tried to think back to the last time he saw a dentist. It must have been at the camp in Market Drayton, all of nine years ago.

Despite his height and a posture that still owed something to his time in the army the man looked older than his thirty-nine years. Heavy smoking, a poor diet and lack of exercise had left him baggy-eyed, podgy of face and with skin the colour of an old handkerchief. His dark hair was combed straight back, greying at the temples and thinning in the early stages of baldness. The severe short back and sides did him few favours. Beneath the worn trousers of his Alexandre suit his legs were white and spindly and a burgeoning paunch overhung his waistband. Nobody saw him naked these days, other than Monica. Fully dressed he still cut something of a figure, he thought, not entirely unattractive to women.

Despite the aspirins he still had vestiges of a headache, but he'd been feeling scratchy since leaving home, legacy of a sleepless night and the early start. Also he couldn't shut out the maddening little voice that kept piping up that a wiser man than he would never have embarked on this madness.

He could have been ensconced this afternoon in his allotment shed with his mates, drinking tea, eating fig rolls and chewing over the latest in the sports pages, and all without the benefit of a broken tooth.

Leaving home without saying where he was going had been stupid. He couldn't remember now how the row with Monica had begun. It was probably money, or the lack of, the usual story. Why couldn't they have a proper holiday like other folk? What was so wrong with wanting a nice little car? Why hadn't he kept up learning to drive when he was in the army? Why? Why? Why?

He belched softly. The two pints of bitter and the cheese and onion rolls that Kathy had pressed on him at the Lord Nelson had been welcome, but they'd be with him for the rest of the afternoon. The bar hadn't changed much since the war. There was a new dartboard and the old curtains had been replaced. The sticky tape on the windows had gone of course, and the blackout blinds, but it all looked comfortingly familiar.

It was nice to see Kathy again and it had been really good of her to treat him. He'd noticed the landlord eying him up and down from along the bar. For a moment he worried that he looked that down on his luck.

He'd first met Kathy in the pub yard, thirteen years ago. They'd pulled into the Lord Nelson car park for directions to the depot. He was crunching across the gravel on his way to the public bar when she'd struggled out with a couple of boxes of empties. Her jaw dropped at the sight of the four lorries and the half-track. He'd helped her take the empties round the back and then offered her a cigarette while she gave him directions. He'd played daft, a bit slow, to spin out more time with her. She'd caught on though. She had those eyes that some women do, that seem to pierce your very soul. They give you a look and it feels as though they're scratching the inside of the back of your skull with long fingernails. Cool, appraising, blatantly sexual. She'd smelled good too. Having caught on she gave him a different sort of look, but they'd laughed together. He'd gone back to the lorry thinking he was on to a good thing. That evening though, Kathy had eyes only for Dave Holt. It hadn't bothered him greatly, especially after he and Ellen had exchanged looks. He was sorry to hear about Dave though.

There was a brief lull in the wind and he inched towards the cliff edge again. A ridge about seventy feet down obscured the beach directly below. The cliff was 226 feet high directly below Beacon Hill, a couple of hundred yards to his right. He had good reason to remember. He'd been up and down it many times. Often very, very carefully, with an anti-tank mine clasped to his chest. Each mine had been roughly fourteen inches in diameter and weighed about forty-five pounds. It was a heavy and lethal load.

The top section of cliff appeared passable enough. It sloped gently and didn't look too sticky. What it was like below the ridge was anyone's guess.

It could be a sheer drop. Even though he was braced, the wind almost caught him and he stepped back hurriedly. He shivered, turned away and huddled deeper into his fawn mackintosh. His cracked shoes let in the damp and cold. Twenty-nine and eleven from Stead and Simpson, but they were well past their best now.

If he was going he had better get on with it. The weather was worsening and it would get dark early. Glancing away to the right he could just make out a couple of arc lights twinkling intermittently at the depot. The sea was so rough that he couldn't make out what the tide was doing. From what he could see of the distant beach there seemed to be sand all of the way.

He wished he was already at the depot, inside the old tar-painted Nissen hut with its hissing lamps, the iron stove, large white mugs of strong tea, plates of toast and dripping. He'd missed it all, that and the camaraderie. Mind you, it was long ago. There was no telling what it would be like now. There was no guarantee that it would be the same. He was prepared for that though.

If he went down the cliff and along the beach he could be there in forty minutes. By road it would take twice as long. He'd be more sheltered on the beach too, under the cliffs. Still undecided, he glanced around. Heavy clouds muscled their way across the sky above him. Over the fields some 300 yards behind him, the Lord Nelson was no more than a dark lump. Away in the distance to his left the sky was black. It looked as though the rain was coming down in stair-rods and heading his way. The two lights twinkled invitingly to his right.

He took a tobacco tin from his pocket. Extracting a hand-rolled cigarette he smoothed it to his liking and then, cupping it with his hand, lit it with a worn Zippo. It was just as well he had made a couple at Ellen's. Rolling a cigarette in this wind would be something of a challenge.

He sucked in the blue smoke. The wind whipped it away as he exhaled. It had been great seeing Ellen again. He'd hoped all along that he might bump into her, but he wouldn't have been surprised if she'd moved away. When Kathy said Ellen lived in Back Lane and that she would be at home he could hardly believe his luck.

Ellen had been surprised, a bit flustered even, but that was natural enough. Like Kathy, she was still a very attractive woman, but in a less obvious way. If anything they'd both improved with age. It was almost impossible to see the scar now.

She must be in her early thirties. Suddenly he was angry with himself. How could he have forgotten? Tomorrow would be her birthday. She would be what, thirty-something, three? He'd have to try to get her a card or some flowers before calling in on the way back. No sign of any man. No wedding ring. There was just the boy, Peter. He seemed a nice enough lad. So was

Kathy's boy, Philip. He regretted giving them his change though. It had left him short. Maybe he could wangle a sub from Wormy at the depot. For a moment he toyed with the idea of trying to get off with Ellen somehow, but the wind caught him again and he staggered.

'Bloody hell!'

Simply standing upright was becoming almost impossible. Another fierce gust and a flurry of heavy rain spots helped make up his mind. Crouched, with his back to the wind the man pulled up his collar and tightened his belt. After a last drag on his cigarette he tossed it aside, straightened up briefly and then stepped over the cliff edge into the minefield.

In the early hours of 30 January 1953 an unremarkable depression measuring 996 millibars began to develop to the south of Iceland. It caused no comment until it began heading east and deepening rapidly. By the evening the depression was close to the Faroes. It had deepened to 980 millibars.

At 11.30 the next day, the Meteorological Office at Dunstable warned of exceptionally strong winds. By midday the depression, now measuring 968 millibars was centred over the North Sea. With each decrease in pressure of a single millibar the sea level had risen by one centimetre. It was a huge volume of water and it was being driven on by storm-force winds.

Within hours the east coast of England would experience the full force of an event reckoned to occur only once in every 250 years. In the late afternoon, the man descending the cliffs in North Norfolk was just one of many thousands of people without the benefit of this intelligence.

TWO

The sun promised all morning on Friday, 14 September 1979 finally broke through just after noon. It lifted the mood slightly but did little to raise the temperature. After some uncertainty and a couple of false starts Kathy Holt and Peter Fincham led the mourners away from the graveside. Kathy's son Philip accompanied Peter's wife, Abigail.

Kathy was just about holding things together. She was not only wretched with grief but also extremely angry. Losing her best friend was bad enough but despite numerous assurances the grave had been dug not in the old churchyard but in the recently opened extension next to the Churchfields building site. Instead of a sunny sheltered aspect beside the wall with the rest of the Fincham family the grave was the first in the new graveyard. It had been dug next to some temporary chestnut palings that were barely keeping the brambles and cow parsley at bay and it would shortly be overlooked by a particularly nasty chalet bungalow. It was not what she'd wanted for her friend.

Even though the day was now bright many of the women regretted their choice of footwear. The uncut grass was still wet and they were relieved to gain the cinder footpath that led through the old churchyard. The mourners clumped, clicked and tapped over the heavy wooden lid of the well and then turned right on to the worn paving that gave access to the church from the lych gate on Church Street. There they bunched, some reserved, some embarrassed, others impatient and most discomforted to some degree as they waited to be introduced to Peter Fincham, son of the woman they had just buried.

Peter and his wife had been late. On arriving at the church they had been dismayed to see the hearse already standing at the lych gate. Fortunately Philip was supervising. He'd given them a quick wave followed by some elaborate mouthing and gesturing. The undertaker recognized that a pause would be appreciated. So, under the incurious gaze of the bearers, Abigail not so much parked as abandoned her maroon Jaguar on the road foreman's sand and gravel heaps on a bank opposite the church. After quickly changing her shoes she and Peter then hurried over to take their places behind the coffin. The church was full. All the extra chairs that had been brought in were taken and there were still people obliged to stand at the back.

Kathy excused herself briefly *en route* to the lych gate to harangue the church warden. He'd affected surprise at her ire and explained that the old graveyard was full. Full meant no spaces.

'Only for some,' Kathy had railed, 'and there's no need to take that tone with me, Bob Watts.' Red in the face and quivering she had hissed that the next time he came scrounging for a bottle for the tombola he'd be getting salad cream rather than cream sherry. Moreover they could whistle for the buckshee sandwiches that she provided whenever they held a meeting at the Lord Nelson. Not that she wanted anything for them but they never so much as said thank you. If they wanted sandwiches in future they could pay for them like everyone else. 'Tit for tat,' she said. 'We can all be like that.'

'And you couldn't even be arsed to cut the grass properly. Look at this! It's a disgrace. Old Mr Bullimore would never have left it like this. I'm upset, Bob. It really isn't good enough.'

Through her angry tears she had watched him hurrying off to bleat at the rector but the churchman had given Kathy a furtive glance, waved Watts away and left for another funeral at one of the other of his churches.

Since few of the mourners knew Peter and his wife, Kathy and Philip did the honours at the lych gate. They were well known. Kathy had lived in the village all her life and was now landlady at the Lord Nelson and Philip had been back in the village for over a year and was a partner in a dental practice in Cromer. Everyone was invited back to the pub for a drink and a buffet afterwards. Most accepted since Kathy always put on a good spread.

Taking her place at the lych gate after giving Peter Fincham a quick hug and a kiss Kathy recovered her equanimity somewhat. Petite, with copper hair piled up beneath a small net hat she caught the eye in an elegant lightweight black suit and high heels. As usual she hadn't stinted on the jewellery and make-up and from time to time she wiped carefully beneath her eyes with her fingertips or the corner of a small white handkerchief. Beside her Philip, short, pink and dapper in a dark suit, blue button-down shirt and a silk tie was equally tearful. Peter and Abigail stood bemused, to Philip's right.

The mourners might have been forgiven for thinking that Peter had stopped off on his way home from an all-nighter. Tall and slim, with the hint of a stoop he had about him the air of a raffish academic. He looked as though he would be most at ease leaning against a doorjamb at a party with a glass of red wine in one hand and a cigarette in the other. His longish fair hair was untidy and his lightweight khaki suit was rumpled. The soft leather slip-ons, denim button-down shirt and loose oatmeal tie didn't quite fit the bill either. It was not really what one would expect of the principal mourner at his mother's funeral. Peter looked tanned and fit but weary, which was not surprising since three days earlier he had been working in Hawaii. He had flown from Honolulu to Los Angeles, spent a few hours with his head down in a motel near LAX and then caught an overnight flight to Heathrow.

Abigail had met him at the airport and they had driven straight to the church in North Norfolk. Unlike Peter, his wife did not have the look of one so employed for the last few hours. A small, dark-haired woman, tending to plumpness, she was immaculately turned out. She looked as though she had just been taken out of a *de luxe* presentation box and set down gently at the lych gate.

Once the line of mourners had expressed their condolences and passed through, small groups gathered on the roadside. Handbags snapped open and pockets were patted. Cigarettes and lighters were produced and funereal reserve was punctuated by the odd cry of recognition and a laugh or two, initially shushed and stifled but eventually ignored. Passage through the lych gate was a relief for most. It seemed to bestow consent for a dropping of gravitas in favour of a degree of lightness and humour.

'Hello, Tom. Hello, Frank.' Kathy greeted two elderly men in fully buttoned blue serge jackets that bulged over lumpy Guernseys. Both were bent and hobbling with the aid of gnarly sticks. Once longshore fishermen, they were brothers born and bred in the village and long time regulars in the public bar of the Nelson.

'Hello, my woman,' Tom bellowed. 'That was nice to hear a proper tune for a change. That'd be down to you and the boy?' He nodded at Philip. 'She'd'a bin well pleased.' His head bobbed up and down as he gripped Kathy by the hand.

'How're you a' holding up, gal?'

It was all Kathy could do not to snatch her hand away. She couldn't look at Tom's hands, terribly misshapen with arthritis and a lifetime of labour with freezing ropes, lines and saltwater and the right one missing the major portion of three fingers, caught in a drifter's winch over sixty years ago.

'Oh, you know.' Kathy shrugged and smiled determinedly for the umpteenth time that morning. 'I'm sad, Tom. But—'

'Good grief, your little hands are like ice.' Tom was eager to get on. 'It's normally me that feels it these days. That don't get any warmer in that church.'

'No. It's bitter. It's warmer outside than in. I shall be glad to get back home.' Kathy quickly withdrew her hand and cast a glance around the churchyard.

'You two are the last, aren't you, Tom?'

Tom had moved on and was shaking Peter by the hand.

'I remember . . . You and that other little bugger chucked sand all over my taters. Right bloody mess. You and' – he inclined his shaven head – 'what's his name? Philip.'

It was up to Frank to answer Kathy.

'Hello, my dear. Yes, we're the last.' The old man began to turn but became distracted. Kathy noticed a large white blob of Brycreem on the back of his left ear. It gleamed greasily in the sun. He tailed off uncertainly and stumped after his brother who had just made some wisecrack that was plainly incomprehensible to Abigail.

'No,' said Philip, 'here's someone else. Oh, it's Margaret.'

'Oh, that's nice of her. I thought she might have to work.'

'I saw her arrive. Smart new red Mini.'

A tall, pale woman elegantly dressed in a charcoal suit and wide-brimmed hat appeared at the foot of the church tower. She waved a brief acknowledgement and quickened her step.

'Sorry,' she called. 'Sorry to hold you up. I was just having a quick look at Father's grave.' She smiled as she approached. 'It's a disgrace. I'll need to come back sometime. Hello, Kathy. I love the suit.'

Kathy gripped Margaret's hands and shook them both.

'Glad you could come. Oh! Your hands are colder than mine.' She reached across her son and touched Peter's arm. 'Peter, Peter! This is Margaret, Margaret Graver, works at the convalescent home. She got to know your mum well.'

'Oh, yes.' Peter smiled and held out his hand. 'How do you do, Margaret? Thank you for coming.' He chanted the mantra yet again. 'Will you be joining us back at the Lord Nelson for a drink and a bite to eat?' Margaret took his hand, smiled and said that she would.

'Excellent. What part of the States are you from?' Peter regarded her quizzically.

'Oh, I'm English but I grew up over there.'

'Ah, thought I could . . . it'll be good to get acquainted.'

Neither Kathy nor Abigail missed the looks exchanged by Peter and Margaret. That they held hands longer than was strictly necessary and that Abigail was not introduced was not lost on them either.

The Lord Nelson Hotel was built during the 1840s. It was an imposing hostelry by any standards and was by some margin the largest property in the village. The fine white-painted three-storey building with its blue slate roof once offered over thirty bedrooms, many with a sea view. It also boasted a large dining-room, a comfortable lounge, a public bar and an off-sales counter. Behind the hotel were two lawn tennis courts and a bowling green and it was a short and easy walk to the cliff tops.

The first inn-keeper was also the village pump-maker and a wheelwright. It was he who had sunk a borehole and installed an iron water pump on the roadside opposite the hotel. Those living between Beacon Hill and Back Lane were obliged to fetch their drinking water from this pump. Some had to labour with their buckets over half a mile home before the belated introduction of a water main in the mid-fifties.

Before the interruptions of the Great War and later the Second World War the hotel flourished. Throughout each summer season it was invariably full, as were the meadows behind it where the landlord rented pitches to those with an inclination to camp on the cliff tops. During the wars the hotel continued to be busy and the bars came into their own. The Lord Nelson was famed for its Saturday night dances, held in what was once the dining-room. The pub also ran darts and bowls teams that contested local leagues. In front of the hotel a tall illuminated inn sign depicting the head and bust of Lord Horatio Nelson stood at the edge of the gravel car-park and the main coast road.

By the early 1970s the Lord Nelson was doing little in the way of hotel trade. The off licence and the dining-room were closed and there was little activity in the bars. The place looked and was, rundown. It began to improve in 1975 after Kathy took over as licensee.

This Friday lunchtime she had opened up the dining-room. By the time the mourners had gathered, a small contingent of black-clad helpers who came in on such occasions was hovering, awaiting Kathy's signal. The buffet was set up on trestle tables and there was quickly a determined line of eager diners, juggling wine glasses, plates, serviettes and cutlery.

Tom caught Kathy's eye. As she rounded the bar she picked up a couple of pint glasses and went to the pumps.

'I know. I know. You can't bring yourselves to drink wine or sherry. You don't turn your nose up at Christmas though, as I recall. You can have a pint each. Everyone gets a drink on the house. After that you'll have to buy your own.'

'Thank you, Kathy. You're a gentleman.'

'Yes, a mug more likely. And don't go advertising that beer. They'll all want some. Go and sit down and I'll bring it over. I'm going to put some more on that fire too. Is everybody warm enough?'

In due course Kathy delivered the glasses of beer.

'Bless you, Kathy.'

'Thank you, my dear.'

'I'll get one of the girls to bring you something over.'

Kathy was gone, gathering up empty glasses as she went.

Frank took a pull on his bitter. 'Lot of people.'

'Yes,' Tom took several swallows, placed his glass on the table and cleared his throat. 'Cars all the way down past the old school. It's always a good one if they're parked that far down. There were some big motors too. Humber, and I saw a Rover.'

'A Rover?' Frank shook his head. 'You show me a Rover boy, and I'll show you an idiot and a bloody awful driver.'

They each took on board more beer.

'How many do you suppose were there?'

'Hmm. Hard to say. I saw young Rollings putting out more chairs at the back. And they were all taken.'

'Yes.' Tom pulled reflectively at his large hairy nose. 'Bloody shame. Fair shook me, I tell you. No age, was she? Fifty what? Nine?'

Frank nodded. 'No, no age. And she was a lovely girl.'

'Kathy'll miss her,' Tom nodded at the landlady behind the bar. 'She's only just about holding up.'

They sipped in silence for a moment.

'How many were there, do you suppose?'

Tom thought for a moment. He shook his head slowly.

'Best part of several.'

'Oh, at least.' Frank nodded in agreement. 'Best part of several.'

Less than a couple of hours and it was all over. Kathy's helpers shared out the meagre leftovers and Philip ran Tom and Frank to the council houses at the far end of the village. The day had gone off, the weak sun giving way to mist and a thin drizzle.

'Let's go through,' Kathy shepherded Abigail, Peter and Margaret towards the public bar. 'It'll be cosier. Someone left the door open and that dining-room's never warm without the fire. I've never known it so chilly at this time of the year. Does anybody want another drink before I sit down for a minute? I shall be glad to put my feet up, I can tell you. Margaret, are you all right?'

Margaret smiled, nodded and held up a glass in which she had a dreg of ginger ale. She pulled a chair up to the fire.

'I'm fine thank you, Kathy.'

Peter drained his pint glass.

'No need to hurry. You can help yourself.' Kathy poked the fire then turned and stood with her back to it warming her hands behind her.' She looked down at Margaret. 'I'll make us some tea in a bit.'

'I never manage to get it quite right.' Peter moved round behind the bar. 'It'll probably be all head and no body. Anyone else, while I'm here? Abby?'

Abigail was still standing, holding her handbag and an empty wineglass.

'No. I've had enough.' She placed the wineglass on the bar. 'I must make a move. I'll tidy myself up and then I'll be off. Do you want to get your bags out of the car, or do you want me to run you up to the cottage?'

'Oh, are you off? I'll fetch my bags. Phil can give me a ride to the cottage.'

'Are you sure?

'Yes, absolutely.'

'Are you not staying, Abigail?' Kathy looked askance.

'No. I must get back. I need to be in the office in the morning. I'd like to get back in daylight if I can.' Abigail went to fetch her coat.

Kathy frowned. 'Why don't you stay here then, Peter? You won't want to be in that cottage all by yourself, surely. We've got rooms made up.'

'Thanks, Kathy, but funnily enough it's exactly what I do want. Phil said there's food and stuff. Just need some milk. I'll be fine.'

'Oh well, if you're sure. Take a bottle out of the fridge before you go.'

'I'm probably going to be here for a while. I've got a fair amount of sorting out to do and I haven't had any time off for ages. The company owes me a ton of vacation. I thought I might take several weeks, might stay till after Christmas.'

Abigail returned, putting on her coat. 'Thank you for everything, Kathy. I'm sorry I've got to shoot off. It would have been nice. . . .'

'Yes. Well, you take care in that big car. Mind how you go.'

'I will. I'll see you. . . .' Abigail put on her gloves.

'Yes, till next time.'

'Are you?' Abigail gestured at Peter, as she picked up her bag and made for the door.

'Yes, here I come.' Peter put down his glass and followed his wife. Abigail turned at the door.

'Bye everyone, thank you.'

'Bye, drive safely.' Kathy wandered over to the window as Philip returned through the bar from the back premises.

'Oh. Are they off already?'

'It's Abigail. Peter's staying at the cottage. That Tom and Frank safely back? She's not going to drive in those shoes, surely.'

'I should think not,' said Margaret, getting up and joining Kathy. 'They're very classy. Cost an absolute fortune. Mind you, she's very well dressed altogether.'

'Trade. That'll be why she's hurrying back. She's got a boutique in London and another in Brighton. Doing very well.'

Philip took off his jacket and loosened his tie. 'Frank fell asleep in the car. How much did he have to drink? I'm sure he has no idea where he's been.' Philip wandered over to the window beside his mother. 'It's chilly out there, for September.'

'Frank's looking very old suddenly. I think he's losing his marbles. Ah. She's changing them, pair of driving shoes. Panic over. I'd have thought she could have stayed. It was her mother-in-law's funeral after all. You'd have thought she could have made a bit more effort.'

'Yes. Well. . . .'

'Oh, I know, none of my business. Well, there she goes. No kiss, no wave, no nothing. Can Peter manage? Oh, he's only got a case and his coat.'

'I don't think things have been great . . . for a while. They live separate lives, virtually. Peter's away for months on end. I suppose we were lucky she came at all.'

Peter shuffled through the door backwards carrying a large blue vinyl suitcase, a pilot's case and a light coat.

'Have you got some warm clothes?' Philip asked. 'If you're going to be up here and the weather stays like this. . . .'

'Yes, thanks.' Peter put the cases down at the end of the bar and hung his coat on a peg by the door. 'I've got stuff at the cottage.'

'That case has seen better days.'

'Yes. I suppose I ought to get another. I'll go to Woollies while I'm here.'

Margaret was curious. 'I'd have thought you'd want something a bit better.'

'No. It's a waste. I got that one in Woolworths and it's been absolutely fine; had it for years. If you do a lot of travelling you really don't want to spend much on luggage. The airlines are going to wreck it anyway, if they don't lose it first. You might as well buy something cheap and cheerful and when it's done get another one.'

Peter sat down beside the fire opposite Margaret, took off his tie, rolled it up and put it in his pocket. He smiled at her and raised his glass. 'Cheers, first of the day. First beer anyway.'

Margaret raised her glass and smiled in return. 'To the future. Let's hope things improve.' They hadn't had much opportunity to talk other than for Margaret to say how sorry she was at Peter's loss and how much she had enjoyed her conversations with Ellen during their brief friendship.

Peter put his glass down and wiped his mouth. He looked over at Kathy who was now doing something behind the bar.

'I suppose no one spotted dear old Dad? He didn't deign to put in an appearance at all?'

Philip glanced up.

'My dad; Nick.'

'Oh. No. Or at least I didn't catch sight. . . .'

'Surely you didn't. . . .' Kathy was still preoccupied.

'Well, I thought he might. . . . If he was ever going to reappear he might just have turned up for Mother's funeral.' Peter stared into the fire. 'Perhaps he didn't know, of course.' He took another sip of beer.

'That reminds me.' Kathy finished straightening some beer mats on the bar and looked at Peter. 'I've got Ellen's things upstairs – you know, from the convalescent home. There's also a letter that came ages ago, in February I think. It was from America, Ventura in California, from someone wanting information about Nick. His daughter. . . ? Someone Stark, I think her name is. Said that she hadn't seen him, no one had seen him, since 1953. It was addressed to Ellen here, at the Lord Nelson. When I gave it to her she had a quick scan and put it away. She was a bit odd about it. There was a photo enclosed. Your mum carried it about for ages. She never got around to replying. She asked Phil to write a few days ago but . . . I only got to know what was in it after she died when we were going through . . . her things – you know. Shall I go and get it?'

'Well, it all sounds fascinating, but not at the moment, if you don't mind. I don't think I can. . . . I'll pick it all up tomorrow, if that's OK.'

'Yes, of course. You won't want to be bothering just now.'

'Do you remember this?' Peter put his glass down and reached inside his shirt collar. He fished out a silver chain. 'Phil?'

Philip peered at the silver coin dangling from the chain.

'Ha.' Philip crowed. 'You've still got it. I remember him giving us one each. I spent mine down at Annie's shop.'

'He gave me a two-bob bit. He gave you change. He said he was sorry that it was all in bits and pieces, but it amounted to the same thing. I drilled mine when I was about fifteen and put it on one of mum's old chains. This must be the fourth or fifth it's been on. It's the only thing he ever gave me.'

Suddenly embarrassed Peter stuffed the coin and chain back inside his shirt. 'Oh, well. It was too much to hope for after all this time, I suppose.' Again he stared at the flames. 'Over twenty-five years.' He shook his head.

'Tell you who I did see,' Philip said. 'Gilbert Reeve.'

'Oh yes, the proverbial bad penny.' Kathy had obviously spotted him too. 'He's been very ill apparently. I haven't seen him for years. How come we didn't see him afterwards?'

'He was at the back on one of those extra chairs they got out. Looked like a toad on a stick. I think he left straight after the service. He was with what's-his-name, used to be foreman at Pond Farm – Slack. They didn't come to the graveside. He didn't look well. Hugely overweight and breathing hard. Bad colour too.'

'Serves him right.'

'What about Robert?' Peter asked.

'No, he wasn't at the service. He won't actually know. He's out in the Far East somewhere. Going to be terribly upset when he finds out.'

'Hmm,' Peter said. 'I never fully understood the thing, whatever it was, between mum and Robert. Were they really close at some time?'

'Oh, surely you must have had some inkling.' Kathy rounded the end of the bar and came to the fire. 'They were soulmates from about the age of three, I should think. They should always have been together. It was a real shame.'

THREE

William and Amelia Fincham rented a cottage on the end of a row of four close to the corn mill. Ivy Cottage was one of a number of properties in the village belonging to Richard Reeve, the principal farmer and landowner who lived a couple of hundred yards along the road at Pond Farm.

Four years before Ellen was born, the farmer took William on to work with the horses. He had arrived with an excellent reference from a large estate in Westwick where he had been one of a number of stablemen. His wife Amelia was an able and experienced seasonal worker. Ivy Cottage went with William's job and, overjoyed with the improvement in their circumstances, the Finchams were initially very happy.

Less than two years later however William spent many months off work after being crushed against a wall by a farm cart. Eventually, after a lengthy convalescence he recovered sufficiently to return to work, but it quickly became apparent that he was not up to the rigours of his old job. Mr Reeve helped him secure work at the local sanatorium and offered to let the family stay on in Ivy Cottage.

The son of a farm labourer and the eldest of nine children, William was a strong-willed man. During their marriage, Amelia found him to possess a particular talent for cutting off his nose to spite his face. In the far corner of the small field beyond the back garden William kept a couple of pigs. At one time when George Ashley, the smallholder who owned the field was down on his luck, he offered it to William for 10/–. Immediately mistaking this opportunity for an attempt on the part of Ashley to do him down in some way, William rejected the offer.

However, there was no doubt about who ruled the roost at Ivy Cottage. Stooped and bent as a result of his injuries William was ever ready to snarl and bark at his family. Frequently in pain from poorly knit pelvic bones, his brown face was lined with disappointment and discomfort. Ivy Cottage was never free of the odour of liniment that Amelia rubbed into his body morning and night.

He began work at the sanatorium on the gardening staff but quickly took over as the carrier. With a well-mannered mare and a light cart he spent his days plying back and forth between the sanatorium, the railway station and the surrounding villages, fetching and carrying patients, goods and visitors.

Amelia never knew that she was the illegitimate daughter of a scullery maid. She had also never known her mother, since the poor girl had died of pneumonia at the age of thirteen, only months after her baby was born. The Seaman family in a neighbouring village took Amelia in, thus lending credence to the generally held belief that the eldest son of that family was her natural father. All her life Amelia remained ignorant of the fact that this was not the case.

Amelia was a pleasant but unexceptional child. While working in service in Westwick she met William at the market in North Walsham. After a short courtship they married and lived with William's grandmother. When John was born Amelia left service and did what she could in the way of seasonal fruit picking and helping with the harvest. She was also an accomplished seamstress. After William secured the job at Pond Farm and they moved into Ivy Cottage Amelia began to take in work from all over the village.

Mercifully, Amelia was in labour only a very short time with her second child. Her firstborn John had taken an age to arrive. Ellen Eliza was born before dawn on 1 February 1920. It being the Sabbath Day and Ellen arriving a full ten days early, Amelia took as a sign. She determined to go to church and give thanks when the weather was warmer. Given her daughter's propitious arrival Amelia was not in the least surprised when Ellen turned out 'bonny and blithe and good and gay'. She was an easy baby; she slept, she ate, she put on weight and she made no fuss. Happy and enquiring, Ellen did all the right things at the right time and in the right order. In short, she was a rewarding child, but not without spirit.

She grew up fair of feature, skin and hair but, as her mother never tired of pointing out her eyes weren't nearly as blue as those of her elder brother John. Ellen was almost sixteen before she realized that her eyes weren't blue at all. They were grey. John might have been blessed with eyes of the most remarkable azure but he too carried a burden throughout his teens after his mother opined in the presence of his friends that he would undoubtedly be bald by the time he was twenty. This intelligence was founded on Amelia's observation that like several of her brothers John had been cursed with the 'Seaman head'.

'You've got the same shaped head as our Norman and he started losing his hair before he was seventeen. And Tim was almost totally bald by the time he was twenty.'

The fact that her assumed kin Norman and Timothy Seaman suffered premature baldness was entirely irrelevant so far as John's head was concerned. The only boy in the village who went to the Grammar School in North Walsham snidely dubbed John 'Spunk-head'. Completely baffled, John endured the nickname until the clever one could contain himself no longer. After listening carefully to the explanation, John gave his tormentor a fat lip and not one but two dead legs. It was generally agreed thereafter that name-calling John Fincham really wasn't worth the candle.

Brought up in a strict but caring home, Ellen developed into a bright, articulate and attractive young girl. She worshipped John. Five years her senior he was big, strong, loyal and pleasant, if a little slow.

One day Amelia announced that they would soon have a baby brother or sister.

'That'll be nice for you, won't it?' she said to Ellen. 'It'll be someone for you to play with. You'd like that, wouldn't you?'

Over the next few months the three-year-old Ellen and her brother watched the growth of Amelia's belly with intermittent curiosity. Their father seemed more resigned than excited and grew angry when asked whether he wanted a boy or a girl.

In the event the newcomer was a brother. He too popped out promptly, but he was so sickly that he was named and baptized immediately. Against the odds, however, George Frederick survived after a lengthy period in Cromer Hospital.

Once home at Ivy Cottage the newcomer cried; he howled and screamed the greater part of each twenty-four hours. When he wasn't howling, he gurned, refused sustenance and yet somehow contrived to fill nappy after nappy. William took to spending long periods away from home. If he wasn't at work he was on the beach, fishing or beachcombing.

Amelia leaked milk and was tired and cross. Eager to escape their new brother's big square mouth and their mother's uncertain temper, Ellen and John made themselves scarce, seeking out the Reeve boys at Pond Farm or going to the beach. George eventually quietened. As time passed he grew into a plump, dark-haired, brown-eyed and watchful child, with a spiteful streak.

Growing up between the wars in a small seaside village in North Norfolk, Ellen's childhood was for the most part quite idyllic. There was the odd low spot but it was essentially a happy time. She knew everyone in the village and she had John to look out for her. She was also best friends with Kathy Priest from along the row and as she matured, a very promising friendship began to develop with Robert Reeve, the farmer's younger son.

By and large Ellen's aspirations were unexceptional. Early on she thought she wanted to train as a schoolteacher or a nurse. Amelia said 'That's nice, dear.' William guffawed, 'Don't be so bloody soft, gal. Don't let anybody hear you. You can get a nice little job down at the San, doing rooms or in the kitchen. Suit you down to the ground. You can go on your bike.'

It wasn't what Ellen hoped for, but since she didn't really know what she wanted she shrugged and said nothing.

It was in the romantic stakes that Ellen knew her mind. After exhaustive discussion she and Kathy both dreamed one day of falling in love, with the right man of course, then marrying and having a family. Ellen's thoughts were much on Robert Reeve, but she acknowledged to Kathy that she was much more likely to marry someone who worked for him. She and Kathy were agreed that three children would be perfect. Neither of them wanted a large family. Ellen's father had been one of nine. Mr and Mrs Priest came from families of twelve and five respectively. Ellen would have one boy and one girl, she decided. She wouldn't mind what the third child was, so long as it was healthy.

They hooted at the thought of Kathy seeing her husband off in the mornings. He would be riding an old lady's bicycle with his hand-me-down coat tied up with binder twine. His trouser legs would flap in the wind as he went off to the fields on the cliff tops. They shook their heads at the thought of a lifetime of topping and tailing beet, forking sheaves and hedging and ditching.

'Think what it would do to your hands,' said Kathy.

They agreed though that it would be pleasant to walk down to the corn-field during harvest to share tea in the late afternoon sunshine with their husbands.

Well aware of Ellen's feelings for Robert, Kathy teased her a little from time to time. She said that they were bound to live at Pond Farm after a big expensive wedding and a honeymoon abroad. Ellen could spot a potential fly in that ointment in the shape of Gilbert, Robert's elder brother, but she saw no reason to disabuse her friend. She enjoyed dreaming of living in the big flint farmhouse and being driven through the village in Dick Reeve's shooting brake. And she would like to go on their honeymoon abroad.

Robert had been to France twice and she was prepared to let him see to that side of things. Ellen did, however, assure her friend that she would never turn into a snob. She would always ensure that she gave Kathy a genteel wave and only a slightly superior smile as she swished past in the big shooting brake. For her part Kathy undertook to pull her bicycle well into the roadside when Ellen was passing and she would try to remember to curtsy and touch her forelock.

By the time they were fourteen Kathy was cycling every day to work in Norah's Noted Hair Salon in Cromer. Three nights a week she worked in the kitchens at the Lord Nelson Hotel. Ellen was still at school and working part-time at Pond Farm where she helped out with the chickens and the animals. She had given up any thought of teaching. Nursing was probably a more realistic ambition, but she would have to talk her father round and that wouldn't be easy. He wouldn't be swayed from the 'nice little job' at the sanatorium.

So in the mid 1930s Ellen and Kathy's hopes and desires tended more towards the mundane than to the exotic. A disinterested observer might have been forgiven for concluding that Ellen was set for an unexceptional life.

This would prove in time to be quite wrong.

The women and girls in the village had their differences. However there was one thing about which there was no argument, namely, that Robert Reeve was an attractive boy. With his thick black hair, vivid blue eyes and skin a shade or two darker than the anaemic norm of the rest of the male popu-lace he had huge appeal. He had an easy manner, an infectious smile and a greeting for everyone. Girls adored him and many confessed that they would have died for hair and eyelashes like those he had inherited from his mother Maria, who was half Spanish.

Ellen was first introduced to Robert when she was a toddler. It was a beautiful summer day but neither child was at their best. Amelia was work-

ing in the barn at Pond Farm and had taken Ellen, in the last throes of
chicken pox, along with her. Spotting the child at a loose end in the yard
Maria suggested that she go and play with Robert who was indoors in the
early stages of the same disease and feeling very sorry for himself. The children hit it off immediately and became very close. Thereafter they spent
much time together, at the farm, at Ivy Cottage and later further afield, at
the beck, on the beach or ranging over the local countryside. Ellen became
a regular visitor for tea at Pond Farm; Robert received similar invitations to
Ivy Cottage. For several years they were inseparable.

By the time they entered their early teens the relationship was becoming
rather more than mere friendship. In their clumsy fumbling way they were
growing much more aware of each other's physicality and eventually chaste
kisses were exchanged. It was that time of heightened senses and much
promise without the burdens of experience or responsibility. That summer
was one of sheer enjoyment as they grew closer together. In later years Ellen
was sure she could identify the very moment it all began to go wrong.

It was one sultry, sticky and airless afternoon. She and Robert were lolling
about under the willows beside the farmyard pond engaged in one of those
pointless, lethargic altercations that occur all too frequently while waiting
for a thunderstorm to clear the air. It was one of those occasions where
neither of them could help themselves. Robert was hacking a willow stick
into small pieces with a penknife and Ellen was dividing her time between
the gentle provocation of Robert, pulling the petals off a daisy and making
a fuss of a stray dog and feeding it biscuits.

'. . . soldier, sailor, rich man, poor man, beggar man. Oh, good, beggar
man. Either we're going to be very, very poor or I'm going to be marrying
someone else.'

'Mm. Give him the biscuit.'

'Do you want it? Silk, satin. . . . Oh, all right, you have it then, but you'll
have to beg for the next one.'

'Don't tease, Ellen. You'll make him cross.'

'Coach, carriage, wheelbarrow, muck-cart, coach, carriage, wheelbarrow
. . . Oh, good-oh, we'll be married in a muck-cart. That's handy. Come on
then, sit up. I'm not going to. . . .'

Ellen would keep on. She goaded both Robert and the dog further.
Eventually the dog snapped and bit her. Ellen screamed and clutched her
face. Robert leapt up and flailed at the creature, appalled at the two ragged
wounds ripped across Ellen's left cheek. Bright red blood was already
welling through Ellen's fingers. It ran down her arms and spread across her
lap. He managed to drag the dog off, but not before it bit him on the wrist.
As he shouted and flailed anew it darted away, finally taking fright and rushing off out of the farmyard gate.

Ellen's screams and Robert's shouts roused Mr and Mrs Reeve in the farmhouse. They both appeared at the run, anxious of face to meet Robert racing to find them. Seeing blood pouring through the shrieking Ellen's fingers, Maria sent her husband to find towels and Robert to fetch Amelia.

'We'll have to get her to the hospital, Dick. Quickly! She's losing a lot of blood. Bring the car.'

Ellen felt sick with pain and shock. She broke out in a cold sweat and lay down. Within a minute she had passed out, coming to in the shooting brake as they left the village for Cromer. Amelia cradled her towelled head in her lap.

Ellen reared up as they entered the hospital gates and panic gripped her for a moment. 'I don't want. . . .'

The next thing that she was aware of was the overpowering smell of anti-septic and the mask that they put over her face. She concentrated on the voice.

'Now, Ellen, I want you to count backwards from ten. Can you do that for me?' Ellen tried to speak but nothing came out. 'Ten,' she whispered, 'nine. . . .' Ellen counted with the voice, 'eight,' until her head was filled with brightly coloured concentric circles. They pulsed for a moment and then with a loud bang, everything became black.

'. . . severe wound . . . cruel to be kind . . . looks worse . . . flap . . . stitches . . . in time.' Ellen heard fragments as the reassuring male voice droned on in the distance. The smell of antiseptic was sickeningly strong.

She learned later that on returning to Pond Farm Mr Reeve had taken out a shotgun and he and Robert set out after the dog. They caught up with it on the cliff tops but things didn't go according to plan. The dog was over-joyed to see them. It raced towards them, greeted them warmly and then squirmed about on its back at Dick Reeve's feet. Shooting was out of the question. Frustrated they shouted and waved it away, but it wouldn't go. In the end they both got down on their knees and made a fuss of the creature.

Despite her injuries Ellen was glad that they hadn't shot the dog. She would have been surprised if they had. They never discovered where it came from or where it went. One of the farm hands spotted it days later heading determinedly east along the main coast road about eight miles from Pond Farm. Robert marched about for several days with his arm in a sling but in truth his injury was slight.

Some weeks later after the dressings were finally removed Ellen stared in revulsion at the horror peering back at her from the surgery mirror. Her eye was distorted, the outer corner sloping downwards and her mouth stretched upwards on the same side, exposing gums and the tops of several upper teeth. It not only gave her a horrible, knowing leer but also a tendency to dribble from the left side of her mouth. The bruising was going down but the ragged triangle of angry red scars on her cheek brought tears to her eyes. She looked doubtfully at the doctor when he rubbed his hands together, nodded and grinned. He was extremely pleased and said that she really shouldn't worry. The wound was healing nicely, rather better than he had anticipated. He would take the stitches out the following week and it would continue to improve and become much less noticeable in time. Amelia gave her a tight little smile and patted her hand but none of it convinced Ellen.

It took her a long time to recover, both physically and mentally. In the days immediately after the dressings were removed she took to hiding her face with her hair or her hand. It was Maria Reeve who persuaded her to dispense with the strategy. Maria was a stunning beauty and had been a mannequin in her youth. Not only did she look good but she moved with great poise and dressed with elegance. Whenever she was around Maria Ellen felt particularly ugly, frumpy and generally disadvantaged.

'It's not attractive, Ellen. People will think you're odd. It gives you a furtive look and it's beginning to affect your posture. Your head's always over to one side.' Maria demonstrated, pulling a face and exaggerating until she made Ellen laugh.

'Those scars look like nothing so much as the result of a duel,' she continued. 'You're tall, Ellen. You need to stand up straight. You must learn to walk your full height. Your scar makes you special, lends a little *je ne sais quoi*, a little mystery. Men will be intrigued. And in any event you can work wonders with a little make-up. You'll be quite a beauty when you grow up.'

One afternoon Maria took her upstairs and together they experimented with make-up. After they finished Ellen persuaded Maria to let her keep a little lipstick on.

'Aaaah!' Gilbert shouted, pointing as she appeared in the farmyard. 'Beetle blood! She's got beetle blood on.' The boys made vomiting noises and ran away. Ellen rubbed the lipstick off. Their reaction rather gave the lie to what Maria had said.

After the accident Robert was particularly attentive for a while. Amelia noticed.

'You two are very lovey-dovey all of a sudden,' she remarked to Ellen, who of course demurred. But Robert was behaving differently. They were quite used to touching each other, frequently hanging around each other's neck. But Robert had taken to pulling his arm around her waist and he had tried to kiss Ellen on the lips once or twice. Ellen had pulled away. Unable to purse her lips she couldn't respond and in any event she didn't want anyone kissing the mess that was her face. One afternoon beneath the willows at Pond Farm Robert fashioned Ellen a whistle with his penknife. It worked beautifully and she was distraught when she couldn't blow it properly to make it work.

The second setback to Robert and Ellen's burgeoning relationship occurred shortly afterwards. Maria was a keen and able horsewoman. She was accustomed to take her horse Rio out every morning around the local fields and lanes. With so much Reeve acreage at hand she had little need to leave farm property or cover the same ground twice. For most of the year she kept a few modest jumps set up under the beech trees in the paddock adjoining the farmyard. Once a year they were cleared away when the village turned out for the Reeves' garden party, but otherwise Maria usually finished off her morning exercise by taking Rio over a few jumps.

Late one morning two of the farmhands came across the horse standing alone in the yard. Rio was lathered and quivering and of Maria Reeve there was no sign. Mr Reeve was out but Ronnie Slack, the foreman, quickly organized a search party. By mid-afternoon Mr Reeve was back but there was no sign of his wife and the entire farm labour force was out. Eventually the hunt was widened and the police were called.

Arriving home for his tea and hearing the news Claud Mercer, the village knife-grinder parked his bicycle at his cottage and clambered through the hedge at the far end of the paddock to go to the farmhouse to offer his services. As he crossed the paddock in the gathering dusk he noticed something in a pool of water hard up against the foot of one of the jumps. At first he thought it was a piece of tarpaulin from the stack yard, blown by the wind. He admitted later in the pub that he nearly didn't bother going to look. Maria's body lay wedged beneath a jump in a slight depression, her torso almost completely submerged in a foot or so of water. Throughout the day numerous searchers had looked across the paddock, but both from the farmyard and the road nothing untoward was visible. The foot of the jump was out of sight in the dip. Maria's neck was broken and she had obviously been dead for some time.

The entire village was devastated. Maria had been well liked. It was Ellen's first experience of the death of someone close.

After the funeral Robert was sent away to join Gilbert at boarding-school. He was far from keen to go but Mr Reeve insisted. Robert and Ellen agreed that they would keep in touch during term time, exchanging letters and Robert would ask his father whether Ellen could accompany him on his visits.

After the boys had gone back to school the farmer was low for a long time. Never particularly robust, his wife's death clearly ripped at the very heart of him. He seemed suddenly always to be unwell. He had cold after cold. Then he was plagued with alopecia and an ear infection. A small dapper man who walked with a stick he shrunk into himself and his limp became more pronounced.

Numb at the loss of Maria, Ellen fell into a routine of going to the farm before and after school and she was there for several hours each weekend. She saw to Rio, the dogs, the cats, the donkey and the hens. She helped around the house and the farm buildings. Mr Reeve had Mrs Quantrill in three mornings a week and her husband did the garden but there always seemed to be plenty to do.

Ellen was in the back kitchen feeding the dogs one morning when the farmer came in with the post. Startled by a sudden sob she looked up. Mr Reeve was leaning on the window ledge clutching a letter, his face contorted, his head bowed and his shoulders shaking. He glanced at her as she stood up and moved to comfort him.

'Ah, lass,' he said, turning towards her. 'I'm so . . .' The letter was addressed to his late wife. 'I so miss Maria. It's just one bloody awful day after another at the moment.' Clutching each other they cried together until Mr Reeve pulled away and stood back from Ellen, holding her at arm's length. He looked at her face and passed a finger gently over her scarred left cheek. He shook his head sadly and gave her a wan smile.

'Look at us! What a pair of crocks.'

Then he grinned and slapped Ellen on the shoulder. 'Come on; brace up lass.' He made to leave, but turned at the door.

'Thank you, Ellen,' he said. 'I do appreciate what you've done. It means a lot.'

Mr Reeve eventually sold Rio, confiding in Ellen that he found the very sight of the poor creature distressing. The horse needed to be exercised properly and only Robert was ever likely to ride him but he was away. Despite having a horseman for a father and willingly feeding and grooming Rio, Ellen had never taken to horse riding. She quite liked horses, but if she was honest she liked them much better from behind a good stout fence.

She and Robert did rather well exchanging letters during his first term, but it was clear to Ellen that Robert wasn't happy. Mr Reeve was called to the school on more than one occasion to discuss the behaviour of his boys. She supposed though that it was entirely natural. Both Robert and Gilbert were distraught at the loss of their mother.

When Ellen left school at the age of fourteen William would hear no talk of teaching or nursing. It was time she grew up, he said, time to stop messing about and make a contribution. Amelia made tentative representations on Ellen's behalf but they were without conviction and she was not in the least surprised when she achieved nothing except to irritate William.

Ellen had an ally in Mr Reeve though.

'So you're leaving school then, lass.' Standing in the back kitchen one Sunday morning and blowing on his tea, the farmer looked at her over the rim of his cup.

'Yes, at the end of term.'

'What will you do?'

'I don't know. Find a job of some sort I suppose.' Ellen turned away to look out of the kitchen window. 'Father wants me to go to the San.'

'Hmm.' Mr Reeve nibbled a biscuit, sipped his tea and stared into the middle distance. After a moment he straightened up.

'Well,' he said, 'you don't need to make up your mind right away and I won't think any the less of you if you refuse, but why don't you think about coming here for the time being?'

Ellen turned back from the window. 'Oh?'

'Mrs Quantrill is getting on. She's finding the house a strain. You know the place well and you've got some knowledge of the farm. You always seem happy here. You could divide your time between the house and the farm until something better crops up. You're very young still and there's plenty of time to think about the future.' Mr Reeve smiled at Ellen. 'Take some time and think about it. There's no hurry.'

Ellen returned the smile. 'Thank you,' she said.

She pondered the farmer's proposal for all of half an hour. Catching him crossing the yard later she accepted his offer. He laughed.

'Are you sure, lass? You don't want to talk to Amelia and your father? You don't have to make a decision now. And we haven't discussed your wages.'

He was obviously pleased. She knew that she should have waited to put the idea to her father. Even though she was doing as he wanted he would be miffed. He would find fault somehow, but it had been an easy decision. Mr Reeve was right. She did like Pond Farm and she was very fond of him. She could still live at home and she would be able to see plenty of Robert during the holidays. What was wrong being paid to do something that she enjoyed?

One morning Mr Reeve appeared for his coffee accompanied by a short, stocky, pale girl with freckles and vivid ginger hair. Introducing her as Veronica Betts he said that Ellen would be spending more time in the fields throughout the harvest and that he had asked Veronica to keep an eye on her until she got the hang of things.

'You'll like Veronica,' he said. 'She's a hard worker, and she knows what's what.' Veronica stuck out a calloused hand.

'Ronny,' she said. A little older than Ellen, Veronica had worked full time on the farm since leaving school. Ellen had heard of her. She was reputed to be foul mouthed and had a nasty temper. Ellen had seen her about occasionally and was under the impression that Veronica was loud, opinionated and rather fierce.

They began working together during the harvest. The weather was fine ·

and sunny and they spent days within a few feet of each other moving steadily over the fields behind the horse and binder. They soon found that they had a lot in common and Ellen quickly warmed to her colleague. A farm labourer's eldest daughter, Veronica lived with her grandmother. She delighted in being thought the owner of a legendary temper and did what she could to foster the impression. However, removed from an audience she was kind and helpful. Ellen liked her enormously and they tried to work together whenever possible.

Ellen was not without friends of the opposite sex either. In the absence of Robert Reeve she went out with one or two of the village boys and eventually struck up an intermittent friendship with a lanky and rather strange boy by the name of Harry Littleboy.

'Wouldn't Gilbert have let Robert know that Mum had died?' Peter was slumped in one of the round-back chairs beside the fire in the public bar of the Lord Nelson. Margaret sat opposite, very upright in a similar chair.

'They haven't spoken for years. Not since Dick Reeve's funeral.' Perched on a stool at the bar Kathy stroked her nose reflectively. 'Robert was in here with your mum not so long ago. When was that, Phil?'

Philip sat in the corner on a bench beside the chimney-breast with his feet up.

'Oh, must be a couple of months, early August. Yes, just after the fête. They sat in the bay window all evening.'

'That was a funny thing too,' Kathy said. 'Ellen got a phone call from Robert early one morning, out of the blue, arranging to meet her here that evening. He's retiring apparently and wants to move back. He asked us to keep an eye out for a house. I don't know why he did that, he's got several estate agents looking out for him.'

'He is married, isn't he?'

'He was. He married an American woman, much younger than him, in 1972, I think. But it was all over three years later. Robert was very late getting married. He's over sixty now.'

'Has he got any children?'

'There were two, she had a daughter by someone else and she and Robert had a son together. They're still out in the Far East somewhere. The son must be six or seven by now.'

'Doesn't he own property here?'

'Yes, but it's our old cottages by the mill and those down Blackberry Lane. He'd hardly want to live there, would he?'

Peter yawned, stretched and cleared his throat. 'Oh, dear. Excuse me.' He yawned again.

'So why didn't Mum and Robert ever get married if they were so keen?

What went wrong?'

'Oh, it was when Robert went off to boarding-school. He got in with the wrong sort. And there was a bit of trouble. . . .'

Peter yawned yet again, ran his hands through his hair and rubbed his cheeks.

'Dear, oh dear.' He rubbed his eyes and then struggled upright in his chair. 'What was that, the trouble?'

'Oh, misunderstanding and mischief-making. I can't remember now. It was a long time ago. You'll be exhausted. Why don't you go and lie down for a bit?'

'Oh. I think I'll hang on, thanks. Get my third wind soon.' Peter stifled yet another yawn. 'I have to say everything seems a bit surreal at the moment. I don't know whether my arse is punched, drilled or countersunk.'

'Peter!' Kathy gave him a look but then smiled. Margaret tried to keep a straight face but then snorted with suppressed laughter.

'I'll have to try to remember that.'

FOUR

Philip made them all tea, after which he insisted that Kathy go to her room to lie down. When she had gone he poured himself a brandy and sat down with Peter and Margaret. The three of them carried on a desultory conversation until Philip fell asleep.

'Hmm,' said Peter. 'I was hoping he'd give me a ride.'

'I can give you a lift. Your stuff should just about fit in the back of the Mini.'

'Are you sure? It won't be out of your way?'

'No. It's Ellen's cottage, we're talking about?'

'Yes, Cowper's Cottage.'

'Why Cowper's?'

'Why the name? Oh, the poet William Cowper was around this neck of the woods at some point. He was a melancholic soul apparently. They sent him here to cheer him up.'

'Oh, really?' Margaret laughed. 'I could think of cheerier places.'

'Someone said he stayed in the cottage but he couldn't have. Mother's place wasn't built until 1851 or so. Cowper died long before that.'

'Perhaps there was an earlier cottage on the site.'

'There might have been. Not on any maps I've seen though. The four cottages at the top of Back Lane were the first to be built. I think it was just someone being fanciful.'

They stared into the fire.

'This is nice.'

'Yes, it is. It's peaceful.'

'It's been a trying day for you.'

'Yes.' Peter leaned back, closed his eyes and puffed out his cheeks. 'It's certainly been long.'

'You must be exhausted if you've come all the way from Los Angeles.'

'I am a bit pooped, I must say. But I did manage some sleep on the plane.'

'I've never been able to do that.'

Peter got up.

'Seeing Phil with the brandy, I think I might pour myself a small medicinal measure. One of the perks of the movie business is first class travel. It does make a difference on long-haul. And you can get some serious sleeping pills over the counter in the States. They'd be on prescription here. Well, you would know that. A pill, a gin and tonic or two and a meal usually does it for me. Can I get you a drink? You're not expected back, are you?'

'No, but I shouldn't. Perhaps just a very small one. Push the boat out.'

'Brandy or whisky?

'Oh. A whisky, please.'

'Excellent. I must remember to settle up. Cardhu? White Horse? Haig? What else have we got? Ah, Bells. Is Bells OK with you?'

'Yes. Thank you.

'Water?'

'Please.'

Peter found glasses, poured them each a double and returned to the fireside. He offered Margaret a small jug of water from the bar.

'You'd better see to your own. I tend to drown mine.'

'I'll have the same. I don't like it too strong.'

Peter added the water and passed a glass to Margaret. She smiled up at him.

They settled again either side of the fire.

'So, you met Ellen at the convalescent home?'

'Yes. She came to Cavell after her operation at Cromer. I saw her address and wondered whether she ever knew my father.'

'Who was your father?'

'Harry Littleboy.'

'Really?' Peter sat up and almost spilled his drink. 'Harry was your dad?'

'Yes.'

'Good grief.'

'I had some long conversations with your mum about him at the convalescent home. She said she knew him when they were young and then again
when he came back after the war. You'd remember that time, when he came
back, wouldn't you?'

Peter nursed his whisky with both hands and stared into the glass.

'I'll never forget the day Harry turned up.' He shook his head slowly. 'It
was Mum's birthday. I came home from school with a card I'd made in
handiwork and a necklace or a bracelet or something of that sort that Kathy
had been keeping for me. I picked it up at Phil's on the way home. I was
expecting a bit of a treat for her birthday tea. She always made a cake. When
I went in she said we had to be very quiet because there was a man upstairs
– in my bed. He was very ill. She'd been down here to phone the doctor. We
didn't have a phone in those days.'

'Did you see him?'

'Not right away. It must have been a day or two before I actually set eyes
on him. I thought at first he was my dad. I kept on about it until Mum got
mad. She said she had more to do than worry about my father.'

Cavell House was a rare surviving example of a nineteenth-century prefab-
ricated timber-framed building. It was set in a small valley among sheltering
fir and pine trees a short distance from the sea. In its time it had served as a
TB hospital and later a home for those with mental problems. Since the
closure of the San where Ellen's father had worked it had become the principal convalescent home in the area, taking most of the post-operatives from
Cromer Hospital.

It took Ellen a moment to remember where she was. Stifling a yawn, she
lifted her head and looked about. It really was a lovely setting and very
peaceful. Stretching gingerly and shifting in the wheelchair she wondered
what had woken her. A glance about the veranda confirmed that little had
changed. Wrapped in their blankets the others dozed, chatted or read.

She hadn't been asleep long. On the far side of the lawn in front of her the
old soul with the walking frame still struggled manfully towards the main
gate. After lurching forward a few inches he took several stuttering little steps
on the spot, a rehearsal for his next effort, always leading with his left foot.
His chin was thrust out aggressively and he looked hell-bent on escape.

It felt cooler. Some of the windows were open and the chill was probably what had woken her. The sun was hidden behind a heavier and darker
cloud than most of the light woolly jobs that dotted the blue sky. They were
all moving fairly purposefully towards the North Sea a mile or so away, so
the sun would reappear shortly.

Ellen hoped that she hadn't been snoring. Even soft lady-like snores were less than attractive in public and she suspected that there was nothing lady-like about her when she slept. She disliked sleeping in the afternoon. Presumably dozing today owed much to the general anaesthetic and her enforced immobility.

After carefully adjusting the blanket around her legs she opened the paperback on her lap at the airmail envelope marking her place. She fretted again over the loss of her leather bookmark. It must have gone missing at the hospital. She hoped she hadn't lost it completely. Peter had given it to her years ago as a Mothering Sunday present and she used it constantly.

She wondered why she couldn't see the print clearly and then realized that she wasn't wearing her glasses. Good grief, she was going off her trolley. She sighed and then smiled at a memory. She had been sitting on the doorstep at the cottage in the early afternoon, shelling peas. After a while she caught herself putting the empty pods into the colander and the shelled peas back into the basket.

'Oh, for goodness sake,' she exclaimed. 'What on earth do I think I'm doing? I'm going off my trolley.'

Peter was busy with a toy at the edge of the flowerbed close by. After a little while he spoke.

'Mu-um?'

'Hmm? Yes, pet?' Ellen glanced up. Peter hadn't raised his eyes.

'Can I come with you?'

'Hmm? Come with me where?'

'Can I come with you on your trolley?'

She had laughed out loud. Peter must have been three or four at the time. She wished he could come and visit, but there seemed little likelihood. He was always so busy. He had been abroad for months. She had hoped to go down to London early in the year to see him, but there was never a good time. Mind you, she wasn't all that keen on Abigail. Not for the first time Ellen wondered what on earth had been the fascination. The woman was attractive enough and she had been pleasant on the few occasions that Ellen met her. She suspected though that her son's partner was a driven woman and as hard as nails.

Perhaps she wouldn't persevere with the book. It was one of several she had been given for her stay in hospital. It was kindly meant but it wasn't her sort of thing. She wished she'd brought *East of Eden*.

The sun reappeared and Ellen settled back in the wheelchair and closed her eyes.

'Hello? Excuse me. Ellen Fincham?'

The voice seemed a long way off.

'Hello? Ellen? Are you. . . ?'

Ellen opened her eyes. She raised a hand against the sun and squinted up at her visitor.

'Hello?'

'Sorry. I didn't mean to startle you. Thought you were just resting your eyes; enjoying the sunshine.' The woman moved round so that the sun wouldn't be in Ellen's eyes. She smiled and dragged over a chair.

'Ah,' Ellen responded. 'As you get older you do tend to rest your eyes more.' They both laughed.

'Would you mind if I joined you for a moment?'

'No. Not at all.'

Ellen had seen the woman about the convalescent home. Tall and slim, she was obviously in a position of some authority. With her pale, almost translucent skin and well-cut dark hair she was quite striking in appearance. Her choice of jewellery was a little bold for Ellen's taste, but she was always immaculately turned out. A dark-grey skirt and white shirt were having an airing today. She wore a silver ring on each finger of her right hand and a substantial trio of engagement, wedding and eternity bands adorned the left. Her nails were immaculate, carefully shaped and painted a dusky pink. Spectacles hung from one of a couple of chains round her neck. Ellen thought she caught an accent, American probably, or Canadian.

'I'm Margaret Graver. I look after admin here.' Ellen's visitor put down a cardboard folder and made herself comfortable on a wing-backed chair.

'How are you? How is the. . . ?' Margaret nodded in the general direction of Ellen's lower half. It seemed to Ellen that her visitor had little idea which procedure the hospital had carried out. 'Are you reasonably comfortable?'

'It's not bad, thank you, a bit tender.'

Margaret nodded sympathetically. 'Mm, yes. It takes time. I'm sure the physios will have you mobile in no time.' They chatted for a while about the weather and holidays until Margaret glanced at her watch.

'Anyway, I'll tell you why I'm here, Ellen. It's nothing sinister. It's just that I noticed the address on your notes, and I wondered if you'd lived there long.'

'Oh? At Back Lane?'

'Do you mind?'

'Oh.' Ellen smiled. 'Longer than I care to remember.' She laughed. 'I first moved into the cottage in 1944. I think it was March. That would be . . . what, thirty five years, wouldn't it? But I've lived in the village all my life.'

'Ah! I thought it might be a bit of a long shot, but perhaps not.' Margaret fiddled briefly with her rings. She frowned. 'I wondered whether you'd remember a man who lived in the village years ago. Harold Littleboy? It's not a name you'd easily forget. He lived there before the war.'

Ellen was gingerly trying to settle more comfortably when she heard Harry's name. Attempting to lever herself up with her elbow she jerked and then gasped with the pain. It was a shock.

'Oh! Gracious.' She grimaced and closed her eyes. 'That was sore.'

Margaret half rose from her chair. 'Are you all right?'

Ellen found herself making a meal of trying to get comfortable. Harry? Why on earth had the woman brought up Harry?

'Perhaps I should go.' Margaret fidgeted with Ellen's blanket ineffectually and then sat down again, but only on the very corner of her chair.

'No, don't go. I tend to forget about it and then suddenly have good reason to remember. It isn't painful most of the time.' Ellen tried a reassuring smile.

'Yes,' she continued after a moment. 'I knew Harry very well.' She glanced up. 'Why do you ask?'

Even as she spoke Ellen knew the answer. Given the prompt she would have spotted it earlier. It was there in the hint of fine blue veins beneath the pale skin and the darkish smudges below the grey eyes.

'He was my father.'

'Of course; Margaret Littleboy. What a surprise. You're not unlike your dad. You were just a baby, the last time I saw you. Eve had you out in the pram. You were a pretty little thing.'

Margaret smoothed her skirt. 'I never knew Harry, my dad. I went back to the village years ago trying to find someone who knew him. That was when we found his gravestone. We didn't know until then that he had lived beyond the war.'

'He saw you, didn't he, before he joined up?'

'Yes, but I was only months old when he left. I don't remember anything about him. Mother had a few photos from when he was young.'

'How is your mother? Eve,' Ellen asked. 'Is she still. . . ?'

'Yes, she's still alive and kicking. Well, not kicking exactly.' Margaret snorted. 'She's got high blood pressure and trouble with her heart. She just got married again.'

'Ah. Eve always was one for . . . a surprise.' Ellen nearly said 'the men', but recovered herself.

'She lives in Florida now. She and Ray, that's her husband, live with Ray junior and his family. The son runs a trailer park. Mum and Ray spend their time fishing on the lake or by the pool. She's as brown as a berry. She keeps reasonably well, all things considered.'

Ellen struggled momentarily with the image of Eve fishing.

'You obviously lived over there. I thought I could hear an accent. Does she ever come back?'

'Yes, I've still got a bit of it. No. She won't come back now. Her parents died just after the war and she had no other family. I try to go over every couple of years or so. I was there last summer. Didn't suit me a bit, it was so humid.' Margaret paused. 'So you did know Harry, then?'

'Oh, yes.' Ellen smiled, and then she too paused, deep in thought. Margaret looked at her expectantly.

'Go on. Did you know him when he was a boy?'

Ellen pursed her lips and frowned for a moment. 'Yes. We were the same age and we lived quite close. We were in the same class at school, but I didn't really know Harry until I started work. He used to keep to himself a lot, with his bird-watching. Oh, and fishing. He was a bit solitary, not much of a mixer.'

'Ah. Would you mind telling me all about him, if I come back sometime? Someone told us that he committed suicide.'

Ellen frowned and shook her head impatiently. 'That's a bit bald. Things weren't quite that black and white.'

'Oh? I can't stop just now, I've got a meeting. But I really would like to know more, if you can remember; if you wouldn't mind.'

'Yes. I'll try to think back.'

Ellen watched her visitor leave, striding purposefully down the veranda. After pausing to have a word with one of the medical staff at the door Margaret turned and gave Ellen a smile and a quick wave.

Left to herself again Ellen looked at her watch. Tea wasn't for another half-hour. The sun was really quite warm. She was sleepy. The operation seemed to have knocked the stuffing out of her. She closed her eyes. A few minutes wouldn't hurt.

Poor Harry. Fancy seeing Margaret again after all this time. She had grown into an attractive woman. Nice clothes. Obviously coloured her hair. Bit nervy though. Ellen wondered what she would tell Margaret.

While they were talking Ellen's eye had been drawn repeatedly to the sliver of airmail envelope peeping out of the book on her lap. Now she almost took the letter out to re-read it but thought better of it. She really would have to stop equivocating and reply. After a while her blanket slipped a little and the book slid gently from her lap. It didn't disturb Ellen. She was a long way away.

The light rain that was falling when Ellen left Pond Farm had turned into a downpour by the time she cycled past the end of Back Lane. She was tempted to go straight home but she had promised Peter a treat for her birthday tea and there was nothing in. He was not going to be impressed by cheese, paste or sardine sandwiches so she was going on to Annie's in the hope that the shopkeeper might have a nice little bit of ham or tongue and a cake of some sort. There was an outside chance of a jam sponge. She could whip up a little icing and put a few cherries on the top. It wouldn't be as good as her homemade cake but she hadn't had time to bake and in truth Peter wasn't all that fussy. He probably preferred the shop-bought one anyway. He was also partial to Swiss Roll, especially the chocolate. If Annie had neither, which was entirely possible, she could usually be counted on for a Lyons Individual Fruit Pie. It wasn't Ellen's idea of a treat but Peter was very fond of them. She could make a jelly too.

As she rounded the bend by the church Ellen had to avert her face and close one eye against the wind and driving rain. She was almost on the figure standing at the roadside before she saw him. She started, yipped and wobbled. Recovering herself she freewheeled diagonally across the road towards the shop. Propping her bicycle against the wall she looked back. The man was standing motionless in front of the lych gate. His hat and mackintosh were dark with water but he seemed oblivious to the cold and wet. Ellen tutted and shook her head as she hurried round to the shop door-way. Anyone with any sense would shelter beneath the thatched lych gate. He'd be there for some time yet if he wanted a bus. There wouldn't be one along for a couple of hours, until the 2.17 p.m. to Cromer.

Ding-ding-ding-ding-ding. The brass bell on the back of the shop door swung crazily as Ellen went in. It made a deafening noise in the close confines of the tiny shop with its stone-flagged floor and marble-topped counter. She paused in the doorway and looked back at the figure. He hadn't moved. Perhaps he couldn't hear the bell above the rain. Annie had heard it though. The shopkeeper's face appeared at the net-curtain in the door in the far corner of the shop.

'Hello, Ellen. Are you all right? Is it still raining?' Stuffy smells of ciga-rette smoke, frying and comfortable squalor followed Annie into the icy confines of the shop. She was small, middle-aged and skinny with lank grey hair pinned up over her right temple. She wore a long, worn, pink cardigan over a faded pinafore and several layers of blouse and jersey. Her cadaver-ous face cracked into a flitting smile and she breathed dregs of smoke.

'Hello, Annie. I'm drenched. Look at the state of me.' Ellen opened the door again and shook her coat and headscarf quickly.

'That rain is like needles. It's bitter.' She paused and looked along the street at the figure by the church wall. The bell continued to jangle until she reached up to silence it.

'Have you seen that fellow by the church gate?'

'No. I haven't seen anyone. But then, I haven't been out since the papers before six.' Annie forced her way through the clutter and rounded the counter to join Ellen at the door. She had a quick look along the road.

'No. I haven't seen him before. He's not local, is he? Perhaps he's one of them refugees you hear about.'

'He almost frightened the life out of me when I came round the corner on my bike. I didn't see him until I was nearly on top of him.'

'He didn't do anything, did he? Or say anything?'

Ellen looked at Annie. 'No; nothing like that. I just didn't spot him. He made me jump.'

Annie shivered and rubbed her hands. She hurried back to her side of the counter.

'Blast, that's cold. Shut the door, girl. Keep the heat in.'

If anything it was colder in the shop than it was outside. Annie set about straightening a few dog-eared newspapers and magazines laid out on the counter. Lifting a buckled box of cereal and a jar of hair cream she looked at them in wonder before placing them on top of a card of plastic combs beside the scales. She paused.

'I tell you who he puts me in mind of, that fellow, the way he stands. What's-his-name, him that was married to Eve. Didn't come back from the war. He was a bit like that, tall and sort of stooped when he stood.'

'Harry?'

'Yes, that's him. He' – she nodded in the direction of the church gate – 'puts me in mind of Harry, Harry Littleboy.'

'Do you know? You're right.' Ellen frowned and went back to the door. The bell swung wildly again. She looked through the rain along the street. 'It does look a bit like him now you come to mention it.'

'That can't be. He was killed, wasn't he? Eve had a telegram.'

'Well, yes. But it wouldn't be the first time they got it wrong. Mind you, it is a bit late . . . .' Ellen peered at the man for a moment and then dashed the rain from her face. 'Whoever it is, there's something not right. You wouldn't stand out in this wind and rain with shelter just a few feet away, would you?' She considered for a moment and then made up her mind.

'I'm going to pop over there and make sure he's all right, whoever he is. We can't just leave him. There's something odd.' Ellen draped her coat over her head and shoulders and let herself out into the street.

'I won't be a minute.'

The bell jangled again as she pulled the door closed behind her. It was still raining hard. She held her coat up above her head, scuttled across the road and made her way along beside the churchyard wall towards the lych gate. The man hadn't moved.

'Hello?' Ellen called as she approached. 'Hello? Excuse me.' The closer she got the more convinced she became that it was Harry Littleboy.

'Hello? Harry, is that you?' Ellen put her hand lightly on the man's arm. With a jerk he turned towards her. Ellen's hand flew to her mouth as she recoiled. The man too shied away and dropped a sodden brown paper parcel from beneath his arm.

It wasn't Harry: it was Harry. Ellen stared. She took in the concave right cheek, the distorted mouth, the red and weeping eye and the battered nose. It couldn't possibly be Harry, surely.

'Oh. I'm sorry.' Ellen was flustered and upset. Of course it was Harry. Harry Littleboy; officially declared dead almost ten years earlier and now much changed from the man Ellen last saw the evening before he went off to war. He averted his face as again she put out a hand to him, but his good eye was watching. He seemed not to recognize her.

'Harry. It is you. Where have you. . . ? It's me, Ellen, Ellen Fincham. You remember me, don't you? Whatever's happened? Are you all right?'

She took him gently by the elbow and at the third or fourth attempt managed to steer him out of the rain and under the thatched roof of the gate. He shivered violently as he began to move.

'Where have you been, love? Where have you come from, Harry? Have you been here long?' Harry gave not a single word in reply. She fetched his parcel and placed it out of the rain by his feet. The brown paper was disintegrating. For a moment Ellen was at a loss as to what to do next.

'You'd better come with me. Come on.' She picked up the parcel, took Harry by the hand and led him across the road to the shop. He followed without resistance or complaint.

'Annie! Annie!' The bell jangled as Ellen pushed open the door. Harry shied away at the noise. Ellen reached up to silence the racket.

Annie's head appeared from below the counter. She stood up grimacing with her hands to the small of her back.

'What's up? Oh!'

'Annie. You'll never guess who this is. It's Harry! Harry Littleboy.'

'Harry? Blast, I thought he was . . . Well, where did you spring from?' Annie fought her way round the counter again.

'I don't know,' Ellen whispered, 'He hasn't said anything. I wonder what we should do. Do you think Gerald's at home?'

'I was just going to say, you want to take him round to Gerald and Olive's. That would be best. Olive'll be in, I should think.'

'Yes. I'll just get him comfortable. He'll be all right here, won't he?'

Ellen sat Harry down on a sack of carrots.

'There. You wait there a minute, Harry. I'll see if I can find your brother. You remember Gerald, don't you?'

'Hello, Harry.' Annie waved her hand at Harry. Getting no response she studied his face and wrung her hands. 'Good Lord. What have they done to him?' For a moment there was a look of compassion on her grey face, but then she wrinkled her nose and flapped a hand at Ellen. 'Don't let him drip over them postcards. They'll be ruined.' Annie was showing distinct signs of agitation. She backed round to her side of the counter. Ellen moved the rack of cards and forbore from pointing out that every single card was creased, faded or scratched. No one would ever buy them.

Annie stood for a moment looking uncertainly at Harry. 'I know. I'll make him a cup of tea. You'd like a nice cuppa, wouldn't you, dear?' She disappeared quickly behind the grubby curtain into her back premises.

'Yes. I'll be back in a minute, Harry,' Ellen took his hand. 'I'm just going to Gerald's. You remember. Hopefully someone will be in.' Ellen patted Harry's arm reassuringly and put her coat on. Harry gave no sign of hearing or understanding and began a soft repetitive whistle through his front teeth. He flinched at the bell again as Ellen opened and closed the shop door.

She splashed through the puddles, past the church and turned left into Cliff Road. Bottle Cottage, the first house on the right was home to Gerald Littleboy, some nine years Harry's senior and his wife Olive, their daughter Charlotte and a Pekinese named Tina. Ellen hurried up the path between the Littleboys' neat lawns and bare flowerbeds and rang the bell. Olive eventually came to the door in her dressing-gown.

'Hello? Oh, it's you, Ellen.'

'Oh, I'm glad you're in, Olive.'

'Well, I hope you're not collecting. I haven't any change. What can I do for you? I can't stop. I'm expecting the hairdresser in a minute. I'm all behind as it is.' Olive was a pale, thin, dark-haired and brittle woman. A malcontent, she had become increasingly sour-faced with the passing years.

'You're not going to believe this but it's Harry, Gerald's brother. He's round at the shop. He's not at all well. Did you know he was coming? Can you or Gerald come and get him?'

'What? Harry? Are you sure?' Olive was obviously not expecting her late brother-in-law. 'I thought he was. . . .' She stopped. 'Oh.' She paused. Wide-eyed and panicky, she began to retreat. 'Gerald's not here. He's up in Norwich all day, and I couldn't be doing with him, not with my head. Can't you see to him? We haven't room now anyway, what with Charlotte. . . .' Olive tailed off and backed into the hall, beginning to close the door. 'You can see to him for now, can't you? I'll tell Gerald to collect him when he gets back.' She made Harry sound like a bag of potatoes. 'I must get on now though.' Olive closed the door. 'Thank you, Ellen,' she said. 'Thank you. Goodbye.'

Ellen shook her head.

The rain eased as she walked back to the shop. She really hadn't expected any help from Olive and, if she was honest, she had no great hopes of Gerald either. They had never had any time for Harry when he lived with them.

She decided to take him home with her. She could at least get him dry and warm and she could feed him. He jumped and looked alarmed as she opened the shop door. She reached up and silenced the bell. Of Annie there was no sign.

'Come on then, Harry,' she said. 'Let's get you home and out of those things.' She called out to the shopkeeper and heard a faint answering yelp. Annie wouldn't return until Harry had gone. Taking him by the arm she led him out of the shop. He followed willingly enough.

By now the rain was no more than a spit in the wind. With Harry's parcel propped in her bicycle basket Ellen walked beside him along New Road and up Back Lane to Cowper's Cottage. Harry squelched along, whistling through his teeth and plucking at a button on the front of his coat. Ellen couldn't recognize any tune.

She quickly got a blaze going with a few pieces of kindling, then added some logs and filled the kettle and put it on. After taking Harry's coat and hat she removed the rest of his clothes and began to towel him dry.

'Oh, Harry. What on earth. . . ?' She was quite unprepared. Harry's back was a web of scars and weals. There were more on his arms, legs and buttocks. Pink, red, purple, blue, some raised and shiny. Ellen had never seen anything like them.

Concentrating on her task she talked to him quietly as she worked, in much the way that she had spoken to Peter when he was a baby. She wept, but she recognized that the scars were not recent. He had obviously been beaten, many times.

Harry stood quietly until she had finished. She wrapped him in a blanket then popped next door to the Hunts, gave Linda a brief explanation and borrowed a pair of Albert's old pyjamas. After getting Harry into them she hugged him and sat him beside the fire, then made him tea and toast. He ate and drank as though he hadn't seen food for days, stuffing the toast into his mouth and glancing about furtively, as if he expected it to be taken from him. While Harry ate she filled a hot water bottle and put it in Peter's bed. When Harry had finished eating she helped him up the stairs. As soon as he was in bed he turned to face the wall. Ellen closed the curtains and left him, leaving the door ajar.

Like the suit and coat that he was wearing, the few pieces of clothing in the parcel were soaked. As far as she could tell it was all in good enough order and clean. She stuffed his shoes with newspaper and placed them beside the range. After washing out his socks she hung everything else up to dry. There were no papers other than a sodden and disintegrating piece of travel warrant. It contained no useful information.

After checking that Harry was asleep she put the guard in front of the range, went next door to ask Linda to listen out for him and then returned briefly to the shop. She bought some ham, some raspberry jelly and three cream horns. Annie asked how Harry was and Ellen was polite but uninformative. She called in at the Lord Nelson and phoned Pond Farm to explain her absence. Mr Reeve asked if she needed anything and agreed that she should perhaps phone the doctor. Riding home she was glad that she was not the one that would have to tell Harry that his wife and daughter had disappeared years earlier. That job would have to fall to his elder brother, the odious Gerald.

FIVE

When he arrived home from school and Ellen explained Harry's presence Peter wasn't altogether convinced that the man upstairs in his bed was not his father. He took to marching about and whistling loudly in the hope that Harry would make an appearance. Ellen hissed at him repeatedly to stop and eventually threatened that there would be no treat if he persisted.

Philip eventually arrived for Ellen's birthday tea but it was a subdued affair. Ellen could be good fun when she put her mind to it but this evening she spent much of the time distracted and listening. If a voice were raised too loudly in query or laughter it was shushed immediately.

Following Ellen's telephone call to the surgery, Dr Hillier called round during the early evening. He examined Harry and later, on his way back from the hospital in Cromer called in with a tonic, eye-drops and ointment. He said that Harry had obviously had a terrible time in the past but he couldn't find anything particularly concerning physically. He thought it likely that Harry had suffered a severe breakdown and he was concerned that they had no information about him. He intended getting on to the almoner at the hospital in the morning to see whether she could discover anything about his recent past. For the time being he suggested Harry be given as much rest as possible. He promised to look in again on his way to the hospital in a few days.

Peter was astonished to learn that he would be sharing Ellen's bed. He wasn't particularly happy at the prospect, but it was only for one night, she said, two at most, and they would be nice and cosy together.

Gerald Littleboy came and went. Sewing by the fireside Ellen heard his Rover approaching. Two cars in one day, she'd be getting a reputation. Ordinarily there were few cars in Back Lane during the day – let alone at night. As usual he got Ellen's name wrong, calling her Eileen. He went up to see Harry and they spent a few minutes together. Ellen could hear his voice booming through the floor. He didn't stay long. There was nothing he could do, he said, when he came down. They no longer had room for Harry and anyway Olive's migraines ruled out any possibility of him coming to them. As he left he placed ten shillings into Ellen's hand and said that she should get in touch if she needed help with anything. Then he was gone into the dark in a miasma of scented hair oil, after-shave lotion and cigar smoke.

Kathy arrived as he was leaving. News of Harry's return was spreading through the village like wildfire and she said she needed to get it from the horse's mouth, so to speak. She also wanted to see whether there was anything she could do to help, perhaps to have Peter for a while. He could share Philip's bed. Ellen declined the offer however and they both stood at the bottom of the stairs listening to Peter still whistling and even singing from time to time in a hopeful manner. Ellen had to go up to whisper at him to stop. Harry would not be up until the morning at the earliest. Kathy stayed long enough for a quick cup of tea and then left expecting a good telling-off on her return to the pub.

They all had a poor night. Despite the cold Harry was beaded with sweat the first time Ellen was woken by his shouts and whimpering. She towelled him down, gave him a drink of water, tidied his bed and left a nightlight on the chest. Within the hour she was woken again by Peter looming over the bed and shaking her arm.

'Mum! The man.'

'What's the matter? Where have you been?'

'Downstairs. I was thirsty. The man said something.'

'What?'

'He spoke to me when I came back. The bedroom door's open a bit.'

'What did he say? Did he want something?'

'I don't know. I couldn't understand. He's smoking.'

'Well, he shouldn't do that. I'll talk to him about it in the morning. Come on back to bed. You've got school in the morning.'

Ellen could smell smoke from the cigarette.

In the morning Ellen found Harry curled up on the floor and covered only in a blanket. She helped him up into the bed and he seemed calmer. After taking him some tea and porridge she called briefly on Linda next door before walking with Peter to the bottom of the street for the school coach.

Mr Reeve enquired about Harry and said she was to ask if she needed anything. He remembered Harry as a boy, a strange lad skulking about the hedgerows with a pair of old binoculars.

Linda looked in on Harry mid morning. Ellen returned at midday and warmed up soup for him. He had obviously eaten his breakfast but he was fast asleep on the floor again at lunchtime.

Ellen did what she could to make Harry comfortable. After a couple of days in bed she got him up, washed and shaved him and settled him in front of the fire. Thin, gaunt and anxious he spent most of those first days at Cowper's Cottage sitting on a kitchen chair with his hands in his lap. He twiddled his thumbs and whistled through his teeth. Round and round, his thumbs chased each other, first one way and then the other. He had some difficulty seeing. He couldn't read print but he was able to look at the pictures in the paper. He quite liked listening to the wireless but he rarely reacted to anything that he heard. Ellen bought him some tobacco and he chain-smoked skinny little cigarettes and stared out of the window or into the fire.

Harry didn't sleep well and as a consequence neither did Ellen or Peter. Almost every night was broken, often several times by Harry shouting and crying out as he was confronted by his latest nightmare. After trying to settle him down Ellen often had to return to ask him not to smoke in bed. Both she and Peter were petrified that he would start a fire.

Word spread that Harry had returned and that his own family had virtually disowned him. The neighbours were wonderful. Some contributed clothes. Others brought food, books and magazines. Food parcels were left on the doorstep after dark, a bag of potatoes, a couple of cabbages, a string bag of tinned food. There was even the occasional rabbit or newspaper bundle of fish. Linda from next door came up with some underwear. A pair of bus driver's trousers, some brown leather shoes, black and white plimsolls and pyjamas arrived from a few doors down. Fortunately someone had the same huge bony feet as Harry. Others contributed a couple of khaki shirts and ties and a fine big cricket sweater arrived from Mrs Pope. Harry was so thin that nothing fitted properly. Ellen bought him a few other items at a sale in the school.

Harry gradually improved. He went for short walks and occasionally peeled a few potatoes or brought the coal in from the shed. He rarely spoke but he had the odd lucid and, for him, communicative moment. One evening as they sat beside the fire in the warm glow of the Tilley Lamp Harry began to talk. It was confused and halting but with a little prompting Ellen elicited a story that made some sort of sense.

Soon after joining up in 1941 he had gone with the Royal Norfolk Regiment to Cheshire and then on to Castle Douglas. Most of them were inexperienced travellers but they were all looking forward to service overseas. When they were issued with light khaki uniforms they assumed that they were off to the desert.

In Glasgow they boarded a ship that they called the *Drunken Duchess*.

Harry couldn't remember its real name but in crossing the Atlantic the ship lived up to its name. In Nova Scotia they transferred to an American ship, the *Mount Vernon*. They then headed down to Trinidad to refuel and provision. After that they went to Cape Town, Mombasa, Burma and finally Singapore. He went on a couple of expeditions into Burma where they were frequently under fire. Their nice light khaki uniforms showed up really well in the jungle.

In Singapore Harry went to work at Battalion HQ in Thompson Road where they were bombed and shelled by the Japanese Army until the order came for them to lay down their arms. He was taken to the Changi Barracks where for a time he worked in the cemetery.

After a brief spell in another camp he got dysentery. He was put on a train, sharing a truck with about thirty others, many of whom were suffering with diarrhoea. On arriving at their destination they were to be put to work building a railway.

At the end of the war he was in a camp up country to the north of Chungkai. The Japanese just disappeared one day. After a long delay because of bad weather he was flown to Rangoon and given a bed in the hospital. The first night there they gave him some rum.

He was on the first ship back to Southampton. He remembered that it was the *Corfu* and that there had been a terrible storm in the Bay of Biscay. After docking at Southampton he and several others caught a train to London and then another one to Norwich. He didn't seem to know what happened after that.

'So you were back in Norfolk in 1945 or '46?'

'I don't know. I remember a railway station. I just can't . . . after. . . .'

Harry said little about the time he spent on the railway. Since he was tall his captors picked on him. Only hours after arriving he had his nose and cheekbone fractured by a blow with a rifle butt. Cholera was rife and for weeks Harry was put to tending the pyre upon which the corpses of those who had succumbed were incinerated. The pyre was a twenty-four-hour operation. The Japanese were terrified of the disease.

Life was grim. Some days the prisoners received a meagre bowl of rice and a cup of water. Occasionally there was the luxury of a little dried fish or boiled vegetables. At other times there was nothing, and like many of his companions Harry was reduced to eating grass or trying to catch a frog.

One of the Malay guards took a particular delight in beating him. He invariably hit Harry in the face, deliberately targeting the cheekbone that had never properly healed. Like the rest of the workforce, in addition to receiving severe beatings at the hands of the guards he laboured day long in desperate heat and humidity. They all suffered over the next few years with malnutrition, chronic dysentery, ulcers and intermittent malaria.

Ellen could get no further except that Harry thought that he had been in at least three hospitals, some or all of them in Scotland. He didn't know how or when he went there. Ellen couldn't tell whether it was recent or not.

Appalled, she spent much of the evening in tears. She tried to talk to him about Eve and Margaret but it transpired that Gerald had told him that they had gone. It must have been almost their sole topic of conversation. Harry made no further mention of his brother or his wife and daughter.

He took to standing for hours at the bottom of Back Lane outside the cottage that he had shared briefly with Eve and Margaret. Kathy invited him in but he wouldn't enter the cottage so occasionally she took him a cup of tea. Dressed in his overcoat and hat and hunched against the wind he looked like a man waiting for a bus that would never arrive.

Ellen was right to be pessimistic about Gerald. He never called again. He pulled up beside her in the street a couple of times and gave her money through his car window. Ellen was appalled. What on earth would anyone think if they saw her taking money from a man in the street? But they needed it.

'Here. Treat yourself and young Harry. I know things can't be easy. I can't spare much but perhaps this'll help a bit.' She despised Gerald for his lack of interest and grand ways. She felt like throwing the money in his face, but in truth they could do with it. Harry had no identity card, health card or ration books. They tried to obtain an entitlement for him but the wheels ground exceeding slow.

At dinner Ellen struggled manfully with a rectangular piece of battered fish and eight pallid chips. The solid green lump of mushy peas was such an unconvincing shade of emerald that she left it untouched. Dessert in the form of crème caramel was better though. She had finished eating and was sipping her coffee when a movement at the door caught her eye. Looking up she saw Philip Holt's pink and freshly shaved face beaming at her from the doorway.

'You look very cosy.' Large, balding and immaculately attired in a light-weight suit and a multicoloured bow tie he looked more like a consultant than a visitor.

'Oh. Philip; how lovely. You made me jump. Have you been spying on me for long?'

'Certainly not.' Philip sauntered across, leaned over to kiss Ellen's proffered cheek and then sat down on the edge of the bed.

'How are you?'

'Hmm. I bet you have. I'm all right, thank you. This is a lovely surprise.'

Now in his mid-thirties Philip had grown up with Peter. They had remained very close until after a borderline result in the eleven-plus Philip went away to technical college while Peter attended the local grammar. Philip pulled himself together while he was away and eventually trained as a dentist. The boys had spent a lot of time in each other's homes and Ellen and Philip knew each other very well.

Philip had lived and worked in London for years and had returned to the village only recently after the death of his partner.

'Just a sec. . . .' Philip left the bed and went over to the door. After a moment he called along the hall.

'There you are. . . .'

'Yes, here I am; don't fuss.' Ellen could hear the clear, carrying tones and the click of heels. The mock cranky voice continued, 'I don't know how you can put up with us mere mortals . . .' The voice tailed off. Ellen smiled with pleasure. He had brought Kathy.

Philip reappeared with his hand at his mother's back. 'Here we are. I've brought the bride of Frankenstein to see you.'

'Surprise! And that's enough of your cheek, thank you.' Kathy wafted a hand at her son. She was resplendent in a cream trouser suit, gold jewellery and a multicoloured scarf knotted at her neck. As usual her hair was pinned up into a complicated confection.

'I wasn't lost,' she whispered to Ellen. 'I just needed the loo. I got a bit turned around when I came out. Anyway, how are you, dear? How was the operation? You're looking well.'

Ellen brought them up to date, both visitors smiling and nodding and then frowning sympathetically at intervals.

'Good, good. Well, that is good news. We brought a little something, didn't we Phil? Where are they? We didn't leave them in the car, did we?'

Philip produced a bag from which he took some grapes and apricots.

'Oh. Lovely.'

'Only the best for you.'

Philip carefully removed the grapes from a brown paper bag and placed them on the bed. He picked two and popped one in his mother's mouth and the other in Ellen's before pulling up a chair. He gave a little laugh and helped himself. 'Thought we might want to pick at them.'

'Yes. Thank you. Dig in. Mm, they're lovely and sweet. Seedless too, aren't they? I just fancy something like grapes. I've just had fish and chips.'

'Oh, I could just fancy a nice fish supper.'

'Well, so could I. It was arguably supper, but you'd be hard pressed to describe what they brought me as nice or fish. The fish was square and I swear it hadn't been near the sea this millennium. The chips weren't done either.'

Kathy looked wistful. 'Do you remember when the chip van came round? They were lovely on a cold frosty night. We've just had quiche with some other worthy stuff. Carrots, apple, salad stuff. Perfect rabbit food! Makes you want a fry-up just thinking about it, doesn't it?'

They chatted for a while until Ellen recalled her surprise meeting with Margaret Littleboy. As she related the incident Kathy squawked with astonishment and they spent some time recalling the scandal when Eve left the village.

Her visitors stayed for over an hour or so chatting and picking at the grapes. As they were about to leave Philip fumbled in his inside jacket pocket. He made great to-do of slipping Ellen a small flat bottle of Bells whisky.

'Help ease the pain,' he said with a grin and the knowing nod of a medical professional. 'I know you enjoy a small one now and again. Won't do any harm. Might as well put your tooth mug to some useful purpose.'

'You'll get me shot.' Ellen took his offered hand, patted it and smiled. 'Thanks Philip. That's far too much.'

'Think nothing of it. We good guys have got to stick together, haven't we?'

After her visitors had gone Ellen watched TV for a while. Several times her attention wandered to the book on the bed. Once during the adverts she picked it up and then put it down again. Eventually she switched the TV off and removed the airmail envelope from the book. She read the return address on the adhesive label in the top left corner again. *10981 W. Kiowa, Ventura, California, 93004 USA.* After staring at it for a moment she took out the letter.

Dear E. Fincham

I am writing to you largely out of desperation. My name is Louise Stark. I was born Louise Nichols in Leeds in 1939. My parents were Monica (née Oldfield) and Peter, or Nick (as he was known) Nichols. I don't know whether you ever knew Mother but I believe that you may have met my father during the war in Norfolk. This is something of a last ditch attempt to discover his whereabouts since nothing has been seen or heard of him since the morning of Saturday, 31 January 1953. You may remember it because it was the time of those dreadful North Sea floods.

He left home early that morning as usual on his bicycle. He was going to see to his pigeons at the allotment and then go on to work. Normally he would have finished at lunchtime and come home for something to eat before going to the rugby or the football in the afternoon. However, the night before he and Mum had had a row.

A dog walker saw him briefly at the allotment, but they didn't speak beyond saying 'Good morning.' The man didn't really know Father but he had seen him about. He said that he seemed normal and cheerful enough. Whatever happened afterwards, Father left his bicycle in the allotment shed and never arrived at work that day. No one saw him at all after the sighting at the allotment.

The police were involved. They searched for days, even digging up part of the allotment, but to no avail. Father still remains a missing person to this day. Mother spent years expecting that he would return. Eventually the stress made her ill.

After she passed away last year we found an old wartime pocketbook of Father's among papers in the loft. Your name, alongside the Lord Nelson's address, was among a number of others written in the back.

There was no indication whether you are male or female or that you lived or worked there. You may have been a guest. We have traced or accounted for all of the names in the book except yours. Sadly most are dead. Yours was a name with which no one was familiar and I am writing in the hope that you or someone at the Lord Nelson can throw some light on Father's movements or present whereabouts. I know that he was stationed in your area for a while during the war, but people who knew him from that time are few and were unable to help. He would have been 38 at the time. He will be 64 now.

I realize that after all this time the chances of even finding you are slim, but I thought I would have one last go at trying to obtain news of my father. If you are able to help with any information at all I will be delighted to hear from you. Please feel free to call collect (reverse charges). I look forward to hearing from you.

Yours sincerely
Louise Stark

Ellen rubbed the flimsy paper between her thumb and forefinger as she read the letter again. She looked once more for the telephone number but it was nowhere in the letter. Louise had obviously omitted it.

The last time Ellen had seen Louise's father was when he left her cottage late in the afternoon on that very same day in 1953. She had no idea of the present whereabouts of Nick Nichols.

'We've let this get a bit low.' Peter prodded the fire. 'It doesn't feel that cold to me but if we let it go out Kathy will have a fit.'

He took a couple of hardwood logs from the basket beside the fireplace and placed them on the embers, wiggling and poking them until one or two promising fingers of flame appeared. Wiping his hand on his handkerchief he stood up. After stretching he picked up their empty glasses and walked round to the business side of the bar. He gestured with the glasses at Margaret.

'Small one?'

She shook her head.

'I'm not sure I should have any more. I've got to drive home. Drinking at lunchtime always sends me to sleep.'

'You're not going to let me drink alone, are you? Not this day. You haven't got to be anywhere for a while. Couldn't you manage the merest smidgen?'

Margaret laughed at Peter's wheedling tone. 'You're a thoroughly bad influence. Just the very merest then, and make sure you top it up with plenty of water, please.'

'I will.' Peter busied himself with the Bells optic. 'I have to say Margaret; I do appreciate you sticking around like this. I know it's a funny thing to say given the circumstances but I've really enjoyed this afternoon.'

'It has been pleasant. It's been good to have a rest for a change. I don't know how you're still awake though.'

'Curiously, I don't feel too bad. I felt awful earlier, especially when we were driving up in the car. I couldn't stop yawning.'

Peter returned to the fireside and after handing Margaret her drink stood with his back to the burgeoning fire.

'Good health.' He sipped his whisky.

'Cheers.' Margaret got up briefly, straightened her skirt and then sat down again.

Margaret poked her head round the door to Ellen's room.

'Hello. Are you decent?'

'Oh, Margaret. Come in.' Ellen was sitting up in bed with a newspaper.

'I've got a little while. I thought I'd see how you are.'

'I'm glad you did. I've been thinking about your father.'

'Oh?' Margaret sat down in the chair by the bedside.

Ellen laughed. 'I was remembering his terrible haircut.'

'Really?'

'It must have been when we were in our mid teens I suppose. My brother John knew him better than I did. He was always fishing down on the beach until he went off to work in service and Harry was often down there. He was a great gangling and awkward thing by the time I got to know him, well over six feet but he stooped.'

Ellen laughed again. 'But it was the hair. For a while he had the worst hair-cut in the world, a real knife and fork job.' She paused a moment and frowned. 'He had it cut on a Sunday morning by old what's-his-name, can't remember, in one of the sheds in his garden at the top of Back Lane. There were bullock sheds up there at one time. The previous owner hanged himself in one.' Ellen paused.

'Harry was really nice once you got to know him, but he was no great pin-up in his teens. He was pale and spotty and his ears and Adam's apple stuck out. He wasn't what you'd call a graceful mover either. His hands and feet always seemed too big for his body.'

'I can see how you spotted the resemblance. Look at these.' Margaret held up her hands, looked across and laughed. 'They're like bunches of bananas.' She went back to fiddling with her rings.

Ellen studied her visitor. 'Your complexion is similar to Harry's, but there's probably more of Gerald about you in looks.'

'You obviously knew Gerald and Olive?'

'Oh, yes. I'm sorry but I never liked them. Your father was very much in awe of Gerald. Of course he was much older than Harry. By the time Harry was sixteen Gerald had inherited Bottle Cottage, their father's house, and he had his own business.'

'What was it that he did?'

'He had an insurance agency in North Walsham. He did quite well I believe. And, of course, he was married to Olive. She was an only child. Father was a builder and she was not without a bob or two of her own. When Gerald inherited the house he got your dad as a sitting tenant. He and Olive were less than delighted. They moved your father out of his bedroom into a poky little room at the top of the house. And he had to pay bed and board.' Ellen paused for a moment, staring into the middle distance.

'By all accounts it was unsatisfactory for everyone. Olive made his evening meal but he had to see to his breakfast and do his own cleaning, washing and ironing. He always had Sunday lunch with them, but Olive was a rotten cook. She had the cabbage on by eleven in the morning for one o' clock lunch and she only ever bought cheap meat. Harry said the food was awful.'

'What did he do before he joined up?'

'He worked in the hardware shop in the High Street in Cromer. It's still there.'

'I know the one.'

'He used to bike to and from work on a big, upright, black bicycle. A Raleigh I think it was. I saw him sometimes in his shop overall. He used to smell of creosote and paraffin, and something else – soap and mothballs.'

'Hmm. That would have the girls falling over themselves.'

'Poor Harry. He was shy, especially with girls. I don't think he spent much time with anyone though. He was a bit of a loner, happiest with his own company. He was nice though, taught me no end about the countryside once I got to know him.'

It was in the evenings and on Sunday afternoons that Harry Littleboy put hardware from his mind, tucked his trouser legs into his bicycle clips and set off in pursuit of his particular passion. Armed with a pair of binoculars and a small canvas bag that together comprised his inheritance from his father; Harry was transformed.

If he was unexceptional in other respects he excelled in the role of countryman. Just like his father Harry loved the natural world and from a very early age had witnessed some rare and wonderful things. One bitter morning, battered by the wind and stinging sand, he had watched seals giving birth on the beach. When the tide was right he could find crabs beneath the clay shelves in the lows. He could literally pick these large and bewhiskered crustaceans out of the pools with one hand.

Harry had seen hares boxing on the cliff tops and had watched a vixen and her cubs in a sandy hollow on the railway embankment. Deer were generally believed to be nowhere in the vicinity but Harry watched them regularly. He had seen a squirrel swimming across the pond in the woods near the beck and had witnessed the odd sight of a female duck perched high on a branch in a tree. He had stood silently above a pair of hedgehogs copulating at his feet in the dark by the pit at the end of Back Lane. Harry had seen a coypu in the same pit years before anyone ever acknowledged that they were in the area.

One night, as he was returning from watching bats, he had been astonished, and in truth more than a little frightened, when the darkness was lit up suddenly by a splash of searing blue light as something huge hurtled across the sky from behind him. Whatever it was Harry was under the impression that it landed in the next field or the one beyond it. With thumping heart he clambered up banks and forced his way through hedges to see if he could spot where it came to earth. Thoroughly excited when he arrived home, he had told Olive about it but she was more interested in her magazine. Days later he read in the paper that it was thought to have been a meteorite that had glanced off the earth's atmosphere and, far from landing locally, it had plunged on at several thousand miles an hour deep into space.

But Harry was lonely. He had no one with whom to share his interests. Known for years as 'Little Harry Boy', his contemporaries continued to ridicule him long after they had all left school. He tried to interest one or two in his hobby but devising ways to harass or kill birds and animals exercised them more.

Harry envied the other boys in the village their easy ways with each other and with the girls. He tried drinking and smoking and for a while he swore with a will but none of these helped. Harry had no real friends and little likelihood, as far as he could see, of ever having any.

SIX

Every weekend Harry endured Gerald and Olive's idea of a traditional Sunday lunch. The misery began in the cold, dusty and grey gloom of the Bottle Cottage sitting-room at 12.35 when they gathered in 'good' clothes for a pre-prandial. Gerald poured Harry and Olive a small glass each of sweet sherry and as ever remarked that he couldn't stomach the stuff himself. With a sigh of resignation he reached for the Haig and poured himself a large whisky and soda. Once Gerald was ensconced in his chair so began the weekly interrogation of Harry. Neither of his inquisitors had any real interest in him, what he thought or what he had been doing, but Olive felt the need to keep up the appearance of such. Throughout lunch Harry was subjected to an hour or more of goading, baiting and unconstructive criticism, some blatant, some veiled.

Sunday lunch was served promptly at one o'clock. It commenced with a bowl of greasy brown soup and a few off-cuts of elderly white bread. This was followed by a stone-cold Willow pattern plate bearing a sliver of grey meat and gristle, water-logged cabbage and potatoes boiled to the consistency of poorly mixed wallpaper paste. Olive invariably covered Harry's plate in a slather of glutinous brown liquid which immediately began to separate into minute drifts of khaki silt surrounded by pools of clear fat that cooled rapidly to form glistening white tidemarks.

The meal concluded with a baked apple so sour and full of bones that Harry was usually forced to give up on it. Eventually, as they brought the meal to a conclusion over cups of milky tea, Gerald and Olive's eyes became heavy and they lost interest in grilling Harry. Gerald divided up the pages of the *News of the World* and he and his wife pored over them, reading out the occasional titbit until they fell asleep. After clearing the table and washing the dishes Harry gathered up his bag and binoculars and let himself out.

One Sunday afternoon Harry was zigzagging slowly down the far reaches of Back Lane towards Bluebell Woods when a female figure on a bicycle appeared in the distance, heading towards him. A year or two earlier he would have turned tail but he was more or less over that.

As the figure drew closer he recognized John Fincham's sister. He knew Ellen from school but they had never had much to do with each other. He had seen her once or twice in Cromer and in the currant field with her mother, Kathy Priest or Veronica Betts. She always smiled and said hello. He didn't find Ellen frightening. Kathy scared him a bit but it was Veronica who was really threatening. She could reduce him to a gibbering wreck with no more than a look.

As she approached Harry, Ellen slowed, put her feet down and scuffed to a halt just past him. Slipping off the saddle she backed up and gave him a grin, still slightly lopsided. Beneath a blue cardigan she was wearing a pale-blue skirt and a white top. She had a white ribbon in her hair. Despite the warm afternoon she looked cool and attractive.

'Whoops. These brakes are past their best. Hello, Harry.' She flapped her cardigan. 'It's warm. I'm not sure I need this.' She removed the hand-knitted cardigan, folded it neatly and placed it in the wickerwork basket on the front of her bike. 'Where are you off to?'

'Hello, Ellen.' He was careful not to call her Ellie. He'd heard someone say that she didn't like it. He smiled and felt his face and neck redden. It was a pleasant feeling. 'Thought I might go through Bluebell Woods and then down to the beck. See what's about. What are you up to?'

'Oh, I just wanted to get out. Father's back is playing up and it's miserable at home. It's too nice to be inside anyway. I was going up to Veronica's on the off chance, but she's probably with her granny or her mum. We haven't anything arranged.' She wrinkled her brow slightly. 'Do you mind if I tag along? I haven't been to the beck for ages.' Ellen put her head on one side and smiled in what she considered to be a winsome fashion.

'Can you actually still get down the lane from the woods? It was overgrown the last time I saw it. Mind you, that was ages ago.'

Harry felt a flush of pleasure. He was overjoyed. He wanted to fall on Ellen's neck with gratitude but he had learned that affecting coolness was the better option.

'I don't know. It's some time since I've been down there. They may have cut a way through. We could manage the bikes between us, though. And if it's too bad we can always come back and go the other way.'

Ellen wheeled round in the road and paddled her bicycle along beside him. Their Sturmey-Archer hubs clicked almost in unison. It was hot enough that little bubbles had appeared in the tar and they meandered out of their way occasionally to pop them.

They negotiated the Bluebell Woods without any difficulty. The lane however was a different matter. Manhandling their bikes much of the way they eventually arrived at the far end hot and red in the face from exertion and laughing. They were both prickled and scratched. Once out of the lane they cycled the short distance to the beck.

'Can you see the bull?'

'No.' Harry was reassuring. 'He hasn't been down here for a while.'

'We can paddle in that bit where the cows go down to drink.'

The beck had been popular with local children for years and it remained one of Harry's favourite places. A shallow stream issued through a wooden sluice from a sizeable pond deep within the woods. Sluggish ditches bordering the trees joined the main stream before it took a dogleg course through a picturesque meadow. The meadow itself was bounded on three sides by mixed hedgerows established hundreds of years earlier. It sustained several ancient oaks, a few clumps of downy thistle and grass kept neatly cropped by a few good-natured cows. A tumbledown cattle shed stood in one corner. Very occasionally the farmer turned a bull out into the field and it paid to check since one or two visitors had found it prudent to leave the meadow at a brisk trot.

The stream left the meadow by means of a culvert beneath the road. It then took a direct course across arable land heading towards the sea. As it crossed Reeve's farmland it was transformed briefly from the shallow and unassuming beck into a wider, deeper and statelier watercourse. Although never particularly impressive it was at its widest just before it rushed through another culvert beneath Mill Road where it provided power for the corn mill. At that point the stream was only yards from Ivy Cottage.

Leaving their bikes against the fence, Harry and Ellen made their way across the meadow. They took off their shoes and, at Harry's behest, placed them neatly side by side well back from the water's edge. Harry had once seen the beck transformed into a torrent when without warning the gamekeeper had opened the sluice gates.

At the water's edge they picked their way carefully through the muddy holes made by the resident cows' hoofs and paddled, gasping at the sudden cold. Their feet were white and bony in the fast running water. Harry was excited to see that Ellen had pink painted toenails. Gathering up the side hem of her dress she tucked it into the legs of her knickers and bent to take a tentative sip from a cupped handful of water.

'Is it all right to drink?'

'Yes, it's clean. It's lovely.'

'Oh, it's cold.'

Walking with some care on the stony streambed they slowly made their way upstream and round the bend towards the woods where the banks became steeper. Harry lurched after a stickleback with his bare hands.

'Did you catch it?'

'It's almost impossible without a net. Would you like to see the pond?' Harry nodded towards the woods beyond the footbridge.

'There's a sign. Isn't it private?' Ellen looked a little anxious.

'Yes, but we're not doing any harm. There's no one about. It's good. Come and see the fish. There are loads of them.'

'Are you sure it's all right? We won't get into trouble?'

'Well, we need to keep an eye out for old Gooch, but he's usually all right. He only gets cross when he's got young pheasants or there's a poacher about. He knows me well enough, and he'll probably be at home anyway. He doesn't go far on Sundays.' Harry and the gamekeeper ran across each other quite often.

He helped Ellen up the bank and they crossed the footbridge and sluice gate into the woods. Lowering the hem of her dress Ellen wondered whether she would need her shoes. Harry thought not.

Where it had been warm and sunny and the insects had chirruped and ticked in the meadow it was cool, dark and still as they pushed their way through·a tangle of rhododendrons towards the pond. It was almost forbidding in the wood.

'Here, Harry.' Turning, Harry was delighted to see Ellen's flapping hand. He took it carefully. With Ellen following him he picked his way through the rhododendrons, the grasses and cow parsley. Flushed with pleasure that coloured his neck and cheeks Harry dare not look back. Despite thinking that his face must look like a beacon there was a detached part of him that saw something quite different. He was a skilled North American Indian scout, singled out most particularly for a perilous mission and entrusted with the care of a uniquely precious thing. He moved with exaggerated stealth, careful to ensure that there was no possibility of Ellen coming to harm.

Despite Harry's best scouting technique they were both startled by the sudden clatter as a pair of wood pigeons fluttered out from an ivy-clad elm above them. But there were no further alarums and they were back in the sunshine as they reached the pond's edge. With no obvious need to continue holding Ellen's hand Harry let go. To cover his confusion he searched his pockets urgently for a handkerchief and then made a business of blowing his nose.

He was relieved to see that the water in the pond was clear. They walked carefully along the bank until, returning to scout mode, Harry lifted his hand and motioned Ellen to be still. He pointed out a shoal of roach keeping station a few feet from the bank. As they moved on Harry spotted a couple of perch deep among the roots of a horse chestnut that was growing on the very edge of the water. The smile of delight on Ellen's face was gratifying. Emboldened by her warmth, he took her by the hand again and led her along the path by the water's edge, pointing out an old swan's nest on the far bank and the remains of a couple of coots' nests.

'Let's see what else we can find,' he whispered. Hand in hand they tiptoed towards a fallen tree that stuck out some distance into the pond. It was a good place for a pike. Harry scanned the water below the jumble of twigs and branches but he couldn't see anything. He pointed out a freshwater clam close to the bank. A little disappointed, he was about to move on when he made sense of something that he had looked at and rejected several times. It was a very large fish, much bigger than anything that he had seen in the pond before.

His eyes wide he pointed to the sleek brown shape lying at an angle to the tree.

'Pike,' he whispered excitedly 'beside the log. Look at the size of it. Do you see it?'

At first Ellen couldn't make it out. Harry explained patiently exactly where it lay.

'It'll be one of those that old Gooch talks about. He's always said that there are some big ones in here. I never really believed it, but that one must be twenty-five pounds or more. It's monstrous.' It took Ellen a moment or two and further whispered instructions before she saw the creature. Harry knew she had seen it by her sudden sharp intake of breath.

'Oh,' she gasped. 'I see it. I see it. It's huge. I didn't know they grew that big. Isn't it beautiful?' Her eyes were wide and shining. Harry felt a rush of tenderness toward Ellen as she turned and smiled. They were so close that he could clearly make out the tiny holes where the surgeon had stitched her cheek. Almost in slow motion he saw himself taking her in his arms. More than anything else in the world he wanted to kiss her and hold her close.

Ellen suddenly jumped, dropped his hand and gasped.

'Ouch! Oh, I've been stung.' She had backed into some nettles. Grimacing and biting her lip she bent to rub the back of her knees.

'I wish I hadn't done that.' Ellen jigged up and down. Harry found his handkerchief and dipped it in the pond. He wished it had been clean and neatly folded.

'Here. It'll take some of the sting away. We'll get you some dock leaves. I saw some by the sluice.' Harry looked one last time for the pike. Unsurprisingly it had gone.

As they returned he picked a couple of dock leaves, wrung them, folded them into a rough pad and gave them to Ellen. By the time they had made their halting way back to the bikes the leaves were beginning to work their magic. While she sat on the grass and tended the nettle rash Harry fetched his bag and a small poke of sweets from the basket on Ellen's bicycle. They lay side by side on their fronts nibbling biscuits and sucking humbugs.

Ellen told Harry a bit about Pond Farm and he reciprocated with tales of the more bizarre customers at the hardware shop. Ellen said that one day she hoped to get into nursing. Some people were talking about war and if it occurred it would probably present her best chance. Until then her father wouldn't hear of it.

'Oh, no you don't, my girl. We'll have none of your highfalutin ways here. You can forget that as soon as you like.'

She mimicked the old man, although not unkindly. They both laughed.

'I haven't seen John on the beach for a while. Is he still over at Hanworth?'

'No, he's down in Epping now. He's general handyman for a Colonel Bell. I wish he wasn't; I miss him. He doesn't get home very often. He wrote that he'd been in London a week or two ago.' Ellen paused. 'I'd like to travel one day too, see a bit of the world,' she continued. 'Have you ever been anywhere interesting?'

'No. I've never been out of Norfolk.'

'The Reeves go to France. It sounds fun.'

'Do you see much of them, Gilbert and Robert?'

'Not really. Robert is rarely at home these days. He's away at school and then off with his friends to the south of France or Italy. Some of them have yachts and houses down there. He's got very pompous. Gilbert's just a pig.'

'You used to spend a lot of time together, didn't you, you and Robert.'

'We did, once. I suspect I'm not really good enough for him any more.'

Harry pulled a face and shook his head. Not knowing quite what to say he chewed on a grass stalk.

'Do you like watercress?'

'Oh, yes. We all do.'

'There's a small bed on the other side of the road. It's hard to get at so not many people know about it.'

'Shall we go and get some?' Ellen prepared to get up.

'Well, the only way is through the culvert. The nettles and brambles are too bad on the banks over the other side. Can you manage it, do you think?'

'I don't see why not. It's not too long, is it? It's only the width of the road.'

They entered the water at the cows' drinking place. Ellen had momentarily forgotten how cold the water was. As they arrived at the entrance to the culvert she crouched low and looked through it. 'It's a little tunnel. I can see sun glinting on the water on the other side. It doesn't look far.'

'Do you want to go first or will you follow me?'

'You go first. I'll hold your hand.'

Crouching double Ellen followed Harry into the culvert. Suddenly it was dark and chilly. The water was icy on her shins. Her hair brushed the slimy roof of the culvert and something fell on to her arm.

'Ooh! What was that?'

Harry took another few steps.

'Oh, I don't like this, Harry. I'm going back. Sorry.' Ellen dropped Harry's hand and stumbled backwards out of the culvert.

'Are you all right?' Harry stopped and half-turned. 'Ellen?'

'Yes. I'm fine. I'm sorry. I'll wait here for you.'

'I'll see you in a minute.'

Harry continued alone and eventually returned with two bunches of watercress carefully bound with reed. Ellen was lying flat on her back in the sun as he clambered up the bank towards her.

'I don't think anyone's been there for a while. Here we are.' Harry gave Ellen the larger bunch. 'No one eats it but me, and this is plenty. Rinse it well before you eat it.'

Harry scuffed around in the grass a little to dry his feet.

'I'm going to have to go in a minute, Harry. I've got to call in at the farm to see to the animals.'

They returned slowly to their bicycles. The sun dipped behind the woods and cast long shadows. It was cooler. Ellen placed the watercress carefully in her basket and put on her cardigan.

'Are you coming my way?'

'I can if you like. Otherwise I'll come as far as the railway bridge and then I thought I'd just nip down Heath Lane to the old barns. There's an owl down there.'

'Oh, you must go and see the owl. I'd come too, but I really should be getting back.'

Harry was sorry that the afternoon was coming to an end. It occurred to him rather belatedly that he had just shot himself in the foot. Ellen smiled at him as they mounted their bicycles.

'Thank you, Harry,' she said. 'It's been a lovely afternoon. I've really enjoyed it. It was fun and nice to see the fish. And thanks for the watercress. We'll have it for tea.'

They cycled side by side as far as the railway bridge where they stopped and gazed out over the railway cutting after the Cromer train. Ellen leaned over and kissed Harry quickly on the cheek and then set off up Back Lane. Harry waited on the bridge ready to wave if Ellen should turn before she was out of sight. He was more than gratified when she turned and called 'Bye, we must go again', and waved not once, but twice before she disappeared from view.

'Harry was quite different from most of the other village boys.'

Margaret smiled and nodded. She looked pleased and then craned her neck to look at Ellen's watch.

'Good Lord, look at the time.' She stood up quickly. 'I must be off. I'm going to be late.'

'Oh, I'm sorry. I've kept you from your work. I've enjoyed our chat though.'

'Heavens, it's not your fault, Ellen. I lost track of the time. It's so interesting to hear about my dad. I'll just have to make sure I've got more time when I come again. I hope I can?' Margaret's eyes sparkled.

'Yes, do. There's more and it'll be lovely to see you anyway.'

'I'm sorry I've got to rush. I've got an entertaining meeting about leg ulcers, incontinence-pads and other uplifting stuff. I'll see you later. Actually I might be able to look in on the way back.'

'Well, whenever you can make it. Bye, dear.'

Left to her own devices Ellen returned to the crossword. She had decided that she would reply to Louise Stark in California as soon as she got home.

Ellen and Harry met from time to time, occasionally by design but more often as they chanced upon each other in the street or on the beach. She had always enjoyed going to the beach but it wasn't until she began to accompany John and later Harry that she really grew to love it. When her children were small Amelia had taken them down to the sands. They had all built sandcastles, combed the tide-lines and the lows and crunched on sandy sandwiches. She had also taught each one to swim in the sea.

Like William, John was an enthusiastic fisherman. Despite not being particularly interested in the finer points Ellen was ready to share her brother's joy when he caught something and to commiserate when he didn't. What she really grew to appreciate though, once she was old enough, was being able to wander off on her own to daydream and poke about in the stones and lows.

The beach played an important part in the lives of all the men that Ellen ever cared about. Her father loved the shore. He needed no excuse to take the pony and cart by way of Cliff Road several times a day to monitor the tide or cast up and down the beach on the lookout for pieces of timber that had been washed up. A woodpile grew steadily in the back garden at Ivy Cottage, bearing testimony to the diligence that he applied to the activity. He sometimes dragged timber considerable distances along the beach before staggering with it on his back up the cliff. As Amelia pointed out to him on more than one occasion, these were hardly activities suitable for a man with a pelvis made of eggshells. And in any case, what was the point of labouring home with all that wood if he never had the time or the inclination to put it to any useful purpose?

If the tide was right in the evening or at the weekend he often went off to fish or dig bait. The long absences and the missed meals irritated Amelia. What irked her more though was the realization that her husband preferred to spend his spare time on the beach rather than with her and his family.

John was the same. As soon as he could ride his mother's bicycle he went off fishing or beach combing. Younger and fitter than William he could carry prodigious amounts of wood up the cliff. He also developed a penchant for gathering up almost anything that he found. Whatever he had in mind for much of it wasn't always immediately obvious.

'It'll come in. We'll be glad of that one of these days.' He filled the old chicken hut and festooned the rabbit hutches at the top of the garden with fish boxes, tangled rope and netting, broken crab pots, oily corks, marker buoys and the like.

Ellen's younger brother George was also passionate about the beach but he took his pleasure in a different way. He had no patience for, nor interest in fishing or beachcombing and he lacked the physique for clambering up and down the cliffs. He wouldn't contemplate going near the beach at any time other than a hot, sunny day during the summer. Then he was happy to spend all day on the sands. After a token dip in the sea he was content to lie in the sun until forced by thirst and hunger to seek sustenance. It was on the beach that he would meet his wife Janice, the daughter of a local fisherman.

Robert liked to climb the cliffs and poke about in the Cromer Forest Bed. Laid down over 500,000 years earlier it was exposed periodically at the foot of the cliffs, especially after those occasions when stormy weather coincided with a very high tide. It was a good place to search for fossils and Robert had accumulated a huge collection of mammal teeth, bits of bone and antler.

Ellen was carrying on a desultory conversation with one of the cleaners on the veranda when Margaret reappeared mid-afternoon with a kitchen assistant bearing a tray.

'They said you were out here. Hello, Doris. Thanks, Deb. Yes, down there will be lovely.'

Doris quickly picked up her box of cleaning things and left with Deborah.

'I've brought tea and I snaffled a few cookies from the meeting-room. Thought we might as well have them. Otherwise the cleaners will take them home.'

Margaret placed the tray on the table beside Ellen.

'Oh, they look lovely. I had a good lunch but I think I might be able to manage a small piece of something or other.'

'Ah, well.' Margaret grinned. 'You're going to have to do a bit of work first, to earn a cake. I need to know some more about my dad.'

As the weeks passed, Harry's nightmares occurred less frequently but they never left him completely. One bitterly cold night in November he woke Ellen and Peter repeatedly with his shouting. Several times Ellen left her son and went through to comfort him. Eventually after making them all a hot drink she slid into the narrow single bed beside the shaking Harry and put her arms round him. He quietened and seemed much comforted. Eventually they slept.

Returning on the bus from Cromer on a Saturday afternoon with Peter,

Ellen spotted Harry standing outside his old cottage at the bottom of Back Lane. A couple of boys and a dog were whirling about him.

'It's Hedgy and his brother,' said Peter. He turned and knelt on the seat to watch them out of the rear window as the bus slowed to stop at the Lord Nelson. Ellen got to her feet in alarm and stooped to peer out of the window. The Hedge boys were ruffians. They were baiting Harry while their dog Brownie darted repeatedly at his legs. Even as Ellen watched, the dog caught hold of the bottom of Harry's trouser leg and almost had him over.

As she hurried down the steps and off the bus Ellen could hear the dog barking and the shouts of the boys as they goaded Harry.

'Yeeeeeaaaaaah, rat-tat-tat-tat-tat-tat-tat. We're coming to get you, Harry.'

'Hey! Stop that!' As she closed on them Ellen shouted. 'Leave him alone! What on earth do you think you're doing? You nasty little beggars!' The boys and the dog stopped and stared insolently at Ellen before turning and running off.

'Aah! It's only old Fanny Fincham,' they jeered and ran off up Cliff Road hooting and laughing. Ellen was furious and ran after them.

'I'll give you what for if I catch you. I shall tell your father when I see him.' She gave them a bit of a scare by gaining on them briefly but they merely lengthened their strides and ran away from her again. Ellen had always been good at running but there was no way that she could match them with an undignified straight-legged scurry in heels and a skirt.

'Yaaah, go on then. Get back to the zombie.' They soon lost her. She hurried back to find Harry sitting on the roadside bank with Peter crouched beside him.

'He's too heavy. Look what they've done.' Peter pointed at a ripped turn-up.

'Are you all right, Harry?'

'There's dog's spit on his plimsolls.' At first Peter had been embarrassed by his association with Harry, but he was all outrage now that the Hedge boys had disappeared. Harry was agitated but unhurt. Ellen helped him to his feet.

'Don't worry. I can mend the hole and sponge his trousers.' As they returned home she calmed down and decided that she wouldn't tell Jack Hedge. He wasn't the most even-tempered man. A bus driver, he was reputed to take his belt to his children, his wife and his dog. He would probably half kill the boys if she said anything.

Crouched over his plate, Harry ate each meal as though it might be his last. He shovelled food into his mouth, his eyes darting and suspicious. When he thought Ellen's attention was elsewhere he sneaked bread into his pockets.

She came across scraps of food secreted about the house and even in the shed. She tried to talk to him about it, saying that it would attract vermin. Harry nodded but continued.

Peter had tried to make friends with Harry during the first few days but for the most part his approaches went unheeded and his questions unanswered. Fascinated by Harry's face he was incredulous to learn that it had not been the result of an accident.

'What? You mean someone did it on purpose?' Ellen could hardly look at her son's anguished and disbelieving face. She did her best to explain.

One day after tea, while they were still all at the table Harry pulled a penny from behind Peter's ear. Soon they were both laughing. Watching Harry, Ellen thought that perhaps he was on the mend. He did the trick several times until Peter attempted to take the coin in order to try it himself. Harry pushed him away roughly and put the coin back in his pocket. After that he and Peter largely ignored each other.

Late one afternoon in November Ellen walked down to Annie's shop. Peter had been suffering with a cold and had come home from school stuffed up and miserable with congestion. She needed butter and matches anyway and wondered whether Annie might have some Friars' Balsam for a steam inhalation. The shop carried a limited range of potions and medicaments. The principal difficulty would be whether Annie could actually put her hand on any one of them.

Despite it being bitterly cold the shop door was wide open as the fruit and vegetable merchant staggered in with produce from his lorry. Ellen had only been in the shop a moment when she heard the man speaking to someone outside. He waddled in bandy-legged, carrying a sack of carrots.

'Are you Ellen? Someone out here asking. That you, love?'

Ellen went to the door. Harry was standing in the dusk beside the back of the lorry. Dressed only in his cricket sweater, trousers and plimsolls he was hunched against the cold, his hands in his pockets. In the harsh light from the shop doorway his face was pale and pinched. He looked frozen.

'Harry? Where's your coat? Is everything all right? What do you want?' Ellen had asked him whether he needed anything from the shop only a few minutes earlier before leaving home. He had been looking at some old magazines in front of the fire and had shaken his head. As she walked down the road he must have been right behind her.

'Good grief, he'll catch his death. Where's his overcoat? And we'll all go the same way if we don't shut this bloody door.' Annie's grey, crabby face appeared from round the side of the shop. She had been shutting up her shed at the back after taking delivery of potatoes.

Harry wanted some tobacco, but he hadn't any money.

'Annie, could you let us have half an ounce of Juggler Mild and a packet of papers, please? I haven't got enough with me at the moment. I'll bring it down tomorrow.'

' 'Course you can.' Annie was magnanimity itself as she rounded the counter. Ellen was a good customer, and anyway being a heavy smoker herself she had some sympathy with the request.

'Well,' she continued, 'I say that, but I'm not sure... Will something else do, if I can't...? I know I've got Seniors ... and Weights and some Woodbines here somewhere. ... Well, I say that ... I know I saw some only the other day. Now where did I...?'

Her voice droned on as she went round to the cigarette and tobacco shelf to look. She eventually found a misshapen half-ounce of Juggler Mild on the floor. Ellen gave the tobacco and some blue cigarette papers to Harry.

'Here you are, Harry. Off you go. Straight home, before you catch your death. I'm just going to pop down to the old school, to the library, to change these and then I'll be back to make tea.'

The table had been laid for ages. Peter was hungry and chafing for his tea. Ellen was angry. It was dark and cold and Harry hadn't yet returned home. It had begun to rain and he had no coat or hat with him. A cursory check with one or two people in Back Lane had been fruitless. No one had seen him or knew where he was. He was well aware of mealtimes and was usually ready for his food. It wasn't like him at all.

Old Mr Bullimore, the verger, spent a lot of time in the churchyard after his wife passed away. A retired farm labourer, he lived in a cottage almost opposite the lych gate and took considerable pride in keeping the churchyard neat and tidy. He visited his wife's grave first thing every morning and last thing each afternoon before he shut up for the night.

Late that afternoon he was on his way to commune with Edith when something on the gravel path on the far side of the churchyard caught his eye. Few people used the path and whatever it was it hadn't been there that morning. The light was fading and it was bitterly cold so he continued on his way. He had spent the afternoon in his garden tending a particularly satisfying bonfire. Having saved a few evergreen twigs he thought that they would look well on Edith's grave.

It was as he was closing the lych gate on leaving that he remembered the thing on the path. He almost didn't go but he took his church duties seriously. By now the light was very poor. When he reached the path by the church wall he was surprised to see what looked like a pair of shoes placed neatly side by side on the path beside the churchyard well. He was even more surprised to see that one half of the heavy wooden cover over the well had been left open, thrown back against the wall of the church. Mr Bullimore picked up the shoes for a closer look. They weren't shoes. He was holding a pair of black plimsolls.

'I thought it must have been some of them kids left them there and went off leaving the lid open, mucking about,' he was later to tell his fellow drinkers in the bar. 'Bloody dangerous. But then I looked at those plimsolls and I thought they're a bit big. I bet they're twelves or more. I nearly didn't bother looking in the well. I still don't know why I did. I suppose I had a premonition. He' – he gestured with his pewter tankard at the ceiling – 'moves in mysterious ways.'

Ellen was pouring water into the teapot when there was a knocking on the door.

'About time. Where on earth has he been until now? What's he playing at?' Harry usually came in without knocking.

Peter answered the door. Ellen heard a brief exchange. It wasn't Harry. She was wiping her hands on her apron and on her way when the police sergeant's head appeared round the door.

'It's the policeman,' Peter explained unnecessarily. 'He wants to speak to you.' Peter's eyes were wide. It wasn't every day that the sergeant came to the door.

'Hello, missus. . . .'

There was a brief muttered conversation on the doorstep. Peter heard his mother gasp. The conversation continued for a short while and then Ellen came in. She closed the door slowly behind her and sat down promptly on one of the chairs at the table. She stared into space.

'What did he want?'

Ellen didn't answer. Peter was worried. He went to stand beside his mother. He tugged at her sleeve.

'Mum?'

'Hmm?'

'What did he want?'

Ellen looked at her son. She gasped suddenly and her face crumpled a little but she caught herself. After a moment she took one of his hands in hers. 'It's poor Harry. They've just found him in the churchyard.' She paused again. 'He's dead.'

'What? What happened to him?' Peter's eyes were huge and his mouth hung open.

'I don't know. The sergeant didn't say. He just said that old Mr Bullimore found him in the churchyard. They've taken him away now.' Ellen's eyes filled. She looked away, then took out a handkerchief and sighed.

'Where have they taken him?'

'I don't know. To the hospital, I expect.'

'Wonder what was wrong with him? Was he killed?'

'I don't know. I don't think so. I expect his poor body had just had enough.'

'Oh.'

'Poor Harry. Poor, poor Harry.'

The well opening was pitch black and Mr Bullimore was about to let the lid fall when he got the impression of something pale below. With chilled and clumsy fingers he felt in his pocket for his spectacles and matches. Eventually he fumbled a match from the box. At the third attempt he lit it. As he stood trying to regain his breath he was taken aback to see a body floating in the black water below.

' 'Course, I knew who it was straight away, poor beggar. I've seen him hanging about at Back Lane. I'd know that cricket jersey anywhere.'

They found the Juggler Mild and the new packet of blue cigarette papers in Harry's trouser pocket, both unopened. The police sergeant was of the opinion that he must have gone to the well immediately after leaving the shop.

'I know it doesn't make much sense. There's no sign of foul play at all. Poor beggar. I should imagine he did it while the balance of his mind was disturbed.' It was a conclusion often reached in the courts and the policeman rather liked the sound of it. 'Still,' he continued, 'he won't feel any more pain now, where he's gone.'

It was a bright and chilly afternoon in late November 1950 when they buried Harry Littleboy. Ellen was touched when Peter said that he would accompany her to the funeral if she really needed him. However, he said that he would rather go to school as usual, if she didn't mind. He didn't want to miss football that afternoon.

Ellen decided to go to work as usual. She took some clothes with her that morning and changed at Pond Farm. Just before two o'clock Mr Reeve picked up Amelia and drove them all to the church.

The service was poorly attended. The church wasn't even quarter-full. A bare handful of mourners clustered in the first two rows of pews. The final irony, which Harry was in no position to appreciate, was that on his way to the grave his coffin passed over the well in which he had drowned. The normal path was impassable since it was blocked by scaffolding as the church tower was about to undergo renovations. Having borne the worst travails imaginable thousands of miles away on the other side of the world, Harry's final resting-place was no more than a few feet from where he was christened and from where he breathed his last.

Obliged by the intensity of public feeling against them, Gerald and Olive took responsibility for the funeral. Olive and a couple of her friends put it about that they would be serving refreshments back at their house afterwards. Everyone in the meagre congregation was invited. Few attended.

Ellen never spoke to Gerald or Olive Littleboy again. She had never seen much of them but for a while she took a savage delight in going out of her way to meet them face to face so that she could cut them dead. She stopped the childish game though after she saw Olive hiding from her one day.

Some years later the entire village was agog at Gerald and Olive's demise in an explosion aboard a holiday cruiser on the Norfolk Broads. For a moment Ellen pondered the thought that perhaps people ultimately got what they deserved. Of course, it didn't make any sense if you considered their daughter Charlotte who was blameless and left bereft. Kathy's thoughts on the matter were that the explosion would certainly have brought to an end Olive's convenient migraines and the interminable yapping of her nasty little Pekinese.

Peter was pleased to get his room back. He and Ellen painted it and Amelia made new curtains for the tiny window. Ellen kept Harry's few possessions in a box. At first she kept them under her bed. Then they were out in the shed for years. Just before Guy Fawkes night one year Peter gave them to a gaggle of small boys who were collecting for the bonfire. It wasn't until much later that Ellen noticed that the box had gone.

Ellen pushed a few cake crumbs round her plate with a finger. 'You almost had a half brother or sister,' she said.

'Oh, really,' Margaret paused. She had been crying. She turned and peered at Ellen, her eyes red and puffy, her handkerchief poised.

'It was just after Harry's funeral. I discovered that I was pregnant. I was so shocked, I didn't know what to do. I began feeling nauseous and at first thought that I must have a stomach bug. Several afternoons I felt so bad that I had to lie on my front on the floor. I think it was Linda next door who said that if she didn't know any better she'd think that I was pregnant. That was when the penny dropped.'

Margaret fixed Ellen with an interrogatory look. 'Hmm. You must have got to know my father quite well.' Ellen looked up quickly. She caught the smile and the twinkle in Margaret's teary eye.

'What happened?' Margaret continued. 'You said almost.' She blew her nose.

'Yes.' Ellen returned to staring into the middle distance. 'Harry and I shared a bed occasionally. He had terrible nightmares. I went to comfort him and sometimes I stayed.' She paused a moment or two, deep in thought. 'Mm,' she said, nodding. 'I had a miscarriage. I lost the baby. I fell down the stairs.'

'Oh, I'm so sorry. Were you all right?' Margaret took out her make-up bag. 'Well, obviously you weren't but. . . .'

'I gave myself a terrible fright. The stairs used to be in the corner of the living-room behind a little door in those days. I had new stairs put in later. Back then they were terribly steep and narrow and they curved round to the right as you went up. There was no handrail or anything. I was coming down one morning with sheets and hot-water bottles when I tripped. I fell headfirst down the stairs and ended upside down wedged between the foot of the living-room door and the bottom steps. My legs were up the wall. I couldn't move at first. My arms were bound up in the sheets and I'd fallen on the stone hot water bottle. It caught me in the ribs. I was winded and I thought I'd broken my back. I did eventually manage to get an arm free. Fortunately I could just reach the latch and the weight of my body pushed the door open. I fell out on to the living-room floor.'

'That must have been frightening.'

'Oh, I was all right after a bit, but I'm awfully glad I could reach that latch otherwise I might have been there all day. I lay on the floor until I felt better. I knocked on the wall and got Linda from next door. There was the most terrible graze and bruise on my chest. I was stiff and sore for days afterwards. Couldn't stand upright and I could hardly walk. I had a jolly good shiner too.' Ellen put a hand to her eye, grimaced and slowly shook her head.

'And you lost the baby?' Margaret prompted.

'Yes, that afternoon.'

They sat in silence, alone on the veranda except for a man dozing in a chair at the far end. He kept jerking awake every few minutes when he disturbed himself making little puffing noises.

After a while Margaret took a compact and lipstick from her bag.

'Look at me.' She tidied her face and ran a comb through her hair. Gathering the tea things on to the tray she peered out of the window and then glanced at her watch.

'I must be off.' She smiled and leaned across to take Ellen's hand.

'Poor you,' she said. 'Thanks for talking to me, Ellen.'

'You're welcome, Margaret. I'm sorry it wasn't a cheerier story. It was nice to see you though. Come again.'

She remained alone on the veranda for a long time after Margaret left. She closed her eyes and eventually slept. When she woke she realized that apart from his terrible eye she couldn't remember what Harry Littleboy had looked like.

SEVEN

Peter woke with a start. His neck was stiff and his mouth was dry. He'd obviously been snoring. He took a quick look across at Margaret but she was oblivious, fast asleep herself. His tongue felt like old carpet and he had lost all feeling in his right leg from the knee down. Levering himself up he massaged his calf muscle. Once the pins and needles abated he stood up and rubbed his face. A hot shower and a shave wouldn't go amiss. They were out of the question so the pub toilet would just have to serve. When he returned having splashed his face with cold water and combed his hair he felt somewhat better. It would have been stretching things though to say that he was invigorated.

He poked the fire, threw on a log and jiggled it about. Margaret stirred. He glanced over at her. She looked very attractive in the flickering firelight and the warm glow from behind the bar. She gave him a quick smile and then stretched. 'Oh, Lord.' She smiled again. 'I was well away.'

'I must have dropped off. I'm sorry. You looked comfortable though and at peace with the world.' Peter grinned at her, hitched his trousers up and then busied himself again with the fire. 'I think we should probably be going.'

He gathered up their glasses and took them behind the bar, rinsed them and left them by the sink.

'We'd better make a move. Phil seems to have disappeared. Are you still OK for a ride?'

'Yes, by all means, always assuming of course that I can actually get up. I seem to be far-welted.'

'Far-whatted?'

'Welted. Far-welted. It's what they say in Lincolnshire or somewhere up in that neck of the woods. When a sheep is on its back and can't get up, I think . . . or something like that.'

'Hmm, far-welted.' Peter grinned. He liked words. 'Can I help you to un-far-welt yourself at all?' He offered a hand.

'I think that might not only be kind of you but also a necessity.' Margaret took hold of Peter's hands and heaved herself upright. She smoothed her skirt and straightened her top.

'I think I shall skip along to the loo and tidy myself up. Actually, I think it will be a case of less skipping and more limping. I must look as though I've been dragged through a hedge backwards.'

'You look fine. Extremely. . . .' Peter was going to say sexy. Suddenly he realized he was staring. 'I'm just going to nip through and see Kathy and then I'll be ready to go.'

Peter went through the bar. There was no one downstairs. He ran up the narrow back staircase and along to Kathy's room and tapped lightly on the door.

'Hello? Kathy? I just–'

'Come on in, love. I am decent.'

Peter opened the door.

'You'll have to excuse the mess.' Kathy was propped up in her bed surrounded by magazines. The curtains were drawn and apart from a table lamp beside her the room was in darkness. She looked over the top of her glasses at Peter.

'Looks fine to me.' Peter went over and sat on the edge of the bed. 'We're off.' He grinned ruefully. 'We fell asleep in front of the fire. I just wanted to thank you and Phil. I don't know what I'd have done without you.'

Kathy put down her magazine and took Peter's hand. She smiled at him fondly.

'Don't mention it, love. We were glad to help.'

'You'll let me know what I owe.'

'Oh, go on with you. I won't hear of it.'

'No, Kathy. Really, I insist. It's how I was brought up. You know that, as well as I do.'

Kathy looked at Peter and squeezed his hand.

'How are you coping?' She stared hard at him. Tears started in her eyes. They looked at each other for what seemed to Peter an age. Suddenly Kathy let out a shuddering sob and reached for her handkerchief.

'Oh, God. I can't believe it. I can't believe she's gone, that we'll never see her again,' she whispered. She gripped Peter's hand tightly. 'I keep thinking. . . .'

'I know. I don't think I've taken it in. . . .'

Kathy let go of Peter's hand. She looked miserable. 'What's..?' She paused for a moment and then seemed to find some strength. She blew her nose. 'I can't cry any more.' She looked at Peter again. 'Give me a hug and then off you go.'

Peter leaned over the bed and he and Kathy embraced. They held each other tight for some time.

'Right.' She slapped him on the back and disengaged. Carefully passing her fingertips beneath her eyes she blinked several times. 'Off you go.' Kathy looked at the clock beside her bed. 'I must get up shortly and get busy. Will we see you tomorrow?'

'Yes. I'll be in at lunchtime, I expect, if I'm up by then.'

'Phil's gone out, I think. Or is he back?'

'It's OK. Margaret's still here. She'll drop me off on her way home.'

'You're sure you won't stay?'

'No. Thanks anyway, Kathy. I could probably do with a bit of time on my own.'

'Yes. Of course. Well, let us know if there's. . . .'

'I will. I will.' With a final squeeze of Kathy's hand Peter left her looking at her watch and wondering aloud whether she had time for a quick bath. She gave him a last teary but brave smile as he closed the door.

In the bar Margaret was sitting on a stool, her handbag in her lap and car keys in hand.

'Sorry. It got a bit . . . you know, up there.' Peter went behind the bar, took out his wallet and left some money beside the till. 'That should do it, I should think.'

'I'm not surprised. How is she? Is she all right? Are you OK?'

'Yes. I think so. I was just saying, I don't think it's really hit me yet. Kathy will miss Mum. They were always very close, since they were little girls.' Peter collected his cases.

'I didn't know your mum for long, but they were quite a pair, weren't they?'

'Oh, absolutely.'

'She's a lovely person, Kathy, isn't she? Genuine.'

'Yes, she is. She's been like a second mother to me, really. With not having a father around I spent a lot of time with her and Phil. We always got on. I've known her all my life.' Peter looked at Margaret, gave her a brief grin and half shrugged his shoulders. 'I love her.'

'Will she be OK this evening? She could probably do with a rest herself.'

'She's got help. People come in. She'll probably take things easy. Sit at the end of the bar and chat.' Peter paused in opening the door. 'She's a tough lady.'

Margaret looked a little sceptical but said nothing.

The car-park was empty except for Margaret's Mini. She unlocked the door and folded the driver's seat-back down.

'Can you get the case in here? Oh, yes, there's room for them both.' They climbed into the car and after wiping the windscreen clear of condensation Margaret nosed slowly across the gravel car-park. 'It shows.'

'What's that?'

'You and Kathy. You're very close.'

'Oh, yes.' Peter looked out of the window as Margaret waited to turn out on to the coast road. 'I'd stake my life on Kathy. She'd never let you down.'

He laughed. 'She always gave brilliant birthday and Christmas presents. Not expensive necessarily, but always fun. Turn left here and we're up at the top on the right. And if she ever gave us sweets or chocolates she always

insisted that we open them there and then and enjoy them. Phil used to like
to hoard stuff, put it away; keep it good. Kathy used to rail at him. What are
you keeping them for? Enjoy them. There are no pockets in the shroud.'

Margaret smiled and nodded agreement.

'Isn't it funny? It took me a while to realize that. I used to buy things and
keep them hanging in the closet. Must have had something to do with the
way we were brought up. Just here?'

Peter nodded. Margaret pulled in and parked on the gravel outside the
front door.

'So this is Cowper's Cottage.'

'Yes. This is where I was born and grew up. Mind you, it's changed a lot
since those days but I suppose I'll always think of it as home. Would you like
to come in? Have you got. . . ?'

'I'd love to. If you're sure.'

Peter hefted his suitcase out of the Mini and then rooted about in his
pilot's case for the keys to Cowper's Cottage. Margaret gathered up her
handbag and locked the car.

'You're sure you can do with me? You wouldn't rather be on your own?'

'No. Come on in. I thought I might want to be on my own but I'm glad
of your company to tell the truth.'

'It's a lovely cottage. Ellen said she enjoyed gardening. You can see that
she did.' She paused and looked around. 'It's funny to think that my dad was
here once.'

'Yes.' Peter wandered over to Margaret. They stood together looking
across the garden. 'Mind you, it wasn't quite so grand in those days. The
cottage has been extended and modernized. The garden didn't exist. There
was just a patch of dirt out here at the front and a few feet of rough grass at
the back.'

Peter sorted out the front door key and moved towards the cottage.

'Tea, I think. What do you remember of Harry?'

'Nothing at all. I was too young. And I never knew until a few years ago
that he had survived the war. It was a bit of a shock to see his grave in the
churchyard. Where did the headstone come from?'

'I'm fairly sure it was the village. People contributed. I think they had
jumble sales, that sort of thing.'

'Oh. People are good, aren't they?'

Peter let them in.

'Phew, it's hot in here. Phil must have put the heating on.' He felt the hall
radiator. 'It's boiling. I'll turn it off. Would you like some tea?'

'Oh, yes please. I can see the kitchen and the kettle. I'll see to it.'

'Ah.' Peter paused. 'We left without the milk.'

'Never mind. I'll have black coffee. That suit you?' Margaret filled the kettle and put it on. Peter nodded assent and opened the hall window.

'Presumably you'd know the Robert that Kathy was talking about earlier?' Margaret called from the kitchen.

'Yes. He's a really nice guy. I haven't seen him for years. I knew he and Mum were friendly – but not that friendly.'

Ellen was happy working at Pond Farm. When the elderly Mrs Quantrill retired Mr Reeve asked her whether she would be able to manage on her own. Given Ellen's assurance that she would, he nodded and left her to it.

'Let me know if you need anything, lass. It may not always be quite so straightforward. But I know you won't struggle on in silence.'

Mrs Quantrill had always insisted on doing things in the same way. It may once have met the purpose, but of late much of what she did entailed significant exertion to no useful end. Kathy had an American client at the hair salon who described that sort of activity as 'busy work'. The girls liked the expression and Ellen concluded that much of Mrs Quantrill's efforts fell into that category. The house was easy for a young, fit and energetic girl, especially since Mr Reeve's social life was much less active than when Maria was alive. Left to his own devices Dick Reeve had become something of a recluse.

Things were not too bad at home, either. Relations with her father had improved after he convinced himself that he had talked her out of her daft notions of nursing or teaching. He knew she'd see sense eventually, he said. He was a little irked that she had not sought a job at the sanatorium and it irritated him further to learn that she earned more at the farm than she would had she followed his advice. Her mother, too, made few demands and, as George grew up, he took his unsettling presence elsewhere. For a while something of a routine prevailed.

Ellen's face gradually improved. The scars faded and to her amazement and then to her delight her left eye and her mouth returned to something not unlike their state before the dog's intervention. She was left with a web of faint scarring which she would never fail to notice but which Kathy assured her wasn't noticeable and would improve further as she aged.

'Nobody running for a bus is going to notice it. And who's going to be looking at you, anyway?'

Several boys in the village and one or two further afield were looking. Ellen concluded that things could have been much worse.

She looked forward to Robert coming home. His mother's tragic death and his father's insistence that he be educated away had upset him enormously. Gilbert had always been disruptive and initially Robert did poorly at school and was increasingly in trouble, although his letters to Ellen made no mention of it. Eventually Mr Reeve was forced to take both boys away

from the school. Only when they had a fresh start together at a new board-
ing school did Robert begin to settle down. He and Ellen continued to
exchange letters and cards and he was as eager to see her as she was to see
him at the end of each term. Things were less good between Robert and Mr
Reeve. It was to be a long time before Robert forgave his father.

One stiflingly hot afternoon during the summer of 1936 when Robert was
away and his father was out, Gilbert Reeve sidled into the hen house where
Ellen was seeing to some day-old chicks. Senior to Ellen by two years Gilbert
rarely bothered to speak to her. In the ordinary way they had little to do
with each other. He was a large youth, very confident in some respects but
curiously immature.

Gilbert had a marked fondness for the contents of his father's drinks cabinet. With fine brown hair, fair skin and a sulky demeanour he had inherited
nothing of his mother's looks or his father's easy manner. This afternoon he
was hot, rather the worse for drink and bored.

Inelegant in a crumpled aertex shirt and stained khaki shorts he flopped
down against the foot of the wall just inside the hen house door. He lit a
cigarette and propped the door open with his foot.

'So, what are you piddling about at, Scarface, you peasant?'

Ellen looked up with a frown.

'Will you close the door please, Gilbert? And you're not to call me that.'

Gilbert ignored her, intent on blowing smoke rings.

'Gilbert, will you please close the door? The chicks will get chilled. And
you shouldn't be smoking in here.'

'God, it's hot.' Gilbert ran his fingers down his plump, hairless chest and
over his midriff. 'How on earth will they get chilled? It's baking in here. And
it stinks. Don't know how you can stand it.' He paused for a moment and
looked up at Ellen. He snorted mucus, turned his head and expelled a thin
stream of spittle before continuing.

'Of course you'll be used to it. You peasants all smell the same, or worse.'

Ellen stopped what she was doing and gave him a hard look. She went over
to the door.

'Your father isn't going to be pleased if he finds out you've been smoking
in here. You could easily start a fire with all this straw about.' Poking
Gilbert's foot out of the way with her toe she tried to push the door closed.

'And who's going to tell him, Scarface? You?' Gilbert held the door.

'No, I'm not, but you shouldn't—'

'Listen to me, me old muck-spreader. I'll put this in words that even
you'll be able to understand. When the old man's away, I'm in charge. I say
– you do. If I want the stupid door open, I'll have it open.'

'I don't know anything about that. I work for your father.'

Gilbert finally let the door go. As Ellen made to return to the chicks he stuck out his leg to stop her. It was as she stooped to push his leg away that he grabbed her and pulled her down on top of him. Taking her by surprise and having the advantage in size he had little difficulty.

Despite her protestations he rolled Ellen over on to her back and sat on her stomach. He rested his knees on her upper arms and sniggered as she struggled.

'Not so hoity-toity now, Scarface, are we?'

She could smell drink and tobacco on his breath. 'Get off me, Gilbert, and you're not to call me that. You're heavy. Leave me alone or. . . .' She struggled as best she could.

'Or what? Just exactly what is it that you think you're going to do, Scarface?'

'Get off. I'll tell Robert.'

'Ooooooohh, and just what do you think the blue-eyed one's going to do? If he can ever be arsed to pitch up here again, that is.'

'I don't know. Get off. I'll tell your father.'

'Oh yeah, and do you think he's going to believe you?' Gilbert blew smoke into her face and laughed.

'Stop it! I'll scream if you don't let go. I will.' Ellen was frightened. Gilbert had never behaved like this before. He put his hand over her mouth. His fingers were rank. Looming over her he snorted. Gathering mucus in his mouth made as though to spit in her face.

Fired now by disgust and real fear Ellen struggled harder. 'You pig! You bully! Get off and leave me alone.'

Gilbert grabbed her wrists in one hand and then very deliberately dribbled spittle on to her face. Ellen shrieked. Sniggering and taking a last drag at his cigarette Gilbert stubbed it out on the floor beside him and then unbuttoned her shirt. With a grin he thrust his hand inside.

'Go on, Scarface, you know you want me to.' Enraged as he fondled and prodded her breasts, Ellen managed to pull Gilbert's other hand close. Frightened and angry, she dug her teeth into the fleshy side of his palm. Gilbert shouted with pain, jerked his hand free and staggered off her.

'Shit, shit. Shit! You bloody cow. Look what you've done.' Blood was already welling through his fingers where he clutched at the wound. 'It was only a fucking joke. I'm bleeding like a stuck pig.' Wrapping his hand in the front of his shirt he took a wild kick at her.

'Bloody buggering peasant!' But Ellen was up and out of the hen house door.

'Serves you right,' she called back at him, wiping her face on her sleeve. 'You are a pig. I shall tell your father as soon as he gets back. You needn't think you're going to get away with that. And I'll tell my father. Even better,

I'll tell John. He won't stand for it. He'll soon come down here and sort you out.'

Gilbert looked at her. He and John had never seen eye to eye. For a moment she saw fear in his eyes, but then his demeanour changed. He snorted, hawked and then spat.

'Oh, I don't think so, Scarface. I shall simply say you led me on, wouldn't take no for an answer, and then you'll lose your precious job. I shall put it about that you're a right little prick-tease, and if I really make a fuss I bet I can get you peasants thrown out of your house too. And . . . if the old man doesn't throw you out I'll certainly make it my business to have you out when he dies and it's mine, you'll see.' Ellen ran to the farmhouse, her eyes welling with angry tears. She felt grubby and she was worried that Gilbert would do exactly as he said.

For the next few days she was apprehensive and it made her awkward with Mr Reeve. Once or twice he asked whether she was feeling well. To her relief Gilbert ignored her completely and she realized that he intended saying nothing. She too determined that it would be best to let that particular sleeping dog lie but she took care to ensure that she was never alone with Gilbert Reeve again.

It was just after Christmas that year that Kathy came round to Ivy Cottage one afternoon. Ellen was alone by the fireside reading. John was home for a few days and he and William had gone fishing on the beach. Her mother was helping prepare for some activity at the church hall and George was off on his bicycle.

'Oh, good. Kath, come on in.'

'I'm glad I've caught you.' Kathy headed immediately for the fire. 'It's bitter out. But I can't stop. We've got Uncle Lenny and Auntie Edie and their tribe coming for tea and I've got to help Mum. But I do need to talk to you.'

'Whatever is the matter?'

Kathy warmed herself at the fire but didn't take off her coat and gloves.

'You're not going to like this.' She lowered her voice. 'Ronny overheard something in the bar. You know, that lot that sit up the corner by the dartboard.'

She lowered her voice yet further. 'They were whispering, laughing and joking. They were going on about you and Dick . . . Mr Reeve, going on about you having an affair.'

'What?' Ellen was aghast. 'Me? With Dick Reeve? Where on earth did they get an idea like that?'

'I don't know any more than that. Ronny was sure that was what they were saying though. She nearly had a go at them, you know what she's like, but then she thought better of it. Not like her, I know. But probably just as well. She didn't want to say anything if Mr Reeve was involved. We know there's nothing in it but he is her boss . . . and yours come to that. I did think—'

Kathy stopped and looked expectantly at her friend.

Ellen wrung her hands.

'Yes. Thanks, Kath. But . . . Robert wasn't there, was he? He is home at the moment.' She paused and her hand flew up to her mouth. 'Or his father,' Ellen was shaken. 'Dick wasn't in the bar, was he? He does go in now and again at Christmas with it being quieter, and he sometimes takes the boys.'

'No, they weren't in. It was late. It was just those slackers.' Kathy gave Ellen a look. 'Ronny reckons,' she paused again, 'that it's Gilbert that's behind it.' She stared at Ellen for a long moment. 'She's sure she heard one of them say.' Kathy took out a handkerchief and dabbed her nose. 'Anyway, I thought I'd better let you know. I'm sorry but at least you can . . . you know. . . .'

Ellen sighed and looked into the fire.

After dropping the bombshell Kathy apologized again and left. She said that she would try to pop back later.

Even though the rumour was completely without foundation Ellen felt ashamed and embarrassed. Just thinking about it made her hot and bothered. What on earth would Robert think if he heard? What about Mr Reeve? When she thought about it Ellen concluded that it probably was Gilbert. It would be just like him. This would be him getting his own back just as he said he would. In a state of some anxiety she went along to Pond Farm earlier than she would normally in order to try to talk to Robert, but she was too late. He had left that morning to catch a train for Scotland. She couldn't believe that he had gone without saying goodbye. He must have heard. Of Gilbert and Mr Reeve there was no sign.

It was obvious that the rumours were doing the rounds. Once or twice Ellen caught people giving her a look and conversations dried up at her approach. Even her mother asked whether there was any truth in what she had heard in Annie's.

'How can you even think it?' was Ellen's response.

'Well, there's no smoke without—'

Ellen had marched off. She worried about the rumours reaching Mr Reeve but he said nothing and she couldn't discern any change in his attitude or behaviour. He had either heard nothing, or had chosen to disregard it.

Ellen wrote Robert a long letter once he was back at school but she received no reply. He didn't come home at half-term. His father said he'd been invited to his friend's place. There were no further letters and she saw very little of him after that. To her chagrin he often accompanied school-friends for the holidays rather than returning to Pond Farm. His visits home became less frequent. When he did turn up he usually had a friend in tow and it became embarrassingly obvious that they stayed as short a time as possible. He was distant with both Ellen and his father. He certainly didn't want to talk or spend time with her. For her part she found him and his new friends patronizing and often downright rude, and after a while she gave up trying to engage with them. Robert had changed, very much for the worse. With some sadness Ellen concluded that he was welcome to his smart, clever friends and their parents' yachts and holiday homes abroad.

She went out once or twice with other boys but nothing came of these excursions. She spent more time with Harry. During the summer they constructed a huge shrimp net and amused themselves in the lows in the evenings when the tide was out. Ellen suggested they go out into the sea with the net and Harry was astonished when they found that they were more than trebling their catch. If the sea was calm they could still push the net when they were up to their armpits in water. They sold what they could and gave the rest away.

One evening they managed to retrieve an Iron Age spear, in one piece, from the Forest Bed at the foot of the cliffs. They carried it home with great care and some ceremony and were surprised at the lack of excitement or interest that it occasioned. Some months later Major Pope arranged for it to be taken to the Castle Museum in Norwich. It was returned with a note to the effect that they had several such spears and couldn't find room in their collection for this particular example.

Neither the Littleboys nor Ellen's parents would have it in their house so they got permission from Mr Reeve to nail it up on the wall of one of the barns at Pond Farm.

It gradually became apparent to Ellen that Harry would probably like to take their relationship beyond friendship but he was hesitant for some reason. She couldn't decide whether he lacked confidence or quite what the difficulty was, but it suited her. She liked Harry well enough, but not in that way. Receiving no encouragement he seemed content enough to leave things as they were. It came as no surprise eventually when Kathy told Ellen that she had seen him in Cromer with a girl on his arm.

'And you'll never guess who.' Kathy shook her head in disbelief.

'Who?'

'Think of a trollop, the worst person in the world for Harry . . . Go on, guess.'

'I don't know. Um. Who?'

'Would you believe Eve?'

'What? Eve Emmett?'

'I know. Can you believe it? And they were with some of those other baggages she hangs around with. They were all in tow.'

'No! Oh, for goodness sake. Why on earth would he want to get mixed up with that lot . . . and a troll like her?'

'Hmm, well, let's think about that for a minute. What could she possibly—?'

'All right, all right. I just didn't think Harry. . . .'

'He's a man.'

'I know . . . but . . . she'll eat him alive.'

'Yes.'

Eve Emmett was the daughter of a funeral director in Cromer. Her mother had run off when she was little and Eve, an only child, had been thoroughly spoiled by her father. She was well known in the town and its environs. Plump and attractive, she was often to be seen hanging around Cromer in the company of a few like-minded girlfriends. Dressed to kill, they spent their evenings and Sunday afternoons perambulating the town in a predatory manner on the lookout for men.

Once he became involved with Eve, Ellen saw much less of Harry. She tried shrimping on her own a couple of times but it was nowhere near as much fun as it had been with a partner.

Before the Second World War the beach played an important part in the life of the community. Marl dug from the cliffs fed the lime kiln on the cliff top just to the east of the Lord Nelson. No matter what the weather the rector stumped down the cliff behind his house with his two black Labradors for an early morning swim.

Throughout each summer the village thronged with holidaymakers. The beach was a great draw. The Lord Nelson was invariably full to capacity and tents abounded on the cliff tops behind the hotel. Many locals took in lodgers throughout the season, a number moving temporarily into their garden sheds in order to offer bed and breakfast to free-spending visitors. Seduced by the general largesse Ellen talked Mr Reeve into letting rooms at Pond Farm to holidaymakers. It worked well enough until one night a visitor was taken ill and Mr Reeve was up at two o'clock to take him and his wife to the hospital. There were no more paying guests at the farm after that.

Washed twice daily by the sea the beach was wide, open and clean. It provided safe bathing and the soft sands offered a pleasant place to while away the time. Negotiating the tall cliffs could present a problem to the elderly and infirm since the gangway was steep and uneven and after rain it could be treacherous.

Sloping gently down towards the lows mid beach, the sands were ideal for children. Here and there fans of mud flowed out at the foot of the cliffs and dried to a soft crumbly crust. Having their origin in groundwater issuing from the cliff face, it was in those places where the water continued to flow that there tended to be much activity. Driftwood and stones were carried not inconsiderable distances to aid the serious business of water diversion and dam building. A few bits of wood, a committed father or two and some buckets and spades could keep an army of children employed all day.

A handful of longshore fishermen made something of a living working from the beach. When they were not actively engaged in fishing, they offered boat trips along the coast. During inclement weather the craft were drawn up on the clay terraces just above the foot of the cliffs. There the fishermen mended nets and pots and exchanged tales of the sea. A paddle steamer also called in from time to time en route between Cromer and Great Yarmouth or Tilbury.

Many of the villagers did a bit of fishing in their spare time. In addition to the weekend fishermen there were those who rose early from the warmth of their beds on dark, frosty mornings to check bank lines laid before the last high tide. Frequently it was a profitless business, but on occasion they enjoyed spectacular success. Then the family ate fish until they were heartily sick of it. Thereafter the children hawked newspaper parcels of increasingly malodorous seafood door to door round the village.

During the eagerly anticipated cod season muffled figures paced the water's edge. Hunched against the bitter wind they stamped their frozen feet and slapped their arms as they shuffled up and down. Periodically they stopped and felt their lines, holding them gently between numb thumb and forefinger; heads cocked the better to divine signs of life at the far end. They shook their heads, lit their pipes or stubs of cigarettes and scowled and brooded.

Heads down and hands thrust deep into pockets beachcombers paced slowly back and forth, always with an eagle eye out for the thing that just might change their lives. Fierce storms and unusually high tides pounded the beach from time to time. They scoured the sand out from the foot of the cliff and exposed the Forest Bed.

The beach, the sea and the cliffs were a naturalist's delight. Birds were many and varied. Gulls picked at the tideline and soared on the thermals at the cliff edge. Coteries of sanderlings rushed in and out with the waves and cormorants kept station just off the beach. Sand martins and the odd fulmar nested in the cliffs and the occasional crow and wood pigeon joined the gulls at the tideline.

In addition to the usual flotsam and jetsam it was amazing just what turned up on the beach. Sometimes there were cuttlefish everywhere. At other times it might be a glut of jellyfish, starfish or razor shells. There were two particularly memorable occasions. After a storm there were oranges as far as the eye could see. People laboured up the cliffs with boxes, sacks and pockets bulging with magnificently juicy Jaffas. Another time the foot of the cliff was littered with brand new pit-props that eventually came to form the framework of many a new garden shed, chicken house and pigsty.

From time to time seals appeared, usually no more than a sleek black head or two bobbing in the sea just off the beach, but they came ashore on occasion, sometimes to pup. Shrimps, crabs and sand dabs inhabited the lows. There were skimming stones aplenty and occasionally someone stumbled across an ammonite. Iron pyrites were not an uncommon find. On the more stable parts of the cliff rabbits ran and poppies, thistles and primroses flourished.

As the 1930s drew to a close much of this was about to change. War was in the offing.

EIGHT

Preparations for possible conflict first appeared in the village during May 1939 when an ARP Centre was set up in the old school. An officer in charge, a recording officer, a road traffic officer, a special constable and a food supply officer were appointed from the ranks of village worthies. Stretchers and other kit were assembled and a decontamination centre was set up in the Old Rectory. The parish made arrangements for the collection of salvage with the Sea Scouts collecting waste paper and a dump for scrap being set up in a corner of the yard at Beacon Farm.

On 1 September, a charabanc in unfamiliar plum and custard livery pulled into the car park at the Lord Nelson. Six small, pale and bewildered faces were pressed to the windows. Eventually the children were coaxed out. They stood in the pub car-park and looked about anxiously, the last of a coachload of evacuees, newly arrived in North Norfolk from Dagenham. Eventually the rector bowled up on his wife's bike, sweating and flustered. He redirected the charabanc to the old school from which the arrivals would be allocated their new homes.

Amelia was keen to offer one of the children a home but William refused to countenance it. Despite the fact that John's room was free since he was away in Epping, William wouldn't be swayed.

Fully cognizant that her husband was a greedy man, Amelia took a small measure of revenge on the evening following the evacuees' arrival. Having baked a batch of sausage rolls that afternoon she placed an extra large specimen on the very top of the pile. William wouldn't be able to resist it.

'Oh, ho, ho, just the job. I think I'll just have this one here . . . .' He helped himself to the outsize sausage roll, gave everyone else at the table a triumphant look, took a bite . . . and almost broke his teeth. Moaning and gasping William poked at the crumbling pastry case, to reveal a wooden clothes peg.

'Oh,' Amelia exclaimed, 'so that's where it went. I wondered what had happened to it.' She smiled and carried on with her own meal. 'Fancy that.'

William was not amused. Amelia said not another word on the subject except to wonder aloud whether she was losing her mind. Ellen couldn't meet her mother's eye.

She was cleaning and oiling her bicycle in the backyard at Ivy Cottage at 11.15 a.m. on Sunday, 3 September when Amelia called her in. Together with George, still fuddle-headed and yawning in his dressing-gown and slippers, they listened to Chamberlain's broadcast to the nation.

England was at war with Germany.

It was not unexpected but Amelia cried a little. On his return from mucking out the pigs William pooh-poohed talk of war and claimed that it would be no more than a storm in a teacup.

The phoney war that followed was meat and drink to William and his ilk. 'Over by Christmas', was a sentiment much bandied about in the pub. However over two million men between the ages of twenty and twenty-seven were conscripted by January 1940. Butter, sugar and bacon were officially rationed and many imported luxury goods were already scarce due to the success of the German sea campaign.

In early May John returned home unexpectedly from Epping. It was with some consternation that the family learned that he had already had his medical the previous month at Leyton Medical Board. He had been found Grade 1.

It was in the early afternoon on Monday 13 May that the Royal Engineers arrived in the village. Four lorries and a half-track travelling in convoy pulled up in front of the Lord Nelson. After some consultation Corporal Nick Nichols climbed stiffly from the front passenger seat of the lead truck and headed for the public bar. He was glad to have the opportunity to stretch his legs for a moment and didn't hurry. Before he got to the door it opened as Kathy struggled out with two crates of empty bottles.

'Here love, let me.' Nick held the door until Kathy was outside and then took one of the crates from her. 'Where to, sweetheart?'

'Good Lord.' Kathy stared at the convoy. 'Where did you lot spring from?' She pointed. 'Just round the side, thanks, inside the garage door. Beside the others.' They walked together and deposited the bottles and then returned to the front of the pub.

'Thanks for that. I didn't hear you arriving. I didn't know you were here.'

'Ah, we're like little mice.' Nick stretched and massaged the small of his back. 'Oh, I'll be as stiff as a board tomorrow. Those trucks aren't built for comfort. My back's killing me. We've been on the road since early this morning.'

He pulled a packet of cigarettes from his breast pocket. 'Smoke?'

'Oh. Thank you.'

Nick lit their cigarettes with a lighter.

Kathy puffed inexpertly. 'Where are you off to? Or is it. . . ?'

'We're looking for Vale Road. This is the right place, isn't it? New depot, Nissen huts. Do you know it?'

'Oh, yes. You're not far now. Just keep going the way you're pointing, up over Beacon Hill then it's about a mile or so, a rough track on your left down to the cliffs.'

'Sounds easy enough.' Nick nodded at the public bar. 'It looks a nice pub. Do you live here?'

'No. No such luck. I work here sometimes. I'm not usually here at this time.'

'Well, lucky for me you were. Will you be in tonight? If we get everything squared away we might be able to look in for a bit. Perhaps I can buy you a drink.'

'Yes, I'll be behind the bar. I will have a drink with you. Thanks.'

Nick looked around.

'Is there anything to do around here?'

Kathy blew smoke and studied Nick's face. Eventually she gave him a grin. 'Not a lot. Watch spuds grow. Stuff like that. Shouldn't you be going?'

'Oh, as long as we're there by four or so we'll be OK.' Nick stretched elaborately. 'So, tell me again how we get there. . . .'

Kathy laughed and stubbed out her cigarette.

'Go on with you. It's a mile and a half at most, then the track on the left. I've got work to do even if you haven't.' Kathy opened the door to the bar. 'See you tonight, Corporal. Goodbye.'

'OK. Thanks. Cheerio.'

During 1940 the Engineers laid mines along much of the coast of Norfolk to protect the country from invasion. Around the county other soldiers built pillboxes and barricades, dug trenches and anti-tank ditches and rigged bridges for demolition. If there were to be an invasion, broadly the plan was to hold the enemy as long as possible on the beaches before withdrawing to fallback positions based on the rivers Ant, Bure and Wensum.

East Anglian soldiers from the Territorials and a workshop section spent much of the summer of 1940 on these activities in and around the village. They also ferried mines for the sappers to plant on the cliffs. These fearsome weapons were B (Beach) Type C anti-tank mines which required only to be placed in position and have detonators attached. Efforts at recording the locations of the newly laid mines were variable at best and even the most diligently prepared maps were quickly rendered questionable after a few cliff falls.

Men with weather-beaten faces and dialects strange to the local ear arrived in lorries weighed down with stakes and coils of barbed wire. Fencing parties erected the wire over more than 2000 yards along the cliff top, hammering and screwing the stakes into the ground and laying entanglements in a seemingly endless snake. The stiff wire with its cruel barbs was wretched to handle. Experienced as most of the soldiers were, and despite their thick gloves, it was a rare day that a voice was not raised in pain or anger as someone shed blood on the wire. The locals ventured out to follow progress. They found the mining of the cliffs incomprehensible.

'Do you mean we won't be able to get down on the beach at all then? Not anywhere?' It dawned on those who hoped to continue their livelihood as longshore fishermen that they were going to have to move their boats.

'Well, where the hell are we going to keep *Lucy*, *Annie B* and *Isabelle* then? We're going to have to go bloody miles, and at two and three in the morning. That's going to be a right game, isn't it? What do you want to be mining the cliffs for anyway?'

'Dunno, mate. There's a war on. We're just doing what we're told. Coast protection; keep Jerry out I should think.'

'You're having a bloody laugh, aren't you? How do you think Jerry's going to get up that cliff if you put a man with a pop-gun on the top? I know that cliff like the back of my hand and I wouldn't want to try it. You just need a few armed men with binoculars patrolling the top of the cliff.'

It took the locals no longer than that to spot the illogicality of mining the high and unstable cliffs. They gestured and muttered in anger and disbelief as the Engineers proceeded with their hazardous task. It was late on in the pub and even later back in their cottages that it dawned on them that they would no longer be able to supplement their incomes through the holiday trade, at least for the duration of the war.

Even old Major Pope was moved to limp down to the cliff top at the end of his garden at Clyffesyde and cast an eye over the activities. He looked across the empty fields behind the Lord Nelson, shook his head sadly and turned away. It would be the end of village life as they knew it.

*

On the evening of 15 May the Fincham family sat down together to a meal of fried fish and bread and butter. It was John's last before joining up. It was an odd meal, the mood swinging between forced jollity and sober foreboding. It got off to a promising start when William announced that they would have a bit of a drink to see John off. He rarely drank beyond a glass or two of sherry or port at Christmas when it made him red of face and sent him to sleep, so it was to general astonishment when he fetched beer, cream stout and cherry brandy from the pantry and they toasted John's health and wished him well.

John had spent his last day of liberty fishing alone on the beach. He returned in the late afternoon with more than enough fish for a meal but his mood was sombre as he cleaned his catch in the kitchen sink.

'That's the end of it. There's barbed wire everywhere. Fellow said no one will be able to get down on the beach after tomorrow. Nice enough bloke, from the Midlands. He came here once on holiday when he was little. They've just about got it joined up right the way along now. And guess what, they're talking about putting another fence about a hundred feet back from the one they're putting up now and then mining the strip between them.'

'Whatever do they want to be doing that for? It doesn't make sense.'

'Oh, it'll make sense to someone, somewhere, Mother.'

'It's going to be funny, not being able to go down on the beach.'

Ellen sat up late into the night with her brother as they chewed over old stories and shared memories. They became more thoughtful as the night wore on. Eventually Amelia's anxious face appeared at the door.

'Aren't you in bed yet? You'll never get up in the morning. And you've got a long journey ahead of you, John. You'll need to get your rest.' Given the assurance that they would follow her up she returned to her bed, only to reappear a few moments later.

'I've just remembered. I've got a tin of corned beef you can have in your sandwiches. I was keeping it. . . .'

The entire family squeezed into William's cart and set out for the railway station before dawn next morning. The early train to Norwich was the first of several that would very slowly and by divers routes, eventually deposit John in Saighton near Chester where he was expected by the army. No one had heard of the place and they'd had to look it up on a map. They were none too early at the station and the train was on time. Along the platform a couple of fishermen and the porter waited to load up what would be one of the final catches of fish from the beach.

An embarrassed John received a hasty embrace from both his mother and

Ellen. He shook his father and George's hands, and after a final hug from Amelia, was soon aboard with his brown cardboard suitcase and his raincoat slung over his shoulder. He had time only to put his case on the overhead rack before doors slammed, the guard's whistle blew and beside the Finchams the porter struck a dramatic pose with his hand held aloft. There was an answering toot from the locomotive and they were off to Norwich. John's head reappeared at the door and he eventually managed to wrestle the recalcitrant leather strap sufficiently to get the window down so that he could wave. A tearful Amelia and Ellen promised letters and parcels and they waved furiously until John's carriage passed under the road bridge and steam from the engine obscured the still waving John. William began to head for the steps up to the road but Amelia remained looking after the train.

'My little boy. I do hope he'll be all right.' She stood wretched at the platform's edge wringing a handkerchief.

Ellen took her mother's arm.

'He'll be all right, Mum.'

'I know, but. . . .'

'He's a sensible lad.' Ellen tried to comfort her. 'He'll do well in the army. He's very good at doing what he's told.'

'I suppose so.'

'He'll be fine,' William grunted. 'It's not as though he hasn't been away before.'

'Do you think I don't know that,' Amelia rounded on her husband, 'but he's never gone where some bugger's going to try to blow his head off every few minutes, has he?'

William grimaced and pulled a chastened face at Ellen. Amelia was almost never given to swearing.

'I bet he'll get a medal,' George added helpfully.

Within days, troops of the British Expeditionary Force were being evacuated from the beaches at Dunkirk and Italy declared war on Britain. Robert returned home briefly from Cambridge where he was studying. As usual he wasn't alone. He appeared sitting beside his friend as they drove into the yard in a small, noisy, open-topped sports car.

Robert was courteous and seemed less patronizing than hitherto, but he remained cool and distant with Ellen and his father. Ellen hoped to be able to talk to him alone but there was never any opportunity. Then he was gone again.

The village was full of the military. There was khaki everywhere and even an occasional RAF man and sailor appeared in the bar of the Lord Nelson from time to time. Ellen had rarely been in the pub until Kathy and Ronny insisted that she really must come along at the weekend, it was such fun.

Some of the soldiers were little more than boys, but they carried themselves with an assurance lacking in most of the local youth. Like numerous girls from the neighbouring villages, Kathy and Veronica had been quick to spot that there were several handsome ones among them.

Some were obviously family men and one or two were old enough to be the girls' fathers. They came from all over, from exotic sounding places: New Brighton, Musselburgh, Castletown, Lyme Regis and Flackwell Heath. All were made welcome at the Lord Nelson. Kathy and Veronica saw no reason not to allow the newcomers, if they felt so inclined to treat them to a drink on a Friday or Saturday night.

Ellen got to know a few of the men by sight. Most waved, whistled or called out from the back of their lorries if they passed the girls on the road. It wasn't long before enquiries were made of Kathy and Ronny about the girl at Pond Farm.

One Tuesday afternoon, as they sorted fruit baskets and trays in the barn, Ronny persuaded Ellen to promise to accompany her to the pub on the Friday evening. During the next couple of days Ellen spent a good deal of time wondering what to do with her hair and what to wear, not that she had much choice. Occasionally she came to with a start from her daydreaming. On the Friday evening, after spending longer than usual getting ready, she felt a distinct tingle of excitement, feeling the eyes of so many soldiers upon her.

Kathy was behind the bar so Ellen and Ronny joined a group of sappers. Several times during the course of the evening Ellen exchanged glances with a dark-haired corporal at the far end of the bar. Everyone seemed to know him. Kathy said his name was Nick. She knew him quite well.

He spent some time playing with his cigarette lighter, flicking the lid up and down. Everyone admired the lighter, passing it from hand to hand, trying it out and exclaiming over it. It was apparently an American lighter, a Zippo, known as a *Windproof Beauty* and much sought after. The corporal hadn't had it long and he took a good deal of pleasure from showing it off. He'd won it from an American soldier in a card school on Paddington Station. Ellen felt sure that he would speak the next time they met.

After closing time, a young Scot by the name of Ken walked Ellen home. He had a girlfriend back in Kilmarnock. As they neared Ivy Cottage Ellen pointed out the back road to the depot on the cliff tops. After a brief and awkward goodnight kiss across her bicycle Ken took his leave. They made no arrangements for the future. It was as well since by the following Friday Ken had gone, posted to somewhere down in Dorset, they said.

Corporal Nick Nichols wasn't in the pub the following weekend. He was in Leeds for a hurried visit home to see his wife and baby daughter. On his way back on Sunday afternoon in a freezing train, he reflected that it had been good to see them again. Monica had lost most of the weight that she had put on with the baby and she had a new hairstyle. She had obviously been looking forward to his leave and had made an effort. It was astonishing how much Louise had grown too. He enjoyed their brief time together but he was worried about his father. They'd been for a drink together down at the club and the old man insisted on getting them a second pint. Watching him standing at the bar Nick thought that he suddenly looked his age. Despite his pugnacious front he appeared small, wizened and frail.

The time passed all too quickly though and he was soon making the tortuous journey back to the depot on the cliff tops. The train stopped for no obvious reason countless times. To his annoyance he discovered early on that he had forgotten his tobacco tin but he managed to cadge a couple of cigarettes from fellow passengers. Fortunately he hadn't left his lighter behind. As he stared out of the rain-smeared carriage window at the darkening Fens, the girl in the Lord Nelson came to mind. He kept thinking about her. Despite the scar on her face she was very attractive. She seemed well mannered and quiet. Not at all like the barmaid or the belligerent ginger-haired one with whom she was obviously friendly.

Ellen. He'd thought she was called Helen but someone had put him right. She had obviously had an operation on her face. She was never going to lose that scar completely. But then, how many people were perfect? He caught sight of his reflection in the darkening window and scowled. Few knew of the vivid purple patch on his left ankle. Nerves, they said. It might never go away. He hated it.

Apart from his ankle Nick was not displeased with his appearance. He was broad-shouldered and slim in the hips. He had a reasonable head of black hair and good teeth. His father always maintained that there was Romany in his blood, but Nick never knew whether to believe what the old man said. He doubted the tale since the old man also claimed at one time to be descended from royalty and on another occasion, a pirate.

If Ellen was in the pub next time he was there he would ask her out. He was sure he had seen more than a glimmer of interest. Perhaps if she wasn't working they could go into Cromer for the afternoon on Saturday. He could borrow a bike and treat her to tea. A bit of female company would be nice and it was going to be a long time until he got leave again.

When he got off the train he was irritated to find that there was no transport. He was frozen, it was pitch dark and drizzling and he had a walk of over a mile and a half to the Nissen huts on the cliff top that they laughingly called home. Planting mines the following day on the cliff was not going to be much of a laughing matter either, even if the rain did let up.

*

The summer of 1940 saw the Battle of Britain. The drone of dogfights caught the ear and complex lattices of vapour trails hung in the sky over Southern England and the Continent. The newspapers and news bulletins on the wireless were full of gloom as Germany attacked Denmark and Norway. Hitler then turned his attention to the Low Countries and France.

Despite her parents' obvious displeasure, Ellen began to look forward to Friday evenings. Her mother was of the opinion that going into a public house was not a fit activity for a young woman, unless, of course, it was in the company of one's husband or young man. She wondering whether William could go along for a drink to keep an eye on things, but William had never made a practice of going to the pub and said he had no intention of starting now. Ellen responded that she was twenty; she worked hard all week and felt that she deserved an evening out. Besides her friends all went and there was nothing else to do in the village.

'Don't you think I don't know what you're up to,' her father called one evening as Ellen was leaving. 'Just you be careful, my girl.'

'I will.'

'I saw that Kathy Priest the other day. Bright red lips and nails, what on earth does she think she looks like? And her skirt so tight and heels so high she could hardly walk.'

'Oh, William, Kathy's all right.' Amelia chimed in. 'Lots of girls are like that. It's the fashion. Kathy's a decent enough girl.'

'Well, she's always hanging about up at that pub.'

'She works there.' Amelia caught Ellen's eye and shook her head.

'Well, she's asking for trouble, you mark my words.' William turned to Ellen. 'Don't you come crying to me, my woman, when you've got yourself into trouble. It'll be no good saying we didn't warn you.'

Each time Ellen went out her parents trotted out the same or similar censorious warnings.

She usually cycled with George up the hill. He went on to the Local Defence Volunteers meeting in the Methodist Chapel. After the meeting the older contingent usually turned up at the pub. Much to his chagrin her brother had failed his medical for the army. Ellen didn't fully understand what was wrong with him other than it had something to do with the occasional fits that he had suffered as a child. George railed and swore since he hadn't had an episode for ages.

One evening Ellen called for Ronny at her grandmother's cottage and they spent an age playing cards with the old lady until she went to bed and they could finally slip away to the pub. The bar was comparatively quiet. A foursome of fishermen sat at their usual table playing dominoes, a couple of farmhands played darts and sipped at glasses of mild, and RAF man Dave Holt sat on what was rapidly becoming his stool at the end of the bar, talking to Kathy. Ellen and Ronny took a couple of stools beside him.

At 9.30 an army lorry drove into the pub yard and disgorged a large party of soldiers. Within minutes others arrived on bicycles and on a motor cycle and immediately the place became alive. Drinks were ordered and a darts tournament got under way, the two farmhands draining their glasses and gladly accepting a drink and an invitation to join in.

Ronny had been very taken the week earlier with a sapper by the name of Mather and they were soon deep in conversation. Ellen had plenty of time to look around. She had no difficulty in spotting the corporal and eventually after a good deal of eye-contact and smiles he came over.

'Hello. Mind if I sit down.' He drew up another stool.

'Hello, Corp.' Mather glanced round, gave Nick a grin and then resumed talking to Ronny.

Ellen smiled in response. 'Hello.'

'You're Ellen, aren't you?' He held out his hand. 'Nick Nichols. Actually it's Peter, but everyone calls me Nick.' Ellen took his hand and shook it solemnly. A sudden hubbub at the end of the bar caused them both to look up. A game had just ended. Immediately there was a surge for refills and the crowd began pairing off for the next game.

'Nick, are you in this time? It looks as though you've got yourself a partner.' Faces turned and someone muttered something that caused laughter.

Nick waved in acknowledgement and took a quick pull at his pint.

'Do you fancy a game?' Beginning to get up, he wiped his mouth on the back of his hand and grinned. Ellen looked about uncertainly, but Kathy was serving and Ronny and Mather were clamouring for more drinks.

'All right,' she smiled, 'but I'm not very good.'

'Neither am I.' But Ellen had seen him play and knew that he was competent enough. During the lengthy hubbub while pairs were finalized and drinks replenished, Nick bought them both a drink and they trooped over to join the crowd by the dartboard. There were so many wanting to play that a huge game of doubles was organized.

Ellen was actually quite good. John had his own darts and a board. During her early teens she had spent many an hour with him and George outside the washhouse in the back yard. There were nods of approval and knowing hoots when she started them off rather luckily with her first throw.

'Aye-aye, look out. Need to keep an eye on this one.'

'Bit of a dark horse there, Nicky boy.'

They didn't win but they acquitted themselves well enough, Ellen going out with a double 19. They played a second game and again did rather well. Ellen was more than holding her end up and by the third game she had several voluble supporters.

'Here she comes again.'

'Aye-aye, it's the doubles queen.'

Ellen was enjoying herself and accepted another drink when someone bought a round. Kathy caught her eye and beckoned her over.

'Robert's in the lounge,' she whispered. 'He came in with a couple of people, man and a woman. I don't know them.'

'They're probably from the university.'

Ellen went back to the game and found it difficult to concentrate. However she eventually became caught up in the general excitement again. It was soon closing time. She had a quick word with Kathy on the way back from getting her coat.

'Is Robert. . . ?'

'No. They can't have stayed long. I didn't see them again. I went through for glasses and they'd gone.'

After helping Ellen on with her coat Nick ushered her outside and snatched a quick kiss round the corner from the pub door before he had to run to get a lift back to the depot. Before he left they agreed to meet the following afternoon.

Even though they were both busy Ellen and Nick contrived to meet most Friday evenings in the Lord Nelson and occasionally again at some point during the weekend. Nick borrowed the night watchman's bicycle from the depot, met Ellen outside the pub and together they cycled east or west along the coast road. They most often headed for Cromer. After wandering round the town or along the cliff tops they made for the Singing Kettle for tea and a scone before cycling home again.

Ellen spoke about her family and her job at Pond Farm. She told Nick about John. They would have been friends, she felt. She was excited about learning to drive. Since the beginning of the war both she and Ronny had been learning to drive the tractor and Mr Reeve was talking about letting her take the lorry out. She had driven it and the shooting brake in the farmyard but she hadn't yet taken them on the road.

Before the war Nick had worked in a furniture factory. He had been there since leaving school and loathed it. Life in the Royal Engineers was much more to his taste. After the war he wanted to go into business for himself. He was far from clear what he would do but he thought that there would be plenty of opportunities for people like him. His passions were pigeons and growing prize vegetables. He was quite eloquent on the subject of his father's allotment, their pigeon lofts and fishing. In their case it was not the sea that they were fervent about, it was the rivers and canals. They had obviously spent a good deal of time together. When Ellen asked Nick whether he had a girlfriend he took her by the chin, smiled and kissed her on the end of her nose.

'You're my girlfriend,' he said.

One dull but warm afternoon, instead of cycling into Cromer Nick suggested they wander down the lane behind the Lord Nelson. They stood together where the track petered out at the wire entanglement on the cliff edge and looked out over the North Sea.

'It used to be called the German Ocean, you know.'

'Really?' Nick was impressed.

The tide was as far out as Ellen could remember seeing it.

'It's beautiful, isn't it? It's such a shame we've lost it.'

Nick turned and grinned at her. He took her by the hand.

'Come on, I want to show you something.' Fifty yards or so to the right among some stunted trees and bushes there was what amounted to a rudimentary gate let into the wire. It was well disguised. Nick moved a wooden-framed barrier and helped Ellen through the barbed wire fence.

She wasn't keen. 'We mustn't go through there. It's the minefield. We'll get blown up.'

'It's all right. We'll be fine.'

'Are you sure? We're not supposed to go through the wire.'

'No, you're not. And you mustn't come through here on your own, or tell anyone about this.' He replaced the barrier. 'Just stick with me. It's perfectly safe.' Nick beamed at her again.

A few feet beyond the fence a rough path stopped abruptly at the edge of the cliff. Ellen could remember when at least six cottages stood beyond where she and Nick now stood. Like many folk before them their owners had become victims of the relentless erosion of the cliffs at this point on the coast.

Taking her by the arm Nick gently propelled her forward. Then he took her hand and helped her over the cliff edge on to a comparatively gentle slope that was carpeted with rough grass and thistles. It certainly didn't look at all dangerous.

'Keep hold of my hand. We'll follow the pegs.' Ellen saw that driven into the cliff face at intervals were small wooden stakes with white painted tops. They looked official. Now that she was on the cliff face she could clearly see a rough path zigzagging in stages to a point about halfway down the cliff.

'Ooh. We're not supposed to be here.' Despite trusting Nick, Ellen was uneasy about being seen by the police or the military authorities. She was also worried about the mines.

Nick was blasé. 'The thing about mines is that you do have to treat them with respect. But don't forget I laid most of them. I know all their names and I know where they're hidden. Bertie's over there. And Horace, Maurice, Doris and . . . and' – he sought another name – 'and Norris, are exactly thirty feet apart in a line just under that little outcrop.' He waggled his eyebrows at her and gave her a quizzical look.

'Oh, you.' Ellen punched him lightly on the arm.

'It's fine, don't worry. I'm quite within my rights to be here.'

Ellen was reassured, but only to a degree.

'Yes, but I rather suspect that I'm not. And I'm going to have to take these shoes off. They were never intended for this kind of thing.'

Nick waited while Ellen removed her shoes. 'Take your time.'

The track down the cliff turned out to be firm and dry. They had to pick their way over debris from the cottages that had once stood up above. An avalanche of brick, pantiles, glass, lead pipe and wiring lay in a surprisingly tidy fan down a hundred feet or so of the cliff face. The remains of a chimney stuck up at a tipsy angle from the sand below.

'We'll be taking these pegs out in the next day or so.'

Out of the light breeze off the land they found it very warm. Midges swarmed about them until they got away from the cliffs. It was one of those dull and absurdly calm days when the surface of the sea resembled an oil slick. Tiny wavelets washed silently on to the sand. The tide was well out and they had the deserted beach to themselves. In the far distance to the east Ellen could just make out the barrier below the Engineers' depot.

She paddled. They skimmed brown stones across the flat water. Nick was impressed when Ellen got one to bounce seven times. Try as he might he could never better five. They walked almost to the barrier arm in arm before turning and heading back as the light began to fade.

Back on top of the cliff, after regaining their breath; Nick took Ellen's hand. He led her through a gap in a stunted hedge into what had been the bottom of a cottage garden. Vestiges of vegetable plots were still visible amongst the colonizing rough grass and here and there a withered sprout stalk stood obstinately to attention.

In the corner, half hidden by elder and almost totally covered in ivy stood a little brick potting shed with a peeling wooden door and sagging roof. A cliff fall a winter or two ago had claimed the cottage but the old potting shed still clung tenaciously to terra firma. Ellen noticed that the dirt path to the door looked well used.

'Hello. Anyone there?' Nick called out as they approached. He knocked on the door and listened with his head cocked to one side. The shed was empty other than for a pile of old sacks and newspapers and some reasonably fresh hay. The soldiers had not been slow to recognize the potential of the isolated shed. Mather, who to general astonishment was training to be a surveyor before joining up, had inspected the cliff below and declared that the garden was perched above a marl outcrop and there was little likelihood of any movement in the near future. Once inside the shed Nick took off his jacket and placed it on the hay and he and Ellen lay together in the gloom for some time.

The Engineers proved tardy in removing the wooden pegs on the cliff and Ellen and Nick were able to visit the deserted beach on several more occasions. The weather was cool but dry and they spent hours snuggled under Nick's coat in the lee of a low finger of clay that was all that remained of a cliff fall years earlier. Despite the exigencies of war Ellen's life was far from unpleasant. Home was bearable, she enjoyed her work, she had good friends and she had Nick.

NINE

Ellen hadn't seen or heard anything from Nick since the previous Sunday and was looking forward to Friday evening at the Lord Nelson. She arrived early to find it quiet in the bar. Ronny and Mather hadn't yet put in an appearance and Kathy's Dave was on duty and wouldn't be in. Early drinkers came and went. She and Kathy pored over a magazine.

Eventually Ronny put in an appearance and soldiers began to arrive in dribs and drabs. There was no transport so they were left with the alternatives of walking, cadging a lift or borrowing a bicycle. Mather finally turned up having walked most of the way before getting a ride on a crossbar. As he kissed Ronny he pulled a crumpled note from the breast pocket of his battle-dress and handed it to Ellen.

'He's gone,' said Mather. 'Yes, please,' he called over Ronny's head to Kathy. 'Usual. And one for. . . .' He gestured down at Ronny and Ellen and then gave them his full attention. 'Sorry. Several of them went first thing this morning. He had a warrant for Wolverhampton but he didn't know exactly where he was going. He asked me to see that you got it. Sorry.'

Ellen opened the note. It was from Nick. It looked as though it had been written in a hurry, pencilled on the back of a buff-coloured form.

'*Dear E, I'm off. Sorry I won't see you. Typical army. Will write c/o Ld Nelson.*' N.

Ellen excused herself and went to the Ladies. She read the note again, several times. There was no indication of where Nick had gone. It was disappointing, but she had no doubt that he would write when he had time. She looked forward to writing back, long newsy letters about what was happening and the people that they knew. It would be almost like their conversations on the beach. She wondered why he intended writing to her at the pub. He knew both her address at Ivy Cottage and that she could be found at Pond Farm. Perhaps he thought that if she went away nursing, or for some other reason, Kathy would still be here and be more reliable for forwarding letters. That was probably it.

As she returned to the bar, busy now with late arrivals Mather and Ronny both glanced up. She smiled, aware that they were checking to see whether she had been crying. The concern on their faces almost made her laugh. They could have passed for twins with their near identical pale skin, ruddy cheeks, freckles and carrot coloured hair. They were not unaware of the picture that they presented, often referring to themselves as Red an' Ginger.

'I was just about to come to make sure you were all right.' Ronny sipped her drink and looked speculatively at Ellen.

'Yes. I'm fine.'

'Sure? You're not upset?' Veronica fiddled with the marcasite drop earrings and necklace that didn't suit her and were altogether too dressy for an evening in the Lord Nelson.

'No, I'm all right. It would have been nice to say goodbye. Still, it's the war, isn't it? It's happening all over.' Ellen shrugged her shoulders and looked out of the window.

The Engineers departed *en masse* a few days later once all of the mines were laid. Despite talk of one final shindig in the pub there was no last hoorah. One day they were there and then they were gone. For a short while the village seemed quiet and the pub takings were noticeably down.

In July the Local Defence Volunteers were officially renamed the Home Guard. George had become an enthusiastic member but chafed because he hadn't yet been given a proper gun. He spent much of his time in the Home Guard caravan on the cliff tops behind the pub or picketed in the Watch House woods at the west end of the village.

During August the enemy commenced bombing raids on British cities and towns. The London Blitz was to last for nine months from September until May 1941. German E-boats sank two ships just east of the village one night in September. These fast diesel-powered vessels equipped with torpedoes and mines plagued the Great Yarmouth section of the North Sea convoy route to the extent that it became known as 'E-boat alley.' November the same year saw an isolated victory against the E-boats when one was rammed and sunk off Southwold. It was the first confirmed destruction of an E-boat.

A handful of elderly NCOs took over the Nissen huts at the depot and thereafter a steady flow of untrained soldiers arrived in the village to receive their first taste of weapons handling. Early each morning the narrow streets pounded and vibrated as personnel were marched to the ranges that had been set up on the cliff tops to the west of the village. The woods echoed to the sound of barked orders and the reports of .303 rifles, machine guns and mortars. Firing points were set up on banks and in ditches and many of the trees and gateposts in the vicinity were quickly reduced to matchwood. After long days out in the cold and wet fields some elements of the soldiery grew bored. Rather than having to fire seemingly endless rounds at disintegrating targets they took to burying handfuls of ammunition. They did anything in order not to fire it.

An old armoured personnel carrier broke down on the cliff top. Since it was beyond repair, rather than move it the army used it as a target for the mortars. The men fired smoke bombs, dummies and live rounds. Inevitably some shots were long and disappeared over the cliff edge. There was a stunned look on the faces of everyone when a long shot with a live mortar set off a mine.

At the end of each day, men were detailed to scavenge the fields to pick up unexploded munitions and other debris. Frequently with their minds on a meal and hopefully for some, an evening in the pub, they did a sketchy job. When they eventually pulled out, in addition to a huge number of spent shell cases there was also a significant amount of unexploded ordnance lying about the countryside.

During November, after days and nights of air activity overhead the peace of a comparatively quiet night was shattered just before two o'clock by three very loud explosions nearby. *Boom, boo-boom.* They were much closer than any of the distant thumps and rumbles that had been heard in the village before. Few of the villagers slept again that night. Several who peered out fearfully into the darkness from their bedroom windows reported seeing a red glow out to sea, west of the village. Theories abounded, a ship hitting a sea-mine, landmines, torpedoes, a plane crash. Someone had run to the pub to phone the police to report a bomber in flames. As the following morning wore on news spread that the explosions had been caused by three German incendiary bombs. They had landed on the New Plantation on the cliff tops to the west of the village. Members of the Home Guard were quickly on the scene. The trees had burned for some time but the fire had at last burned itself out. It was a talking point in the pub.

'Why on earth would they want to bomb the plantation? There's nothing much there. They must have been looking for the Watch House woods and the Home Guard caravan. I bet that was it.'

'Don't let anyone hear you, boy. Don't you know anything? Are you stupid?'

'What? Why?'

'They don't like trees, your Germanics. Specially pines. They can't abide them. Your average German will go miles out of his way to destroy a pine.'

'Oh.'

'Thought everyone knew that.'

The more informed view was that it was a damaged German bomber ditching its bomb load before trying to limp home across the North Sea.

Christmas was very quiet both at Ivy Cottage and Pond Farm. John was in Wales and unable to get home. Robert had joined the RAF and was in Kent. Gilbert Reeve was in the Middle East. Kathy and Ellen sought each other out since Ronny was in bed with flu and Dave was on duty.

Less than three months into the New Year the villagers witnessed the full horror of the war right on their doorstep. A pack of E-boats destroyed seven merchant ships within sight of the cliff tops as two convoys passed each other. One of the stricken vessels drifted to within a few hundred feet of the shore roughly equidistant between Bottle Cottage and the Lord Nelson. There the hulk lay on its side disgorging fuel oil and cargo into the sea.

Within hours the beach was littered with debris. The fuel oil was everywhere, as was the accompanying stench. Many of the villagers made their way down to the barbed wire fence on the cliff tops to look out at the carnage. As their hearts bled for the victims, most also cursed their luck that the spoils of the conflict that lay on the beach were out of reach. How they cursed the minefield. However it struck a small and more enterprising minority that it would be criminal simply to leave the treasure to spoil and rot. In the dead of night certain of them stumped across the fields and braved the cliffs and minefield in order to scavenge.

Anyone on the cliff tops in the early hours of the morning might have been surprised to see a fleeting glimmer here and there of a flashlight beam down below. And the observant too, might have caught the faint whiff of tobacco smoke on the breeze or the brief glow of the police constable's cigarette as he waited in the shadows, specifically to ensure that no bold adventurers undertook such trips for illicit gain.

The cigarette that the policeman was sucking on was almost certainly a Craven A, only slightly stained by sea water. He had learned early in his career that it invariably paid to be standing, fully alert and ready for action in the right place. Occasionally it paid to be looking the wrong way. The constable fully expected to find a few packets of cigarettes in the saddle-bag on his bicycle when he came out of the Lord Nelson after his Sunday lunchtime visit.

A few weeks after the convoy disaster Ellen left work early. She had been working long hours and Mr Reeve suggested she take the afternoon off. He was going to Great Yarmouth and would have his lunch out and wouldn't be back until late. There was cold meat in the pantry for a sandwich if he wanted anything.

It was a dull afternoon but neither cold nor wet. After a piece of toast and one of the individually wrapped Cox's Orange Pippins that her mother had been storing all winter beneath the bed in John's room, Ellen took her bicycle and set out for Cliff Road and the cliff tops.

The tide was out and the beach looked enormous. There were a few ships away on the horizon and a plane droned somewhere overhead. In the gentle breeze off the land the sea was calm. It reminded her of her first visit to the beach with Nick. It looked so inviting. Away to her right the sands were deserted all the way up to the depot and beyond. To the left, beyond a headland she could just make out the top of the wreckage of the vessel that had come ashore from the convoy. If she turned her head so that she couldn't see the ship it all looked lovely. The smell of fuel oil seemed less but the breeze would be taking it out to sea.

Ellen pushed her bicycle along the cliff tops towards the rear of the Lord Nelson. She had no particular plan in mind that she would acknowledge but when she came upon the barrier that Nick had shown her she knew that she was going down the cliffs to the beach – if she could find the path and if it was passable. She was aware that one or two locals had been down and helped themselves to all manner of stuff that had been washed up. There had been careful footsteps in the street late at night. Tinned goods, candles and soap had come ashore in some quantities. There had also been bodies, clothing and personal items that had belonged to the unfortunate sailors. The police and the military had had to take a half-track from the depot to recover the bodies.

Despite the fact that the marker pegs had long been removed Ellen could make out the faint line of a footpath down the cliff face. So long as it continued all the way to the bottom and she stuck to it she would be fine. After concealing her bicycle in the woods and taking a quick glance around to ensure no one was looking, Ellen walked purposefully to the cliff edge and stepped down. The going was good, particularly at the top. There were one or two sticky places lower down where water welled out of the cliff face but the descent was easy. Once she gained the sands she wondered about marking the position of the track but there was little need. There was a huge amount of rubbish on the beach. Close by the path was a sizeable drift of shingle that had built up beside a piece of hatch cover that had washed ashore. She could certainly find it again.

The beach away to the east was deserted and when she peeped round a headland to the west there was no one in sight. Being seen from above was her worst fear but if she kept close to the high tide line she would be visible only occasionally and then very briefly.

It was a joy to be on the beach again. Ellen took off her shoes and squidged the sand between her toes. Despite her plan to stay close beneath the cliffs she thought that a paddle on the way back wasn't out of the question. But she couldn't wait. Picking up her shoes she walked out to the water's edge. She wished that Nick was with her. He would have made her laugh. She thought back to their clandestine visits to the beach and wondered where he was and what he was doing. There had been nothing from him since that hastily written note. She supposed that he was busy – and the post could be erratic. Letters from John often arrived late and out of date order.

Ellen was not particularly religious but for a moment she stopped. The beach was silent other than for the gentle swash of the waves at her feet. She looked out to the horizon and muttered, to herself mostly.

'Please Lord, keep him safe, please Lord, keep him safe. And John and Robert.' She paused and then continued, 'and all of us really, everyone.'

That was the trouble with prayers. Where did you stop? What about Gilbert? If you kept on and on it was hard eventually not to make a case for the enemy.

Mr Reeve had heard again from Robert. He was up in London from time to time but increasingly in Kent and Dorset, dodging the bombs and working on something called radar. Whatever he did, it seemed to be important. He was working all hours.

Ellen returned to the high tide line but found little of interest that wasn't covered in oil. She stopped well short of the depot. The beach was still deserted but there was no point in taking unnecessary risks. She turned back. The tide was coming in and some of the lows were beginning to fill. She wondered whether Harry still came down. She hadn't seen him to speak to for ages, but she supposed that Eve kept him occupied.

There was a tremendous amount of timber on the beach. Her father and John would have been in their element but she couldn't carry it so there was no point in concerning herself with it. She found a large piece of parachute material which she rolled up and took with her. Amelia would be delighted. Once washed it would come in for something.

Arriving back at the hatch cover she thought she might push on a little the other way. She had hoped to find some cigarettes for John and her father but those that she had seen were ruined by seawater. It would be necessary to keep an eye on the incoming tide since a few small cliff falls had left headlands stretching out across the beach. She didn't want to be cut off by the tide and have to sit it out or take her life in her hands and chance climbing the cliffs.

There were cigarettes galore washed up in the clay crevasses behind the first headland. Craven A. They appeared to be free of oil and water damage so she gathered up as many as she could and wrapped them in the parachute material which she then hid behind a clay boulder. There was no point in encumbering herself at this point. She found a few more which she put in her pockets. It wasn't a bad haul. She decided to take a quick peek around the next headland and then go home.

It was hard to tell who got the greater fright, Ellen or the fisherman. As she rounded the headland she spotted footprints and a piece of broom-handle stuck upright in the sand. Ellen looked around in time to see a beret bobbing down among the clay boulders in the cleft where the headland joined the cliff face. Aware he had been rumbled the man stood up. He was short, burly and red in the face. Ellen laughed. She was relieved to see Dave Holt.

'For goodness sake, you gave me a terrible fright.'

Dave grinned sheepishly and came out from his inadequate hiding place. He picked his way over the boulders to join her.

'You're not the only one. I didn't hear you until you were almost on me; thought I was in dead trouble.' He grinned. 'I can't tell how pleased I am to see that it was you.'

'You didn't come that way?' Ellen cast back to look the way she had come. 'I didn't see any footprints.'

'No.'

'How did you get down? I didn't know there was another way down to the beach.'

'Below the Beacon, just to the right. The coastguard showed us a way down after the convoy was hit. We've been scrounging ever since. I sometimes come down fishing. The cod have been good. You just have to be careful of the oil. It doesn't seem so bad along here. It's really awful further back. Anyway what are you doing down here? How did you get down?'

Ellen explained.

'Ha. We knew there was another way but it didn't matter since we had a path right opposite the camp.'

'Have you got anything?' Ellen walked over to Dave's hand-line.

'Hang on.' Dave went back to where he had been hiding and returned with a canvas bag. 'Feast your eyes on this little lot.' He held open the bag so that Ellen could see his catch. There were several dabs beneath a much larger fish.

'Bass,' she said. 'That is a beauty.'

Dave looked at her.

'Not many girls would have known.'

'Oh, I've been down here fishing with my dad or my brother John for years. They always do pretty well – did well. Don't come any more now though. John's away of course.'

'Oh, yes. He's in the army?'

'Yes. Wales, last we heard. Are you staying?'

'I was about to call it a day. It's been slow for a while now. I'm dying for a cuppa.'

Dave pulled his line in, winding it neatly in figure-of-eight fashion round the length of broom handle with the nail in the end that he used to throw the line out. As they were on the point of leaving he went back to where he had hidden and picked up a fish box loaded with tins and cigarettes.

'Oh, that reminds me. I've got some.'

'Which way are you going?'

'I thought I'd go the way I came, but I can go your way.'

'Well, I could do with a bit of help. I've got some more stuff stashed away a bit further along.' Dave grinned at her. 'I'll make it worth your while.'

'Oh, that's all right. I can as easily come your way. Be interested to see where you came down.'

By the time they reached the top of the cliffs just below the Beacon they were both red in the face and blowing.

'It must be thirty feet higher here than the other path.' Ellen paused and gazed out to sea. Between them they were carrying the bag of fish, the pole and line, the parachute parcel bulging with cigarettes, a fish box and a sack of tins and other booty.

'Let's go and dump this and I'll make us some tea. Then I'll give you a hand home with your stuff.' Dave led the way along a narrow path through brambles and gorse bushes and out into a field just to the east and below the Beacon.

He and a small group of others had been living for some time in an encampment of huts and tents located between the railway line and the cliffs. There they lived and worked among a veritable forest of tall aerials. The encampment was some distance from the road so few people had much knowledge of what went on there. Ellen asked him what he did.

'Oh, we're just testing some new equipment.'

As they approached one of the huts a head popped out of another. Dave gestured with his bag. 'Frying tonight, Nigel.' The head grinned, nodded and disappeared. All around there was the hum and crackle of radio equipment.

They deposited their spoils in the hut that Dave shared with two others and what Ellen took to be a radio transmitter. Much other equipment cluttered the floor and walls.

'You won't touch anything, will you?' Dave went off and returned almost immediately with tin mugs of tea and a cracked willow-pattern plate bearing assorted broken biscuits. They sat side by side on his camp-bed.

'So what exactly do you do? Or can't you say?'

Dave was a little reticent. 'We test radio equipment.' He laughed. 'You should have seen us the other night. We had a right do. These things' – he nodded at the transmitter – 'they pump out so many kilowatts that anything metal induces current. Some of the huts have got more equipment than this. We were all getting shocks, going off like fireworks in the dark. Even touching the door handle was hazardous.'

It wasn't until after the war that Ellen learned that Dave was part of a hush-hush specialist radio unit, No 80 (Signals) Wing. Its purpose was to chart and calibrate the navigational radio signals of Luftwaffe bombers and then by 'bending' them send the bombers off course, away from cities and other strategic targets. Even Kathy never knew exactly what Dave was doing.

'There's the train.' Ellen heard the Cromer train approaching and went to the door. 'It's very loud here. But of course you're closer to the track than we are.'

'Oh, yes. They're loud all right, especially those ruddy troop trains at one and two in the morning.'

'We sometimes hear them, if the wind is in the right direction.'

'Well we get the full benefit here.' Dave went to join Ellen at the door. 'See if they whistle. They might lob some coal out.'

Ellen went to the door. 'What do they do that for?'

'For our fires.'

'Oh.' Ellen paused. 'No. I don't think . . . Yes.' The whistle blew several short blasts. Ellen yipped in excitement. 'There's the fireman. He's shovelling something out. It must be your coal.'

'Good-oh. We'll take the buckets over there after we've finished.'

As it turned out by the time they finished their tea two of Dave's colleagues were returning with the coal.

Dave helped Ellen home with her cigarettes and parachute silk and some fish. He stared at the Priests' cottage as they passed.

'I'll drop some stuff off for them,' he said.

'Kathy's in Cromer this afternoon,' Ellen offered the titbit of intelligence.

'Yes, I know.'

During April, under the direction of a visiting naval officer, the Sea Scouts and the Home Guard built a tall, four-legged wooden structure on the cliff tops. Dubbed the Outlook, it was obviously intended as some kind of observation platform. The locals had no real inkling of its purpose until the following month when rooms were requisitioned at the Old Rectory and one morning the postman was surprised to come upon a small band of WRNS marching down the main coast road. As he cycled back along Cliff Road he spotted them up on the Outlook. From then on it was manned in shifts full-time. Eventually word spread that the WRNS were using direction-finding aerials to monitor radio signals. They were trying to locate the source of enemy transmissions out at sea.

Clothing rationing was introduced during June. Everyone had sixty points for the year. The locals were amused to learn that a man's suit could be purchased in Selfridges in London for twenty-six points. By December all mobile women aged between twenty and thirty were being called up. Ellen thought that it might be a good time to get into nursing. However, Mr Reeve said that as a farmworker she was in a reserved occupation and making a major contribution. Quite apart from that, he said that he couldn't do without her.

TEN

They had both taken off their shoes. Margaret was curled up on the two-seat sofa. Peter was slumped in an elderly armchair with his feet on the big square coffee table between them. The blinds in the conservatory at Cowper's Cottage were partly drawn against the evening sun and Simon and Garfunkel were playing quietly in the background on Ellen's record-player.

'Look. It's a beautiful evening now.'

Peter half-turned.

'Yes. Arguably a case of too little, too late however.'

'Oh, don't be such a misery.' Margaret laughed. 'Do you want another drop of coffee.'

'Ah, yes, please.'

'I'll see to it.' Margaret was briskly off the sofa and gathering up their cups.

'Do you know,' she called from the kitchen, as the kettle came to the boil, 'I've got a great fancy for a cigarette.'

'Oh, really?'

'You haven't got any, by the remotest chance, have you?' she asked, as she returned with the steaming coffees.

'I didn't think you smoked,' said Peter, still supine in the armchair.

'Only occasionally, sometimes with a drink.' She paused. 'You know what I really fancy?' Margaret wrinkled her nose.

'What's that?

'An American cigarette. English just aren't the same. I haven't had an American cigarette for yonks.'

Peter smiled and heaved himself up out of his chair.

'Well, let's see what we can do.' He went to his pilot's case, knelt down and opened it up. After rifling about for a second or two he pulled out a packet of 200 Lucky Strike. He broke it open and tossed a pack of cigarettes into Margaret's lap.

'Oh, Luckies. I don't believe it.' Margaret picked up the cigarettes and beamed. She broke open the seal, removed the cellophane and then sniffed deeply.

'Mm. Don't they smell just heavenly?'

'I think I've got some Chesterfields open if you'd prefer. . . .'

'No. These will be just perfect. Thank you so much.'

Peter returned to his chair and smiled at her.

'Glad to be of service.'

'I haven't seen you smoking today, have I? I didn't think. . . .'

'No. Like you I indulge occasionally. When I'm reading – or with a drink.'

'Do you want one?' Margaret offered the open packet. Peter hesitated for a moment.

'Oh, why not? Might as well be hung for a sheep as a Mongolian rat-snake.'

'A Mongolian what?' Margaret laughed.

Peter grimaced and grinned at her as he took a cigarette. 'It's been a bit of a day.'

Margaret took a gold lighter from her handbag and lit their cigarettes. She blew out smoke and sat back and looked at Peter.

'Isn't it funny? We only met a few hours ago but I feel as though we've known each other for ages. Or at least I feel as if I've known you.'

'Funny you should say that. I feel exactly the same.' Peter smiled. 'It's weird, isn't it? How does that happen with some people and not with others?'

'I don't know. On the same wavelength? But I do feel terribly comfortable with you. It's a bit disconcerting in some ways.'

'Hmm.'

They smoked in silence for a moment.

'They're not expecting you back?' Peter gestured at nothing in particular.

'No. I took the afternoon off. They owe me plenty.'

'No one at home expecting you?'

'No. My husband's away. He left earlier this week. He's with a party surveying in the Antarctic. Back in a couple of months.'

'Oh? What does he do?'

'He's a marine biologist.'

'Sounds an interesting job.'

'Well, he seems to enjoy it. He's gone more than he's ever at home.'

'No pets, no children to see to? If you don't. . . .'

'No. The dog died a couple of years ago and we haven't any children. We'd both like a child, but it hasn't happened. You?'

'No, we haven't any either. Abby didn't want any so that was that. I wouldn't have minded. In fact I think I really would like children. Mum kept hoping. She would have liked grandchildren, to see someone carrying on the line but it looks as though it isn't going to happen.'

'Plenty of time. But, of course, if Abigail doesn't want any you're a bit stymied, aren't you? What about the rest of the family? Haven't you any aunts or uncles, cousins?'

'Only George. Mum's younger brother.'

'Did I meet him? Was he at the funeral? I didn't see—'

'No.'

'Really? That's a bit. . . .'

'He was never likely to be. The whole tribe are barking. He lives two doors down, but George doesn't hold with funerals. Mother hardly saw any of them of late.'

Peter shook his head.

'That's their cottage.' He leaned towards Margaret and pointed through the window to a tar-painted cobble cottage with drawn curtains. The back yard was full of stacked timber.

'They'll be sitting in there in the gloom, slumped in front of some rubbish on the television. They're a strange pair. George wouldn't pee on you if you were on fire. And his wife, dear Aunty Janice, well, she's nothing but a bad-tempered, foul-mouthed harridan.'

'Mm, close family then.' Margaret laughed.

'They've got a couple of unpleasant children too, but they've moved away. And an equally nasty dog, if it's still alive.'

Margaret laughed again. 'No one else then?'

'No. You wouldn't want any more like them. There was John, mum's older brother, but he was killed in the war. I never knew him. No children.'

Margaret stubbed out her cigarette in the Swedish glass ashtray on the table beside her.

'It's funny. I'm trying to imagine my father here. Which is difficult since I never knew him; but I did know Ellen. I know you said it had changed but surely something . . . some of it must be like it was in those days.'

'See that chair, behind you.' Peter pointed to an old bentwood chair in the hall. 'Harry used to sit by the range on that. In fact, both of our fathers sat on it, at different times of course. The Tilley Lamp on the windowsill in the hall was all that we had to light the cottage before we had electricity. That and candles. Harry used to sit on that chair with his hands in his lap and his thumbs chasing themselves round and round, first one way, then the other.'

'I remember your mum saying, about the thumbs, and the interminable whistling. He must have been in a bad way, poor soul.'

'Yes. He'd obviously had a terrible time. They all did on that railway.'

'I'm so glad we weren't caught up in the war. I know it was appalling for some but it must have been bad enough for almost everyone in one way or another. Imagine having to try to carry on at home here with the threat of bombs at any time, invasion, shortages and rationing. And if you had a husband or son or daughter stationed away, in the thick of it, it doesn't bear thinking about.'

'Mm. Yes.' Peter smoked in silence for a moment. 'Mum saved Kathy's life during the war. Just behind the pub.'

'Oh.'

'Before I was born, in 1941.'

Ellen was cycling to Pond Farm from Annie's shop. It was early afternoon. She was vaguely aware of the drone of aeroplanes. The RAF had been at it for weeks. Sometimes there was only one bomber, usually there were more. Two Blenheims were up today and they were driving people potty with their continual circuits.

Starting far out at sea they were making high speed runs on the wreckage of the ship that lay on its side just off the beach. After dropping a smoke bomb they climbed up over the cliff tops somewhere between the Lord Nelson and the bottom of Back Lane. Then they turned left over Bluebell Woods and slowly droned off out to sea ready for another high-speed approach.

As Ellen was passing the Lord Nelson, a bomber roared over from behind the pub roof. Even though she had heard it approaching she bobbed her head involuntarily. She pulled into the roadside and sighed as she watched the plane head off inland to begin another long anti-clockwise loop that would take it far out to sea again. Ellen was sure she felt the wash from the two engines as the bomber climbed away.

Kathy was in the garden behind the Lord Nelson taking in washing as the next Blenheim began its bombing run. As she popped pegs into her apron pocket it seemed to her that the bomber was approaching faster than normal. She paused for a moment to watch. The plane rushed low across the sea towards its target and then disappeared briefly below the cliff tops. They all did that and then reappeared with a great roar as they climbed to clear the cliffs.

Kathy said later that she knew something was wrong. The engine note was different. She had watched plenty of bombing runs. From the back windows of the top floor of the pub the wreck of the ship was visible and you could see whether the bomb-aimer had been successful. On this occasion the pilot had got it all wrong. The plane's port wing clipped the cliff top as it climbed. Kathy watched in horror as the bomber staggered briefly before cart-wheeling into the stubble field to her left. The disintegrating plane threw up a lot of dust and made a horrible noise, the screaming engines competing with the crump and screech of the collapsing airframe. As the doomed bomber continued to career along she lost sight of it behind the garden hedge.

Kathy dropped her washing and ran to the garden gate. She crossed the lane and, as she dashed through a gap in the bank opposite, she was showered with earth, stones and other debris. He eyes were filled with grit and something hit her violently on the nose. Through her tears it was apparent that the plane had come to rest. From what she could see it appeared that the bomber fuselage was still largely in one piece, albeit misshapen and upside down. It was enveloped in a great cloud of dust. More ominously black smoke appeared as she watched. The plane was much closer than she had expected. A little more and it would have been in the lane or on the pub tennis courts.

She had no idea of what she was going to do as she ran towards the wreckage. There was no sign of life that she could discern. She was only a few feet away when she saw the flames. In the smoke and dust she was having difficulty breathing and she wiped the back of her hand across her nose and mouth. It came away covered in blood. Shocked, she stopped and looked down. Her front was red. Even as she watched more blood poured from her nose, dribbled down her shin and on to her shoe. She took another step or two.

'Kath! Kathy!'

She turned to see someone running towards her from the road through the drifting dust and smoke. It looked and sounded like Ellen. There was a sudden woof from behind her. She turned back to the plane. The flames had now engulfed much of the bomber. She could just hear Ellen's voice.

'Get away! Kath . . . Get down!'

Kathy's legs buckled as the aeroplane exploded.

She came to rest face down in the hedge. Unconscious and bleeding she lay among debris and burning brambles. By this time others were arriving on the scene. A tractor driver who had been ploughing just to the east of the field was running towards them and the rector's old car rattled to a halt in the lane.

'Keep away. It's probably going . . .' The rector's words were lost in another explosion. Pieces of burning plane showered down around them. Ellen rushed towards her friend and half-dragged, half-carried her out of the burning hedge. She and the rector had just got Kathy into the lane and behind the bank when there was another explosion, much bigger than the first. Deafened and disoriented Ellen managed to get them both back to the Lord Nelson while the rector stood in the lane white-faced and shaking his head. The bomber was now a huge conflagration, sending pillars of greasy black smoke high into the air. The second Blenheim roared overhead, its crew having abandoned their bombing run. It continued heading south rather than beginning another loop out to sea.

Other than Kathy's nose bleed and loosened front teeth they were both scratched and bruised and temporarily deafened. For Ellen it was the shock that was the worst thing. Once the landlady had Kathy's nose-bleed under control she seemed to recover quite quickly but Ellen sat in the back premises at the Lord Nelson shaking until Mr Reeve appeared in the shooting brake to take her home. Amelia put her straight to bed. The next morning they learned that unsurprisingly the crew of three had all perished in the crash. The hedge where Kathy had lain was burned out.

'Are you hungry? I suppose we should do something about food.' Peter looked at his watch.

'I am a bit peckish.'

'I don't know whether there's anything much in. Phil got the basics, I think. I suspect they thought Abby would be here. Still . . . We could go out, I suppose, if you know anywhere.'

'Let's have a look and see what there is.' Margaret got up and went through to the kitchen. Peter roused himself and followed.

'Bread. Oh, there are eggs. Cheese, bacon, tomatoes. What's over here? There's soup. Beans. Peas. And there's fruit.

'Does any of that take your fancy?'

Margaret stood for a moment looking in the fridge. She turned to Peter.

'What about a fry-up?' She grinned. 'We could be really wicked and have fried bread. I haven't had a decent fry-up for ages. It never seems worth it for one.'

Peter returned her grin.

'That's a great idea. And some toast. I could just eat something tasty like that. Is there any HP Sauce?'

Between them they found all that they needed including both HP and tomato ketchup. Peter set a couple of places at the kitchen table and made toast while Margaret found an apron and set to work with bacon, eggs, tomatoes and beans.

'So what else did you and Mum talk about at the convalescent home?'

'It was mostly about Harry. I don't remember getting on to very much else. My dad was what I was really interested in and Ellen seemed quite happy to talk about him.'

*

They were on the veranda at the convalescent home. Ellen smiled and shook her head.

'I remember the evening Harry told me that he was getting married. I'd got a dreadful cold and I was late leaving work. I just wanted to go home and go to bed. I met Harry. He was really excited and obviously wanted to talk. He pulled his bike across in front of mine. "You'll never guess, Ellen", he said. "What?" I asked. And he leaned close and whispered; "Eve and me, we're getting married". "Oh, Harry", I said, "I'm so pleased for you. When's the . . . happy day?" "Soon", he said. I thought then, there's something else. He kept me there talking for ages. He eventually came out with it: Eve was going to have a baby. That would be you, Margaret.'

'Isn't that just typical of me, conceived out of wedlock?'

'Well, never mind. You weren't the first and you won't be the last. Your parents were certainly married before you arrived. Eve was just beginning to show.'

'They moved into the cottage at the bottom of Back Lane. Where Kathy and her husband lived later?'

'Yes. Kathy and Phil. Dave was never there. Your parents went on honeymoon to somewhere near Felixstowe, I seem to remember. They went on the train. That's right, and that same night the Germans bombed the village. Parachute bombs. They were after the troop trains that came through late at night. The railway station was damaged and so was the gamekeeper's cottage in the woods. I remember someone saying it was a good thing Harry and Eve had got away when they did because the railway was disrupted for days after that. There were several more bombs, but they landed in the fields. It sounded like the end of the world. I don't think we got much sleep that night, kept listening out for aeroplane engines.'

That same evening Kathy and Philip visited Ellen.

'Margaret was asking if I remembered her being born.'

'I do,' said Kathy, 'or at least her christening. They had a bit of a do at the Nelson.'

'I've got some memory of it, I think. We've been to so many dos at the pub. I did remember seeing her out in her pram. I thought it was with Eve but it might have been her mother.'

'Oh.' Kathy clapped her hands. 'She was a funny old stick, wasn't she?'

'Well, so would you be, living away in that ramshackle farm of theirs, miles from anywhere, with that old man. It would be enough to make anyone peculiar.'

'Did you go to the wedding? Were you invited?'

'No. It was a very strange affair, by all accounts. But then it would be.

Olive and Eve's mother arranged it. Gerald and Olive were the only people to go from Harry's side.'

'They moved into our old cottage when they came back from their honeymoon, didn't they?' Kathy said.

'Yes. Then it wasn't long before Harry was called up.'

'That's right. It was just after Margaret was born. She was tiny when Harry left. Too young to have any memory of him.'

'Yes. Far too young.' Ellen frowned. 'I remember Harry coming round to Ivy Cottage the night before he left. He came to say goodbye, but I think what he really wanted was to see if I'd write to him while he was away.'

'Yes. You did, didn't you? Do you suppose he had a premonition of what was going to happen?'

'What, him being captured?'

'No. Eve running off like she did.'

'No. The reason he wanted me to write was because Eve couldn't. She was just about illiterate; could barely read, let alone write. I think she could just about manage her name.'

Throughout 1941, in addition to the normal routine the hands at Pond Farm worked hard at clearing woodland and scrub and preparing the land for arable crops. Across the country odd corners and field edges, scraps of land hitherto considered unworthy were cleared, ploughed, raked and seeded. The country was desperate for food. Everyone on the farm was working at least ten hours each day.

Ellen tried to persuade her father to get someone in to plough the field at the top of the garden. It had been left rough for years. He said he would need to talk to George Ashley. It was his field. He, William, only rented part of it, and in any event the old gateway was overgrown and it would be impossible to get a tractor in. Ellen asked him to talk to Ashley if he saw him. After a fortnight William had done nothing about it. She asked him again and he lost his temper.

The following evening Ellen took the tractor and a plough from Pond Farm and forced her way into the field through the hedge from the road at the top end. It wasn't until the following morning when William went to feed the pigs that he discovered the newly ploughed field. He was furious. He was even angrier when he discovered that it was by Ellen's hand.

'Who said you could do that? Did you get Ashley's permission?'

'Mr Reeve talked to him. He's going to pay for the seed if we do the work.'

'Oh, well. That's all right then. God bless Mr Reeve.'

'You've got no reason to go miscalling Dick Reeve,' Amelia chimed in. 'He's been good to us. He's been good to you.'

'Yes, and I might have known whose side you'd be on.'

'I'd have thought you of all people would have good reason to be grateful to Mr Reeve.'

'That's right, that's right. I might have known it'd all be my fault. Well, bugger the lot of you.' Boot-faced, William limped off out. Normally when feeling sorry for himself William went over the field to lean on the wall of the pigsty to commune with the pigs. He made to go over the field but couldn't bring himself to walk on the newly turned earth. Instead he went into one of his sheds and shut the door.

'That's him,' said Amelia. 'He'll be stuck in that old shed till dinner. He'll be mucking about with those old fishing lines. John won't thank him for it.'

In the evenings Ellen and her mother unravelled old woollen garments and reused the wool knitting gloves, socks and scarves for the troops. If she wasn't at the pub Kathy came round but she was a poor seamstress compared with Amelia and Ellen.

Petrol and soap were rationed and bananas had disappeared altogether. Now that they were no longer available even people who never ate them swore that they fancied nothing quite so much as a banana. There were queues at the shops, even in Cromer. Unusual items began to appear on the table. The Finchams sampled a sheep's head for dinner one day. They declared it tasty enough but neither Ellen nor Amelia could meet the sheep's eye. The carrot marmalade that Mrs Pope pressed on Amelia was not greatly admired either.

With the cliffs mined and the beach closed, fishing as a source of sustenance was no longer feasible. Along with others in the village William took to snaring rabbits on the railway embankments and where he could get away with it, in the woods, fields and lanes. There was an old gun in John's room. William sneaked it out of the house and secreted it in his shed. When Amelia was otherwise engaged he tucked the gun beneath a sack on his cart and went off into the countryside for a little poaching. He saw no harm in it so long as operations were conducted at sufficient distance from the village. After a bit of a fright when the police constable from a nearby parish almost caught him with the gun and the rewards of a good evening's work, he made a rather ingeniously concealed hidey-hole beneath the cart. There was plenty of room for the gun and more game than he was ever realistically likely to catch.

Ellen received a letter from Harry. He was camped somewhere up north and was rumoured to be leaving shortly, possibly for the desert. The censors had blacked the word out but it was still possible to read it held at an angle to the light. Ellen wondered how on earth Harry would get on. He had never been out of the county before he joined up.

There was some excitement towards the end of the year when the army set up another listening post on the cliffs by the Beacon. For a short while the WRNS manned the Outlook, the army were at the Beacon and just down the way amid their forest of aerials; the beam benders plied their covert trade. Just when the village seemed to have every conceivable kind of listening facility located on the cliff tops the RAF appeared, bringing with them rumours of yet another.

After a period of training the gentle and naïve Harry found himself on board a troop ship bound for North Africa. His war was turning out to be something of a great adventure. Eve moved back home. Her mother was happy to look after Margaret and Eve was left with sufficient time on her hands to begin an affair with one of her father's employees. She had received a short letter from Harry just before he left the country. Her mother read it to her. It was the very last communication that she had from her husband. The only other news that she ever received concerning Harry was a telegram from the War Office stating that he was missing in the Far East, and presumed dead.

As time passed and there was no further word from or about her husband, Eve finished with the labourer and took up with a black American airman who was billeted temporarily at Seaview across the road from her cottage. Besotted, she returned to the cottage at the bottom of Back Lane in order to be near him. They were in the pub together almost every night and few were fooled by the loud calls of goodnight that rang out at the bottom of Back Lane before two figures crept up the path and into the cottage.

Some months later the airman transferred to a US base in Suffolk. He asked Eve to go with him. The village woke up one morning to find that Eve, her daughter Margaret and the airman had all disappeared. No one had any idea where they had gone.

ELEVEN

On 27 April 1942 the Luftwaffe launched their first attack on Norwich. Numerous other cities were targeted in what became known as the Baedeker raids. The bombers were back over Norwich a couple of days later. Significant portions of the city were destroyed and well over 200 people killed. Almost everyone seemed to know of some poor soul who had perished.

More RAF men arrived in the village. They erected a mast, over 200 feet high, on Beacon Hill and placed a huge dish on the top. This occasioned some muttering among an element in the community who felt that such an obvious structure would be like a red rag to a bull and make the village a target. However the unrest died down as time passed and the Luftwaffe found business elsewhere.

It became known eventually, in the way that things do, that all radar activity in the village was now under the jurisdiction of the RAF. The WRNS packed up and left and the Home Guard took over the Outlook. They immediately erected a canvas shelter to keep the wind and rain at bay and installed a few home comforts in the form of deckchairs, a small table, a primus stove and tea-making requisites.

At Christmas, George announced that he and Janice Woodhouse had got engaged and would be getting married the following spring. This revelation came out of the blue. Equally surprising was the fact that they had already made arrangements to rent one of the old fishing cottages in Back Lane.

'You're very young. Are you quite sure you know what you're doing? That it's what you really want?' asked Amelia. Throughout the meal Ellen spotted her mother's vain glances and covert signals to enlist William in her cause but he wouldn't be drawn.

'There's no going back once. . . .'

'I know.' George's responses were becoming terse.

'Boy's old enough to know his own mind,' William sat back in his chair. He plainly didn't share Amelia's misgivings.

'Well, I hope you do know what you're doing, that's all.'

'We do.' George was becoming sulky and petulant.

'And those cottages,' Amelia continued, 'they're terribly poky if you're ever thinking of having a family.' She stared hard and meaningfully at George but could elicit nothing on the current or intended state of Janice's belly.

'Oh well, so long as you're sure.' Amelia gave up. She hardly knew the girl at all.

After New Year she was asked to run up a wedding dress for the heavily built Janice. She spent a lot of time and took a good deal of trouble fitting her future daughter-in law's burly frame and was outraged when she never received a word of thanks.

'Mind you, it's no more than I would have expected from that lot. There's not one of them knows how to behave.'

Ellen was a reluctant bridesmaid. She was grateful when it was all over. It was one embarrassment after another. Her misery was complete during the evening festivities in the Woodhouses' cramped sitting-room when she was cajoled into doing the hokey cokey with two of Janice's brothers, one home on leave from the navy and both very drunk indeed. Able Seaman Woodhouse fell over, dragging Ellen and the other brother with him.

He was heard to say the following day in the bar of the Lord Nelson that the wedding had been, at least for him, a memorable occasion.

'Hell of a good do that was. Blast, boy, we sunk some beer. That Ellen's a bit of all right. I wouldn't kick her out of bed. I might just have to look her up when I'm back again.' He took a pull on his pint.

'Tell you what though' – he laughed and shook his head ruefully – 'I had a right rotten head this morning. Woke up in the backyard with my head in the taters. Blast, I was as sick as a dog. Right good night that was.'

It was on a Sunday afternoon almost a year later that George and Janice put on their best clothes and strolled down the hill with their firstborn to take tea with William and Amelia.

'Have you decided what you're going to call him?' Amelia cast a glance at the fat face cradled above her left breast. She found the baby's washed out blue eyes unsettling, and looked away. Cold and impassive, not unlike his mother's eyes, she decided. They were sitting comfortably in the sitting-room at Ivy Cottage drinking tea and eating cake only slightly past its best. The cake was William's doing.

He had spotted it tucked behind a curtain on a back windowsill at the sanatorium. It was there all Wednesday and Thursday. Nothing had changed on Friday morning. On the spur of the moment he stopped and tried the window. It opened easily. Closing it carefully he promised himself that if the cake were still there at the end of the day he would give serious thought to taking it home. He didn't consider himself a dishonest man but the cake had obviously been forgotten and it would be a shame if it went to waste.

To his delight it was still there as he headed for the stable at the end of the day. He stopped the horse and looked around. All was quiet so he eased the window up and reached inside. It was the work of a moment. He didn't even have to leave the cart. Back at the stable there was a padlocked wooden box permanently strapped to the carrier of his bicycle for just such an occasion.

Once she became aware of its provenance Amelia hadn't wanted anything to do with the cake. She had to admit later though that it was very good.

'What are you going to call him?'

George and Janice exchanged glances.

'Have you thought of a name yet?' Amelia persisted.

'Shall we tell them?' Janice shrugged her thickset shoulders in what she considered a winsome manner. Amelia thought that the girl's pink dress was far too tight and dressy for a Sunday afternoon. She was also sporting jewellery altogether too dainty for someone of her build. Her necklace disappeared into the numerous folds of flesh around her neck and the tiny ear-rings looked lost on her fat lobes.

She beamed at George. As usual her smile never quite reached her eyes. George shook his head and sighed. The principal reason for their visit was so that Janice could impart this intelligence.

'William John has a nice ring to it, don't you think?' Amelia continued pleasantly, 'after Granddad and his uncle. Or John William, or something George, I suppose.' She spoke softly since the subject of their conversation was rubbing his face and showing signs of nodding off. It was nice to have a rest from his big square mouth.

'No.' Janice looked fondly at her son. 'We want something classier than that.' She stared at George. 'Don't we, boy?'

She returned her attention to Amelia.

'Have a guess. You'll never get it in a month of Sundays. Go on, have a guess. Have a go.'

'Oh, I don't know.' Amelia tried a few names although she already knew that it would be fruitless.

'Come on, Granddad.' Janice turned on William, smoking quietly beside the empty fireplace. 'You have a go too.' If he thought he was going to be able to get away without participating Janice's shrill entreaty soon put him right.

'Oh, I don't know, girl. Call him Fred or Eric. That's a thought. Why not call him Eric?'

'We can't call him that.' Janice looked at them both expectantly. She was plainly disappointed at the lack of enthusiasm.

'Just tell them,' George interjected.

'Do you want to tell them? They're your parents.' Janice took exception to the interruption. George frowned in irritation but without waiting for an answer Janice continued excitedly.

'You wouldn't never have guessed anyhow. We're going to call him – duh-dah – wait for it' – she raised her arms like some demented conductor – 'duh-dah!' Again she paused. 'Kingsley!' She looked at Amelia and then at William expectantly.

'Kingsley Ambrose,' she continued.

'Aren't we, sweetheart?' she bawled at the baby. 'We thought about Edwin after my dad, but then we thought Kingsley because it's got class. Or Ambrose, after my granddad. Then we thought we could call him Ambrose as well. Do you think Kingsley Ambrose or Ambrose Kingsley sounds best?'

There was silence apart from the clock ticking on the mantelpiece. George was suddenly absorbed in pushing cake crumbs about his plate.

'Dad?' Janice pressed for an answer but William looked too thunder-struck to respond.

'Mum?'

Amelia wished that the girl wouldn't call her that. She wasn't comfortable with that level of familiarity.

'Oh.' To say that Amelia was surprised would have been something of an understatement. 'I really couldn't say,' she continued after a pause. Unable to bring herself to look anyone in the eye she stood up carefully, handed the potential Kingsley Ambrose to his mother and busied herself with the teapot. William cleared his throat and spat genteelly into the fireplace. It was by no means certain that it was a shred of tobacco that had caused his discomfort.

Amelia was further surprised when John wrote from Iraq to say that he was working in the cookhouse.

'I didn't know he liked cooking. He never showed the slightest inclination when he was here, at home. Nor washing up neither.' She laughed. 'Soon as there was anything like that to be done he was off.'

She found the news encouraging. 'Perhaps it'll keep him out of harm's way. Stands to reason, they won't have the cookhouse right on the front line.'

William wasn't sure that John's expertise in the kitchen, or lack of the same held much sway, nor was he convinced that an army at war worked quite like that. For once he kept his thoughts to himself. Amelia and Ellen tried to write to John every week, sometimes twice or three times, and sent him the occasional newspaper and parcel of cigarettes, razor blades and soap when they could get them. Throughout the following year they would be able to follow his progress from Iraq into Egypt and then on to Libya.

Mr Reeve received more news of Gilbert. He was in Palestine and newly promoted to captain. Ellen thought privately that the promotion would probably make Gilbert even more insufferable than before but she said nothing. Robert was still busy with radar down on the south coast. Mr Reeve rarely mentioned his youngest son these days although he probably worried about him more than he did Gilbert.

The highlight of the summer was Kathy's wedding to Dave Holt. Kathy's mother conjured up sufficient pieces of suitable material and she and Amelia ran up dresses for the bride and her sisters who were bridesmaids. It was a bright spot in the year. The newlyweds moved into the cottage next door to Annie's shop in Church Street but the idyll was short-lived. By the onset of winter the beam-benders had gone and in the New Year Dave was posted to Africa.

It was a bitter Wednesday evening early in February when Amelia answered the door at Ivy Cottage to find Kathy on the doorstep. She seemed excited.

'Hello, Mrs Fincham. Is Ellen in, please?'

'Hmm. Hello, Kathy.' Amelia had been sewing. She mumbled a greeting through a mouthful of pins. 'Sorry. Yes. She's upstairs. What's got into you? Ants in your pants? You'd better come in. You look frozen.' Amelia ushered Kathy into the living-room. 'Get yourself warm by that fire. I'll give her a call.'

But Ellen was already on her way down the stairs.

'Oh,' Amelia paused in the hall, 'there you are. How's your grandmother, Kathy? She better now?'

'Yes, thanks. That'll teach her to climb up on chairs.'

'She was lucky she didn't break anything.'

'Yes. Oh, by the way, while I remember, someone was saying today that they've started clearing the beaches of mines.'

'What here?'

'No, other side of Cromer, but they're supposed to be heading this way. It might not be long now till they open the beach again.'

'Oh, wouldn't that be good? I've really missed it. We might get a few holi-daymakers in the summer and the fishermen will be able to bring their boats back.' Amelia paused to see whether she was to be included in whatever it was that had brought Kathy round. It looked unlikely so she headed back into the front room.

Kathy waited until Amelia had closed the sitting-room door and she and Ellen were alone. Gripping Ellen's arm she whispered. 'You'll never guess who I saw on my way home today.' She began to remove her coat.

'Oh? Who?'

'An old friend of yours.' Kathy paused for effect. 'I nearly telephoned the farm to tell you.'

'Who? Who was it?' Ellen poked the fire into life and put a couple of pieces of coal on.

'Nick. Nick Nichols.' They stood with their backs to the fire, warming their hands behind them. Kathy nudged Ellen and grinned.

'Oh.' Ellen looked a little uncertain and then smiled.

'I was biking back from Cromer in the dark when this lorry pulled along-side. It almost frightened the life out of me when this voice said "Hello, Kathy." They put the light on in the cab. Not that it was much help. He's back but he won't be here long, he said. He asked about you, what you were doing but he couldn't stop. What he did say though was that he would see you in the bar on Friday night. If you want, that is.'

Ellen smiled. 'He's back then.'

'Yes.' Kathy could still barely contain herself. 'You'll see him, won't you? 'Course you will.'

Ellen smiled again and turned to gaze into the crackling fire. They chewed over the names that had come and gone in the last few years. These days most of the younger men in the pub were from the radar station.

'And guess what else?' Kathy had another reason for her visit.

'Oh, I don't know. What?' Ellen waited expectantly.

Kathy grinned but stayed silent, willing Ellen to get it right.

'What?' Ellen pulled a face. Kathy smiled smugly, half turning and looking down pointedly at her stomach.

'What?'

Kathy placed both hands on her belly and grinned.

'You're not! You're not going to have a baby?'

Kathy nodded and beamed.

'You are! How long have you known? Oh, you. When?

'I am. I'm going to be a mummy. September.'

'Does Dave know? What does he—?'

Kathy frowned. 'I don't know. We haven't heard from him. I've only just sent a letter telling him.' But the solemnity lasted only a second or two. The pair shrieked, hugged and cavorted round the living-room. Amelia pushed the hall door open to see what all the noise was about. On hearing the news she insisted that Kathy sit down at once.

'That's no way to be going on if you're expecting,' she said. She went to the sideboard and poured three small glasses of ginger cordial.

Ellen had been out once or twice since she had last seen Nick but she had no steady boyfriend. Several RAF men had asked her out but they had all moved on. There had been a sporadic exchange of letters with one of them but she had no real expectation that anything would come of it. She was not really looking for anything serious.

Ellen determined to meet Nick. At worst they would spend an evening catching up on each other's news, not that she had anything very interesting to tell.

Arriving at the Lord Nelson early after a couple of days of mounting excitement she was surprised just how much she was looking forward to seeing him again. It was quiet in the pub. He was leaning on the bar talking to Kathy and fishermen Tom and Frank Clarke.

'Here she is.' Kathy had been keeping an eye on the door. Ellen smiled and called hello. Nick promptly straightened up, and grinned back. He adjusted his sleeves and walked over to the door where Ellen was unbuttoning her coat.

'Hello, stranger,' he said very quietly.

'Good evening, Corporal Nichols. How are you?'

Nick snuggled his nose into the nape of Ellen's neck for a moment and then helped her off with her coat.

'I'm fine thanks. Better for seeing you. And if you look very carefully I think you'll find that it's Sergeant Nick these days.' He hung up Ellen's coat on the hooks by the door. 'Mm,' he whispered, 'you smell wonderful.'

'Why, thank you, kind sir. And congratulations.' Ellen turned and gave him a smile.

Nick bought drinks and after a few minutes banter with the Clarke brothers they were heading for a table in the corner when Kathy called after them.

'Why don't you go into the lounge? There's a nice fire and I don't think there's anyone in there at the moment. It'll get busy in here and you won't be able to hear yourselves think.'

'Ah, that old trick,' called Tom. 'You want to make sure she don't charge you lounge prices, together. You'll pay a premium for sitting on them fancy seats.'

They laughed and walked through to the empty lounge and settled themselves comfortably beside the fire.

It took some time for them to grow comfortable with each other again. Nick said that when he left the last time he expected to go abroad but he went first to Yorkshire and then after a few days on to training camp in Whitstable. He stayed there for some time as an instructor before moving on to Market Drayton where he spent almost a year. His visit to Norfolk was going to be fairly short, although he had no real idea when he would be leaving. He seemed much the same, although he looked tired and he was beginning to lose his hair.

They both drank a little more than was prudent. At closing time it was a crisp clear moonlit night and as they left Nick suggested that they wander down the lane behind the pub to look at the sea. Ellen asked why he hadn't written.

'Ah,' Nick said. 'I'm sorry about that. I always meant to. I just never seemed to get around to it. I suppose I'm not much of a writer really.'

By the time they reached the cliff top they had stopped to kiss several times. When Nick suggested that they go to see whether the little potting shed was still standing Ellen was in no mood to decline.

They had to negotiate some relatively new barbed wire fencing to reach the shed. Nick climbed through first and then placed a heavy boot on the middle strand and pulled the top one up so that Ellen could get through.

'Mind your coat. This stuff is vicious.'

'Gosh, the edge is a lot closer than the last time we were here.'

'It is. Don't go too near. This path is a bit overgrown too. I doubt whether many people come this way these days. I suspect that the radar boys have found somewhere else.'

Nick had to lean on the potting shed door to open it. He flicked his Zippo. Other than for a slightly fusty smell it seemed dry and clean inside. Flicking off the lighter he gently backed Ellen into a corner and kissed her.

Nick and Ellen didn't see much of each other since they were both working long hours. They met occasionally in the Lord Nelson and they returned to the potting shed twice more. On the sole occasion that they visited the beach Nick was much less assured on the way down than he had been a few years earlier. He walked well ahead of Ellen and trod slowly and warily, hacking marks with the heels of his boots as they descended. Since the last time they negotiated the minefield the villagers had actually heard several mines explode. It certainly got people's attention when it happened.

As things turned out Nick stayed less than three weeks. Early one morning as Ellen was returning to the farmhouse after seeing to the chickens an army lorry was backing into the yard. Nick leapt out before it came to a halt.

'Hello. What are you up to?' She was pleased and surprised to see him. Nick seemed hot and flustered.

'Ah, I'm glad you're here. I won't need to leave this.' He waved a crumpled brown envelope before stuffing it into his breast pocket. 'I'm off again. I didn't want it to be like last time. I talked Mac into coming round this way on the off chance. I haven't got many minutes. I hoped you'd be here.'

'Where are you going? I suppose you can't say.'

'Transit camp. We're off to the station just now. I'll write. I will this time, I promise.'

'Yes, do. I'll write back. I'd like to know you're safe.'

Nick took Ellen in his arms and kissed her, rather clumsily since she had a bowl of eggs and a few wrinkled apples from the barn in her arms.

'Look after yourself.'

'I will. You be careful too.'

They were still in an ungainly embrace when the lorry horn sounded. Ellen could see the driver gesticulating through the cab window, but he had a wide grin on his face. Nick gave her a final kiss on the tip of her nose, squeezed her hand and then ran across the muddy yard towards the lorry. He gave her a last wave from the cab window as they disappeared behind the paddock hedge on their way to the railway station.

Ellen slipped back into the old routine. A few weeks later she was unwell. For several days she felt nauseous, mostly in the afternoons. Sometimes she felt so bad that she had to lie on her front on the floor until the feeling passed. Mr Reeve was worried.

'Do you want to go home, lass?'

'No, thanks. It'll pass in a little while. It must be one of those twenty-four hour things. It's just going on a bit.'

'Well, if you're sure. If it keeps on you'll need to see the doctor.'

It didn't dawn on her until comparatively late. She was pregnant.

Pregnant outside wedlock. After several disturbed nights and much soul-searching she confided as much to Ronny and Kathy one Saturday afternoon in the Singing Kettle.

'No! Are you sure?'

'What? Oh, for goodness sake.' Ellen's companions gaped at her with a mixture of consternation and pity. Kathy lowered her voice. 'Nick?' She and Ronny stared.

'Of course.' Ellen was indignant. She had never been with anyone else.

'How long? Are you sure? Have you told anyone, your mum and dad?'

'Of course I'm sure. No. I haven't told anyone.' Ellen stared dully at the empty teacup in front of her and sighed. 'Not yet.' She wasn't looking forward to telling anyone else, least of all her parents. It was a pity that John was not at home. She grimaced and shrugged her shoulders.

'Will you tell him? Nick?'

'Well, yes, if I can. He'll want to know, won't he? I don't know where he is though. He's never written. He said he would. I expect they'll know how to contact him down at the depot.'

Kathy and Ronny swapped glances. Kathy puffed out her cheeks and looked doubtful. Veronica chewed at her lower lip. She began to fiddle with her cup and saucer. After a moment they both sighed.

'What?' Ellen would have had to be blind not to spot the exchange.

There was another lengthy silence.

'You do know he's married, don't you?' Ronny finally took the bull by the horns.

'What?'

'He's married.' Kathy leaned back in her chair and began to push her cup and saucer about with the tip of a finger. 'Surely you knew he was married. And he's got a daughter at least, maybe more children by now.'

Ellen stared at her teacup. Her cheeks burned and tears started in her eyes. It wasn't what she wanted to hear.

'We thought you knew. You must have known.'

'Ah,' she said. She found a handkerchief and blew her nose. 'It never occurred to me. . . .' But of course it had and after a moment she admitted as much. It had crossed her mind more than once: it had actually worried her. However, no mention was ever made of any wife or family so it had been easy to put it to the back of her mind. Being with Nick had been sufficiently diverting for it not to have been difficult.

It was recognized by all three that Ellen's bombshell merited full and proper consideration so they ordered more tea and a bun each to sustain them as they did the subject justice. Now that it was out in the open Ellen was glad to talk. By this time Kathy was considered an expert on all aspects of pregnancy, and the subject was covered in some depth. The discussion continued, occasionally in shouts as they cycled home, sometimes three abreast, sometimes in single file. After Kathy left them Ellen and Ronny continued in the dusk outside the church.

They concluded that the baby must be due the second week in November. There was talk of whether like Kathy Ellen wanted a boy or whether she would be happy with a girl. They covered the subject in greater detail the next day as they moved over the fields hoeing beet. Now it was no longer theoretical. Unsurprisingly they concurred that it wouldn't matter so long as the baby had all its bits and pieces in working order and in the right place. During a discussion on whether she would keep the baby they touched briefly on subjects as diverse as hot baths, gin and knitting needles. It was no more than a red herring. For a short time the problem seemed less significant and the cold twisted knot of fear that had lain inseparable from Nick Nichol's seed in Ellen's belly abated.

Sleepless in the early hours for several mornings the fear returned. However the question of whether or not she should keep the baby ceased to be an issue. Ellen had assumed that Nick would want the baby as much as she did. That he was married altered nothing in her eyes. Her parents and most of the village would be scandalized and that would be difficult. When she thought about Mr Reeve her stomach lurched and it positively squirmed at the thought of Robert. What on earth would they think?

Ronny and Kathy would be fine. They would be fiercely supportive. It was bound to be difficult and there would be some unpleasantness but she made up her mind that she would have the baby and keep it. She just hadn't worked out quite how it was all going to turn out.

She made the mistake of confiding in George. John would have been a much better bet. He would have been surprised, shocked even, but he would have been sympathetic and he would have wanted to help.

She cycled up the hill one evening to seek George out. He had just quarrelled with Janice and taken refuge in a newly built but ramshackle shed in the front garden. He was in an evil temper.

'Oh, shit! Bloody hell!' Ellen heard her brother's raised voice before she saw him. Something crashed against the shed wall. She found him hopping about in the doorway having whacked his ankle with a hatchet while trying to knock the front wheel out of an old bicycle.

Ellen was prepared to admit later that the sensible thing would have been to get back on her bike right there. George calmed down a little though after Ellen inspected the wound and padded his handkerchief inside his sock. They talked of this and that for a while until Ellen reluctantly announced her news.

'You what?' George stared at her for what seemed like an age. 'You stupid cow.'

Ellen was appalled at her brother's reaction. She was even more aghast at the lengthy tirade that followed. Eventually George limped indoors to tell Janice. Her cunning brother wasn't about to let pass such a heaven-sent opportunity for a conciliatory overture to his wife. The ploy obviously worked since Janice wasted no time in hurrying out, with Kingsley Ambrose in her arms, to join in heaping sarcastic approbation on Ellen's head. George and Janice were reunited against a common foe. After learning that their parents hadn't yet been told George climbed on to Janice's bike and despite Ellen's entreaties sped off to carry the glad tidings down the hill to Ivy Cottage.

Ellen took refuge in the Lord Nelson for the rest of the evening. Between customers she and Kathy debated George's reaction and the likely scenario at Ivy Cottage. It wasn't difficult to imagine. Eventually it was closing time and Ellen was forced, reluctantly, to leave. Kathy offered to go with her or provide a bed for the night, but they decided that there was little to be gained by putting off the inevitable. Leaving the bar unattended for a moment Kathy accompanied Ellen outside where she gave her a hug and squeezed her hands before Ellen trudged across the gravel to get her bicycle.

Having put her bike in the shed at Ivy Cottage Ellen could see her parents and George waiting for her through the living-room window. Despite the darkness they couldn't have avoided seeing and hearing her but not one of them looked up. She dreaded going in but made up her mind to try to brazen it out.

Her mother and father sat in their usual chairs either side of the fireplace. Amelia was clutching a screwed up handkerchief to her chin. Her father sat rigidly, drumming the fingernails of his left hand on his tobacco tin on the arm of the chair. Every few moments he flicked ash with the other hand into the fireplace. She had seen them like this before and knew that there was going to be no easy way of dealing with it.

'Hello,' she said brightly, as she went in unbuttoning her coat. 'Anyone like some tea?'

'I could do with a cup.' George leaned forward on the sofa and rubbed his hands together expectantly, but he wouldn't meet Ellen's eye. No one else spoke. Ellen went into the kitchen to fill the kettle. She hung up her coat and paused briefly, closing her eyes and biting her upper lip. After a moment of trying to compose herself she returned to the living-room.

Primed by her brother, her parents reacted in exactly the way that they had always said they would, should the occasion arise.

'Well, my girl' – Amelia levered herself out of her chair and turned as Ellen entered the room – 'what have you got to say for yourself?' For a moment Ellen could have sworn that a look of grim satisfaction crossed her mother's face. Amelia faced her, arms crossed tightly beneath her bosom, her mouth clamped into a thin line. Then suddenly her face was tearful again. 'Oh. No need to ask is there? You have been busy, haven't you? Well, I hope you're satisfied now.'

George stared out of the window, still unable to meet her eye. Ellen recognized the barely concealed look of smugness on his face; she had seen it many times before. It was no more than she expected from him. What on earth was wrong with them all? George couldn't help himself; he had always taken joy from the misfortune of others. For a moment she hoped that his ankle was sore. A quick glance at her father's face confirmed her belief that he would fail to take any satisfaction from the situation.

'How long have you known? When is it due?' Amelia dabbed at her nose and then sat down again.

Ellen's hope of brazening it out crumbled now faced with the reality of her parents' anger and disappointment. She stood in the doorway with her head bowed, plucking at her skirt. She was frightened by the look on her father's face. He hadn't yet said anything. He didn't get up from his chair and he took his time lighting the stub of his cigarette before addressing her.

'Well, girl?' He glared at Ellen. 'Your mother's waiting.'

'What?'

'What?' With some awkwardness he pushed himself up out of his chair, took his hat off and threw it on to the floor. 'What the bloody hell do you mean *what*? Don't you bloody *what* me, my woman.'

The white dome above his lined brown face with its big droopy moustache gave him a comical look. He rarely took his hat off. Standing bent and questioning he looked like some exotic monkey. For a moment Ellen almost wanted to laugh.

Mr Fincham could go from silent, pent up fury into kitten-kicking mode in an instant and he now demonstrated that ability. Ellen had seen it before, but her father's reaction frightened her.

'You know bloody well what we're talking about. What the hell do you think you've been up to?' Flecks of spittle appeared on his chin as he worked himself into a froth. 'Come on. I'm talking to you.'

Ellen remained silent.

'I don't know,' her mother said. She turned away, shaking her head, her shoulders sagging. 'Where did we go wrong? What on earth will people think?'

William sucked angrily on his dead cigarette and then threw it into the fire.

'I don't know either. You spend your bloody life scrimping and saving and struggling to do the best you can for your kids and this is all the bloody thanks you get.'

He turned away to rearrange the cushion on his chair. His back was obviously giving him pain and he winced as he sat down.

'Well, you've gone and done it now, girl, good and proper. That's what comes of hanging around in pubs. You wouldn't listen. Oh no. You knew best. Well, you know what you can do now, don't you? You can get up those stairs and pack your things. You've brought nothing but disgrace on this family. Now you can pack your bags and bugger off.'

'Language, William!' Amelia turned and barked at her husband. 'There's no need for that.' She turned back to Ellen before looking away again.

'We won't be able to look anyone in the eye. We'll never be able to hold our heads up again. I never thought it would come to this. I always thought you were a decent girl.'

She sat down and added, somewhat bizarrely, 'I'm just glad that poor John isn't here to see this. It would break his heart.' Amelia snuffled into her sodden handkerchief. 'And who's the father, may I ask?'

'Who's the father? I doubt whether she knows who the bloody father is,' William shouted nastily. More spittle gleamed on his chin. He wiped it away angrily with the back of his hand.

'Whoring about up there at that pub with that trollop Kathy Priest – or whatever her name is – and her so-called mates. It's enough to make you bloody sick.'

Her mother turned to look at her. 'Well, do you? Do you know who it is?'

Ellen was not surprised at her father, but she could hardly believe that of her mother. It was the last straw. She didn't answer. Averting her eyes she hurried through the living-room and ran upstairs. Her barely contained composure broke long before she got into bed but she took care to weep silently. She was not going to give any of them the satisfaction of hearing her cry.

TWELVE

With her mother raising the subject at every opportunity and her father ignoring her completely Ellen spent as little time as possible at home. Running up the stairs that evening she had heard her father.

'She can sling her hook, as soon as she likes.'

Her mother's weary response had been inaudible, but she would have to leave, that much was obvious. She couldn't live at home any longer. It would be intolerable.

Several evenings later when they were alone Ellen told her mother that the baby was due in November and that the father was a soldier who had now gone away. Beyond that she had nothing to say that her parents wanted to hear or that would make them feel better. Since Dave was away she accepted Kathy's invitation to join her in the tiny cottage next to Annie's shop. All being well they would be giving birth within weeks of each other.

The matter that really exercised Ellen was the need to tell Mr Reeve. It wasn't that she was frightened, but she knew that they would both find it embarrassing. She felt as though she had let him down. As hard as she tried she could think of no way to broach the subject.

It turned out to be unnecessary. Preparing his lunch one day she butter-fingered a jar of pickled onions on to the quarry-tiles in the pantry.

'Oh! For goodness sake,' she railed at herself, 'you stupid girl.' The farmer had just come in and was washing his hands at the kitchen sink.

'That sounded a bit terminal. Are you all right, lass?'

'Oh hello, I didn't hear you come in. Yes. I've just dropped the last of those pickled onions and the jar has broken. I'm sorry.'

'Ha! How many onions were there? There can't have been many.'

'Three. They're the last, I'm afraid.'

'Don't be afraid, lass. Run them under the tap. They'll be fine.' He chuckled. 'Any more of that and I won't be able to afford you. You'll be getting the heave-ho.'

Instead of a rueful laugh, Ellen burst into tears.

'That's not you laughing at my misfortune I hope, young lady.'

Receiving no reply the farmer wandered through to the pantry as he dried his hands. Ellen was kneeling on the floor, her shoulders shaking.

'Good Lord, Ellen. Whatever's wrong?' He went to her. 'It was only a joke. Ellen? Have you cut yourself? Let me see.'

Taking in the pool of vinegar and the broken glass on the floor he helped her up and led her out of the pantry and sat her at the kitchen table. Once he was satisfied that she hadn't cut herself he fetched the coal shovel and gathered up the glass and onions. Between dabbing her eyes and blowing her nose Ellen fetched a floor cloth and bucket of hot water. She began wiping up the mess.

'What a waste. I'm sorry.'

'Never mind, there were only a few. Here's another one. We'll run them under the tap. Accidents happen. It's not as though you make a habit of it, is it?' Mr Reeve tried a jocular approach. 'When was the last time you broke anything? I can't remember and I bet you can't either.'

'No.' Kneeling on the quarry tiles Ellen's shoulders slumped and she began sobbing anew. Concerned, the farmer put a hand on her shoulder.

'Whatever is the matter, lass? Ellen?' He kneaded her shoulder gently and gave her his handkerchief.

'Nothing.'

'It's not the onions, is it?'

Ellen plucked at the hem of her skirt. 'No.'

'Well, what's the matter? Can I not help?'

'No. No one can.'

'Oh.' Mr Reeve paused. 'Well, Maria was a great believer in a problem shared . . . as you know.' He paused and gazed out of the window before turning and looking at Ellen. 'Think about it,' he said gently. 'Let me know if I can help. You know I will if I can.'

Ellen nodded. She stared at the floor for a moment before resuming in a small voice. 'I'm going to have a baby.' She peeped up at Mr Reeve through her hair and gave him a tight little smile. Then she looked away again.

'Oh.' The farmer looked dumbfounded. 'Ah. I see.' After a moment he straightened up and took the broken glass out to the backyard. When he returned he pulled a kitchen chair over beside Ellen and perched on the corner of the seat. He rubbed his hands together lightly and winced. 'Ouch!' He sucked at his finger. 'I suspect that your parents are less than delighted. You have told them, I suppose?'

Ellen was still kneeling on the floor. 'Yes. Father says I've to leave home. I have, more or less left.'

'Where are you?'

'At Kathy's. Her husband's away.'

'Ah.' Mr Reeve rubbed his chin and then sucked his finger again. 'Look at this. I've cut my finger. It's only a nick but it's pouring. Can I trouble you for my hanky?'

'I'll get you something to put on it.' As Ellen stood and tried to pass him the farmer stood up too and put his hand on her shoulder. He pulled her gently towards him.

'Come here, my lovely lass.' He wrapped the handkerchief round his hand and then hugged her. After a moment he held her at arm's length and looked into her eyes. 'How do you feel about it, Ellen? I'm sure it's all been a bit much. Are you all right with the prospect? Do you want the baby?'

Ellen nodded, sniffed and gulped. 'I was a bit shocked at first. But I'm getting used to the idea.' She paused, nodded her head and then continued fiercely, 'I'm going to keep the baby, somehow. No matter what it takes.'

Tears started again and Ellen wiped them away, angrily this time. Mr Reeve pulled her towards him again and hugged her tightly.

'There, there, come on. Don't cry, lass.' He kissed the top of her head.

'And don't worry. We'll sort something out. I promise.'

That afternoon when he called in for his tea Mr Reeve raised the subject again. Perched on the edge of a kitchen chair with his elbows on the table he nibbled a jam tart and sipped tea from his oversize cup. Steam rose about his face as he blew urgently on the tea. He always drank it as hot as possible.

'When is your baby due, Ellen, if you don't mind my asking?'

'November. Second week, I think. I haven't seen the doctor yet but that's when it's due.' Ellen was folding sheets and pillowcases. Mr Reeve considered her reply.

'And what about the father? Does he know? What does he think?'

'He doesn't know.' Ellen stopped and gazed out of the window into the darkening farmyard. 'I don't know where he is. He's in the Royal Engineers. And he's married, but I didn't know that.'

'Hmm.' Mr Reeve finished his jam tart. 'You're probably not going to be able to rely on him just at the moment then, certainly not in the short term. Will you tell him, if you can find him?'

'I don't know. I was bursting to tell him.'

Mr Reeve pushed his cup across the table towards Ellen. 'Pop another drop in there, will you, lass? And your parents, they're upset?'

'Yes. Father went berserk. He says I have to leave.' Ellen's lower lip trembled and she gave a sob. 'He won't have me in the house.'

'And your mum? What does Amelia say?'

'Oh, she's upset. Left to herself she probably wouldn't make me go. She went to pieces at first but she'd face it out. But she hasn't got much choice, what with Father. . . .'

Sitting at the kitchen table with his tea and another jam tart Mr Reeve pondered for a while.

'Dear, oh dear. Still, worse things happen at sea.' He stood up, took his cup and plate to the draining board and then turned to look at Ellen.

'You'll know Back Lane?'

'Yes. My ratbag brother lives up there.'

'Oh, yes. Of course. You'll know Cowper's Cottage then, at the end of the row.

'The one at the top?' Ellen was paying the farmer full attention.

'That's it.' He poked around his upper back teeth with his tongue before continuing. 'If you're leaving home, what would you say to moving into it? It's not much but it belongs to the farm and it's empty at the moment.'

Ellen's eyes widened. 'Oh.' She thought about it for a moment, but quickly came to a decision. 'Well, it's very kind of you but I would never be able to afford it.'

Mr Reeve frowned, a little impatiently.

'Well, let's not concern ourselves with that for the moment. If you carry on working here, and you should be able to after you've had the baby, I can't see that there would be any difference between your situation and that of any of the hands that live in a farm cottage. Your parents did, and in fact still do, despite that fact that your father doesn't work on the farm any more.'

'Oh.' Ellen was quick to see the possibilities. A place of her own and being able to keep her job sounded almost too good to be true. 'But I won't be able to do much after the baby . . . not for a while anyway . . . and Dad won't be pleased. He'll think you're interfering.'

Mr Reeve shook his head.

'We can worry about the job later. There's no reason why we can't be a bit accommodating. Most of the time there's only me here anyway. And if I am interfering, well, that's because we're friends. You've always been our friend. Maria thought the world of you, and that goes for me too. I rely on you a lot, I did especially after Maria died, and I still do. Now it's my turn to help you, if you'll let me.'

Mr Reeve cleared his throat as his voice began to wobble. Embarrassed at his speech he looked hard at Ellen and then ducked behind his cup for a moment before reappearing to resume sipping his tea.

'Besides,' he smiled, 'it might be a bit selfish but I don't want to lose you. Where else would I get such a bargain?' He grinned and then shook his head. 'It would be handy if you lived in, but we can't do that, certainly not at the moment.' He gave another brief shake of his head. 'Your father's not totally heartless. I know he's proud of you because he's told me so.'

'Hmm. That was before.'

'Well, I expect he's angry and upset at the moment but I'm sure he loves you. I'll try and have a word with them. See if we can soothe things a bit. Anyway, at least in principle; what would you think about the cottage as a possibility?'

'That would be wonderful. Are you sure? Oh, thank you.'

Ellen had ridden past Cowper's Cottage many times but she had barely given it a second look. Her impression was of damp and dilapidation. The place had been empty for months. It was falling down. Old Mr Ash, the last tenant had died there. His next-door neighbour had found him lying on his face in the outside lavatory.

The nurse brought Ellen a drink and a painkiller. She eventually dozed off and after some lurid dreams woke again hot and generally feeling out of sorts. The same tune ran through her head over and over again. Eventually she recalled that it was the music that Mr Reeve played on his gramophone when Maria danced the flamenco. And there was Maria, up on one of the hay carts, all flashing smiles, stamping feet and swirling skirts.

When the music stopped she lifted the hem of her dress. She looked directly at Ellen through the crowd and pointed to the vivid purple patch on her ankle.

'Come and see,' she called. 'It won't bite.' Everyone stopped talking as Ellen pushed through the crowd to the cart. Standing on tiptoe in order to reach she put her hand on Maria's ankle. The purple patch began to squirm. Ellen squawked and jerked her hand away. Mr Reeve was sitting on the shafts of the cart tuning a fiddle. He winked at her, grinned and inclined his head.

'Got you that time,' he said. Ellen had never noticed before that every one of his teeth was black. Then everything was black.

Later she was lying in the thick dust at the edge of the footpath in the blackcurrant field. She must have caught her foot in some rough grass and fallen. Her basket had to be close by but she couldn't find it. She felt like weeping. Now she'd have to pick up all those wretched currants and try to clean them. The man at the weighing machine wouldn't take them if they were dirty. She tried to get up but she couldn't move. The more she tried the more helpless she felt. There was no feeling down one side of her body and she thought that she was probably dribbling again. She gave up struggling and lay still. After a while she realized that everything was grey. Later there were voices. Someone called her name. More people. Shadowy, insubstantial, they were lifting, bending, whispering and doing things. Different voices called her name. They helped her up. Then it was light again and she was reassured to find that she was propped up in bed. She felt exhausted, but it must just have been a bad dream.

One morning a couple of days after the pickled-onion incident Mr Reeve beeped the horn of the shooting brake as he drove into the farmyard. Returning to the house from the back garden with a basket of washing, Ellen waved in response. She stopped and waited as the large vehicle splashed through the puddles in the farmyard and drew alongside. The farmer leaned over and wound down the passenger window.

'Are you busy with anything you can't leave? I thought we might nip up and have a quick look at the cottage.'

'Oh. Yes, if you're sure you've got time. That would be nice. I just need to tidy myself up. Would you like your coffee before we go?'

Mr Reeve glanced at his watch. 'Yes, I'll have a quick cup. It's a nice bright morning. We'll be able to see the place properly.'

Twenty minutes later they drove up the hill.

'I went round that way yesterday. It looks in a pretty poor way from the lane, needs some attention.' Mr Reeve patted his jacket pockets and sighed.

He laughed. 'I've left the key on the window sill. Still, I think Mrs Hunt's got one.'

Ellen had ridden past the cottage on her way to call on Kathy. It looked dilapidated, but she thought that it might be cosy inside. George and Janice and the two-year-old Kingsley Ambrose lived a couple of doors down and she'd popped in to see them and mentioned that Mr Reeve had mooted the idea.

'It's a dump.' Sitting in the sole comfortable chair in their small kitchen rolling a cigarette George shook his head. 'There are vermin, I've seen them. Old Ash was a dirty old beggar and that stinking dog of his didn't help. Neither did Dick Reeve for that matter. It must be ages since anything was done there. The place is a disgrace. It's falling down.'

'He wasn't right was he, old man Ash? And the dog was on its last legs. Should have been put down long before, both of them.'

Red of face and with her hair swathed in a towel Janice glared at Ellen.

'It's not as big as ours, you know. Hasn't got a separate kitchen for a start. And no one's got electric or water up here. How on earth are you going to manage on your own with a new baby? You'd be better off at home.'

'Well, I can't stay; Father has made that quite clear. I'm not going to stay where I'm not wanted, and besides it's time I had a place of my own. Mr Reeve said they'd do the place up. I'll manage, thank you.' Ellen would make up her own mind about the cottage. George and Janice certainly wouldn't sway her.

Mr Reeve pulled the shooting brake off the road into a field gateway just past the cottage. The small yard in front of Cowper's Cottage was no more than a compacted cinder rectangle bounded on one side by a low outhouse and on the other by the sparse remains of a sagging wire-netting fence. Rough grass struggled in the poor soil around the edges amid the skeletal remains of thistles and cow parsley. Previous inhabitants had obviously been in the habit of emptying the ash pan in the yard. A crumbling cobble wall separated the property from Back Lane. There had been a gate but all that remained of it was a rusty hinge at thigh height, projecting just enough to catch the unwary.

Mr Reeve paused at the roadside to take in the cottage. There was little to admire.

'We'll get you a new gate, and that gutter looks past its best.' A variety of weeds and a buddleia sprang from the gutter in question. It sagged along its entire length beneath a jumble of lichen-covered tiles. Water stains were much in evidence on the front wall of the cottage and there was a steady drip, drip, drip on to the disintegrating doorstep from a gutter joint above.

They went first next door to get the key. Mrs Hunt had been watching from the window and the door opened promptly.

' 'Morning, Linda.'

'Good morning, Mr Reeve.'

A small brown-skinned woman with streaky grey hair pinned into a bun at the back of her head, Mrs Hunt almost curtsied. She wrung her gnarled hands and smiled nervously.

'I saw your motor car from the upstairs window.' Her face was lined and cross looking, although it quickly became apparent that she had a ready smile and was not nearly as crabby as she looked.

'I'm sorry to bother you. I wonder whether we might trouble you for the key for next door. I believe you've got the one that Mr Ash had. I've come out without mine.'

Mrs Hunt hurried back into her living-room and returned with two large keys attached to a twist of wire.

'I thought someone might call for them.' She handed them to Mr Reeve and smiled quickly at Ellen. 'I gave them a good scrub. They weren't very nice.' She wrinkled her nose. 'And you're George's sister.'

Her eyes flicked down over Ellen's belly. News of her condition had obviously preceded her.

'I've seen you passing once or twice. He said you might be coming.'

'Hello, yes. I'm Ellen Fincham. I'm pleased to meet you.'

'I see your mum about sometimes. I used to see William, but I haven't seen much of him lately. And I know your George, of course.' Mrs Hunt's stern face again broke into a shy smile as she shook Ellen's hand.

'Everyone calls me Linda.' She wrung her hands again.

'You've got a bit of a job on there.' She nodded towards Cowper's Cottage next door. 'But I hope you'll like it. Mr and Mrs Fairhead always kept it nice when they were there, and so did Mrs Ash. The place has gone to rack and ruin a bit since she died though and Mr Ash of course... It'll be nice to have someone next door again.'

Mr Ash lived in the cottage with only his dog for company for several years after the death of his wife. Mrs Hunt's husband had spotted him early one morning in January, crumpled in the doorway of the outside lavatory in only his shirt and long johns. Almost ninety, he had died during the night from an unhappy combination of old age, malnutrition and pneumonia. His ancient mongrel Brandy was dying inside on a filthy piece of blanket.

Ellen began to get an inkling of what lay inside the cottage as she tried to peer through the almost opaque glass of the living-room window while Mr Reeve fiddled with the lock.

'I think this could do with a drop of oil.'

He discovered that leaning on the door eased the turning of the key. The door opened suddenly, taking the farmer by surprise.

'Ah! Oh!' He recoiled and stepped back sharply. 'Good Lord.' They were both unprepared for the stench. Mr Reeve turned and looked at Ellen, his nose wrinkled and his mouth shouting a silent 'Oh!'

He gave a short laugh.

'I'm not sure we want to go in there. That's an awful smell.' He pushed the door wide and stepped back. After several rapid breaths he poked his head inside the cottage. He recoiled again as though someone had taken a pot shot at him.

They waited in the yard for a while. After further cautious sniffing Mr Reeve took a deep breath, ran inside and with some difficulty forced the window open wide. It was such a small aperture that Ellen wondered whether it would make any difference.

'Goodness knows when that was last opened.' The farmer hurried out again and they waited together in the yard. Eventually he judged it safe to try again. With some trepidation they stepped down the four inches or so on to the worn stone-flagged floor in the gloomy living-room. It was dark and bitterly cold inside despite the sliver of sunlight that fell across the floor from the tiny window.

Clearly nothing had been done since Mr Ash was taken away. The sad odds and ends of the old man's last days still lay about the room. There was nothing of value. A discoloured stump of candle stood lopsided on a wax-encrusted tin lid. Condensed milk and sardine tins with jagged lids and a half-eaten bowl of something brown lay mouldering on a homemade wooden tray. Crusted cutlery, crumpled clothing, medicine bottles, dog-eared playing cards and old newspapers lay on a ruined dark-wood table in the middle of the room. Mr Ash's pipe, a white tide-mark round the mouth-piece and burnt away on one side of the bowl lay with spent matches on the greasy arm of the only armchair. An unwashed safety razor, a piece of shaving stick, a filthy comb and hairbrush and a small rusting mirror lay on the windowsill beside a can of Brasso and a bottle of rubbing liniment. Plates and a pan lay half-submerged in a bowl of grey water beside the match-strewn hearth. The dog's foul blanket and the remains of a knucklebone lay almost welded to the floor beside the chair. A jacket, hat and coat and a dog lead hung on a nail behind the door. It wasn't much to show for a life.

Mr Reeve glanced back to ensure that he had left the door open.

'Dear Lord, I didn't realize things were this bad. Poor old beggar. I'll get Ronnie and one of the men up here with a cart and we'll clear everything out, take it away and burn it. I doubt whether there's anything here that you or anyone else would want.'

They glanced round the room at the few pitiful sticks of furniture. The wallpaper was mouldy and peeling and the curtains looked as though the only thing that held them together was the greasy dirt and cobwebs with which they were festooned.

'There are stairs, in the corner.' Mr Reeve crossed the room and opened the door, his right shoe detaching itself reluctantly from the tacky floor with every step. He had trodden in something. He set out bravely and must have been almost at the top of the narrow staircase when Ellen heard him gasp.

'Oh, heavens!' The farmer hurried back down the stairs with his nose buried in his coat sleeve. 'Ugh! The ceiling's fallen in and there are mice.'

He shut the door firmly behind him and shepherded Ellen out of the cottage. After closing the door and locking it he wiped his hands on his trousers. He took out a handkerchief and blew his nose several times and then paced about the yard swallowing hard and taking deep breaths. Eventually he halted and stood with his hands in his pockets looking up at the front of the cottage.

'Sorry. That's better. Got to my stomach. I didn't realize things were that bad.' He paused and glanced at Ellen. 'What do you think? There's an awful lot to do. You won't have seen enough to get much idea. But it will all be cleaned up and repaired. We'll make it as good as new.' He paused.

Ellen nodded. She didn't know quite what she had expected but it wasn't what she had seen. She didn't know what to say.

'There are a couple of small bedrooms upstairs, a lavatory just round here,' he gestured at the peeling green painted lean-to, 'the shed and so on. We'll get Mr Crowe over to look at it. He can fix it. The range looks all right. Just needs a bit of a clean and polish. When we come up I'll fill a cart with logs from that tree that came down a year or two ago in the grove and you can keep them in the shed.' He looked round the front yard doubtfully. 'I know it smells to high heaven and it doesn't look much at the moment but by the time we've finished it'll be fine. What do you say? Think you can make a go of it?'

Ellen looked up at the front of the cottage. In truth she was dejected at what she had seen. It was horrible but it was the best chance that was likely to come her way. She turned and smiled. 'Oh yes, thank you. And I can help get it ready too.'

'I think we're going to have to do some work first. And you don't want to be doing too much now, do you? Not in your condition.'

Suddenly overcome by the man's concern and his great kindness, Ellen's eyes filled with tears.

'Thank you,' she said in a small voice, smiling at him. 'I'll make it nice. It's so kind of you.'

'No, Ellen. We'll be doing each other a good turn. You can see what a state the place has got into. I blame myself. It'll be good to have someone living here.' He smiled at her and put his hand on her arm. 'Come on, cheer up.'

He squeezed her arm gently and then turned away. 'We'd better be getting back. I'll have my lunch and then I'll need to be off to Norwich. Come on. Oh, and you'd better have one of these. I'll give the other to Ronnie. You can get it when the work's been finished.' He undid the wire loop and pressed into Ellen's hand a key to Cowper's Cottage.

A few days later Ellen was repairing the hem on a curtain in one of the back bedrooms at Pond Farm when she heard an aeroplane approaching. Bombers had been crossing the coast all morning, returning from raids over Germany. The early morning arrivals had for the most part announced their approach with a purposeful engine note. As the day went on an increasing number of stragglers began arriving, planes staggering in low and faltering with tail-planes and wings shot up. Some looked as though they might not get much further.

It was just after one o'clock in the afternoon when Ellen heard the latest arrival in the distance. It didn't sound good. The uncertain engine note was intercut with popping and banging. Suddenly there was silence. She ran through to the front of the house just in time to see a Liberator bomber clip the tops of the beech trees in Maria's paddock. It was trailing smoke and obviously in serious trouble. She hurried to the back of the house, terrified that the plane would hit the barn. There were people working inside.

The farmhouse shook as the bomber hit the ground. As horrified as she was Ellen saw with some relief that it had missed the barn and crashed in the meadow beyond. Farmhands were already rushing from the barn towards the burning plane. By the time she had gathered up towels and blankets and rushed downstairs and out into the yard five of the crew had been pulled from the wreckage. Two more were extricated as she arrived on the scene.

'We need water, hot and cold, towels and bandages. Bring some sheets.' Mr Reeve had been in the office and was taking charge. 'And Ellen, I have phoned. Can you make tea? Lots of it, thanks.'

More people arrived to help, among them two nurses from the sanatorium. Eventually a doctor appeared, closely followed by the police constable and the fire engine. Ellen ran back and forth with tea, with water, bandages and eventually sandwiches. She held the hand of one of the crew as he lay on a trestle table in the barn. He was badly burned and drifted in and out of consciousness. Not more than twenty years of age, he died as Ellen held him.

Six of the crew were taken to Cromer Hospital with cuts, fractures and burns. In addition to the man who had died in the barn three other crew members perished in the fire. Their bodies wouldn't be recovered until the fire was out and the wreck cooled down, if there was anything left to recover.

As the last of the rescuers was leaving, Ellen stood alone in the dark yard.

There was still the foul acrid stench of burning. She felt shocked and worse, a failure. Surely there must have been something they could have done, *she* could have done.

'You all right, love?' One of the nurses called out as they left on the bicycle upon which they had arrived. They laughed and swore as they wobbled out of the gate, one on the seat, the other standing on the pedals and bobbing up and down in order to sustain some sort of forward motion. 'You daft ha'p'orth. I thought you were going to have us in the bloody pond. Bye.'

'Oh. Goodbye.'

Ellen was impatient to be getting on and during the next few weeks she cycled up or down Back Lane several times to check on the cottage. Going yet again, she had the key in her pocket and was intent on doing something useful. However she found Ronnie and a couple of farmhands on the point of leaving with the contents and a good deal of rubble on the back of the farm lorry.

'I wouldn't go in there if I were you, Ellen.' They paused in securing the load. 'You'll get filthy and it stinks to high heaven. There's vermin everywhere.'

After tying off the rope Ronnie walked over.

'We've cleared everything out, like the boss said. Crowe is coming on Monday. Mr Reeve seems to think it should all be done in a couple of weeks or so, although I'll be a bit surprised myself if they're that quick. They're doing a lot of work up in Norwich at the moment after the bombing and this place needs gutting. I'd wait until they've finished if I were you. You won't be able to do anything and there's a good bit more to do than the boss seems to think.'

Ellen was disappointed. After the lorry had gone she wandered round the front yard. At the end of the shed nearest the cottage stood a large galvanized water tank that took rainwater from the shed roof. It was so full that when she nudged it with her knee water cascaded down the side. Nice soft water for washing, she thought. Poking at something half submerged on the surface she recoiled when she realized that it was a dead blackbird. She lifted the carcass out with a couple of sticks and threw it over the wall into the field.

When she opened the shed door and peered into the darkness something skittered over her foot and made her jump. The creature disappeared into the pitch dark at the far end. Her skin crawled. She could make out a few lumps of coal and some odds and ends of wood propped in the corner by the door. Slivers of sky were visible here and there where tiles had slipped, but it seemed dry inside. It smelled of rodents and something else, rotting potatoes. Closing the door she wandered round to the lavatory. The green paint was peeling, revealing the remains of a light green undercoat and grey deal beneath. She opened the door and promptly slammed it shut again. Lying among the blown leaves on the floor was a decapitated cat.

The yard petered out behind the lavatory into a narrow strip of rough ground. It ran the length of the cottages and led directly into a field planted with winter wheat. Immediately behind the cottage she spotted the answer to the question that had been troubling her for some time. She would have to empty the contents of the lavatory into the hole hidden beneath some green and slimy boards. As she picked her way cautiously through the wet grass behind the neighbouring cottages she could see that the Hunts, George and Janice and much of the rest of the street had similar arrangements. It was going to be a change from life at home. Her parents had had proper sewerage, running water and electricity for years.

On the way back to Kathy's she detoured and stopped opposite the Lord Nelson to look at the village pump. She'd passed it a million times but had never before gone through the gap in the hedge to actually take a look at it. She gave the handle an experimental pump or two. Sure enough, water gushed out purposefully. Once she moved into the cottage every drop of water for drinking and cooking would have to be carried the 300 yards or so. Just her luck she thought, to be moving into the cottage furthest from the pump. She made a mental note to ask George how he managed.

As Ronnie surmised Mr Reeve's estimate was hopelessly optimistic. Ellen rode past the cottage numerous times in her impatience and was disappointed to see that work hadn't begun. Then one day there was a huge heap of dark yellow sand in the yard and the door hung wide open. Two bicycles leaned against the wall and purposeful hammering and whistling came from within. Ellen decided against stopping and rode on greatly cheered.

On the next occasion she passed, clouds of dust issued from the upstairs window as someone swept energetically. The following week the walls were newly cement-rendered and she watched from outside the yard wall as a workman in white overalls came out of the cottage with a brush and paint kettle and began painting the lower window. The door and the newly straightened gutter were already gleaming with fresh chocolate gloss.

As the man painted he coughed. He had the meanest stub of a cigarette in the corner of his mouth and it wasn't long before he was racked with coughing. It began with a little *heh, heh, heh, heh* and culminated with him bent double, hacking helplessly. At some point he took the cigarette from his mouth, gulped air and wiped his eyes. No sooner had he recovered than the cigarette was back and after a moment or two it began again. *Heh, heh, heh. . . .*

It was after lunch one day some weeks later that Mr Reeve proposed a visit to the cottage. He was obviously excited and conceded that he had been there a few days previously.

'I think you'll be pleasantly surprised,' he said. 'Things are nearing completion.'

A wooden gate hung in the gateway and a newly erected wooden fence now stood between the cottage yard and the Hunts' front garden. The shed boasted a small window and a new door. Both the shed and the cottage roof had been re-tiled and the cottage walls were painted cream. All of the woodwork had a fresh coat of the chocolate-brown paint. The outside of Cowper's Cottage looked a picture.

Inside there was no sign of the squalor of their first visit. The stench of old had been replaced by the smell of fresh timber, plaster, cigarette smoke and above all, gloss paint. The living-room was much lighter and seemed larger than on their first visit. It was empty apart from a stepladder, a small table and the tools of the paperhanger neatly in one corner. Ellen could hear him upstairs: *heh, heh, heh. . . .*

The walls were newly decorated with a light coloured paper of floral design. The doors, windows, skirting board and picture rails were all painted cream. Shiny brown patterned linoleum covered the floor and despite the fact that there was no water or drainage a deep kitchen sink and wooden draining board had been fitted in the alcove beside the range. In the corner the brick copper was now chocolate brown and fitted with a brand new pine lid.

'Hello?' Mr Reeve called up the stairs. 'Is it all right if we come up?'

'Oh, Mr Reeve. Yeah, *heh, heh.* You want to watch yourselves on the paint. It's still *heh, heh,* still wet. *Heh, heh, heh.*'

Mr Reeve ushered Ellen ahead of him. Their eyes prickled with the new paint and cigarette smoke as they made their way up the narrow stairs. At the top there was a tiny landing with a short banister, and two battered but newly painted doors into the bedrooms. The room at the front of the cottage was marginally the larger. It had a new ceiling, new wallpaper and freshly varnished floorboards. There was a cupboard built into the corner and just enough room for a double bed, a chest and a chair. The room even boasted a small fireplace. It was the tiniest that Ellen had ever seen.

'There's a bit of a draught in that chimney. If you're not going to use it you might want to block it up. I'll find a bit of board to go over it, if you like.'

Mr Reeve marched about touching the paint here and there to see if it was wet.

'Ah,' he muttered. He had found some that was.

The back bedroom had a tiny window and exposed beams. It was just big enough to accommodate a single bed, a chest and a chair. The decorator was crouched over the skirting board in the corner.

'Nearly done, Howard. I must say it's looking much better now.'

'Yeah, *heh, heh, heh.* Look a bit different, don't it? *Heh, heh.* Lord; that was rank. Don't know as I've ever come across a place so bad, and I've seen a few. And the rats, my Lord, big as heifers some of them. *Heh, heh.*'

Howard showered the newly painted skirting board with ash, before pausing to take the cigarette from his mouth. 'Be finished by dinner tomorrow. I've got this to do and the floor to stain and varnish and that'll be about it. Be out tomorrow.'

'Have you done the what's-it outside?'

'Oh no, *heh, heh*. You're right. I've still got the top coat to do, and I'll get young Will to dig a new hole like you said when he gets back. That won't take him long if the rain keeps off. You soon get down to nice loose sand.' Howard replaced the stub of cigarette and with his next breath began coughing again. Ellen and Mr Reeve went carefully down the stairs.

'*Heh, heh, heh. . . .*'

'What will you do for furniture, lass?' Mr Reeve had raised the subject before and he enquired again as they drove back down the hill to the farm.

'Well, I've got a few things. I can have my own bed and a chest from home. And I've got several pieces of curtain material that will do. The windows are all small so it shouldn't be too difficult. I've got a piece of matting and a rug too.'

'We've got some stuff that you might like to look at out in the back barn. I didn't mention it before because I wasn't sure what was still there. Most of it came from a sale at North Walsham. We were going to use it in one of the cottages but then didn't need it for some reason. I had a quick look yesterday and there are one or two decent bits that are not too big. There's a nice gate-leg table and chairs and a couple of small armchairs. They're all good solid pieces too, oak. They've been covered up. They're not damp and there's no worm. Just need a clean and a polish.'

'Oh yes, I'd like to have a look, if I may.' Ellen had given up even token discomfort at Mr Reeve's largess.

THIRTEEN

Philip called at the convalescent home at lunchtime and was turned away.

'Ellen's a little bit under the weather. It's probably just a reaction to the anaesthetic. It happens sometimes.'

Philip left, promising to phone. Margaret received the same information later in the afternoon.

'Oh? Has she got an infection? I thought she was doing well.'

The nurse raised her eyebrows. 'TIA,' she mouthed. 'They think.' She shook her head, grimaced, and then continued *sotto voce*. 'She seems to have had a little stroke during the night.' She frowned and continued, 'They say they can't be sure, but that's what they think.'

'You don't share their view?'

'Oh. Not for me to say.'

'Is she all right now?'

The nurse screwed up her nose and mouth. She continued quietly. 'I saw her this morning and I think she's doing OK. I've seen enough of them over the last thirty years. Unless she's very unlucky and if they're right about the TIA she could be all right in twenty-four hours or so. I think they'll probably keep her here unless things suddenly deteriorate.'

Ellen moved into Cowper's Cottage at the end of April in 1944. Since the farm lorry was in use elsewhere Mr Reeve and Robert (of all people,) loaded up a tractor and cart with the few pieces of furniture from the barn and then collected Ellen's bed, her clothes and other items from Ivy Cottage. Ellen got a terrible shock when she looked out of the window and saw Robert at the wheel of the new Fordson tractor. She was excited to see him but mortified that he should see her in her reduced circumstances. He must know that she was pregnant and that she had been forced to leave home. He greeted her warmly enough however, and throughout the rest of the morning was civil but no more.

Since the day that Mr Reeve first made the offer of Cowper's Cottage Ellen had been looking forward to leaving home. The farmer's intervention had made all the difference. Predictably her father was angered and had withdrawn even further from Ellen. He had gone out earlier than usual on the morning of the move. Amelia had come to some sort of terms with Ellen's pregnancy and became increasingly agitated as the removal day drew near. Now that the actual day was upon them she was clearly unhappy.

Ellen had expressed her regrets about her unexpected pregnancy and for any shame that she had brought upon the family. Saying the same thing over and over again though achieved nothing. She didn't know what more she could say or do. Mr Reeve had apparently talked to her father but to no avail. Ellen was not prepared to beg.

After the tractor and cart left for Back Lane she quickly dusted and swept her bedroom and gathered up the last few items to go in her bicycle basket. Her mother stood in the back door unhappily twisting the hem of her pinafore.

'Are you sure you're doing the right thing, love?' she asked. 'Let me talk to your father again.' But she had spoken to William until she was sick of the subject and of him. She knew that further representations would be useless.

'I'll be fine, Mum. It's time I was off anyway.' She smiled at her mother ruefully. 'It's not what I'd planned and I know it's not what you and Dad wanted for me, but there you are. I'll just have to make the best of it, won't I?'

'You will come and see us, won't you?'

'Of course I will, and you must come and see me, although I'm not sure that Father will want to.'

' 'Course he will, dear. He'll come round. Give him time. He's a stubborn man. It's difficult for him.' As Ellen mounted her bicycle the last remnants of Amelia's composure crumbled. She stood in the back doorway wringing her hands and weeping, a picture of misery. Ellen stopped and leaned her bicycle up against the washhouse wall. With her own face set with the effort of maintaining some sort of control she put her arms round her mother's shoulders to comfort her.

'Oh, come on, Mum. Hush. I'm only just up the road and I'll still be at the farm every day until the baby comes. We'll see plenty of each other. If I don't see you anywhere else you can bet I'll see you in the currant fields.' Amelia smiled and then laughed briefly. They both hated picking blackcurrants.

Amelia clung to her daughter for a few moments longer.

'You've all gone now. We're alone, me and your father.'

'We haven't gone far. John will be back and George and I are only up the hill. Come on, cheer up. I'll pop in to see you tomorrow.' Giving her mother a final squeeze she let her go and went to her bicycle again.

Giving her mother a wave as she freewheeled down the path Ellen forced herself not to hurry. She was desperate to get to the cottage to supervise the unloading, before they scraped the paint or the paper and put everything in the wrong place.

After the furniture was installed more or less to Ellen's satisfaction Robert wished her happiness in her new home and left with the tractor and trailer. Mr Reeve drove down to the pump to fetch water. Since he was opposite the Lord Nelson he popped in and returned with several bottles of ale.

'I'll look out an old milk churn. You can put it in the pantry and top it up with pump water. It'll give you a decent supply and keep it clean.'

They lit the fire in the range and then sat either side of it with beer and shortcakes that Linda Hunt had brought round.

'You'll be fine and dandy here, won't you, lass? By the time you've put a few things on the wall, put your own stamp on it, you'll be as snug as a bug in a rug.'

'It's lovely. I'm very lucky. You've been very kind.'

Mr Reeve as usual was uncomfortable with the compliment. Ellen changed the subject.

'You'll be pleased to see Robert home for a bit.'

'Oh, he's off back tomorrow. I shan't see much of him, I'm afraid.'

'Is he all right? He looks tired.'

'I think he is exhausted. Still, that's the war for you.'

Kathy and Ronny appeared early in the evening bearing a jug of cider from Ronny's grandmother. The three of them toured the cottage. All aspects of it were subjected to as close scrutiny as was possible by candlelight, until both visitors declared themselves green with envy. They lit more candles and rigged up a temporary curtain in the living-room and talked, drank and laughed until very late. After waving the girls off Ellen went up the narrow stairs to spend her first night in her new home. She was glad that she had had the foresight to make her bed before the girls came round. With a hot-water-bottle she was warm and comfortable. As she lay in the dark she suddenly realized that she had taken quite a step. There was no going back now. Tears started but she quickly got the better of them.

'Dratted paint fumes,' she muttered.

After the first night it was clear that she needed better lighting. Mr Reeve donated an old Tilley Lamp and an oil lamp that he had found in one of the outhouses. He also came up with a wireless. It was a bit knocked and scratched but it worked well enough with an aerial wire draped along the picture rail. Ellen walked most of the way home with the wireless upended in her bicycle basket and the lamps and a couple of accumulators in a sack on her handlebars.

The Tilley Lamp needed a mantle and a shade. Ellen picked them up at the hardware shop in Cromer in which Harry had worked. Once they were fitted and it was filled with paraffin it gave an attractive soft light. It also generated a good deal of heat and Ellen found its soft hiss comforting. Thus equipped she began to settle down to life in her own home. Linda and Albert Hunt next door turned out to be good neighbours. Linda introduced Ellen to the tradesmen who called regularly and she offered the services of her thirteen-year-old daughter Penny for a bit of future baby-sitting and odd jobs, if and when required.

Kathy and Ronny were regular callers, sometimes singly, sometimes together. They gathered at Kathy's house too and on one memorable occasion at Ronny's grandmother's cottage. They brought each other all manner of items. Jars of jam, pickled onions, elderberry wine and ginger beer. The two expectant mothers began to accumulate numerous knitted and other items for their babies.

The spring and summer passed and as her stomach grew Ellen slipped into something of a routine. She carried on working at the farm, sometimes having to ignore or sabotage Mr Reeve's attempts to restrict her to light duties. But she was sensible and she and Kathy went to see the doctor and the nurse periodically. She bought a few small items and in her spare time made or mended a number of other things to improve life at the cottage. She spent a weekend cleaning, repairing and painting a hat stand, a towel rail and a small bedside chest. After clearing the worms and wood lice out of a meat safe that had been dumped at the entrance to the local sandpit she carried it home on her bike. The perforated zinc was whole and the wood showed no signs of rot or worm. Once it was thoroughly scrubbed out she reckoned that it would be good for a few years more. At a sale in the school hall she bought a couple of pictures, a framed mirror, a washboard and a mincer.

One evening as it was getting dark, Major Pope's wife appeared at the door. A tall, thin woman in thick tweeds, she was wheeling a pram.

'Hello, Ellen. Sorry to descend on you so late. I wondered whether you had a pram.'

A little nonplussed Ellen shook her head.

'No? Splendid, I won't have to take it back. We thought you might like this. One of the wheels is a bit stiff but otherwise it isn't bad. Something started to squeak a bit too as I came up Back Lane. Probably just needs oiling. It's been out in the stables for ages. I'm sure you can get someone to see to it.'

Ellen nodded. 'Oh, are you sure? Thank you. That is kind. Yes, I'm sure I can fix it.'

'I expect young George will be happy to help.' George had done a bit of gardening for the Popes when he was younger. Ellen smiled and nodded. She wondered whether Mrs Pope would be of the same opinion if she had seen George trying to remove the wheel from a bicycle with an axe. He was about as adroit with anything mechanical as a cow with a gun.

'You're not superstitious, are you? About having the pram in the house before the baby. . . ?'

'No.' Ellen gave a little laugh. 'At least I don't think so.'

'Good-oh.'

She helped Mrs Pope manoeuvre the pram over the step and into the living-room where it took up an enormous amount of room. Once inside the old lady pushed the door shut and gave Ellen a conspiratorial grin.

'And that's not quite all.' She whipped the cover off the pram rather like a conjuror concluding a particularly baffling illusion. Inside the pram was a large metal preserving pan, a presentation box of fish knives and forks and an assortment of ornate serving spoons and ladles.

'I thought you might like these too, dear. I fibbed and told the major they had all gone for salvage ages ago. They were Mummy's and I couldn't bear to let them go. I've got some others that I still use that used to belong to my grandmother. These have been in a trunk in the attic for ages but of course I can't bring them out.'

'I'm not sure my dad would be able to tell you what Mother uses every day.'

'Oh, I never thought of that.' Mrs Pope laughed. 'You're probably right. Still, I'm sure you can find a use for them.' She laughed again. 'I'll be able to look the major in the eye if he asks about them. I can truthfully say that they are being put to good use. I won't feel so guilty.'

Mrs Pope was a funny old duck. She stopped for a cup of tea and then asked Ellen to show her round. Despite living at Clyffesyde which was a huge house in enormous grounds the old lady was genuinely interested and impressed with what Ellen had accomplished in such a short time. There was little doubt that she was a bit eccentric but she was terribly kind. She wrote poetry and compiled crosswords and there was a persistent rumour in the village that she worked for the government from time to time. Nevertheless, as soon as she left Ellen lifted the pram out through the front door and wheeled it into the shed where she carefully covered it with an old curtain. She wasn't about to have it in the house yet. She told herself that there really wasn't room.

Ellen bought three galvanized baths, a chamber pot and two buckets from Paraffin Pete who called at Back Lane in his van each week. The baths fitted neatly one inside the other and she hung them on a nail in the shed. They were very suitable for doing the washing and the largest was perfect for bathing in front of the range. She put up a short clothes line between the end of the shed and the cottage and she dug and planted a modest flowerbed beside the fence between her and the Hunts' front garden. A couple of brown earthenware ink bottles turned up while she was digging so she cleaned them up and they looked very well on the living-room window sill with dried flowers in them.

Emptying the lavatory into the hole at the back of the cottage was a trying business, although she felt much better about it once she had a new bucket from Paraffin Pete. Another initiative was the placing of a candlestick and a box of matches in the lean-to after she blundered and fumbled about in the dark unexpectedly one night.

Before the war a number of tradesmen delivered regularly to Back Lane. Groceries, fruit and vegetables, bread, milk, fish and meat could all be ordered from and delivered to the door. The coal lorry, Paraffin Pete and the laundry van also called. Most of the tradesmen struggled on as best they could during the war. Ellen left notes on the doorstep for the regulars and Mrs Hunt next door was happy to take in deliveries since she was always at home.

Ellen tried to get George to help her with the water but he was wholly unreliable. After being let down she found that she could manage a couple of buckets on her own quite well. If two became a struggle when the baby was due then she would just make do with carrying one bucket at a time. She used less than one a day on her own but she knew that she would use much more after the baby was born. Mr Reeve was keeping an eye out for a purpose built galvanized water container with a lid that she could fill up and keep in the cottage, but they were in short supply. A suitable old milk churn was also proving difficult.

She continued cycling down to work at Pond Farm every day. According to Mr Reeve he deducted the rent from her wages but it seemed to Ellen that her pay packet dipped a little one week and then returned to what it had been. If pressed on the matter the farmer said he had given her a raise and after deductions, astonishingly her pay worked out to what it had been. In any event he said that there would be plenty of time to sort things out once the war was over.

Ellen popped in to see her mother two or three times a week, usually staying long enough for a cup of tea and to be brought up to date with the news. Her father was always at work. The sanatorium was extremely busy with the many casualties of war. Amelia knitted for the baby and walked up to see Ellen with her finished articles one Sunday afternoon. She didn't make any attempt to hide these activities from her husband although he steadfastly refused to accompany her.

Most Saturday afternoons Ellen, Kathy and Ronny cycled into Cromer unless they were particularly busy on the farm. On Friday nights they went to the Lord Nelson together. Both Dave Holt and Ronny's boyfriend were away so they all wrote letters.

One sunny evening towards the end of September Ellen arrived home from work hot and weary and looking forward to a wash, something to eat and an early night. Slowing as she passed George's gate she caught a glimpse of Janice heaving herself up off their woodpile. Ellen thought that she heard Janice call her name. She freewheeled to a halt outside the Hunts' cottage and then paddled her bicycle backwards. She wondered what on earth Janice could want. They rarely sought each other out.

'Ellen! Ellen!'

Ellen frowned and sighed with annoyance. She and Janice had never hit it off and she really couldn't be bothered with her now. The infrequent appearances of her sister-in-law usually presaged rumour, gossip or more likely a request for something. The woman begged and borrowed all the time and never repaid or returned anything.

'Oh, I'm glad . . .' Red-faced and agitated Janice wheezed up as Ellen was about to dismount.

'Hello, Janice. What's up?'

'I'm ever so glad I've seen you. I've been looking out for ages.'

'Why? Whatever's the matter?' Ellen took off her sunglasses, pushed some hair out of her eyes and frowned. Her sister-in-law had an irritating habit of dramatizing the slightest thing.

Janice stood in front of Ellen with a leg either side of her front wheel. She gripped the handlebars with both hands and tried to control her breathing. Lowering her head slightly and looking up at Ellen from beneath her untidy eyebrows she took a deep breath. 'It's John. Your John. There's been a telegram.'

'Oh.' Ellen froze. 'What?' Slowly she got off the bike. She looked away. After a pause she spoke in a small voice. 'It's bad, isn't it?' She glanced quickly at Janice and saw that it was.

Janice bit her lip and sniffed. She nodded but wouldn't meet Ellen's eye.

'Oh, no. No. Not John.'

Janice wiped her nose with her fingers and nodded. 'Italy, somewhere, I'm not sure. I can't remember the name.' She sniffed again and looked down at Ellen's front tyre. 'About three weeks ago.'

'What? No. There's been some mistake. I wrote to him earlier this week, in Italy. Sent a photo. Kathy and me, we had it done in Cromer to send . . . It happens all the time. You read about cases like this in the paper.' Ellen was gabbling. She stopped and stared dully at her sister-in-law. 'No, there's no mistake, is there?'

Janice shook her head. Tears prickled at Ellen's eyes. Her face crumpled.

'Not John. Oh, God. What am I going to do without my big brother?' She dropped the bicycle, put the back of her hand to her mouth, turned away and howled. She put her hand on the wall to steady herself. Janice let the bicycle fall and quickly caught Ellen round the waist as her legs buckled. She lowered her sister-in-law to the ground.

'Sit there a minute. Put your head down.' She pressed Ellen's head forward until it was almost between her knees. 'Stay there, I'll get you some water.' Distraught, Ellen flopped over and lay on her side in the weeds at the foot of the wall.

Janice returned with a cup of water. She pulled Ellen upright and made her drink. Eventually Ellen quietened. After a few more sips of water she felt able to speak.

'Does George know? And Mum and Dad?'

'Oh yes.' Janice hitched herself up to sit on the wall. 'We knew early this morning before work,' she said chattily. 'Your father got Dolly to call in on her post round.' Janice was suddenly very talkative. She was much more comfortable now that the deed was done.

'What?' Ellen looked up sharply. 'You knew this morning? Why didn't someone let me know?'

'I don't know. George rushed off down to your parents' house. I thought he'd say.'

'But I saw you this morning as I was leaving. I waved. You waved back. You were feeding your chickens.' Ellen was incredulous. She slowly levered herself upright. 'You must have known then. Why didn't you say?'

Janice looked away. 'I didn't like. You'd gone past anyway. Here, let me. . . .'

Ellen stared hard at Janice. Pushing her sister-in-law away she struggled up.

'You knew. You knew all the time and you didn't say. You stupid woman. How could you?' Ellen was furious. Then she was crying and shouting at Janice.

'I've been at work all day and nobody saw fit to tell me. I was less than a hundred yards along the road from Mum and Dad. I don't believe this.' Linda Hunt looked through her window, then quickly appeared at her door and hurried down the path.

'Whatever's the matter?' She wrung her hands.

'It's her brother, John. He's been killed. In Italy. She's upset.'

'They didn't tell me. Nobody told me,' Ellen sobbed. 'You stupid woman,' she rounded on Janice. 'How on earth could you be so simple-minded?'

'Of course she's upset. I'm not surprised. Anyone would be.' Linda took Ellen by the shoulders and steered her through her gate. 'Anyone with half a brain, that is,' she muttered under her breath. 'Come on, Ellen. Let's get you inside. Help me get her into mine,' she added to Janice. Linda led Ellen towards her cottage.

'I'm not coming. She can't speak to me like that. It's not my fault her brother's dead. I never liked him anyway. I was only trying to help.' Janice flounced off into her own front garden.

Over a cup of tea in Linda's cottage Ellen wept. Eventually she calmed down and an overwhelming sadness replaced the rage. She didn't know what to do. She felt that she should go and see her parents but she couldn't understand why they hadn't been in touch. Eventually after thanking Linda she went next door to wash her face. As she brushed her hair she decided that she had to go. Her bicycle was still out on the roadside. Someone had picked it up and propped it against the front wall. Ellen turned it round and set off once more. At least it was downhill most of the way.

George's bicycle was leaning up against the wall outside Ivy Cottage. As she wheeled her bike round to the back Ellen could see her mother and father sitting either side of the fireplace. They were motionless, staring at the empty grate. Faced with a crisis it was what they did. There was no sign of George. Her father looked up briefly as she let herself in.

He looked years older. After glancing at Ellen he returned to the empty grate. He never spoke. Her mother had a handkerchief to her face. 'Hello, love.' Amelia's eyes were bloodshot and puffy and her face was flushed. She too went back to staring at the grate and sniffing intermittently.

'What a thing,' she said. 'What a dreadful thing to happen. You live in fear, but you never really think it's going to happen to you.' They were both obviously wretched with grief. Ellen went to her mother and kneeling, gave her a hug. They remained clinging to each other for some time until Ellen got cramp.

She staggered up, rubbing her left leg. 'I'll make some tea.' She dried her eyes and then busied herself with making her parents' tea and scones.

Having ascertained that the pigs hadn't been fed she found George when she went across the field beyond the top of the garden. Her brother was sitting on the ground in the last of the evening sun with his back against the pigsty.

'It's a bastard, isn't it?' He began crying. Ellen was a little surprised that George was so upset. He and John had never got on as children. She didn't have the heart to berate him for not telling her earlier.

'It's not fair. He never hurt anyone.' He fumbled in his jacket pocket and pulled out his tobacco tin. Ellen sat down, put her arm round him and pulled his head on to her chest. She held her little brother tight. George was racked with sobbing. Ellen tried to soothe him, occasionally wiping away her own tears. Eventually George quietened. They sat together until some time after the sun had gone down. He eventually pulled away, wiped his face with his sleeve and opened his tobacco tin. He rolled a cigarette.

Ellen asked him to make her one. She had never smoked but she noticed that a lot of people seemed to take some comfort from it.

'All the poor beggar ever wanted was to be on the beach fishing. He never asked for any more than that. Down on the beach with a line and a few worms and he was as happy as a pig in muck.'

'I know. Poor John. He did love fishing.' George lit her cigarette and after a tentative puff Ellen levered herself up, fetched the bucket of swill that she had carried across the field and emptied it over the fence into the trough.

'Did you see the telegram, George?' she asked.

'Oh, yes. Bloody thing.'

'Have you got it? Can I have a look?'

'You'll have a job.' George barked a teary laugh. 'One of the pigs got it.'

'What?'

'One of the pigs ate it.' Suddenly George began to laugh. 'The piggy-wig ate it.' Just as suddenly his voice cracked and they were both tearful again.

As they walked slowly back over the field to Ivy Cottage Ellen asked whether John had a girlfriend.

'No, I don't think so. Not anyone special, anyway. He used to go to see some girl, but I think that came to a sudden halt when her boyfriend came back. I don't know if there's anyone down south where he worked. He never mentioned anyone.'

Ellen tossed the cigarette away as they reached the top of the back garden. It went out after that first puff. She couldn't see what people saw in them.

Their parents were still sitting either side of the fire in the gloom. They had drunk their tea and William had eaten something but Amelia's plate was untouched. Despite their protestations Ellen stayed and made them a meal and then walked in the dark along to Pond Farm to tell Mr Reeve.

John's old employer in Epping wrote a letter of condolence to Amelia and William. He spoke highly of John and said that he would be sorely missed. He had also taken the liberty of informing Miss Mattocks. This latter information left the Finchams puzzled.

John's suitcase eventually arrived at Ivy Cottage. His personal effects were delayed, having initially been sent to Epping. Their arrival upset his parents anew. At first Amelia couldn't bring herself to touch the case. The man who delivered it left it in the back doorway. As the day went on it was in the way and eventually she steeled herself to move it to the foot of the stairs. When he arrived home from work William carried the case up to his son's old bedroom. He sat on the foot of the bed and looked at it for a long time. Eventually he blew his nose, wiped his eyes and moustache and levered himself up. He placed the case unopened under the bed where it had lain before John went away.

The family received a letter from John's commanding officer. Delayed by snipers and shelling while delivering dinner one night on a Bren Carrier up the line John was caught in a heavy barrage. It had been a shambles and it was days before anyone was certain that he was missing. The officer said that Mr and Mrs Fincham should be proud of their son and take comfort from the fact that he died bravely in the service of his country. He felt sure that John had died instantly, so heavy was the barrage. The officer did not mention that despite as thorough a search as could be made at the time, of Sapper John Fincham there remained absolutely no trace.

On a Sunday morning some weeks later, the family attended a memorial service in the local church. Heavily pregnant by this time, Ellen opened up her brother's suitcase that afternoon and sorted out his possessions. Along with clothing she found a bundle of letters and airgraphs. There were several from Amelia and she recognized George's writing and her own. She was not, however, prepared for the pile of letters that John had received from a certain Violet Mattocks from Epping.

She also came across a small red diary for 1943. John had never been good at spelling or grammar and he wasn't a tidy writer, but flipping through it Ellen discovered an entry for most days. She put it in her bag to read later.

Back at Cowper's Cottage that evening she sat by the fire and in the soft glow of the Tilley Lamp she read John's diary. He was in Iraq at the beginning of 1943. She remembered writing to him there. He was greatly exercised at the time by the lack of cigarettes and baths. They had been on manoeuvres and had supplemented their rations with a 'gazzle,' wild pigs and some Tigris salmon. It took Ellen a moment or two to conclude that John meant a gazelle. He had tried to cure the skin but it hadn't been a success and he had thrown it away.

Mid-March they were travelling in convoy via Kirkuk and Ar-Rutbah across Sinai into Egypt. Mid-April they were near Tripoli and at the end of the month north of Sousse in Tunisia.

Ellen knew that mail from home was important but she had never really appreciated just how vital it was. They lived from one mail delivery to the next in a world turned upside down. There were brief instances of horror and extreme danger but most of the time they had to put up with crushing boredom. All this took place in a climate of rumour, privation and lack of real information. Every piece of mail that John had received or sent was faithfully recorded in the diary. Occasionally they went without mail for many days. During such periods everyone was invariably 'browned off.'

In the middle of June they were 'bullshitting' for the visit of King George VI to Tripoli. In July John reported sick with tonsillitis for several days. On 4 September they set out by landing craft from Tripoli. They landed in Salerno Bay in western Italy five days later. John was in action immediately carrying HQ's wireless. They built a bridge over the Volturno River and at the beginning of December John was taken to the 65th Gun Hospital with jaundice. He spent the last days of the year recovering in Sorrento, on light duties at the museum. He seemed to have enjoyed his Christmas.

Ellen was wrung out by the time she got to the final entry. As a postscript John recorded that on 4 January 1944 he was still waiting for a fifth day at reinforcement camp. Having wept for much of the evening Ellen fell asleep in the chair and eventually woke, cold and stiff in the early hours of the morning.

For weeks afterwards she thought about her brother, recalling moments that they had shared. As the initial keenness of her grief began to fade she determined to set aside a moment to think about him every day. She was fearful that if she didn't make a conscious effort she would forget him altogether. However the bulge in her belly was occupying her increasingly and one night she wept when she realized that John hadn't been in her thoughts for over a week.

Eventually a cross was erected on the grave of Sapper John Fincham in the cemetery at Coriano Ridge. Ellen visited the grave many years later while she was on holiday on the Adriatic coast. It was to be another thirteen years after he died that the fact of John Fincham's life and death would be properly recorded in the graveyard in his home village.

FOURTEEN

Since Dave was still away Kathy returned to her parent's house to have her baby. In due course a pink and wrinkly boy was safely and quickly delivered early one evening. As a result Kathy managed a half decent night's sleep. Next day Mrs Priest sent a telegram to Dave Holt saying that mother and baby son were both doing well. The child would be named Philip as agreed.

Ellen called round to see them every day since it was only a short walk from Pond Farm. By this time she envied Kathy. To look at her you would never guess that she had just given birth. Ellen felt increasingly large, cumbersome and ugly.

After an uncomfortable day on Saturday, 18 November she had to knock up her brother just before midnight. Janice answered the door and both she and her husband groaned at the sight of Ellen in her coat with her little suitcase in her hand.

'Sorry. I think the baby's coming. Can you get Dennis?'

'How often are you getting the. . . ?'

'Oooh. Here we go again.' Ellen doubled up, leaned on the doorframe and groaned.

Dennis, the landlord at the Lord Nelson had offered to run Ellen to the hospital when she was due. He was an insomniac and said that whatever time of day or night it was he would be on hand to do the necessary. If it was at night the plan was that George would run and fetch him.

The door behind Ellen opened and Linda Hunt's head appeared.

'What's up? Is it baby?'

Linda pulled her door to and ran round to George's.

'How often are you getting contractions?'

'Oh, I don't know, quite often. Oh, I think something's . . .'

'You'd better forget hospital,' Linda was suddenly all business. 'I think we're past that. Let's get her home and into bed.' She took Ellen's arm and helped her down the path and back to Cowper's Cottage. 'You should have let us know sooner.'

'They started some time ago. I think I fell asleep though. Oooh.'

Linda shouted across the gardens to the emerging George.

'Run down to the pub and phone the surgery.'

George was back after a few minutes.

'Did you get through?'

'Course. Where's Jan?'

'I haven't seen her for a bit. I think she's gone back to bed.'

'I'm off too. Got work early tomorrow. See you.'

'So what did they say at the surgery?' Linda called after George. 'Is anyone coming?'

'Oh. The quack's out but they'll tell him when he gets back.'

'Thank you.' Linda shook her head disbelievingly.

Linda Hunt delivered the baby in Ellen's bed at Cowper's Cottage on Sunday 19 November 1944 at 2.29 in the morning. Her daughter Penny ran up and down the stairs fetching and carrying at Linda's behest. Ellen was fortunate in having a comparatively short labour and a normal delivery with no complications.

'Is it all right? Is it a boy or a girl?'

'He's a sweet little baby boy and he's just lovely, aren't you, sweetheart?' Linda handed Ellen's newborn baby over.

'Are you sure?'

'I'm sure. He looks perfect. Got all his fingers and toes and everything else is in the right place. And if I'm not mistaken there's the doctor.'

After examining both the baby and Ellen the doctor pronounced them fit and well.

'The nurse will be round. I wish everything was as straightforward,' he said over a cup of tea that Penny had made. 'It sounds as though it was just like shelling peas. You can't beat a short labour.' Ellen muttered to Linda that perhaps if it were so simple he should have a go himself.

Ronny and Kathy called in during the morning with the recently christened Philip. They were both excited. Ronny was as pleased as Punch since Mr Reeve had said she could pop in for a little while since she was working only a couple of minutes away down Back Lane.

Kathy had still heard nothing from Dave.

'Hello, mum,' they squealed. 'Oh, look. She's got baby with her.'

'Oh, let me see. Ah, isn't he lovely. It is a he, isn't it? Thought so. You're looking ever so mumsy, Ellen.'

Finding herself an odd mixture of weariness, pride and embarrassment Ellen smiled a little tiredly. 'Hmm, you can talk. How's the bold Philip?'

Kathy looked down at her son. 'Oh, he's fine. Don't talk about him though. I swear he knows when we're talking about him.' She turned her attention back to Ellen's son. 'Look at this one. Isn't he gorgeous?'

'He's quite big, isn't he? He's nearly as big as Phil. And look at all that hair.'

'What are you going to call him?'

'Yes, have you thought of a name?'

'Well, I haven't decided for certain. I thought Peter.'

'Yes, that's Nick's proper name, isn't it?'

'Mm.'

'What about a second name?'

'I don't know. I was toying with Richard or maybe John.'

'Oh, yes. That would be nice.' The visitors lowered their voices briefly in deference to Ellen's recent bereavement.

'Richard's a nice name. Where does it come from?'

'I just like it.'

'That's Mr Reeve, isn't it? Dick.'

'I just like the name.' But in truth Kathy was right.

'Peter John Richard, what about that? P.J.R. Fincham, it sounds good, doesn't it? Or will you call him Nichols? Either way it's got a bit of a ring to it.'

'I'm going to give him my name, Fincham.'

'Look at his little fingers. Isn't he sweet? Hello, Peter.'

'Let me have him for a minute.' Ronny's fingers were twitching. 'Oh, there. Hello, Pete. Aren't you beautiful, hmm? Oh, yes you are.'

'Peter! We'll have less of the Pete, thank you. You'll be calling him Pete Jack Dick next!'

The girls stayed as long as they could. Mr Reeve arrived as they left. Bearing a small posy of flowers the farmer seemed a little embarrassed. He kissed Ellen's cheek and admired the baby. He was surprised and pleased to hear that Ellen's son was to be named after him. He had a surprise for Ellen too. His second name was Peter, he said. They laughed and wondered what the chances would be against that happening. He said that it was just a pity that he hadn't been named Richard Peter John.

He reassured Ellen that she was to take whatever time she needed. They had discussed the matter at length well before the baby was due and he had arranged with Mrs Quantrill's daughter to help out at Pond Farm until Ellen was able to return.

When the weather was better and if she felt up to it he would come or send someone to pick her and the baby up mid-morning. She could work in the house with the child there with her and he would drive them back during the afternoon. She could do as many days as she wished. Ellen thought that it seemed workable. They could certainly give it a try and see how things went.

During the afternoon Mr Reeve brought Amelia. William was at work. He wouldn't come.

'He's not been himself,' said Amelia, 'not since John. . . .' It was true that it was still less than two months since the dreadful news had reached them. Ellen nodded but privately she thought that even if John were still alive her father would still not have been able to bring himself to visit his trollop of a daughter and look upon her bastard son.

Amelia was smitten with Peter immediately and held him for most of her visit. She convinced herself with no trouble at all that he had John's nice blue eyes. She even laughed briefly when Ellen said that they should be pleased that the baby hadn't inherited John's ears too. By the time visiting was over Amelia was overwrought and tearful having convinced herself that Peter and John were part of some fearful symmetry. Peter too was fretful by the time Ellen took him from her mother.

'It's funny how things work out, isn't it,' Amelia said to Mr Reeve as they were leaving. 'It's almost as if it was meant somehow. Poor John's gone and little Peter has come to take his place.' She smiled and her eyes sparkled brightly but her voice trembled and her knuckles were white as she wrung her handkerchief. Mr Reeve put his hand gently on her elbow as they left.

Ellen received numerous visitors. Kathy reappeared bearing a parcel of yet more used but good baby clothes that her mother had sent. Linda and Penny popped in from next door with bottled blackcurrants and the instruction that she had only to bang on the wall any time she needed anything. One or other of them would be round immediately. Ronny turned up after work bearing eggs and a knitted jacket and hat that she had laboured over ever since Ellen announced her pregnancy. It was intended to be identical to the one that she gave Kathy for Philip. They were both terrible shapeless things. Kathy was back yet again bearing sherry and there was quite a little party for a while. Eventually the gathering broke up and the visitors went on their way. Ellen decided that at least for one night she would have Peter in bed with her rather than in the second-hand cot that Mr Reeve had bought and that he'd had a couple of the hands repair and paint. Somehow they had managed to manoeuvre it into the corner of the room.

'Just you and me now, precious, hmm?'

After what seemed an eternity, the war in Europe finally came to an end on 9 May 1945. Those who had been away and survived began returning. They came in dribs and drabs, by bus, by train, dropped off after a lift or footsore after having to walk. Usually unexpected and unannounced, there was often nobody to greet them. They turned up, pale and exhausted, some with the shakes, some normal enough, others with a worryingly fixed grin and a stranger peering anxiously from the depths of their eyes. Some were accompanied by new wives and children to be absorbed somehow into the family home that they left years earlier.

Within days many began the heartbreaking business of trying to find a job and somewhere to live. The village celebrated with a garden party and dance at Pond Farm but the celebrations were somewhat muted with most people mindful that the village had lost five of its sons.

Robert was home for a few days and seemed rather friendlier towards Ellen than he had been when he helped move her into Cowper's Cottage. Late on in the evening he ran in to her on his way back from the bar and asked her for a dance.

It was a waltz. Ellen could scarcely believe how happy she felt when Robert took her in his arms. It was as if they'd never been apart. His smell was just the same. It was all she could do not to bury her nose in his neck. He was saying something.

'How's your little boy doing? Peter, isn't it?'

'Yes, Peter. He's fine thanks. He's with the next-door neighbours at the moment. They'll be spoiling him rotten.'

'How old is he now? Six months or so?'

'Yes, in a couple of weeks.'

They grinned at each other when the dance finished.

'What will you do now?'

They parted, uncertain, almost embarrassed.

'I'm not sure. I'm waiting to hear about something out in the Far East.'

'Oh,' Ellen was taken aback. 'Will you. . . ?'

It was at that point that the band began the next dance and Robert was whisked away in a ladies excuse me by a tipsy Poppy Mercer, Claud's daughter. Ellen looked around and was immediately gathered up by Janice's brother, ex-Able Seaman Woodhouse, who had already bored her with tales of how he intended getting a job on the trawlers. He began where he had left off.

She saw no more of Robert but took some comfort from the fact that in the few minutes they were together they had exchanged more words than they had in all the years since Robert went away to school.

The war with Japan continued until 14 August. Unlike the war with Germany its conclusion passed almost unnoticed in the village. In total both conflicts had lasted for just twenty-six days less than six years.

One sunny morning Ellen turned into the yard at Pond Farm at the same time as the postwoman. She had taken to cycling down with Peter in the basket seat on the back of her bicycle.

'Hello, Dolly, lovely morning.'

'Oh, it's grand. It's not supposed to last though, rain by this afternoon. Are you going to take these in for me?'

Dolly dug in her bag and pulled out a thin sheaf of letters.

'There's something for you, I think. A card. I'm sure I saw one.'

'Me?' Ellen didn't normally receive post at the farm. She riffled through the mail.

'I can't see . . . Oh, you're right. It is for me.'

'Good news I hope. I do like to bring good news.' Dolly wheeled round in the yard and set off again. 'Busy, busy, must get on. Bye, Ellen.'

'Bye, Dolly.'

Ellen watched as Dolly cycled to the far end of Maria's paddock. She smiled as the postwoman then cast around quickly before turning left into Heath Lane. Dolly would cycle a quarter mile or so up the hill to Storey's smallholding. There she would wheel her bicycle round the back of the house before spending the next hour or so with Gerry Storey. They'd been having an affair for months. Dolly's husband had been missing for over two years.

The postcard was from Nick.

Dear Ellen, I've survived! All best to everyone at Lord Nelson and you and yours, Nick. PS. Hope you have too (survived!).

There was no address. The postmark was Bradford and the card had been posted only a few days earlier. She wondered whether she might hear something further from Nick once he was settled.

Kathy too received news. An official airgraph arrived from Alexandria. It was dated over seven weeks earlier. Dave had been injured. His truck had run over a mine many miles out in the desert and he was in a field hospital. The prognosis was not good.

Two days later another letter turned up. This one was only three weeks old. Dave had been moved to a military hospital in Cairo. His condition was grave. Despite a number of phone calls to the War Office Kathy could find no further details.

Weeks later an airmail letter turned up. Dave had been moved to yet another hospital. He was under the care of a nurse by the name of Hoda and was as well as could be expected. The nurse would be in touch when there was something more to tell. Kathy was frantic to learn more and contacted numerous people who were recommended to her as someone who could perhaps help. All enquiries came to nothing. Kathy discovered not one useful lead. Eventually a letter arrived from Hoda. It was written in pencil on flimsy paper. Dave was still gravely ill and not expected to live. She would look after him until the end.

On a bright but cool morning in September 1949 Ellen and Kathy walked their sons to the bus stop in front of the Lord Nelson to await the coach that would take them to their first day at primary school two and a half miles away. Once the boys were on the coach Kingsley Ambrose taunted them with promises of teacher brutality. When they stopped at the west end of the village another newcomer made such a fuss in separating from his mother that the coach driver had to get out and lift him bodily into the coach. Fortunately for Peter and Philip the bawling newcomer was treated to Kingsley's undivided attention for the rest of the journey.

Little had changed in the village. Any hope that the mines would be cleared from the cliffs and the beach reopened had been dashed in 1946. Cliff falls, both massive and minor and continual erosion had changed the cliffs and beach to such a degree that mine clearance looked well nigh impossible. Few maps existed and those that had survived were useless. Things looked so bleak that an Act of Parliament was passed authorizing the sealing off of the beach in perpetuity. Even so an optimist made application to the parish council for a stand on the beach from which to offer pony and donkey rides.

The continued success of mine clearance elsewhere was galling for the village. Other beaches opened up and the holiday trade rekindled with the appearance or reappearance of hotels, guest houses, bed and breakfast establishments, tea-rooms and cafés. Ice cream sellers, hirers of deckchairs and providers of boat trips were not slow to seize their opportunities. Fishermen relocated their boats and anglers returned.

The village was fast losing opportunities for regeneration. The parish council agitated for the beach and cliffs to be cleared of mines. After a mine washed up on the beach at Great Yarmouth the villagers signed a petition and sent it to the Secretary of State for War urging clearance of 200 yards of beach at the foot of Cliff Road. After a while the Secretary responded that 2000 yards of beach had been cleared, yielding thirty mines in one week. Ominously, more mines were found in the swept area the following week. The Secretary could not accept the risk of removing restrictions.

Before leaving the cottage every morning Peter and Ellen crossed Back Lane to gather eggs and feed the hens in the field opposite. Mr Hunt had made them a modest chicken house and together they had erected a run from wire netting and fencing stakes, not a few of which had originated in the barbed wire fence above the mined cliffs. When it was finished Mr Reeve dropped off some point-of-lay birds and an elderly cockerel that they named Ginger Ted.

'Are you coming, Peter? Let's go and feed the chooky-birdies. See if there are any eggs. Fill up the watering can from the tank and bring it over.' Ellen waited at the gate with scraps and grain in one hand and a heavy headed stick in the other. She had carried the stick ever since surprising a rat in the chicken coop. If she saw another one she felt that she might be able to kill it with the stick. However, by far the greater reason was that she needed it to ward off the attentions of Ginger Ted.

From the outset the old cockerel disliked Ellen. He'd flown at her enough times for her to ensure that she never entered the run without the stick. Ellen was frightened of Ginger Ted and he knew it. She was miffed by his antipathy towards her. He was as nice as pie with Peter. Couldn't the stupid bird see that she brought his food and water and that she meant him and his harem no harm?

Peter lugged the galvanized watering can over to the chickens. 'I'll feed them while you get the eggs.' His mother was not keen. No sooner was she inside the run than the cockerel began to bristle and cluck a warning. When she made a tentative move towards the hen house Ted flew at the back of her legs.

'Aah! Get off me, you old beggar.' Ellen hopped about and flailed at the cockerel. 'Go on, get off.' This particular morning Ted prosecuted a vicious and sustained attack. Ellen waved her stick at him ineffectually but he kept coming. He scratched the back of her legs and was driving her out of the chicken run when she caught him with a lucky swipe. It wasn't a hard blow but it struck the cockerel on the head. Ted staggered and halted. Ellen swore later when she was telling Kathy about it that the bird had shaken his head, cleared his throat, dusted himself down and then refocused, just like a professional fighter. However, when he came again she was ready for him. She gave him a sharp whack across the back. Still the cockerel advanced. She whacked him again. On he came. By now Ellen's blood was up. She reversed the stick and then measured her next blow carefully like a golfer preparing a drive. Very deliberately she raised the stick above her head.

'No! Mum! Don't hit him!' Peter was alarmed by the look on his mother's face.

Ellen paused. She looked at Peter.

'You'll kill him,' he said in a small voice.

The apprehension on Peter's pale face slowly registered. Ellen blinked and then slowly lowered her stick. The cockerel still bristled, clucked and glared at her. She began to shake.

'Aah! Get away from me, you wretched creature.' She turned her back on Ginger Ted and stalked out of the chicken run, leaving the gate wide open.

Peter and Margaret sat at the kitchen table. Margaret surveyed the remains of their meal.

'I'll say this for you. You certainly know how to give a girl a good time.' They grinned at each other good-naturedly over their greasy plates.

'I offered to buy you dinner in Cromer. A drop more?' Peter reached across and poured wine into Margaret's glass and then topped up his own.

'I know. Mm, thanks. I'm just joking. That was delicious. Sadly we'll both smell of fried food. Did you ever have someone like that standing next to you in the early morning on the London Underground?'

'Yes. Lots of times, people who lived in a bed-sit.' Peter looked at his watch. 'Coffee?'

'Yes, please.'

'I think I might allow myself another one of those cigarettes with my coffee.'

'Do you ration yourself?'

'Sometimes.'

Margaret began to gather up the plates.

'Leave those. I'll have plenty of time to see to them tomorrow.'

'I'll just put them in the kitchen, then you take the wine through and I'll bring some coffee.'

Peter was lying on his side on the sitting-room floor, propped up on one elbow with his back against an armchair. Margaret had taken off her shoes and was sitting on the sofa opposite with her legs tucked beneath her.

'When I got back from school that day I really thought Harry was my dad. I thought he'd finally come home.'

'You'd be disappointed then, when it wasn't him.'

'Well, up to a point. But I have to confess that I found your dad, Harry, a little bit frightening.'

'Why was that?'

'Well, I was only five remember and then suddenly there was this bloke I'd never seen before in my house, in my bed. That was another thing. I was scared stiff Kingsley, my stupid cousin, would find out I was sleeping with my mother. Anyway, there was Harry. He looked terrible most of the time, with his face, you know. . . .'

Peter waved his hand and screwed up his nose. 'And he wasn't all that friendly. He gave me a fright the very first night. Shouting out and moaning in his sleep.'

Margaret nodded and sipped her wine. 'He did improve though.'

'Yes. He had a little wooden rifle that he'd made. It was a cracking little thing. He'd whittled it out of a scrap of wood. I don't know whether he made it when he was a POW or later on. We were sitting in the sun on the doorstep and he went and fetched this little rifle, it must have been a model of a .303. He sat down and took it out of this cloth and polished it. He let me hold it for a bit. Then he took it back.'

Margaret smiled and shook her head.

'He wrapped it up in the cloth again before he put it away.' Peter became animated. 'That's right! He said it was for Maggie, little Maggie. That would be you.' Peter stared at Margaret.

'And I'll tell you something else I've just remembered. I think it might still be here somewhere. I'm sure I kept it after Harry died. We kept his few bits and pieces for a bit but I think most of it went later. There wasn't anything of value or use. But the rifle, I'm sure I kept it.'

'Really? Do you remember what you did with it?'

'Ah, now that would be the clever bit. Leave it with me. It'll come.'

'So what about your dad? Nick?'

'Nick? I only met him once. He came round here. I recognized him from a photograph. I don't think he ever knew I was his son. I'm not sure Mother ever told him. Mind you, she never knew where he was so it would have been a bit difficult.'

'Did you miss having a dad?'

'I did early on. I suppose I couldn't understand why I was different from a lot of kids. But Phil was the same. It was Kingsley who told me about Nick.'

They were trailing home from the beck in a thoroughly ill humour, having wet feet from going in over the top of their boots. Most of the way home Kingsley baited Peter about his absent father. During a lull in the hectoring Peter slashed at some roadside cow parsley with a stick. He then tried a rather fanciful gambit.

'My dad was a Spitfire pilot.' He paused for effect. 'They gave him a medal.' He waited again, longer this time, before resuming. 'What was your dad, King? What did he do?' They all knew that Uncle George had been in the Home Guard after failing his medical for the army.

'He was on special duties. Just as important as anything else, my mum says. And your dad wasn't a Spitfire pilot. He wasn't even in the RAF.'

'Your dad didn't fight in the war because he was too scared. He stayed at home and hid behind Granny's coat-tails.'

'No he didn't, bloody knock-knees. That's all lies.'

The memory of Peter's splinted legs was still fresh in Kingsley's mind but he hadn't yet worked out how to use it to best advantage. Before Peter went to school Ellen was convinced that her son had knock-knees. When he stood with his knees together his ankles remained over five inches apart. It was a fashionable affliction at the time since it was widely rumoured that the young Prince Charles suffered with the condition. After a period of being bandaged into aluminium splints as he went to bed every night Peter was relieved when the doctor abandoned that approach. He said that medical science now favoured the view that the errant limbs would straighten themselves. He'd frowned a good deal and looked serious.

'I expect it'll happen when they're good and ready.'

Ellen had fretted but in time the doctor was proved correct.

'He was a Spitfire pilot. And you don't know anything about my dad.'

'Yes I do, because my mum told me.'

'Your mum's a fat liar. Just like you.'

'No, she isn't. Your dad was called Nick, see. He was a traitor and a deserter. And when they caught him he was shot.'

'No, he wasn't.'

'Yes he was. That's why you've never seen him. And it serves him bloody well right.'

The wrangle continued until Kingsley grabbed Peter's head in an arm-lock.

'My mum told me all about your dad. She said he was stupid and not even good looking. And she should know because he asked her out once, and she wouldn't go. That was before he asked your mum.'

'I don't care.'

With Peter's head still in an arm-lock the pair made crab-like progress in irritable silence. Unusually it was Kingsley who offered a small olive twig.

'Nah,' he said, 'he wasn't really.' He let Peter go. 'He wasn't a traitor or a deserter and he wasn't shot. He was just one of those soldiers that laid the mines in the cliff, Royal Engineers.'

'I don't care. He could be the King of China and I still wouldn't care.'

' 'Course, you're really a bastard, aren't you?' Kingsley's change of heart didn't last long. 'My mum says so. And your mother's no better than she should be. Mum said that as well.'

'Your mum is a fat pig and she picks her nose and eats the bogies.'

'No, she doesn't.'

'Yes, she does. And you and your stupid sister wet the bed and your sister smells of wee.'

'No one went to your christening because you're a bastard and your mother's a troll. Mum and Dad didn't go and neither did Granddad. You brought shame on us. My mum says you're lucky to have cousins like Jeannie and me.'

After Kingsley explained his understanding of the terms as fully as he could Peter trudged along behind his cousin wiping away angry tears and mulling over what had been said. From time to time Kingsley turned to goad anew.

None of it squared with Peter's view of his mother. As Cowper's Cottage came into view he studied the back of his cousin's head. Kingsley had a partic-ularly stupid-looking back of head. From forehead to crown, it was too long. There was altogether too much head sticking out and back above his collar. When they were only a short distance from home Peter hit Kingsley on the back of his stupid-looking head with his stick. Because of the disparity in height and the fact that Peter hurried the blow it was a good deal less effective than he intended. It certainly took Kinsley by surprise though. He howled and stum-bled. Peter took off as much like a scalded cat as he could in flapping Wellington boots. It was imperative that he reach the safety of Cowper's Cottage before Kingsley caught up with him. He judged the distance to a nicety.

As Peter removed his boots on the doorstep Kingsley called across the

Hunts' front garden. 'I'll get you this afternoon, you little bastard.'

'No, you won't, Fatty. I'm going out with Mum, so there.'

'I can wait. And you're definitely going to get beaten up for calling me Fatty.'

'Ooh, I'm scared, Fatty bum-hole.'

It was neither the first nor the last altercation between the two. An over-weight and irritating child, Kingsley had the unhappy knack of upsetting everyone. Few of the children who lived in the street sought him out.

His sister, Jeannie Flora Morag, born in 1947 was an odd child too. She was quite as wilfully destructive and disruptive as her brother. With spiky blonde hair and a perpetually running nose, Jeannie was rarely to be seen without a mucus moustache. Once she could walk she was also rarely seen without a disintegrating sandwich clenched in her podgy fist. Far from being laden with bogies, the sandwiches that Janice made her typically comprised thick layers of margarine and sugar, condensed milk, or tomato ketchup.

Jeannie rarely finished eating anything. Copious amounts of the filling slathered her front. Of the remainder, it wasn't unusual for someone to step in it later on the roadside.

Peter asked Ellen what his father looked like. He had asked before and been fobbed off. On this occasion though she ran upstairs and went to the old writing case on her chest of drawers. She took out the only photograph of Nick that she had ever possessed. It was a small and poorly focused black and white affair, taken with a cheap camera and by a shaky hand. Someone from the depot had given it to her in the pub after Nick had left. They said that she might as well have it if she wanted it since no one else did.

Nick was clowning in the doorway of a Nissen hut. He was wearing an over-large boiler suit with torn knees and his beret was perched upside down on his head. Holding a tin mug and a cigarette in one hand and brandishing a lavatory brush in the other he leered at the camera. Peter had seen the photograph before when he had been rooting in his mother's writing case when she was out. Unaware of its significance he had simply thought that the man looked stupid.

'What, him? He looks mad.' He was not impressed.

'Yes. It's not a very good photograph, is it?' Ellen had to agree. 'It's not much like him actually. But it's the only one I've ever had.'

'I thought he was a soldier in the Royal Engineers, a sergeant.'

'So he was. Who told you that?'

'King. He doesn't look like one. What's he supposed to be doing?'

'I don't know, having a bit of a joke. I expect they were in the middle of some dirty job.'

Peter held the photo out at arm's length, examining it through narrowed eyes. After a moment he chortled. 'Ha! He looks just like old Mercer cleaning the lavvy.'

'What? He does not.' Ellen rounded the table quickly to stand behind her son to peer at the photo over his shoulder.

'He does. You look. He looks just like old Mercer.'

'Oh, for goodness sake, so he does. I see what you mean.' Ellen laughed briefly. 'Well, you can take it from me that he never really looked like old Mercer. Do you think I would have gone with him if he had? It's just a bad photograph.'

Claud Mercer was well known in the village. Something of a character he lived in a rundown cottage close to the far end of the paddock in which he had found the body of Maria Reeve. For years he supported his wife and daughter by means of poaching and knife grinding. At the former pursuit little was ever seen of Claud; at the latter pursuit he drew an admiring audience wherever he went.

Claud journeyed round the villages on a big black bicycle. Mounted on a spindle above and parallel to the handlebars was a set of abrasive wheels. It was a clever arrangement. When Claud propped the bike on its stand and fitted a belt to the spindle he could drive the abrasive wheels by means of pedalling. Children, the unemployed and pensioners soon gathered to watch, drawn by the screech of metal on wheel and showers of sparks.

However Claud abandoned his enviable lifestyle in favour of the bottle after his wife Biddy committed suicide, throwing herself from the station bridge in front of a goods train bound for Cromer. After the funeral Claud continued to share the cottage with his daughter Poppy. She was a tempestuous girl with wild black hair and a fondness for rather more than one drink. However, she remained sufficiently sober to support the pair of them by means of a little cleaning and farm work and for the price of a drink or a packet of Woodbines she was not averse to a quick fumble round the back of the Lord Nelson.

'I don't take after him, I hope.'

Ellen smiled and ruffled Peter's hair. 'No. You're my handsome boy.'

'Where does he live?'

'I don't know. I haven't seen him since before you were born and I haven't heard anything from him since the end of the war, and that was just a postcard. I don't know where he is.'

'Why doesn't he come and see us, at least.'

'I expect he's busy.'

'I think he doesn't come because he doesn't like me.'

'Oh, I'm sure that's not true.' Ellen was indeed sure since Nick knew nothing of Peter.

'Well, if he doesn't like me, I won't like him back.'

Propped up in bed at the convalescent home Ellen finally started a letter to

Louise Stark. It wasn't easy. She had spent ages thinking about what to say and how to frame it. Several times she thought that she had it sorted out but faced with the sheet of paper she couldn't remember exactly what it was that she wanted to say. She never used to be like that. And her handwriting was awful. It was illegible. Her pen hand didn't seem to work properly. At first she had been unsure whether she wrote with her right hand or the other one. It had taken quite a while for her to remember that the other hand was called the left.

Dear Mrs Stark

Thank you for your letter . . .

Ellen stopped and stared. Who on earth was Mrs Stark? She glanced at the airmail letter again. Oh, yes. She found herself thinking about Robert. She missed him. Why she was thinking about him now? He popped into her head for some reason. She had always had a soft spot for him. Fancy him thinking for all those years that she and his father were having an affair. It was true that she had always liked Mr Reeve. She supposed that she had loved him in a way, but not like that. He was obviously very fond of her too, but there had never been even the slightest suggestion of anything untoward between them. She shook her head. Why was she thinking about them?

. . . which came as something of a surprise.

Mr Reeve never remarried. He really should have. Maria would have been appalled had she known that he had not. She wouldn't have wanted him left on his own. He had not been entirely without women friends though. There had been that Irish widow, a schoolteacher. She was nice. An infant teacher at a school in Cromer, she would have been perfect. Ellen didn't know what had gone wrong there.

Eventually, he seemed content simply to have one or two lady friends that he invited out for a meal occasionally. With Gilbert and Robert both away and troubled increasingly with his health, he left much of the everyday business of farming to the farm foreman. Then he took to playing golf and got in with a group who played several times each week. He began to look fitter than he had for a long time.

I'm sorry that it has taken me so long to reply but I have not been in the best of health. My name is Ellen Fincham. I am 59 now . . .

Good grief, where on earth has all that time gone? I'll be sixty in a few months.

and I did know your father, Peter, or Nick as we knew him during the war. We became friendly when he was stationed nearby.

Friendly? We were a bit more than friendly.

He was one of the soldiers laying mines on the cliffs.

. . . and there were times when I was with him when I thought that we would always be together, once the war was over.

I never lived at the Lord Nelson but we often met there in the evenings. I still live in the village a short distance from the pub.
   You say that you last saw your father on 31 January 1953. I know that twenty-five years have passed and my memory is not as good as it once was, but I think that it was on that same day that he came to see me. I have talked to a friend who also knew him during the war and we are sure that was the date.

Of course it was.

It was a surprise. I was not expecting him. I hadn't seen him since 1944 or heard anything of him since the end of the war. He arrived in the afternoon on 31st and only stayed for a short while. He didn't stop long because the weather was bad. He had a cup of tea and a piece of cake and we chatted for a little while. Then he left to go to see some-one about a job on the sea defences, or something like that. I think it was to be in Lincolnshire, in which case I don't know why he came down to Norfolk. He said he might look in the next day if he had the time, but I never saw or heard from him again.

And I got all dressed up and waited for him.

I assumed that he had returned home.

Exhausted, Ellen put the pad and pen down and lay back. She still hadn't reached the thing that she really wanted to address. She would write some more later.
   Lying back in bed Ellen realized how desperately tired she was. The Filipina aide had washed her hair earlier that morning. While she was look-ing in the mirror with a towel wrapped round her head and wondering whether she could be bothered to put on a little make-up it dawned on her

how like her mother she looked. Amelia wore little or no make-up and towards the end of her life she took to wearing a small dark-blue beret. Ellen had tried pointing out that it did little for her appearance and at times gave her a positively foolish air, but her mother took no notice.

Amelia had died just before Christmas in 1956 after suffering a stroke. She was picking sprouts in the back garden. Confined to bed, she was dead in less than a week after another stroke. Ellen took Peter to see her the day before she died and he had been aghast at her appearance. Propped up in bed with her head lolling on her left shoulder and her mouth open her eyes followed him round the room. She wasn't able to speak. A long string of dribble hung from her chin on to the front of her bed jacket. No sooner did Ellen wipe it away than another thick, syrupy string slowly replaced it. Peter had watched, mesmerized.

They went to the funeral with Mr Reeve, but they stood beside her father during the service. George and his family hadn't gone. Peter discussed it with his mother later and they agreed that it was very odd behaviour. He wondered whether it was because Amelia had never liked them. She positively loathed Janice and had never forgiven her daughter-in-law for the names with which she and George saddled their children.

'Kingsley Ambrose? What kind of highfalutin nonsense is that? Who on earth does she think she is? Then she goes and burdens that stupid girl with Jeannie Flora Morag and there's not a Scottish bone near any of them. That girl's going to have enough difficulties without the added bonus of names like that. I don't know where they get their daft ideas sometimes.'

Even at his wife's funeral and in the few months that remained of her father's life William refused to speak to Ellen. Less than four months after Amelia's funeral he too suffered a stroke which killed him outright. His next-door neighbour found him dead in the garden in a puddle of pigs' swill only a few feet from where Amelia had collapsed.

William had been devastated when he lost Amelia. He had never looked after himself in his life. After her mother's death Ellen tried to help with washing and ironing and making him a meal occasionally, but he shouted at her to bugger off. She still went round to Ivy Cottage when he was out.

As he signed the death certificate the doctor said that he thought that William had quite literally lost the will to live. He had never really recovered from John's death and Amelia's demise was the last straw.

Only hours after William's funeral and under cover of darkness, George and Janice were down at Ivy Cottage with a friend and his van. The next-door neighbour told Ellen that they were there until very late. By the time Ellen called round after work the following day it was apparent that they must have made many trips back and forth. Anything of value had gone. Ellen really didn't want anything but she was heartbroken to discover the remains of old family photos, keepsakes, mementoes and documents among the ashes of a bonfire in the back garden. Once they had everything that they wanted George and Janice were conspicuous by their absence. They never set foot in Ivy Cottage again and Ellen was left with the real business of clearing up.

Within the week George had sold the pigs and hens and pocketed the proceeds. The next few weekends Ellen and Peter spent hours at Ivy Cottage sorting through what remained in the house and the old tack and rubbish in the sheds at the top of the garden. Mr Reeve limped along occasionally and lent a hand.

The rag and bone man made two visits and went off heavily laden. Eventually all that remained were the countless items that John had brought home from the beach years ago and dumped on top of the rabbit hutches. It was all still there together with the remains of the homes of countless creatures that had taken refuge within it. Generations of vermin, birds and insects had been born, lived and died there. All any of it was fit for was the bonfire. As they removed John's treasures the hutches collapsed and Ellen burned them too.

Several times during those days Ellen was in tears. She cried as she thought of poor John, dead now for over twelve years. She cried for her stupid, stubborn father. The foolish man had barely spoken to her for almost as long a time and he had completely missed Peter growing up. And then there was her mother in her silly little beret, her face a mask of anxiety every time Ellen saw her. Amelia seemed perpetually torn between her daughter and the obstinate William. She had to resort to subterfuge and occasionally lies in order to see her grandson at all.

Between them Ellen and Mr Reeve organized a headstone. It recorded the lives and deaths of her mother and her father, and also finally of her brother John. She asked George if he wanted to contribute. He had hummed and hawed but she never heard from him again on the subject. It didn't surprise her since she heard Janice shrieking at him that same evening in their front yard about how he didn't want to be wasting his money on that old squit. They were all dead. What good was it going to do any of them now?

Ellen did stumble upon one interesting item that had eluded George and Janice at Ivy Cottage. Tucked away in a worn leather writing case among a pile of knitting patterns she found George's birth certificate. She glanced at it and tucked it in her bag to give to him later. It wasn't until she arrived home that she actually read it. She was astonished to see that William had not been George's father. George was the product of a union between her mother and George Ashley, the man who had owned the field beyond the back garden at Ivy Cottage. No wonder her father had always been cool towards them both.

FIFTEEN

'Good grief, is that the time?'

Margaret roused herself sufficiently to look at her watch. She glanced for confirmation at the clock above the fireplace.

'It's almost midnight. I'd better be off.'

'Have you got work tomorrow?' Peter propped himself up on one elbow and peered at her. They were both sprawled on the rug in front of the fireplace in the living-room. Ellen's collection of LPs lay round about them and Leonard Cohen droned in the background.

'No, fortunately not. But I'd better be off anyway. Do you realize we've spent the last twelve hours together? Before that we'd never set eyes on each other.'

'Ah, and what a penance it's been.' Peter put the back of his hand to his brow and feigned distress.

'Pig.'

Margaret struggled to stand up and then sat down immediately on the sofa.

'Whoa. I think I'm a bit squiffy.'

'Are you OK? You probably shouldn't drive.'

'Oh, I'll be all right. It's not the first time and it won't be the last.'

'It might very well be the last. You're welcome to stay, if you'd like. There's plenty of room.'

'That's you plying me with all that wine. I told you we didn't need to open another bottle.'

'Well, speaking for myself, I have to say I've had a very pleasant evening.'

Margaret stood up. 'Yes, it has been good. I'll just pop to the loo and then I'll be off. I should think you'll be glad to have a bit of peace and quiet, won't you?'

'Oh. I sometimes think it's overrated.' Peter clambered to his feet and busied himself with clearing away their glasses and emptying the ashtray. 'You do realize,' he called, 'that we've smoked ten, no, twelve cigarettes between us.'

'How many? Good Lord. You're a thoroughly bad influence, you know.'

'You'd have to say that's pretty good going for people who don't really smoke.'

When Margaret returned she sat down on the sofa.

'Do you know, I think I might take you up on your offer to stay if that's OK? I suddenly feel pooped.'

'Certainly. It's probably the sensible thing. We've put away a fair bit, haven't we? I'll nip up and get you a towel and stuff.'

'Oh, I'll just crash on the sofa. There's no need to go to any trouble.'

'I couldn't possibly let you sleep on the sofa. We've got plenty of room and the beds are made up.'

Upstairs, Peter showed Margaret to the spare bedroom and fetched towels from the airing cupboard.

'What a lovely room,' Margaret called. 'Beautiful shade of blue, corn-flower.'

'It used to be Mum's before the place was extended. It's a good bit bigger now. And it's rather less spartan. Used to be whitewashed in those days. And it boasted the smallest fireplace I've ever seen. We had to shove an old cushion up it to stop the wind howling.'

Peter joined her in the doorway. 'You go ahead and use the bathroom,' he said. 'There are glasses if you want water. I need to fetch my case up and sort out a few things.'

Peter ran down the stairs, switched out the lights, locked up and returned with his case.

'I know this is going to sound odd,' he called from his room, 'given the circumstances, but I've really enjoyed this evening.'

'I'm glad. So have I. Given the circumstances I suppose it could have been unutterably miserable.'

'Yes. Well, at least you've helped me avoid that. Do you need a nightdress or a T-shirt or anything?'

'No, I'll be all right. You haven't a spare toothbrush, have you? I really could do with brushing my teeth.'

'I have. I've got several in my toilet bag, courtesy of TWA, KLM and Braniff, I think. I got another one today, yesterday – or whenever it was. They're all still in the cases or wrappers.'

They met just outside Peter's door. Margaret had hung up her suit and removed her shoes and was now in a black petticoat.

'There you go.' Peter handed over the folding toothbrush. 'I suspect they're only intended to do the one time so it may not be up to the job in the morning.'

Margaret took the brush out of its plastic case and fitted it together. 'It seems sturdy enough. Thank you.'

Peter looked down at her.

'You've shrunk.' He grinned.

'I've taken off my shoes. I'm just over three inches shorter than I was a few minutes ago.'

'I really meant what I said – about enjoying our evening together. It's been so good.'

'It has.' Margaret looked Peter in the eyes a moment. Then her gaze dropped to his lips. Gently she rubbed the back of her hand against his chest.

Peter kissed her on the mouth and then quickly they were in an embrace.

'Mm, suspenders,' said Peter. 'Black stockings and suspenders.'

'You like?'

'Mm!'

'I have to say that when I set out this morning I didn't expect to finish the day quite like this.' Margaret took the proffered cigarette.

'No, me neither. Although speaking for myself, I have to say I can't think of a better way to round off any day.'

Margaret gave Peter a look of mock exasperation.

'Yes, well.' She waved the cigarette. 'How many is this?'

They were propped up on pillows side by side in Peter's bed.

'Oh, don't worry about it.' Peter lit their cigarettes. 'Might as well be hung for a sheep—'

'I know – as a Mongolian rat-snake.' Margaret laughed. They smoked in silence for a bit.

'Another thing that's worth commenting on, it's a little weird finding myself making love in the very same room as my father and your mother nearly thirty years ago.'

'Yes. You'd have to wonder what the odds against that would be.'

The bedroom was at the back of the cottage and the sun didn't intrude until late in the morning. Peter and Margaret slept in the darkened room undisturbed until after ten o'clock. On waking, Peter lay quietly and looked up at the ceiling for some time. It had been a weird few days. Eventually he turned to look at Margaret still asleep beside him. She had forgotten to take out her ear-rings and had made a rather sketchy job of taking off her make-up. Her hair was all over the place but she was still extremely attractive. An impressive pile of rings and chains lay beside her on the bedside table. Peter had hardly been able to believe his good fortune when she had clambered up to sit on him. Small breasted, slim and elegant in her expensive lingerie, she had been an enthusiastic lover.

He must have dozed off again. When he woke later Harry's model rifle came into his mind. He remembered hiding it under a floorboard in this very room. The trouble was that the cottage had been altered and extended. He thought it unlikely that the rifle would still be where he put it.

Casting around the room he came to the conclusion that the corner in which the loose board had been located would now either be beneath a pine chest of drawers, the stud partition wall immediately behind it or the landing beyond. He determined to move the chest and pull back the carpet later. It would be the quickest and easiest approach.

He got out of bed quietly and went downstairs. A piece of torn cardboard had been thrust through the letter box and lay on the mat in the hall.

Milk on doorstep. Nice Mini!!! See you later, P

Kathy had sent Philip up with the milk. Peter was willing to bet that reports of Margaret's Mini outside the cottage had kept them both going for quite a while on Philip's return to the pub.

He made tea and took it upstairs. Margaret's eyes snapped open as he pulled the curtains back a little.

'Oh, lovely. Good morning. What time is it?'

'Getting on for eleven. Do you have sugar in your tea?'

'No.' Margaret sat up and stretched. 'Thank you. You've got milk. That looks very welcome.'

'Phil must have left it. Did you sleep?'

'I did, like a log. You?'

'Yes. I feel much better. It was worth keeping going. It seems to have taken care of the jetlag – or at least the worst of it, for the time being. I'll probably fail again a little later.'

They sat side by side in bed drinking their tea.

'What are your plans for the day?' Margaret asked.

'Oh, I thought I might have a day off. I've got loads to do here but I really don't feel like getting started on it.'

'No. I should take your time, if you can.'

'I thought I'd potter about here and then go down to the Nelson for a pint and a bite to eat. What are your plans? Would you like to. . . ?'

'I must go home and change. I need a bath and—'

'You can have a bath here.'

Margaret laughed. 'I need a change of clothes. I can't spend all day poncing about in my best suit.'

'Mm. Don't know why. You look great.'

'Yes, well. I could meet you at the pub after I've been home. We could have lunch and then do something this afternoon perhaps.'

'Excellent. In the meantime however, we could just have another little go at that rather interesting thing we tried last night.'

'Whatever can you mean?' Margaret leaned over and kissed Peter on the cheek. 'All right, but I must go to the bathroom first.'

They arranged to meet at the Lord Nelson at 1.30 p.m. After Margaret had left, Peter wandered round the cottage. Other than being uncharacteristically tidy it looked as though his mother had just popped out and would be back shortly. Everywhere there were poignant reminders. Car keys, a half eaten roll of Polo mints, a ring, countless paperclips, buttons, pins, ball-points and blunt stubs of pencils lying in a bowl in the hall. In the kitchen there were appointments on the calendar. Hair – 3.15, dentist – 9.00, both next week. He supposed that he had better cancel them. After digging out another pack of Lucky Strike he lit a cigarette and mooched out on to the patio. A pair of secateurs lay forgotten and rusting on the coal bunker but otherwise everything looked spick and span. His mother had taken to gardening in a big way sometime after he left home.

At the end of the garden he turned to look back at Cowper's Cottage. He and his mother had never discussed wills but she had always intimated that it was her intention to leave him the cottage. It was tempting to stay. There was little enough for him in London. He could carry on doing his job from almost anywhere in the world.

An upstairs curtain twitched two cottages along. He assumed it would be Janice, having a nose. He almost waved but changed his mind and turned his back.

Looking across the field he recalled once taking an apple to a labourer out there. He had been very young, four or five perhaps. It had been pouring and the man was standing up to his knees in mud, topping and tailing sugar-beet. He had a sack folded over his head and he was dressed in oilskins but he looked drenched. Peter had cajoled his mother into letting him take the man an apple. He had slithered and splashed across the heavily rutted and muddy field to deliver his gift. Thinking back on it, he smiled and shook his head. A stone cold apple must have been the last thing that the man wanted on such a day. He'd said thank you though, and there had been a twinkle in his eyes beneath the dripping sack.

Turning back towards the cottage, the curtains two doors down again caught his eye. Someone was watching. He stopped and very deliberately thumbed his nose. The curtains snapped together immediately. It was some time since he'd given in to such an infantile gesture. It took him back to altercations that he'd had with King. He gathered up the secateurs, dried them and left them in the conservatory on his way back.

It didn't take him long to move the chest of drawers and peel back the carpet. He was right. There was the short board beneath which he had hidden anything that he preferred to keep from his mother. The stud partition wall partly covered it but with a little judicious levering with a screwdriver from the garage he managed to ease the board up without too much difficulty.

At first he could find nothing. The void beneath the board was empty. He felt around beneath the surrounding boards. There seemed to be nothing there. He went downstairs to the kitchen and returned with a torch. By lying on the floor and squinting beneath the floorboards he could just make out something a few inches out of reach. A wire coat-hanger did the trick. He gently raked the little parcel closer until he could pick it up.

The model rifle was intact. It had remained untouched since the day he placed it beneath the floor. There was a little bloom on it but still wrapped in the oily cloth that Harry had kept it in, it was well preserved. Peter took it downstairs and rubbed it over with a little furniture polish. He buffed it up with a yellow duster and was well pleased with the result.

Peter walked down to the pub just after 1 p.m. The bar was busy with what he took to be regulars. Most had the look of people in for a quick pre-prandial before heading home for a substantial lunch. A barmaid that he hadn't seen before was serving. Kathy was sitting at the end of the bar reading the local paper.

'Peter. How are you, love?'

'Hello, Kathy. Not so bad, thanks. Not a bad morning.'

'No. What would you like?'

'Let me get you one.' Peter addressed the girl behind the bar. 'I'd like a pint of bitter please and a. . . .'

'I'll have a small sherry please, love. Dry, the Fino. There.' Kathy pointed at the bottle. 'Yes. That's it. Just a very small one.' She turned to study Peter.

'Did you manage any sleep?'

'Yes. Out like a light.'

'Not immediately, I suspect.' Kathy peered at Peter over her glasses.

'Oh. Yes.' Peter tried hard not to grin, but couldn't help himself.

'I don't know.' Kathy shook her head in mock sorrow. 'What are you like?'

They discussed Margaret for a few minutes, Kathy telling how they had got to know her during their visits to Ellen.

Margaret drove into the car park a few minutes before the appointed time. She had changed into jeans and a sweater beneath a black leather jacket.

'Oh dear, oh dear,' she said, as she sat down on a stool beside Peter. 'We're going to look like Bill and Ben.' Peter too was in jeans and leather jacket, albeit a brown bomber style.

'More like Tweedledum and Tweedledee,' said Kathy.

'Easily remedied,' Peter said. 'I've got a suede jacket less than five minutes away.'

'I wouldn't worry about it. You're nowhere near the same,' said Kathy.

Peter got Margaret a half of beer. 'I thought we might get a sandwich here. It would save messing about at the cottage trying to make lunch.'

Margaret nodded her agreement.

'Have you got any sandwiches, Kathy?'

'We have. What would you like?'

'Oh, ham and salad, thanks.'

'And I'll have roast beef and salad and a dab of mustard, if you have any.'

'We do.' Kathy went through to place the order.

'Look what I've got here.' With some ceremony Peter produced the model rifle from the inside pocket of his jacket. 'Feast your eyes on this little number.'

'Oh, you found it. Was it where you thought? Did you have much trouble?'

'It was exactly where I thought it would be, give or take an inch or two. I cleaned it up a little, gave it a bit of a polish. It looks good, doesn't it?'

Margaret took the model rifle and looked at it carefully.

'Is that what they're like? Look at the detail. It must have taken him ages.'

Margaret stared closely at the rifle and then suddenly put it down on the bar. She gasped once and reached for her handkerchief.

'Are you OK?' Peter placed a hand on her arm.

'Yes.' Margaret stared at the optics behind the bar. 'I was just thinking of him spending all that time making it. It breaks your heart.'

'It does. I never knew whether he made it while he was a POW or later when he was in hospital.'

When their sandwiches came they took them over to a table in the bay window.

'Your mum told me that she got pregnant by my dad.'

'Really? I didn't know that. Is there another. . . ?'

'She had a miscarriage after she fell down the stairs at the cottage. Lost the baby.'

'Oh. I remember that, her falling down the stairs, not the baby. She was in bed when I came home from school. There was a terrible bruise and graze on her ribcage. She was in a right old mess, could hardly stand upright for ages.'

'So we both nearly had a half-brother or sister.'

'Hmm, I suppose so.'

Philip joined them as they finished eating. He was newly shaved and dapper in a blue blazer and severely creased slacks.

'So, boys and girls.' He stood beside their table and jingled coins in his pocket. 'And how are things in Gloccamora?'

'Hi, Phil. Thanks for the milk. I forgot it yesterday. Thanks to your good offices we were able to have a proper mug of tea.'

'Hello, Philip. Yes, thank you.'

'Well, you had other things on your mind yesterday.'

Peter looked at Philip sharply.

Margaret excused herself and went over to the juke box that Kathy had just had installed on a month's trial. Philip sat down opposite Peter and grinned.

'You certainly haven't lost your touch, have you, matey?'

'What?'

'Got in there a bit smartish, didn't you?' Philip inclined his head in

Margaret's direction. 'Mind you—'

Peter frowned. 'It wasn't like that at all.'

'Oh. Well.' He seemed not to know how to go on. 'Anyway, I'm off up to the big city. Going to the cinema and then dinner afterwards.'

'What are you going to see?'

'Haven't a clue. We'll decide when we see what's on.'

'OK, well, have a good one.'

'I will.'

As Margaret returned Philip took his leave. They watched him through the window as he got into his Austin 1100 and cautiously made his way out of the car-park and on to the road.

'It'll take him ages to get to Norwich at the rate he goes,' said Peter. Margaret got up and looked at the sky through the window.

'It's a lovely afternoon. Shall we go for a walk?'

'Good idea. Let's go and get some fresh air.'

After their lunch they said goodbye to Kathy and once outside, after some discussion, turned left into the lane that ran down to the cliff tops.

SIXTEEN

Ellen, Peter and Philip had just finished lunch as the first heavy spots of rain battered the living-room window. A few ragged diagonals slashed the glass and then dribbled erratically down the window panes.

'Goodness. Look at that. If it gets any darker I'll have to light the Tilley.' Ellen popped the last of her toast into her mouth. She swept a few crumbs off the table into her hand and tossed them into the glowing grate in the range behind her. They crackled and flared briefly.

Peter and Philip had been playing with other children down at the far end of the village all morning. They had appeared on the doorstep as Ellen arrived home from Pond Farm weary after cycling up the hill into a strong headwind all the way. It was curious how wind could be so exhausting.

She couldn't be bothered changing out of her work clothes and had made them all a boiled egg and toast soldiers. The eggs had built up a bit of late and it wouldn't hurt to use a few. She thought she might make a fruitcake later. The boys had made the toast in front of the range on a toasting fork that John had fashioned years earlier from heavy-duty wire he had brought home from the beach.

'Phil? Would you like another egg?' Peter had turned his empty shell upside down in his eggcup. Lolling with one elbow on the table he pushed the plate towards his friend. Ellen and Philip winked at each other and shook their heads, but it was a ritual of which they never tired.

'I was just going to offer you one.' Philip turned his eggshell upside down in the eggcup and tapped it gently with his spoon. Unsurprisingly it sounded hollow.

Ellen surveyed her mangled eggshell and the hardening dribble of yolk that had overflowed down the side of the eggcup. She had never been able to eat a boiled egg tidily.

'I think mine is probably past. . . .'

She stopped suddenly to listen. The unmistakable sound of running feet, heavy and hurrying, was coming closer. They looked up at the window and then at each other.

'I'll go.' Peter slipped down from the table. The rain hammered anew at the window.

'Who on earth can that be? They'll be soaked.' Ellen craned across the table to look out of the window but the visitor was already out of sight and knocking. Sliding across the linoleum in his socks Peter opened the door. The wind rushed in and rain spots darkened the doormat.

'Oh. Hello. Does Ellen live here? Ellen Fincham?'

'Ah, wait a minute. . . .' Peter looked at the visitor. 'Mum!'

'Who is it, Peter? You'd better ask them in . . . they'll be soaked. Hang on a minute. Here I. . . .' Ellen wiped her mouth.

'Who. . . ?' Peter continued to stare.

'Nick.' The visitor coughed and gasped for breath. 'Nick Nichols.'

The climbing roses beside the door rasped and scraped on the wall and behind Peter a picture tapped the wallpaper in the draught.

'It's Mr Nichols.'

Ellen rounded the table, removing her apron as she went. She arrived at the door slightly flustered. Peter slid back to his chair.

'Hello? Can I. . . ?'

'Hello, Ellen.' The man in the long fawn mackintosh hunched his back against the wind and rain and smiled shyly. He looked unsure of himself. Ellen's chest lurched the moment she saw him. Despite the balding head and the lined face averted from the weather she recognized him right away.

'Nick?' She fiddled with her hair. 'What are you doing here? Come in!' She stood back and gestured him in. 'Come on. You'll be soaked.'

'Thanks. It is a bit grim.'

'You'll catch your death.'

Nick stepped down into the cottage and Ellen quickly closed the door.

They looked at each other in the gloom. Peter and Philip watched closely from the table.

'Here, let me take your coat.'

'Thanks. It's probably only a shower. It's been like this on and off all morning.' Beneath his coat Nick was wearing a sports jacket and a pair of trousers that looked as though they had once belonged to a suit. He pulled the material away from his ankles and stamped his feet.

'Are you very wet?'

'No. They'll dry in a moment or two by the fire, thanks. I saw Kathy down at the Nelson and she said you were living here. I couldn't believe it. Lucky for me you were in.'

'Come on, sit down. Have the chair by the fire. Would you like something to eat or drink? We've just . . . but I can easily make you something.'

Nick shook his head. 'No, thanks. I've just had a sandwich at the pub. It hasn't changed much, has it?'

'Are you sure? I was just going to make some tea.'

'Oh, well. I will have a cup, thanks.'

'Mum, we're just off to Phil's.' Peter and Philip had slid off their chairs and were pulling on their coats and boots.

'You'll get soaked.'

'No. Look. It's stopping and it's brighter again. We'll be all right.'

'OK, love. Don't get in Aunt Kathy's way and don't go far in this weather. We're in for a rough do according to the wireless. See you later. Bye, Phil.'

'Bye, um. Bye.'

Ellen smiled. Philip had not yet got used to addressing her as Ellen, which she had suggested.

'Bye, boys,' Nick called after them. 'Nice lads,' he continued after the door closed. 'Yours?'

'Peter is mine, the one who answered the door. The other one, Philip, is Kathy and Dave's son. You remember Dave Holt?'

'Yes. I've just been talking to Kathy. I was sorry to hear that Dave didn't make it.'

'Yes. We all were.'

Nick shook his head. 'He was a nice chap. How's she. . . ?'

'She's doing OK. She's got a nice little hairdressing business at home and she does part time at the pub. As you can imagine she's not short of admirers. She and Phil live at the bottom of Back Lane, on the left, the cottage with the blue gate.'

Nick took out his tobacco tin and lighter.

'Do you mind?'

'No.'

'You still don't?'

'No, thank you.'

Nick rolled an untidy cigarette and flicked his lighter open.

'You've still got the "Windproof Beauty?" '

Nick held it up briefly.

'Certainly have. It's getting on a bit now.' He flicked the lid shut and then opened it again. 'It's started playing up a bit, probably needs a good clean.'

He blew on the lighter. 'It was brand new in 1937, I think. So it's getting on. I got it in '39 or '40.' Nick flicked it open and then shook it. He frowned and blew into the top again. The lighter sparked but it wouldn't light. He shook it and blew on it again.

'I'll have to take a proper look at it when I get back.' He held it up. 'Had my name engraved on it, both sides.'

'Oh? Well it's been a jolly good one, hasn't it?'

'Yes. They come with a lifetime guarantee. I could get it fixed free of charge if I sent it to the States. Postage would probably be prohibitive though.'

Nick put the lighter in his pocket and took out a box of matches. They were unlike any that Annie sold. Ellen hadn't seen the box before. The match flared with an awful lot of blue smoke and it smelled rather nasty, she thought.

Nick coughed and flapped at a few strands of smouldering tobacco that dropped on to his lap. 'Damn, sorry.'

'So what brings you here today, anyway?' Ellen made the tea and then fetched a cake tin from the cupboard. There was a small piece of her last fruit cake remaining.

'Would you like a piece? It's probably past its best. I thought I might make another this afternoon.'

'Oh, well. Just a small . . . I'm down about a job.'

'Are you thinking of moving to this neck of the woods?'

'No. The work's up in Lincolnshire, sea defences. But the fellow I need to see is at the depot, where we used to be. Do you remember Wormy? Probably not. He's in charge. Been down here for ages apparently, putting in revetments and breakwaters, but they're coming to the end of the contract. They're looking for people to work up there, somewhere north of Skegness. Good money, too.' He sipped his tea and grimaced. 'Aah! I broke a tooth this morning.'

'Oh, it'll be sore. Do you want something for it?'

'No, thanks. Kathy gave me some aspirin. I'll just have to eat and drink on the other side.' He blew on his tea. 'It'll be funny to see the depot again. Has it changed much?'

'I don't know. I haven't been near but it looks much the same from the road.'

'Kathy said they still haven't cleared the mines.'

'No. They haven't even begun. They're supposed to be making a start this year. There was a bit in the paper some time ago that said they had started but it was a false alarm.'

'The other beaches around here are clear now, aren't they?'

'Yes. Isn't that just typical? Apparently our beach is more difficult because of all the cliff falls and erosion. But it's my belief that they don't know how many mines were laid and now they don't know where they are.'

'Hmm, you're probably right.'

'Didn't you tell me you kept maps?'

'Yes, but some were better at it than others. Some never bothered at all. I bet most of the maps have been lost or mislaid.'

'Typical!'

Nick shrugged his shoulders and gave her an apologetic grin.

'You still work on the farm then? The same one?'

'Yes. Pond Farm, I'm still there.' Ellen laughed. 'I haven't moved far since you last saw me.'

'And what about Peter's dad? Is he at work?'

Ellen's heart fluttered. 'Oh. No. We haven't seen him for a long time.' She gave a wry smile and busied herself with clearing away the boys' plates. 'Not for years.' The response was automatic these days.

'Hmm. I'm sorry to hear that.' Nick paused. He frowned but then thought better of pursuing it. 'You and Kathy haven't been all that lucky then – in the marriage stakes.'

'Heavens, I wouldn't say that.' Ellen laughed. 'I'm not sure that we'd agree with you. It has its compensations. Anyway, where are you these days? Where have you just come from?'

'Leeds. I hitched down.'

Nick pulled a worn brown leather wallet from his back pocket. He extracted a couple of small photographs and slid one across the table to Ellen.

'That's the wife, Monica, and her mother, the wicked witch of the west. It was at Skeggie several years ago. She's put on a little weight since then.' He passed over the second photo. 'And this is the kids on the beach at Scarborough last year. Louise is thirteen. She's the eldest, wants to be a model, or a stewardess on an aeroplane. And the one pulling the silly face is Raymond. He's nine. He's football crazy and a future England centre forward. Or likes to think he is.'

Nick took a bite of cake and winced again.

'Mmm. I'll need to get this seen to when I get back.'

He asked whether she saw or knew anything of any of the others they had known during the war. Ellen said that Veronica had married an airman from the RAF station and that they were now in Cyprus. She hadn't seen them for ages but they did exchange cards at Christmas. Nick had lost touch with everyone although he had heard that Mather was killed in Italy in 1944.

Ellen said that John had died there the same year.

'How are your mum and dad?'

'Oh, they're OK, thanks. Still at Ivy Cottage.' Ellen shook her head. 'Father is still as miserable and cantankerous as ever.'

Sitting either side of the fire with their tea they reminisced. An hour and more quickly passed.

Looking out of the window Nick sighed and said that he had better be on his way. He took out his lighter, flicked it open and worked the wheel. It lit first time. Nick shook his head, tried it again and then returned the lighter to his pocket. He rolled another cigarette, put it in his mouth and then made a couple more which he put carefully into his tobacco tin.

'I can't say that I'm all that keen to leave this fire but it looks as though it's a bit brighter. I'm not sure that the wind isn't even stronger than it was. Listen.' It had been booming in the tiny chimney upstairs for some time.

'I'll have to shove something up that chimney tonight or we'll never get to sleep with that racket.'

'Can I use your. . . ?' Two pints of bitter and the tea were demanding Nick's attention.

'You can as long as you don't mind putting on your coat. We've still got an outside lavatory, if you can believe that.'

'What, really?'

'Yes. And we've got no running water, no electricity, and no sewer. In short, we've got very little. It's a disgrace. The council keep saying that they'll put in water and electricity but nothing ever happens.'

It was mid afternoon when Nick finally left to walk to the depot. The rain had stopped but as soon as they opened the cottage door it was apparent that the wind was much rougher. Nick stopped to button up his raincoat.

'Well, it's been good to see you. Will you be in tomorrow? I'll look in again, if I can. I've got to go past on the way back.'

'Yes, I expect so, after I've been to the farm. But I haven't anything much to do down there. Just see to the animals.' Ellen smiled. She would be able to tell him then.

'OK. Well, I'll be off. Lovely to see you. You're looking well. I'll see you tomorrow.' After hesitating he kissed her lightly on the cheek.

'Yes. And good luck with the job.'

'Thanks. Bye then.'

'Bye, take care.' She watched him down the path. He had quite a definite bald patch at his crown. Nick turned at the gate, pulled up his collar and gave her a smile and a quick wave. He left the gate undone. It wasn't until she closed the door that Ellen thought that she should have taken his address. She would get it tomorrow, she thought.

*

Buttoned up snugly in his newly dried raincoat Nick strode down Back Lane in high good humour. Fancy seeing Ellen again. Of course he had hoped all along that he might hear something of her but he never dreamed that he would actually see her. He could hardly believe his luck. She looked great, obviously improving with age. Her figure was much as he remembered and she still had the best legs and ankles he'd ever seen. Marching along he realized that he had barely noticed the scar on her face. Shorter hair and make-up obviously suited her. He decided that he really must make time to call in on the way back.

At the end of Back Lane he spotted Kathy's cottage. In the garden an overgrown apple tree leaned alarmingly in the wind, a motor tyre swinging maniacally on a rope from one of the branches.

The rain was still holding off and the skies directly overhead had actually lightened by the time he reached the Lord Nelson. No longer within the shelter of Back Lane it was extremely rough, but the wind was behind him. He ducked behind the garages beside the pub. There was bound to be a car along any time. He would try to hitch a lift.

Peter and Philip came slowly into view, returning from the cliff tops behind the pub.

'Hello, Mr Nick,' called Philip.

'Hello, lads. Been down to the cliffs?'

'Yeah. It's really rough down there. We nearly got blown over. And the sea is really bad.'

'Which way are you going?' asked Peter. 'There isn't a bus for ages.'

'I'm going to the depot. I was hoping to cadge a lift, but I'm not having much luck. I'm probably going to have to walk it.'

'On the road?' Philip shook his head. 'You'd be quicker along the top of the cliffs.'

'No,' replied Peter. 'You can't go past the radar station. It's fenced off.'

'Oh, yes.'

'You could go along the beach. Only the cliffs are mined. That would really be the quickest.'

'Well, I think I'm going to have to go one way or another. It's very quiet and I've not had any luck so far.'

The boys were leaving when Nick called them back.

'Here.'

'What?'

Nick felt in his pocket and pulled out some change.

'Go and get yourselves some sweeties. Is Annie's shop still there?'

'Yes.'

'And does she still own it?'

'Yes.'

Nick handed over a florin to Peter and then carefully made up the same amount into Philip's outstretched hand, a shilling, a sixpence, a joey and the rest in pennies and halfpennies.

'There you are, lads. Sorry about all the coppers, mate, but it's all I've got.'

'Gosh, thank you.'

'Yes. Thank you very much.'

'Go on and enjoy it. Does she still have those liquorice bootlaces?'

'Sometimes.'

'Well, you have one for me. Take it easy, lads. Goodbye.'

'Bye.'

As the boys drifted off Nick suddenly felt alone. He peered along the road but there was nothing to see. It was not so surprising. The weather was rotten and he recalled how things ground to a halt out in these rural areas for an hour or two after Saturday dinner. He was pleased when first Philip and then Peter looked back. They both gave him a vigorous wave which he returned before turning on his heel to set out along the coast road.

He crunched across the gravel and hadn't left the pub car-park when on impulse he changed his mind. Instead of the road he decided to go down the lane behind the pub and have a quick look over the cliff edge. It might just be possible to walk along the beach if the tide wasn't too high.

The lane wasn't without difficulty. It was a good deal more overgrown than Nick remembered and he had to negotiate several sizeable puddles in the rutted surface. Ellen had told him years ago that the ruts were made by the lime-burner's horse and cart. He could well believe it since he could see the deep ruts made by the heavy cartwheels and between them a broader and shallower groove worn by horse's hoofs as they hauled marl from the cliffs up to the lime kiln. The kiln of course was long gone, marl no longer available after the mining of the cliffs.

The lane seemed shorter too, but of course, it was shorter. More land had slipped into the sea. The top of the cliff was still fenced off even though much of the barbed wire was in poor condition.

As soon as he left the shelter of the hedges bordering the lane Nick felt the full force of the wind. It whipped along the exposed cliff top, pressing his trousers against his goose-pimpled legs. He was astonished to see that remnants of the little potting shed were still just visible beneath a tangle of thorn bushes, bare elder and cow parsley stalks. Mather had been right about it being safe. It looked as though the roof had fallen in though.

He shivered, hunched further inside his raincoat and pushed his hands deep into his pockets. The wind and cold was enough to take the breath away and the sea was rougher than Nick had ever seen it. White horses were everywhere, obliterated further out by what looked like a huge fog bank, although in the gale that was blowing it could only have been spray. There was no horizon. Close in great combers rolled from left to right before crashing at an angle on to the sand.

There was still a strip of beach visible away to the right towards the depot. Undecided Nick stood on the cliff top for a moment. Buffeted by the wind he stepped back a little. It was easily strong enough to blow a man over the edge. He shivered again and cast a glance back over the Lord Nelson and further west. It began to rain again. He made up his mind. It would be more sheltered below.

In truth it had been in his mind since he left the house that morning. He had dreamed for years of walking on this beach again. It was the best beach he had ever seen. He would never get another chance. If he went down the cliff now he would have a short walk to the depot. The cliff didn't look too bad. He couldn't see all the way down but the upper reaches looked OK. It would probably be all right.

Moving to his right, Nick stepped over the sagging barbed wire, crossed several feet of rough grass laid flat by the wind and rain and looked over the cliff edge. After some indecision he found a gentle slope that would take him about a third of the way down to the beach. It looked as though there was a bit of a path. Even though the mines hadn't been cleared he thought that certain of the locals were probably up and down all the time these days. He had a bad moment when he slipped and almost fell but he recovered himself. His shoes weren't ideal for the job.

After backtracking a short distance only once Nick reached the beach without any mishap other than getting mud on his shoes and trouser legs. Breathing heavily he was relieved to reach the sand. However, once on the beach he was in danger of getting sandblasted and soaked. The wind was whipping sand along the beach at a ferocious rate. It stung his face and got into his eyes and ears. The boiling water and breaking waves sent clouds of spray and spume high into the air. Filthy-looking froth rolled across the wet sand like soiled streamers. Turning his back on the needling sand he set off immediately towards the depot. He made good progress with the wind pressing him from behind.

It began to rain. Visibility was deteriorating by the minute and the sea was a good deal more terrifying down below than it had seemed from the top of the cliff. Suddenly the beach up ahead looked frighteningly narrow. It looked as though the tide was on its way in too. He would have to get a move on.

Dodging across a rapidly diminishing triangle of sand towards a small headland and misjudging the waves, a comber caught him and almost had him over. He was soaked from the thighs down. The freezing water made him gasp. A substantial cliff fall had formed the headland a year or two earlier. Wave action had eroded much of it but it still reached out a fair way. Safely round it, apart from the wet and icy legs, to his dismay he saw that less than 200 yards ahead the beach disappeared. A much more recent and heavier fall reached out far into the sea. It hadn't been visible from the cliff top. Waves were bursting over its furthest reaches, sending spray hurtling thirty feet or more into the air. As he arrived at the huge sprawl of sand, gravel and clay he could see that there was no way round it.

He would have to climb over it or turn back immediately. There was little time to think since the small piece of beach that he was standing on was fast disappearing. The next wave might well swamp him unless he moved to higher ground. Suddenly keeping his clothes clean and dry seemed a lot less important than survival. He tried to scramble up the soft, wet, crumbling side of the headland but his shoes slipped and then sank in up to the knee with every step. Moments later it began to pour.

Nick was exhausted and his tooth ached. He was soaked to the skin and frozen and he had clambered less than ten feet up the side of the headland. There was probably another forty feet to go before he would reach the top and there was no telling what lay on the other side. There was no going back now though. Wave after wave smashed over the little wedge of sand below and the water had begun to claw at the cliff face beneath his feet. He simply had to get over the headland. He lay for a moment on his front in the mud trying to regain his breath.

His chest ached and he had difficulty getting his breath. He regretted not phoning Monica's sister from the Lord Nelson. She could have popped round the corner to let her know where Nick was. Hearing at the pub that Ellen lived close by had put it right out of his head. He had tried earlier in Cromer at the bus station but the phones were all in use. He would do it as soon as he got to the depot. Monica would certainly worry if he wasn't home or if she hadn't heard from him by teatime. What on earth had possessed him? What was he doing in the middle of this god-forsaken minefield? A spur of the moment thing, it had only taken shape in his mind last night. It had seemed a good idea at the time, a bit of an adventure.

He levered himself up another inch or two but then slithered down, well over a couple of feet on the slippery clay. Sobbing with the effort and the unfairness of it all, as he pushed himself up again he felt something solid under his right foot. He kicked at it. Yes, there was something firmer there. He glanced down but couldn't make out anything in the gloom.

He levered his left foot out of the glutinous mud and transferred his weight on to his right leg. It occurred to him as he pushed upwards that Peter, the boy who had opened the door at Ellen's cottage, reminded him of someone.

SEVENTEEN

The gale that had its origin 1000 miles out in the Atlantic on Thursday rushed towards the Hebrides and Northern Scotland. A depression of less than 970 millibars caused the extreme north-westerly gale that blew down the entirety of the North Sea. The weather station on Orkney recorded a wind speed of 125 mph. Combined with a high spring tide and the narrowing and shallow topography of the southern North Sea these factors produced a storm surge. Sea level grew rapidly until it was eight or nine feet higher than the highest tide expected under normal circumstances.

That night on the east coast of England the water breached sea defences and flooded nearly 200,000 acres of low-lying land. It prompted the evacuation of 32,000 people. Miles of road and railway became impassable and 46,000 head of livestock were lost. The floods claimed the lives of over 300 people.

Perched on top of the cliffs with nothing to shelter its upper storeys from the wind the Lord Nelson lost many slates from the roof and several sea-facing windows were blown in. At some point during the night the sign out in the car-park crashed to the ground. The wind uprooted trees and damaged most of the properties in the village. The police constable and one or two fishermen noted that the waves pounded the cliff face at a level higher than anyone could remember before. Large chunks of cliff fell. Mercifully, situated as it was well over 200 feet above sea level; the village remained safe from the sea.

During the evening the telephone at the police sergeant's house barely stopped ringing. The sergeant himself had been out on duty for hours but his wife took one telephone call after another, most of them reporting damage or requesting assistance. Among the calls that she logged was one reporting a loud rumble or bang, certainly some kind of noise, from the cliffs. The caller said that it could have been a cliff fall. It was hard to tell in the howling wind. No one else called and the report remained unconfirmed.

The police and emergency services were severely stretched that night, many of them called to the low-lying coastal villages to the south of the minefield. It wasn't until the following afternoon that a weary policeman on a bicycle made a sketchy search of the cliff and beach from three points on the cliff top. Apart from the boiling sea and a few new cliff falls he saw nothing untoward and returned to other more pressing matters. He had never seen the sea looking so evil. It was almost black.

*

In the morning Ellen had little time to give much thought to Nick or to her thirty-third birthday. A quick check from the bedroom window at first light confirmed that several tiles were down. She and Peter were up very early and glued to the wireless. They hadn't slept well. Peter had crept into Ellen's bed just before one o'clock. Huddled together they'd listened to the roar of the wind and the tiles on the roof lifting and sliding. Somewhere a piece of corrugated iron flapped and banged. Ellen was prepared to bet that it came from the mess that was her brother's front garden.

In the grey light of morning Peter noticed from Ellen's window that the chicken hut was lying on its side and the fence was down. Of the chickens and Ginger Ted there was no sign. After casting about the field they trailed up to the top of Back Lane. There Peter spotted the birds on the far side of the field beside the railway.

Ellen's heart sank. 'We'll need to round up those hens before they stray any further. We don't want them on the railway line. If they get into the cutting we'll never get them back.'

'I'll run down to Phil's and see if he can come and help. I can check that Aunt Kathy's all right too.'

'OK. But don't be many minutes. I'll start making my way over.'

'OK.'

'And Peter.'

'Yes?'

'Walk in the middle of the road, just in case. And watch out. There may be more tiles flying about.'

Ellen was closing cautiously on the hens when Peter eventually returned with Philip. They had news. Almost every house in Back Lane was missing tiles. Others had lost gutters or had a window blown in and someone had lost most of a chimney. Otherwise it was greenhouses, trees and shed roofs that seemed to have suffered most. The milkman told them that in Church Street and beyond the telephone and electricity wires were down. They tutted but remained largely unmoved at this intelligence since they had access to neither service. Apart from losing felt from their shed roof the Holts had come through the night more or less intact.

They tried to drive the hens. Most co-operated but in the end they had to pick some up and carry them. Of Ginger Ted there was no sign. He had either come to a sticky end or taken the opportunity to make good his escape.

'Good riddance,' said Ellen, as she put the finishing touches to the wire netting fence. 'I'm not sorry to see the back of him, horrid creature.'

'I always liked Ted.' Peter was hurt at Ellen's words.

'So did I,' said Philip. 'Wonder where he's gone.'

'Oh, I expect he'll find some other chickens to rule the roost over.' Privately Ellen was thinking, that is, if the fox hasn't already got him. Peter was obviously thinking along similar lines.

'Hope the fox doesn't get him. Still, I wouldn't want to be any fox that went after Ted. He can be really fierce. He'll make Foxy wish he hadn't bothered.'

'Yeah. He'll probably peck his eyes out.'

Ellen thought this slightly optimistic but she didn't say anything. As they shut up the gate to the chicken run Peter changed tack.

'Who was the man who came round yesterday?'

'Mr Nichols?'

'Yes. What was his name, Nick?'

'His real name's Peter, like yours, but his friends call him Nick. We knew each other during the war. He was stationed down at the depot on the cliff top.'

'Was he . . . is he my dad?'

The question somehow took Ellen by surprise. She didn't answer immediately, not knowing quite what she wanted to say. Philip stood motionless, watching the pair of them closely.

'Is he? Mum?'

'Why do you ask?' Ellen fenced still, but Peter could see the answer on his mother's face.

'He is, isn't he? I recognized him anyway, as soon as I saw him, from that old photograph in your writing case. That one where he looks like old Mercer.'

'Yes. It was your father.'

'Thought so. I'm glad he doesn't really look like old Mercer. What did he want?'

'He's down to see someone about a job. He was passing so he looked in.'

'Is he coming back? Is he going to live here?'

'No. He said he'll try to pop in today on his way back, but it all depends.'

'On what? Where's he going back to?'

'I don't know. Leeds, in Yorkshire, I think. He's busy. But he did say he would try.'

'Mum?'

'Yes, Peter?'

'What did he think of me? What did he say?'

'He thought you and Phil were both very nice lads.'

'Oh.' Peter paused before continuing. 'Mum?'

'Hmm?'

'At least he doesn't smell like old Mercer.'

'No.' Ellen laughed. 'And a good thing too.'

'Oh, urrrgh!' Philip roused himself, wrinkled his nose and then ran around holding it ostentatiously between finger and thumb.

'Have we finished? Can we go and play now?'

'Don't you want to stay, in case he does come back? It would be nice if you could get to know him.

'Oh.' Peter paused, but only briefly. 'I'll come back after a little while and see if he's here. Can I? Please?'

'Aren't you going to Sunday school?'

'There isn't any.' Philip volunteered. 'Starts again next week, I think.'

'Oh. Well, yes. I suppose so. Don't get under Aunt Kathy's feet though, and make sure you're back in good time for dinner. And don't get mud on those trousers.'

'I won't. I will. I won't. Bye.'

'Bye, missus – Ellen.'

'Bye. Bye, Phil.'

Down the hill and enjoying more shelter than Back Lane, Pond Farm had survived the worst excesses of the storm. The wind had taken several branches off the willows by the pond and there was a tree down in the grove but there was nothing that required urgent attention.

'Are you all right, lass? Anything you need help with?' Mr Reeve had been out since first light.

'We've lost a few tiles, but Albert Hunt next door said he'd see to them when he does his own.'

'Well, let us know if you need anything.'

Ellen called at Ivy Cottage but they too had survived. Her father was out in the back garden sawing up an apple tree that had come down across the path. She arrived home to find Albert coming down his ladder from the roof. He was watery of eye, red-faced and windblown.

'Dear Lord! It's rough up there, and bitter. It's perishing.' He blew on his hands and rubbed them together. 'I've put your tiles back, Ellen,' he called. 'You weren't too bad. One's in two pieces but I've wired them together and it looks as good as new. Should be fine, now.'

'Thank you, Albert. I heard them sliding and rattling in the night. Thought the chimney was coming down. Did you lose many?'

'Oh, a few. Funnily enough none of them broke. Most of them fell on the grass at the back. Thought it would be worse. We could hear them in the night. We were obviously lucky. George lost several but the new people down by the chapel have lost nearly all the tiles off the back of their roof. I'm just off down there. See what we can do.'

'Oh, dear. Let me know if I can help.'

Once inside the cottage Ellen washed and then went upstairs to change. She put on a little lipstick and one of her better skirts and a jumper. She painted her nails with pink varnish, and found a pearl necklace and ear-rings that she had inherited from her grandmother, William's mother. It was the first time that she had worn them. Downstairs she spent the rest of the morning fiddling about at little jobs that didn't entail getting herself dirty. It was hard to concentrate and she found herself going to the window several times.

Peter reappeared at lunchtime and asked whether his father had been back. Since Ellen had nothing new to report he bolted his food and rushed off again down to Phil's house. He paused as he was going out of the door and grinned at Ellen. 'You look nice,' he said.

Ellen smiled.

'Thank you.'

She had read somewhere about someone having a sphinx-like look on his face. It might well have been an accurate description of Peter as he left.

Ellen eventually fell asleep in her chair beside the fire. When she woke it was dark. Her ears were sore and she took off the ear-rings.

She lit the Tilley Lamp, stoked up the fire, drew the curtains and made a cup of tea. Nick wouldn't be coming now. He must have gone straight home, either because of the weather or perhaps he got the offer of a lift. As she sat by the fire with her tea she acknowledged that she was disappointed. It might have been pleasant to chew over some of those old times with him. There was no one else with whom she could share their particular memories. And there was still the matter of Peter. Nick deserved to know. Not that she wanted anything from him on that score.

Peter returned at 5.30 for his tea.

'Did Dad come back?'

'No. I haven't seen anything of him.'

'Perhaps he'll call in later.'

'I expect he's gone by now. He only said that he might look in, if he had the chance.'

'Where does he live again?'

'Leeds. In Yorkshire.'

'Oh. We've been making a dragline with Phil's Meccano.'

'You haven't been getting in Aunt Kathy's way I hope.'

'No, course not. Can I go back later? It's enormous and we want to finish it. Aunt Kathy says it's OK. What's for tea?' The possibility of his father looking in had obviously not been weighing too heavily with Peter.

'I thought I might make us a fried cheese sandwich for a treat. And we've still got some scones and a dribble of Mrs Hunt's goosegog jam.'

'Good-oh.' Peter washed his hands. 'I'll set the table.'

During the floods the cliffs and beach received a terrible pounding. The waves scoured out huge tracts of sand and the level of the beach fell drastically. Locals who braved the weather to look over the cliff edge marvelled at the height and roughness of the water. The fishermen stared at it moodily through thin slit eyes before spitting and returning to the bar of the Lord Nelson or their firesides. Most of them were on half-pints if they were drinking anything at all. They hadn't been able to get off the beach for ages. Few of them had seen anything like it before. Tom Clarke swore he'd been in bigger seas round Cape Horn and in the Southern Ocean west of Australia, but not much bigger. The fishermen nodded. They believed him but it wasn't what they wanted to hear. They'd seen how black the sea had become and its malevolence frightened them.

As the North Sea wreaked havoc, damaging huge swathes of property and claiming lives up and down the east coast, there were one or two minor events that in the minds of the locals helped even the score. A few days after the storm beachcombers discovered that the lows on the beach were thick with fully grown lobsters. Men hurried home for sacks and boxes anxious to take advantage of this unexpected bounty.

The year improved. A Bomb Disposal Unit arrived in the village and set up headquarters at the old depot. A considerable talking point for some time was that among their number were seven German ex-POWs. At first they were discussed in lowered voices but then someone spoke to someone else who was working with them and it seemed all along that ordinary Germans were actually no different from anyone else. Down at the depot Karl I and Karl II, Josef, Franz, Uwe, Gunter and Max were nice enough fellows, and if they kept themselves to themselves, well, that was understandable.

At the end of May the entire country was captivated, first when Hillary and Tenzing stood on the summit of Everest and again a few days later with the Coronation of Queen Elizabeth II. The village entered into the celebrations with a will. Bunting and flags festooned the fronts of most of the houses and the Lord Nelson was got up to resemble an ocean liner.

A fancy dress parade assembled in the pub car-park. After the judging it set off round the village behind a stream of decorated cars and bicycles to terminate at a fête in the meadow behind the church. Kathy was a clear overall winner in the fancy dress. From the tip of her gleaming top hat to the soles of her highly polished riding boots she was every inch a convincing Johnnie Walker. Philip came first in the children's section making an equally impressive guardsman in plumed helmet, polished breastplate and thigh-boots. Having spent weeks researching, designing and making their costumes it was generally acknowledged that they deserved to win. There were however one or two disgruntled souls who felt that Kathy had taken it all a bit too seriously. Certainly nothing quite so sophisticated in the way of fancy dress costumes had been seen in the village before.

Peter resisted entering the fancy dress competition until the very last minute and then turned up in a hastily assembled and entirely unconvincing pirate outfit. Standing in line for the judging, surrounded by Chelsea Pensioners, Beefeaters and heralds he wished that he had made a little more effort.

Ellen won the ladies race at the fête, as usual. She had always been good at running and had won many such races over the years. No matter how many times she did it she never failed to get a kick out of it. Peter won the boy's sprint and he and Philip came third in the all-comers three-legged race. On something of a winning streak, Kathy outdid them all by guessing the number of peas in a jar and winning a box of groceries.

Later in the year the local paper reported that the Bomb Disposal Unit was actively searching for 'several thousand' anti-invasion mines on the beach and cliffs. Periodically a lorry from the unit drove through the village with a hand-cranked siren wailing on the back. It was the signal that they were preparing to detonate mines and that a prudent housewife should open her windows. The village half held its breath until after the explosions.

Peter asked less and less about his father. If and when he did, it tended to be at moments of stress, doubt or disappointment. One such occasion followed his very first game of football for the school team. It was quite an occasion since he was team captain.

After the eagerly awaited posting of the team selection on the school noticeboard there were elements of the untried team that spent the next day and a half before the match in a state of growing excitement, talking up their chances. By the time Peter left home at eight o'clock that Saturday morning he had been seduced by the team's belief in its invincibility.

He arrived home after the game well after two o'clock in the afternoon. Cold, hungry, dirty, stiff and sore he was thoroughly dejected. They had lost by eight goals to nil. Peter knew deep in his heart that his side had been no more than an ill-disciplined rabble of ball watchers, gossips and malcontents and that their opponents had fielded a far more disciplined team. It had been a fair enough game and unquestionably the right result. However, after their ridiculous expectations it was hard to swallow. Peter was having difficulty holding back the tears as he told Ellen how they fared.

After washing his hands and face he sat beside the fire with his lunch balanced on his mud-encrusted knees. Sausages, peas and mashed potato, it was one of Peter's favourites. Ellen sat opposite and did her best to comfort and commiserate. It was over cups of tea later that Peter raised the subject of his father.

'Mum?'

'Hmm.'

'Was Dad a good footballer?'

'Oh.' Ellen had to think for a moment. 'Do you know I have no idea? They used to have a kick about sometimes but I never actually saw him play.

I would have thought that he would be quite good. He was well built and he could certainly run fast. We used to race each other on the beach. He could beat me, and you know I'm quite good, or I was when I was younger.'

'Wonder if he was good at any other sports? I bet he was a good batsman or a boxer or something.'

'He was a slow bowler once for some village team, I think. I don't think he boxed. He liked fishing and he kept pigeons. I only ever saw him play darts at the Lord Nelson. He was quite good at it but I don't think he played that often.'

So, his father was a slow bowler, an occasional darts player, a pigeon-fancier and a fisherman. As he finished his tea Peter resigned himself to the probability that his father was not a great sportsman. Still, one of the great benefits of an absent father was that with a little imagination he could be anything that one chose. One simply had to resist the temptation to go overboard.

It wasn't until months later as he was driving up to Lincolnshire that Wormy Dale realized that Nick Nichols hadn't been in touch. He'd probably found another job or changed his mind. Wormy thought he had Nick's address somewhere. He might look him up one day.

EIGHTEEN

'Hello?'

Ellen opened her eyes. There was no one there.

'Ellen? Hello? Are you awake?'

She turned her head. It took her a moment to recognize Margaret.

'How are you?'

'Oh.' Ellen rolled over. She winced a little and then smiled. 'I think I must have been dreaming.'

Margaret pulled up the chair beside the bed and perched on the arm. She was very businesslike in a black jacket and trousers.

'I can't stop. I thought I'd just pop in to say hello since I was passing.'

'That's nice of you.'

'Have you got anyone coming to see you this afternoon, any visitors?'

'I don't know.'

'I'll try to look in later if I get finished in time.' Margaret stood up. She nodded towards the door and smiled. 'I think you've got a visitor now.'

Ellen looked round. Philip stood in the doorway.

'I'll leave you to it, Ellen. See you later perhaps.'

'Yes. Bye, Margaret.'

Margaret and Philip exchanged hellos and smiles as they passed.

'Permission to come aboard?' Philip grinned. He was looking very relaxed in a light-blue short-sleeved shirt and chinos. Ellen waved him closer. He gave her a peck on the cheek and put down a brown bag of fruit.

'I've just been at the Links. Had an hour on the driving range. I've brought you some figs, good for the bowels. I hope they're OK. I left them in the car and they're a bit warm. How are you feeling?'

'Oh, that's lovely. Thank you.' Ordinarily Ellen might have responded with a sally about the state of her bowels being none of Philip's business but she had other things on her mind.

'I'm glad you've come,' she continued, 'I need some help,' she paused and frowned, 'with something or other. Now what on earth was it?' Ellen frowned again. 'Oh, I know. Can you pass me my bag and the writing pad in there,' she gestured at the cabinet beside the bed.

Ellen opened the pad and showed Philip the letter from Louise Stark and what she had managed to write in response.

After reading both letters carefully Philip looked up. 'Mm, Mum mentioned the letter.' He gestured with the airmail envelope. 'Fascinating.' He paused a moment, wondering quite what to say. Ellen saved him the embarrassment.

'I know. I know. I'm finding it terribly difficult, Phil. I can't seem to concentrate. And I can't write properly. I know what I want to do and say, but I can't always do it. It's ever so odd. My head's all over the place. And I get tired so quickly.'

'So what would you like me to do? How can I help?'

'Well. I wondered if you would write the letter for me if I tell you what to say.'

'Yes, of course. I can type it up at home, if you like. It wouldn't take a minute.'

'Good boy, Philip.' Ellen took him by the hand. 'Well, what it is . . . I want to tell this Mrs Stark that she and Peter are probably related. You see, Nick' – she leaned towards him and tapped the letters – 'Nick Nichols was Peter's father too.'

'Ah, yes.' Philip frowned and pulled at his nose. He had known the identity of Peter's father for as long as Peter had although when they were boys Peter had told him so many tales. One minute his father was a whale hunter, then a doctor, then a missionary and even a test pilot. The occupation of Peter's father tended to change with Peter's enthusiasms.

'Peter never met his father until that day in 1953. You met him too. I'm sure you were there. I don't think Peter was very taken with him.'

'Yes, I remember.'

'Well, Peter won't know anything about Louise Stark. I didn't know myself until that letter arrived out of the blue.'

'Well, where is Peter's father now? You really don't know? You haven't seen him since 1953?'

'No. I haven't the faintest idea.'

'Phil?'

'Mm?'

'Phil! Philip!'

'Mm. What?' Philip jerked awake. 'Oh, gracious.' He sat up and rubbed his face.

'For goodness sake. I must have dozed off. I'm sorry, Ellen. It's so stuffy in here.'

'Yes. I think I must have drifted off too.' Ellen gazed out of the window. 'I was thinking about all those bombs and bullets and things.'

'Oh? What bombs?'

'Those that you boys collected in the fields. What happened to them? Peter had some, didn't he?'

Philip laughed. 'Oh, yes. Peter had a rather fine collection.'

'What happened to them? They're not still at the cottage, are they?'

Philip glanced at Ellen. 'No. What made you think that? The Bomb Disposal people and the police took them away at the time. It was years ago. They blew them all up on the beach. Why?'

'I must have been dreaming. I suddenly thought that I didn't want Sally coming across all that stuff while she was cleaning and blowing herself up.'

'Don't worry. It's all long gone.' As is Sally, Philip thought. Ellen's old cleaner had gone to live with her daughter down in Chichester years ago.

When Peter and Philip were ten or so one of the members of the little gang of which they were an occasional part devoted the best part of an hour to digging .303 bullets out of a rotting gatepost on the cliff top. Not much more than a mangled stump, before the war the post had held a heavy five-barred gate. There were several such posts and riddled trees on the cliff top, a legacy from the 1940s. Casting about someone else found a .303 shell case in the field nearby. Without much effort the gang soon found several more.

'We ought to collect these. If we can get enough we can sell them to the rag and bone man and get money.'

Within minutes they were all on their knees. In the days that followed they discovered that three fields on the cliff tops to the west of the woods were littered with ammunition. It had been discarded or deliberately buried by troops undergoing weapons training during the war. By the end of the week the gang had accumulated a considerable haul of spent shell cases and several live rounds.

From that moment a fervour gripped the youth of the village. Boys turned up equipped with trowels and forks, others with sticks and rakes. They devoted much time and energy to grubbing about in the fields, on the banks and in the drainage ditches west of the woods. It wasn't long before someone unearthed a clip of live .303 ammunition. The group immediately concentrated its efforts on that bank and quickly amassed hundreds of live rounds along with many spent shell cases.

Further rich seams of ordnance were unearthed and they found their first live mortar shell. In the weeks that followed more and more ammunition came to light. Every boy in the village soon had his own personal ammunition dump.

'It's a wonder any of us survived to tell the tale.' Philip rubbed his hand across his chin and grinned at Ellen. 'Mike what's his name used to walk about swinging a live mortar on a length of rope. Used to whirl it round and then let it go like someone throwing the hammer. We piled mortars in a heap in a field and then threw stones at them. When that didn't work we tried to set fire to them. We lobbed them at trees and dropped them from the bridge on to the railway line. When the police arrived at the Hedges' they found little Hedge with a live mortar clamped in the vice on his father's bench. He was only going at it with a hammer and chisel, trying to get it open.'

'Dear, oh dear.'

'Some of the shells contained powder and some contained cordite sticks. We used to dismantle them, empty the contents into tin cans and then set fire to them. It was always disappointing. Never as spectacular as we thought it would be. Mind you, there's no telling what might have happened if Beefy's mum hadn't banged her leg.'

'What happened?'

'You remember Beefy. Lived down in the council houses?'

Ellen nodded.

'He went home for his dinner and hung his jacket on the back of his chair. Mrs Gee got up to answer the door when the baker came for his money and damn near broke her shin on a live mortar bomb that Beefy had in his jacket pocket.'

Ellen laughed. 'I must have forgotten that.'

'Anyway, that was the end of it. Beefy's parents just about had apoplexy when they discovered the bomb. They made him show them where he kept the rest of his collection. I think he had four or five live mortars and a bag of bullets hidden in the back yard. The Gees got the police out that afternoon and they visited every house in the village where children lived. They found thousands of live .303 bullets, machine-gun ammunition and a fair number of mortar bombs. Kids had them in their bedrooms, in cupboards, in their father's sheds, buried in the garden. I had a collection in an old shoe box in the top of the wardrobe. I used to polish them up when mum was out. And, of course, you probably remember now where Peter kept his ammo – under the water tank.'

'Hmm. Yes. I had no idea he had all that stuff in there until those bomb disposal men brought it out. And that wasn't all. He had more under a floorboard in the corner of his room. He thought I didn't know about it, his little hidey-hole. I found all sorts of things there over the years, cigarettes and matches, love letters from a girl called Valerie. She couldn't spell for toffee. A sheath knife he thought I didn't know about, a packet of condoms, later of course. And a CND badge. All sorts. Oh, and those mucky pictures you gave him, Philip Holt.'

'Hmm, what was that?'

'Oh, some scantily clad women. Out of a magazine, I should think. They weren't terribly racy by today's standards. You weren't very old.'

'Ah.' He passed his hand over his chin as though checking his shave and then continued. 'I forget what the total haul was. I think they got several hundredweight of explosives of one sort or another. Took the lot down on to the beach and blew them all up. Then they went back to where we found it all with their mine detectors and cleared up the rest of it. Mind you, they didn't get it all. You can still find the odd shell case on the cliff tops. They're terribly corroded now, but they still exist.'

Philip read the letter from Louise Stark again. 'Well,' he said, 'I think that this is extraordinary.'

It was in late 1952 that the village became aware that the railway would be closing. It was another knock to the hopes of those who yearned for the pre-war boom times when the beach was open and the place was heaving with holidaymakers.

Initially the line was to close in March 1953 but the date slipped to April. The local paper reported whimsically the day following the closure that 'the coast railway line went into its final slumber last night.' The last train to run through the village was a fifty-five-year-old tank engine pulling four coaches and carrying approximately a hundred passengers. The sole remaining member of staff at the station placed detonators on the line through the station yard to give the train a suitable send-off.

Less than a couple of months later tragedy struck the village when two members of the Bomb Disposal Unit were killed by a mine as it exploded on the cliffs. Everyone heard the explosion since it occurred mid morning. It led to the usual uninformed debate about whether the explosion had been caused by one mine or two, or even more and whether it was intended or otherwise. There were those who were adamant that they could tell from any explosion exactly how many mines had been dispatched. It wasn't until the next day that the village learned that two sappers had died. The mine in question had been partly excavated and was clearly marked. No one had seen what actually happened.

Later in the year news leaked round the village that the RAF underground bunker beneath Beacon Hill had become operational. Since little was visible it made no difference to anyone other than that an increasing number of RAF vehicles sped through the village.

Shortly after Ellen buried her father, electricity and water finally arrived in Back Lane. Located at the very top of the lane Cowper's Cottage was inevitably the last property to be connected in both cases. Peter chafed at the delay. The arrival of water and electricity gave the inhabitants of Back Lane a tantalizing glimpse of modern life. Sewerage and the telephone however, remained something to which they would have to aspire for several years more and a gas supply would only become a reality more than forty years later.

Installation of the water and electricity services was a nightmare. Trenches, holes and rubble despoiled the normally pleasing, smooth, slate-coloured surface of Back Lane for months. 'Road Up' signs, wooden barriers and a corrugated iron workmen's hut turned the lane into an obstacle course. Heavily laden lorries and the noisiest dump truck in the world churned up and down leaving an ankle-turning surface and diesel and tar spills to trouble the unwary.

Some time after the tamping down of the last temporary patch a gang from the council highways department hove into view at the bottom of Back Lane with a monstrous resurfacing machine, trucks and a steam roller. To the horror of the residents they proceeded to coat the entire length of the lane with the same cold grey granite chips that they used on the main coast road. What with that and TV aerials sprouting from every chimney Back Lane was changing forever.

For Ellen and Peter, modernization meant the installation of a single cold water tap above the sink and a new soak-away in the front yard. Suddenly water carried in buckets from the pump opposite the Lord Nelson became a thing of the past. They revelled in the novelty, although like everyone else in the lane they were a little irritated that the water pressure was so high that water splattered down the front of their clothes as it issued from the new tap. It was Kathy who solved the problem with a little rubber pipe that slipped over the end of the tap and ensured a much more manageable flow. She bought a green one for herself and a red one for Ellen from Harry's old hardware shop in Cromer.

The Finchams also took ownership of a cooker point and a single electrical socket in the living-room alcove. Peter was elated. He would be able to plug in an amplifier and play an electric guitar, if and when he was ever able to afford them. Despite his assurances to the contrary Ellen wasn't convinced that the socket was designed for that purpose. She felt that an electric kettle was what had been intended. It remained academic however, since they could afford neither electric guitar nor kettle.

A single light bulb suspended on twisted brown flex from the ceiling of each room prompted partial retirement of the Tilley Lamp. Ellen put it away in a cupboard, but kept it fuelled and ready for those none-too-rare occasions when the electricity supply went off, either during a thunderstorm or at other times quite inexplicably. Unable to afford another wireless and even less able to afford an electric cooker she soldiered on with the range and the old wireless powered by accumulators.

To the delight of both Peter and his mother, he passed his eleven-plus exams and started at the grammar school in North Walsham. Philip turned out to be a border-line case and after much humming and hawing on Kathy's part went off to school in South Norfolk as a boarder, coming home at weekends.

By 1957 little of the original barbed wire fence remained on the cliff top. The few bits of any vintage that had survived the ravages of numerous cliff falls were rusted, sagging or broken. An odd warning sign or two could still be found, pockmarked by stones, half buried and rotting in the rough grass. Despite the fact that the cliffs were still not clear of mines the fence no longer gave the appearance of serving any real purpose.

During the spring officers from GOC Eastern Command visited the minefield. The official party was greatly impressed as men from the Bomb Disposal Unit pulled out all the stops and put on a show for them. Men dangled on the end of 100-foot rope lifelines as they swept the cliff face with their mine detectors. On the beach later, armoured Bren carriers hosed down the cliffs and the visiting general and his party was ushered over to witness men in shirtsleeves engaged in excavating a hole in the sand. Surrounded by stakes and official tape it looked an impressive undertaking.

A few locals, having got wind of the visit, stirred themselves from the public bar and wandered down to the cliff edge. They fell about at the units' antics with the ropes. Most had never witnessed such energetic or acrobatic activities before and believed that the entire show had been put on especially for the benefit of the cameras. Others swore that the rope trick was no more than standard procedure. Back in the bar later however, those assembled admitted to admiration for the unit's ingenuity.

The nurse was trying to keep up with the show jumping, and she switched on the TV when she brought Ellen's medicine. Ellen wasn't much interested, but she left the programme on when the nurse hurried off in response to her pager. She watched the screen with half an eye but with the sound low. After a little while her eyes closed. The commentators' voices droned on in a comforting manner. She couldn't hear what they were saying but they sounded relaxed and full of self-assurance. Periodically she could make out the sound of polite applause. Now and again there was a roar and the commentators' voices rose in mannered excitement. She knew little about the sport but it was gentle enough and she didn't feel up to the struggle of trying to read or do the crossword.

True to her word Margaret looked in later. Ellen had forgotten that Philip had been there until Margaret mentioned it. She told Margaret something of their conversation and then felt obliged to elaborate about Nick, Peter, Louise Stark and her letter. Looking round she was relieved to see that Philip had taken the letters with him. Not like him to leave without saying goodbye though.

'You said that you never married, Ellen.' They had been chatting for some time when Margaret raised the subject.

'No, I never found anyone who would have me.' Ellen looked up and then smiled at the concern on her visitor's face.

'There must have been men, surely, in all that time?'

Ellen smiled again. 'Oh, yes. The odd one or two, and some of them were very odd indeed, believe me. I've mentioned Nick.'

Margaret laughed. 'And what of the others?'

'Oh, I wasn't short of suitors. It was amazing though, how quickly they lost interest once they found out that I had a child.'

'Wasn't there anyone who you thought might do?'

'Well, there was an officer from the RAF station, Ralph, but he was posted abroad, to Cyprus. We wrote a few times but then the letters dried up. Found someone else I expect.'

'Hmm.'

'I was quite hopeful about a lecturer from Norwich for a while, but he couldn't leave his elderly mother. Michael, his name was. No idea what happened to him. He was a bit of an old woman, I suppose, looking back. All leather patches, cord trousers and desert boots. It finally foundered. I've never seen him since.' Ellen paused. 'There were others but nothing serious. I suppose that in all honesty the only one who really mattered was Robert.'

At seventy Mr Reeve seemed fit and well. He was still very much involved in the farm but had handed over the day-to-day business to Ronnie Slack's son Gordon. In the absence of any real interest from Gilbert or Robert he'd spotted Gordon's enthusiasm and potential early on and paid to put him through agricultural college. He'd then sent him to work on a sheep station in Australia for eighteen months. Gordon's return coincided precisely with his father's retirement and he was appointed farm foreman in Ronnie's place.

Ellen still looked after the house and helped with the animals but since

Mr Reeve was out a good deal she had reduced her hours. Semi-retired, the farmer still led an active and well-ordered life. After his tour of inspection of the farm each morning he played golf or bridge in the afternoons, with an occasional visit to the cinema or the theatre.

It was something of a shock when he was discovered late one Saturday afternoon dead at the wheel of his shooting brake. He had been to visit an old friend in the south of the county. His car was parked neatly in a lay-by at the roadside. It was presumed that he'd felt unwell and pulled in, to die alone of a heart attack.

Gordon Slack appeared at the door of Cowper's Cottage the following morning with the unwelcome news. He and Ellen sat at the table in the living-room and shook their heads and wiped away their tears. They both had good reason to be thankful to the farmer. Gordon stayed no longer than it took to drink a mug of coffee since he wanted to break the news personally to the rest of the hands. After he had left Ellen sat alone in her bedroom. How like Mr Reeve, she thought. He had died as he had lived, quietly, tidily and without fuss.

It had been more than a year since either Robert or Gilbert's last visit to Pond Farm. Both returned for the funeral. Gilbert arrived alone by taxi, having taken the train from Liverpool Street to Norwich. Ellen knew that he was separated from his wife and children. His father had been to see the family several times but Gilbert had never brought them to Pond Farm. He was still overweight and scruffy despite his City clothes, and Ellen was perturbed to see that he had been drinking. However he barely acknowledged her presence beyond refusing her offer of a cup of tea or something to eat, saying that he had eaten on the train. He helped himself to a glass and the whisky decanter and went off upstairs to his old room.

Robert arrived in a plum-coloured Alvis coupe, accompanied by an attractive blonde woman. Dressed in a flying jacket and cord cap he looked as dashing as ever. They snorted into the yard at Pond Farm as Ellen was about to leave on her bicycle. She stopped and paddled backwards to the car.

Robert was obviously pleased to see her.

'Ellen! Goodness! What a lovely surprise.' He levered himself up and out of the low-slung car grinning with pleasure and gave her a hug and a kiss before introducing her to his companion, Rowan. Ellen was surprised at Robert's enthusiastic welcome. She was also surprised to see in the limited illumination offered by the porch lights that the glamorous female was a good deal older than Robert.

'I'm so sorry about your dad. It was a shock.'

'Yes. It was a bit of a blow, I must say. I thought the old man would go on yet a bit. Seventy's no real age these days, is it?'

'No. And he's seemed and looked so well.'

'Ah. It was the old problem apparently, the family heart. Many a Reeve has gone the same way. Still, if you've got to go it's as good a way as any, short and sweet. He wouldn't have suffered for long. Hope I'm as lucky.'

Robert helped the tall and angular Rowan up out of the car. Ellen offered to stay to get them something to eat, but they said that they would manage with eggs or cheese on toast. Ellen assured them that there was plenty in.

'We'll be OK as long as Father didn't drink all the whisky before he went.'

'Or the brandy. I need a couple of big ones. I'm frozen stiff.' Rowan teetered beside the car in a pair of elegant shoes that the designer had never for one moment envisaged in a Norfolk farmyard. She rubbed the arms of her suede coat trying to restore circulation. 'My feet are like blocks of ice. I wish I'd put some boots on or that we'd come on the train.'

'There's a good fire in the kitchen and the sitting-room fire is laid. Just needs a match. Would you like me to see to it?'

'No. Thanks anyway, Ellen. You get off. We'll make do with the kitchen. It's cosy enough in there. Is Giblets here?' Robert looked about briefly for his brother's car before opening the boot and taking out cases. Ellen hadn't heard the nickname for years.

'He arrived a little while ago, in a taxi. He's upstairs.'

'Oh, joy,' muttered Rowan. Robert glanced up at her quickly. Ellen thought that she saw a flash of anger but nothing was said.

'Oh, and he took the whisky with him. But there are a couple of bottles of Famous Grouse in the sideboard.'

Robert nodded. 'We'll see you tomorrow then, Ellen. Can't say I'm look-ing forward to it much.' He looked up. 'Whatever else happens though, we must find time for a chat. We need to catch up.'

'Yes, we will. I'll see you tomorrow. Goodnight.'

'Goodnight.'

The following afternoon Ellen and Peter cycled down to Pond Farm together. They joined the cortège for the walk of less than a mile from the farm to the church. As they passed the mill and walked alongside the river Ellen smiled to herself. Mr Reeve had always maintained that he didn't want any fuss when he died.

'I'm relying on you, lass. Pick me up on the tractor and sweep and take me up to the five-acre beside Bluebell Wood. Pop me in a hole on that sandy crest that runs away from the stand of beeches. It's well drained there and I'll be nice and dry, and warm on a sunny day. It's the highest point on the farm. I'll be able to keep an eye on things from up there.' The farmer hooted at the thought of being able to put the fear of God into some of his men as they passed that way.

'Morning, Walter, morning Edward, I could say, when they're hoeing beet. I think you've missed one or two there. Can you imagine the look on their faces?'

The church was full. Walter and Edward and their colleagues were crammed into their best suits with their hair newly cut and slicked down. They stood red of face and uncomfortable beside their wives and the eldest and youngest of their children. Men hurried back and forth between the rectory and the church with more chairs to accommodate the mourners. When all the chairs were out there were still people standing several deep.

It was a moving occasion. Dick Reeve was widely recognized as one of those thoroughly decent men that most people chance across seldom in a lifetime. It was a nice service, Ellen thought, although low on family mourners. There was no one to attend from Maria's side and Mr Reeve's two brothers were both dead. A couple of cousins stood beside Robert and Gilbert. Robert spoke briefly about his father and read a passage from Burns that his father had always admired.

As the coffin-bearers passed on their way out of the church Robert indicated that she and Peter should accompany the family to the graveside. As they buried Dick Reeve beside his wife Maria in the corner of the churchyard in the warmth of the late summer sun, Ellen wept one last time. Not simply for the farmer or her employer, more for the loss of a good friend.

Back at Pond Farm, Peter stayed long enough to eat more than his share of sandwiches and sausage rolls. He talked briefly to Robert and even more briefly to Gilbert before returning home to complete work for school.

After helping to serve tea and coffee Ellen eventually got the opportunity to talk to Robert out in the yard beside the pond. It was late in the afternoon and most people had gone. He was crouching beneath a willow tossing stones into the water when Ellen sauntered up beside him.

'Aha,' he said. He stood up and turned to face her. 'By golly, Ellen, I must say that black suits you. You're looking extremely elegant if I may say so.'

'You may say so, thank you.' Ellen poked him in the stomach. 'What's all this? Eating too many doughnuts?'

'I'm sure you're well aware that in certain societies a little pod like this is greatly admired. It's highly desirable in a potential husband or sugar-daddy. Presumably it's an obvious sign of the wherewithal to eat well.' He pulled his stomach in for a moment. 'It's fine if I do this.' He laughed and relaxed again. 'It's even better when I'm lying on my back.'

He turned and took Ellen gently by the chin and tilted her face upwards.

'Mother was right. You'd never notice, looking at you now, unless you already knew about it. Damned dog, it turned out to be his lucky day, didn't it? I thought Dad was going to shoot him for sure. He was so upset.'

'It could have been worse, I suppose. I've got you and your mum and dad to thank.'

'Ah,' Robert grimaced and shuddered. 'I'll never forget it. I thought you were going to die. That piece of your cheek hanging, and all that blood.' He shook his head. 'Fancy a wander round the paddock?' He put his hands in his pockets, turned away and they began to saunter together towards the gate.

'Peter's a nice lad. You'll be proud of him. I was talking to him earlier.'

'Yes, he's a good boy, despite the nasty hairstyle and the spots, poor soul. He's pretty good for a teenager, most of the time.'

'He was telling me that he wants to study languages. We had quite a conversation. Plenty of jobs for a good linguist, I believe.'

'Yes, if he can tear himself away from his group. He's music mad. First it was skiffle, then it was rock and roll and now we're into rhythm and blues. He's in a band, the Overtones; he's got a second-hand Spanish guitar. They practise in the old school.'

'Ah, some of it's pretty good. I like it.'

'He's saving up to buy an electric guitar and an amplifier.'

They chatted of this and that until Robert enquired about Peter's father.

'Do you see anything of him these days? I believe that he was in the Royal Engineers here during the war? I seem to remember Father saying so.'

'I thought you. . . .'

'What?'

'Oh, nothing. Never mind.'

'Do you see him at all?'

'No. I've seen him once, briefly, since he left in 1944 with me pregnant, although to be fair he didn't know that at the time. I didn't know where he went or that he was married. Then he turned up out of the blue for an hour or so one afternoon a few years ago and I haven't seen or heard anything from him since. I suppose he's up in Yorkshire somewhere still.'

'You obviously manage well enough though, by the look of things.'

'Yes, we're very happy. Your dad was brilliant. He saved our bacon with Cowper's Cottage. And do you know – he would never take anything for it.'

Robert laughed. 'Ah. That sounds like him. But you were always a great favourite, Ellen. You must have known that. We're all going to miss him. I am. . . .' Robert pulled a face and looked away. He sighed. 'I wish I'd made more of an effort.'

They wandered on together into the paddock. After a few steps Ellen stopped and slipped off her shoes. 'I can't walk in these in the grass.'

'Do you remember the garden parties?'

'Yes. I was thinking about them earlier. I'll never forget your father in that dreadful old brown hat and waistcoat, with his red neckerchief, doing the bowling for the pig. And Maria doing teas and then getting up on the tumbrel and dancing the flamenco. At the end they got together and danced.

Your dad was shorter than your mum, they looked really sweet.'

'I found them out here in the dark after one do. They were smooching to that old wind-up gramophone. They were good times. He never went to a garden party after Mother died.'

'No.' They walked on in silence for a bit. 'They were good people, your mum and dad.'

'Yes.'

'So what do you do with yourself these days? I thought you were abroad. And who's the glamour puss? Is she your fiancée, or girlfriend, or what?'

'Good lord, no. She's old enough to be my mother. Rowan's a friend. She's got a flat in the same building as mine. I see her occasionally when I'm in London. She's in the antiques business these days, very successful. Used to be a model. She offered her car if I brought her with me. She's a bit eccentric but nice enough.'

'Did you never get married? Your dad never mentioned any—'

'No. Never really found the right woman. There was never anyone really special.' He turned to look at Ellen and took her hand. 'I should have come back and made an honest woman of you, shouldn't I?' He took Ellen's other hand and smiled at her. Then he realized. 'Sorry. I didn't mean. . . .'

Ellen shook her head and smiled back. 'I know,' she said. 'That might have been interesting.'

'Ha. Well, maybe one day. You never know how things will turn out. But I suspect that I've become something of a confirmed bachelor now. I'm used to having my own way.'

Hand in hand they wandered round the paddock a second time. Robert became expansive. When the war ended he got a job with the government, still in the radar and communications business. His work took him abroad frequently, often to the Middle East. He had developed something of an interest in antiques over the years and after leaving the communications business he went to work for an international dealer. For the last two years he had been working for an auction house in London, which was how he'd bumped into Rowan. She ran her own business and it was Robert's intention to do the same eventually. He lacked the capital to get started at present.

They were heading back towards the farmhouse when Rowan appeared in the yard.

'Yoo-hoo. Robert.'

He waved an acknowledgement. 'OK,' he called. 'She's flying off to New York tomorrow,' he said to Ellen. 'So I suspect that we're going to have to leave.'

Ellen managed to see them briefly before they left.

'Sorry,' Robert said. 'I would have liked to talk more. I've enjoyed seeing you again.'

Once Rowan was installed in the passenger seat and their cases were in the boot, he walked over to give Ellen a kiss on the cheek. 'Let's keep in touch. I'll write,' he said. He gripped her hands for a moment and then turned to get into the car.

'Take care, Robert. It's been lovely to see you. Bye.'

Ellen could have wept anew.

After Mr Reeve's funeral there was less to do in the house. Robert had gone off abroad and Gilbert had returned to London. Pond Farm seemed in a state of limbo. Finding time hanging heavy around the farmhouse Ellen worked in the fields and helped Gordon with paperwork. She had kept up her driving and could now drive on or off the road. One of her greatest joys was giving the shooting brake a largely superfluous clean and polish and taking it for a spin once a week. It was the one activity in all her years at Pond Farm where Ellen took liberties. The weekly jaunt was not strictly necessary. She often drove for miles along the coast road, such was the joy she derived from driving.

Things carried on much in this vein until one morning when she arrived for work to find Gilbert asleep on the sofa in the living-room. When she returned from seeing to the hens he was awake, sitting at the table with a cup of coffee and a cigarette.

'Hello, Gilbert. How are you? Would you like some breakfast?'

'No, thank you.' Gilbert coughed and cleared his throat noisily.

'Sure I can't get you something? Nice fresh boiled egg? Toast soldiers?'

'No. I'm not hungry, thank you.'

Ellen went to put the eggs away. When she returned, Gilbert was standing with his back to the fireplace.

'Look here, Ellen. You might as well know that I'm back. I've packed up working in the city and I'm here to stay now. The old man's left me the farm and I shall be running things from now on. There are going to be some changes.' He dragged on his cigarette and then flicked ash into the fireplace.

'The thing of it is, I shan't need you here any more. We'll be doing things a bit differently around here from now on, and I'm afraid that there won't be any place for you. There's an envelope on the hall table with your money in it. There's a bit extra for the lack of notice and as a gesture of goodwill.' Gilbert's mouth was smiling but his eyes were not.

'Perhaps you'll be good enough to gather up your things. Oh, and leave the keys on the table when you go, thank you.' With that Gilbert nodded at her, and produced a grimace that was presumably intended as a smile. 'All right? Good.' He belched softly, tossed his cigarette end into the fireplace and stalked out.

Ellen was stunned. Gilbert obviously intended that she leave right away. She considered trying to discuss matters with him but quickly decided against it. A few days were neither here nor there and if he really was back then she didn't want to stay. She gathered up her few possessions, a basket, boots, odd hats, gloves and scarves and the cardigan that hung on the back door. She left her keys on the hall table and was on the point of leaving when Gilbert reappeared.

'Oh, and there's one other thing.' He gave her a hard look. 'You'd better start looking for somewhere else to live. As you know Cowper's Cottage is a farm property. I expect I shall want it before very much longer.'

Ellen was shocked. She was on the point of protesting but changed her mind immediately.

'Well, thank you, Gilbert,' she said. Her face was burning with anger and disappointment. 'Thank you very much.'

With that she left. She had worked at Pond Farm for over twenty-five years and she had been in Cowper's Cottage for fifteen or so. As she cycled slowly up the hill she wondered what on earth she and Peter would do. She was suddenly jobless and would shortly be homeless with Peter coming up to his O Levels the following year. She stopped at Kathy's house on the way home to break the news and for a restorative cup of coffee.

'Don't worry, girl,' said Kathy, after they were seated at the kitchen table. 'Gilbert Reeve always was a nasty piece of work. You're better off out of that. You know you and Peter can come here. Peter can share with Phil. He's not here most of the week and they can double up when he's home. And you can have the spare room. Unless of course, you want to go and stay with you-know-who.'

'Who's that?'

'Your George.' She laughed. 'And Janice the Hun.' Kathy waggled her eyebrows in the same way that Nick used to when he was making a joke. She had probably picked it up from him, years ago. She was looking a little bizarre since she was experimenting with an elaborate strawberry blonde hairstyle and fearsome eye make-up.

'Oh, no fear,' said Ellen. 'I'd rather be in the workhouse.'

'That's settled then. You can come here until you get yourself sorted out.'

'Kathy, that is kind of you. Thanks. I hope it won't come to that though. We wouldn't want to impose. I love my cottage. I'll go back and speak to Gilbert, see if he'll reconsider.'

The next few weeks were a worrying time. Despite Kathy's offer Ellen looked for somewhere to live. There was nothing that she could afford in the village. The only possibility within her means was a single bedroom chalet on the cliff tops just below the radar station. It wasn't actually in the village and access was by means of a rough track from the road down the side of a field. It was a ramshackle construction of timber, corrugated iron and asbestos sheets. Left empty for years it was small and dilapidated, in worse condition than Cowper's Cottage was when she first saw it. Ellen couldn't bear the thought of having to do without water and electricity again. The round trip to the pump alone would be almost a mile.

Peter was quiet and withdrawn. He was outraged at having to leave the cottage and threatened to go to see Gilbert Reeve. After they'd seen the chalet he flatly refused to live there. Kathy had invited them to stay and he intended accepting her offer. He couldn't understand why Ellen wouldn't graciously do likewise. Ellen tried to explain but he was in no mood to listen.

She began to gather a few things together preparatory to moving. It crossed her mind that she could write to Robert and try to get him to intervene, but she concluded that it would be unfair to involve him. She tried to see Gilbert on two occasions but he wasn't at the farm when she called.

Finding a new job wasn't going well either, other than the odd hour here and there in the fields and a bit of shop work in Cromer occasionally. Running into Ronnie Slack in Annie's shop she asked him whether Gordon needed anyone. He shook his head and said that Gordon was looking for work. Ellen was astonished to learn that Gilbert had sacked him. She couldn't believe anyone could be that stupid. Mr Reeve had been the first to admit that the farm had improved immeasurably under Gordon's hand. Ellen wondered what on earth Gilbert Reeve thought he was playing at.

In the event Ellen's lack-lustre attempts at packing proved needless. A long, crisp brown envelope arrived at Cowper's Cottage one morning in the post. It was from Mr Reeve's solicitor. As she sat at the table with a cup of tea Ellen was astounded to read that in recognition of a long and much valued friendship Mr Reeve had left her something in his will. She was to receive a ring and peridot pendant that had belonged to Maria. There was also a set of antique wineglasses that Ellen had always admired. The real surprise though was lower down the page: Mr Reeve had left her Cowper's Cottage and the sum of £2,000.

The farmer had also left Peter £500 in the hope that it would go some way towards helping with further education. The solicitor continued that he would be pleased to see Ellen at his office at the earliest opportunity to finalize these matters. Ellen put her head in her hands and wept.

After a while she went upstairs and found a smarter frock, put on her face and then walked briskly down Back Lane in the hope that Kathy was at home and not busy with a perm or cut and blow-dry. She was in luck. Without any enthusiasm whatever Kathy was oiling her lawnmower preparatory to cutting the patch of grass that passed for a lawn in her back garden. She didn't have a customer until mid afternoon.

It was well after two o'clock when Ellen returned home, not a little unsteady from the several glasses of sherry that Kathy had insisted upon. As she walked up Back Lane she was glad that it was Kathy and not her who was about to embark on cutting someone's hair. She was equally glad that she wasn't the one about to receive the haircut.

A few weeks later Ellen arrived home from shopping in Cromer to the sight of Linda Hunt gesturing from her living-room window. Linda's front door was ajar. She had obviously been watching for Ellen's return.

'Ellen! Ellen!' She scurried down the path in a state of some excitement.

'I took this in, second post.' She brandished a small flat package. 'You'll never guess where it's from. America!' Her eyes sparkled and her lined and nut-brown face was unusually animated.

'Really?' Ellen stopped at the Hunts' gate. She took the neatly tied package and frowned. 'I wonder what it can be. I don't know anyone over there.' Sure enough it had US stamps.

'It says Reeve in the corner. There.' Linda pointed and gave Ellen a knowing glance. 'That would be Robert, I expect.'

'Hmm. I think it must be.'

Linda shrugged her bony shoulders, grinned and wrung her hands. 'Isn't it exciting?'

'Yes. Thank you for taking it in.' Ellen had her hand on her gate when she realized that Linda was beside herself with curiosity. She was going to be desperately disappointed if Ellen didn't open the parcel.

'Oh well, only one way to find out.' Ellen smiled at her neighbour and began to pick at the knots. Linda's fingers twitched in agitation.

'I've got some scissors here.' Impatient with Ellen's efforts, Linda produced a pair of dressmaking shears from her pinafore pocket.

Ellen laughed. 'You're well prepared, Linda. I'll say that for you. You never go anywhere without them, I bet.'

'I thought we might need them.' Linda grinned and had the grace to look a little embarrassed.

They placed the parcel on Ellen's garden wall and between them opened it up. It was double wrapped. Inside was a dark-blue box accompanied by a single sheet of cream deckle-edged paper. Ellen glanced briefly at the letter and put it in her pocket. She was not prepared to air its contents in the street. Pressing a small brass catch she opened the box. Inside, backed by dark blue velvet lay a silver and turquoise necklace and a pair of matching drop ear-rings. Pasted in the box lid was a discreet slip of paper from a jewellery store in Taos, New Mexico.

'Oh,' Linda gasped, her eyes out on stalks. 'My goodness, aren't they beautiful?'

'Gracious, yes they are.' Ellen carefully detached the necklace and an ear-ring. She passed the ear-ring to Linda.

'Oh, these are gorgeous, aren't they, and so different. You wouldn't get anything like them here. They're so elegant. You'll be able to wear them when you go out somewhere special.'

Ellen put on the necklace. 'Hmm. I'll have to get my ears done. How's that?'

'Oh, that is nice.' Linda adjusted the necklace and then held the ear-ring against the side of Ellen's head. She inclined her head to consider the effect. 'Yes. That's lovely. You want to get Poppy to do it. She did mine years ago with a needle and half a potato, in the currant field. She'll do it for half a crown or so. Poppy Mercer, you know, Claud and Biddy's daughter.'

'Ah.' Ellen frowned slightly. She could rather too readily bring to mind Poppy's nicotine-stained fingers and long grubby nails. 'I think I might go to the jeweller's in Cromer.'

'Oh, well. It'll amount to the same thing. Just cost you more.'

They admired the jewellery again.

'Oh, you are lucky.'

'Yes. I certainly am.' First the cottage, she thought, and now this. 'What a lovely surprise.'

She waited until she was inside before she read Robert's letter. He obviously knew about the cottage and congratulated her on joining the ranks of property owners. He said that by the time she received the parcel he would probably be back in London. On business in Albuquerque he had spent a day in Taos. He had been very taken with the Indian jewellery and thought that she might like some. He continued that he had greatly enjoyed seeing her although he could have wished that it had been under different circumstances, and that they mustn't leave it so long before meeting up again.

Ellen wondered what the present meant, if anything. After a few moments she concluded that it probably meant no more than Robert said in the letter. She sent a note to his London flat in reply, thanking him for the kind thought. Thereafter she sent him a Christmas card every year and even remembered his birthday on occasion. Robert didn't always manage a card at Christmas but he sent Ellen postcards from time to time. She received cards bearing views and a few words of greeting from all over the world. The stamps she kept for Philip since Peter wasn't at all interested in them.

NINETEEN

The inheritance changed the lives of Ellen and Peter. Ellen opened bank accounts for them both and set about extending and modernizing Cowper's Cottage. She prevailed on Hutchinson, the farmer who owned the field next door to sell her a strip of land adjoining the cottage. In addition to providing space for a garden it allowed for a much needed extension to Cowper's Cottage. Crowe's were engaged to do the work, turning the cottage into an L-shaped building. The old living-room became a decent-sized kitchen. Otherwise downstairs they gained a porch, a living-room and an inside lavatory. The stairs were relocated and a bedroom and bathroom created above. While she was at it, Ellen had the soak-away replaced by a septic tank and the far end of the shed converted into a garage.

Despite being an enthusiastic and able driver Ellen took a course of lessons. It was with some trepidation that she went up to Norwich one gloomy morning to take her test. She needn't have worried since she passed at her first attempt. Such was her excitement that in the afternoon she went into Cromer and bought the 1955 Morris Minor saloon in Clarendon grey that she had been coveting for some time. On their first outing in the car together Ellen drove Peter to Norwich to buy the Hofner electric guitar and Vox amplifier that he had long wanted. While they were in the shop he managed to inveigle Ellen into stumping up the money for a microphone and a stand too.

George and Janice weren't slow to notice the change in Ellen's fortunes. They began visiting. Ellen had seen nothing of them for months, but round they came now, asking questions, probing, Janice's piggy little eyes darting. She told them that Mr Reeve had left her the cottage and enough money to cover the alterations. Once they were convinced that there was nothing in it for them they stopped visiting as quickly as they had begun.

Ellen could have been forgiven for thinking that all her eggs were double-yolked when she succeeded in landing a rather good job as part-time receptionist at the country club in Cromer. The work was clean and easy, the pay was good, the flexible working arrangements suited her and transport was simple since she had her own car.

Having sacked Gordon Slack after a very public row, Gilbert Reeve brought in an old school crony to manage Pond Farm. Recently returned from years in Australia Noel Orr assured Gilbert that he was more than qualified to look after a piddling little farm in a Norfolk backwater. The remoteness of Orr's place of previous employment precluded obtaining references but Gilbert recalled that Noel had been a good laugh at school. Discovering that he enjoyed a drink or two at lunchtime further endeared him to Gilbert. After several familiarization tours and long discussions in the pub the new manager took over.

Orr soon set about distancing himself from Gilbert. He also shunned the fields and the farmhands. Closeted from 10.30 or so each morning in his office, chain-smoking Gold Flake and drinking tea laced with Teachers he shuffled paperwork into drawers. Mid morning he drove off in his Vauxhall

Wyvern, ostensibly for meetings with suppliers, buyers and merchants. It was usually the last anyone saw of him until the next morning. Far from working on farm business he was conducting a steamy affair with the sluttish divorcee who worked part time in the mill accounts office. Within weeks he moved in with her and from her cottage on the outskirts of the village the pair set about defrauding both the mill and Pond Farm.

Free from the tiresome day-to-day business of the farm Gilbert put his heart and soul into presenting himself in the county as a gentleman farmer and all-round good bloke. Resplendent in army fatigues and sunglasses he tore round the farm, the village and its environs in an old ex-military jeep. From the driving seat he exchanged wisecracks with the farmhands before stamping on the accelerator to roar off again. The labourers chuckled and shook their heads. 'He's a rum-un,' they said. 'He is an' all.'

At lunchtime he exchanged the jeep for his Rover and drove to the Conservative Club in Cromer. There he ate smoked salmon sandwiches or pork pie and drank beer and whisky chasers as he regaled the old buffers with reminiscences and tales of wartime derring-do in the Middle East. As the afternoon wore on he moved seamlessly into the multitude of grandiose schemes that he intended implementing at Pond Farm.

Over the next few years Gilbert abandoned arable farming in favour of more fashionable pursuits. He dabbled with chickens and then with mushrooms. After they failed he planted thousands of Christmas trees in partnership with someone he met at the golf club. He excavated lakes beside the millstream and stocked them with trout. He reared pheasants and arranged shoots. There was a brief but disastrous foray into orchids. Elsewhere people were doing very nicely thank you, engaged in those very activities. All of Gilbert's initiatives foundered while he sat in the Conservative Club.

The morale of the farm workforce was at rock bottom. Hitherto energetic and trustworthy farm hands slacked off. With no supervision and direction they went absent, they hid and they pilfered. They grew accustomed to going through the motions and took it badly on the rare occasions that Gilbert or Orr demanded action. Gradually the members of the old workforce left in despair. One after another Johnny-come-lately appeared to take their places. Without exception the newcomers had little knowledge or expertise and absolutely no loyalty.

Farm machinery, buildings and other monuments to Gilbert's stupidity soon lay about the property abandoned, idle and rusting. Other examples of poor husbandry abounded. Hedges that had flourished since Saxon times were rooted out on a whim. Gilbert filled in drainage ditches and had ancient footpaths and rights of way ploughed up or fenced off. He was frequently in dispute with the public and neighbouring farmers. Finally he antagonized his suppliers and customers and fell out with the bank.

*

Peter left school in 1963, taking a job for the summer as a kitchen porter at Butlin's Holiday camp in Skegness. After securing his £9 bonus for seeing out his six week contract he went home for a couple of weeks and was then off again, this time to London to begin a degree course in History. Philip had also done well with his A Levels and had been accepted to study dentistry. They left the village together and for the first few months shared a flat in Crouch End. It was during the spring term that Peter dropped out of university and left London to accompany his girlfriend to Manchester. She was the singer in a band and he was hopeful of making something of a career in music.

Kathy was leaning on the bar reading the paper with a cup of coffee at her elbow as the first customer of the morning arrived. The sun had just gone in and sleet hammered on the windows as the door opened.

'Morning, Tom. Cold enough for you?'

Just inside the door of the Lord Nelson Tom Clarke took off his creaking oilskins and woolly hat. He opened the door again, shook them and then closed it quickly.

'Good Lord, Kathy, it's bitter out there. Bloody April showers. It was beautifully sunny just a minute ago. Look at it now.' He hung up his oilskins and went over to the fire, turned his back to it and warmed his hands and buttocks. 'Oh, that's better. It's nice and warm in here. I'd keep this well stoked up if I were you.'

'Have you just been out?'

'Been out since four. Give us a pint, gal. Better make it two. Frank will be in any minute.'

'I will, but in the meantime this'll warm you up, give you a bit of a laugh.'

'What's that?'

'In the paper this morning, about the minefield.'

'Oh, what now?'

'It says, and I quote "that a clerical oversight at the Ministry of Defence has kept the beach closed to the public for six months longer that it need have been. A limited clearance certificate should have been issued six months ago, in October 1965. It seems to have been pigeonholed at the Ministry of Defence." '

'That'll be right.' Frank shook his head in mock bewilderment. 'Still, what's another six months when we've waited all this time?'

'You'll be able to bring *Isabelle* and *Lucy* back, won't you.'

'I don't know.' Frank looked sceptical. 'I'm not sure there's anywhere we could get down now, nor whether there's anywhere to pull the boats up. Cliff's changed a lot since we were last down there. We're pretty well fixed where we are. And anyway, if I went down that cliff now I seriously doubt whether I'd ever be able to get back up again. I have enough difficulty getting up the stairs to go to bed.'

'Yes. I think I'd have a bit of a job myself.'

On 1 August 1966 the beach reopened. It had finally come to pass after being closed for twenty-six years. The authorities considered that the beach was as safe as any other on the east coast. Well over 500 mines had been located and detonated by the Bomb Disposal Unit. The newspaper reported that the beach was open; however the cliffs remained a dangerous risk. The public was warned not to climb or trespass on them. People were further advised not to touch any unusual metal object, but to report it immediately.

After some initial excitement and enthusiasm it quickly dawned on the locals that if the cliffs weren't safe there would be no way down to the sands from within the village. Anyone wanting to go down to the beach would have to go either to the depot to the east or two and a half miles to a neigh-bouring village in the west. The fishermen quickly concluded that there was no point in even thinking of moving their boats.

One or two enterprising souls attempted to dig out a gangway but all efforts foundered for one reason or another. There was an understandable apprehension over remaining ordnance as well as fear of the authorities, the potential for disaster from cliff falls and the lack of permissions to use land on the cliff tops. In the face of these drawbacks the chance of holidaymak-ers returning in any numbers to the village looked as remote as ever.

By the early 1970s Gilbert Reeve's capital, his manager and the workforce had all gone. He was reduced to selling off what remained of the farm bit by bit until nothing but the house remained. Eventually he had to sell that too.

He moved in with Poppy Mercer who had been left to her own devices since the death of her father Claud. Their bedroom window overlooked the paddock at Pond Farm in which Maria Reeve died. It was rumoured that Gilbert tried his hand at knife grinding with Claud's old bike but no one actually saw him thus engaged. Gilbert settled down to a very orderly life, dividing his waking hours between the public bar of the Lord Nelson and the grubby sofa in Poppy's living-room.

Ellen almost ran over him one afternoon as she was driving past the pub on her way to work. Waiting to turn out of Back Lane she watched him wobble out of the Lord Nelson car-park on an old ladies' bicycle. Having spotted his condition she was particularly circumspect as she drove up behind him. She had just made up her mind to pass, giving him a wide berth when his foot slipped off a pedal; he lurched across in front of her and fell off his bike. Ellen stopped, backed up and parked.

Gilbert lay in the road, helpless. He was so drunk that he couldn't get up.

Ellen ran to help. Heavy as he was she got him up and sat him on the bank at the roadside, where he promptly vomited over his shoes. She picked up his bicycle and propped it on the bank beside him.

'Gilbert Reeve, what on earth do you think you're doing?'

Gilbert looked up and attempted to focus on his saviour.

'Who's that?' He wiped his mouth on his sleeve and squinted up at Ellen, his mouth open.

'It's me, Ellen. Are you all right? Have you hurt yourself?'

'Oh.' Gilbert laughed. He snorted and then blew his nose, pressing his right nostril with his finger and blowing, expelling the contents on to the grass beside him. He repeated the procedure with his left nostril.

He sniffed. 'Hello, sexy. I'm all right. I'm in the pink.' Gilbert gave a short laugh and then spat in the dust at the roadside.

'You're a disgrace, Gilbert. What am I going to do with you?'

Gilbert leered up at her. 'Ah well, now you're asking. You could always give us a quick poke.' He held up his arms. 'Come on. Do yourself a favour. I bet you haven't had a good seeing to for a while.'

Ellen looked at him, disgusted. She shook her head and backed away.

'Ah, still the pig you always were, Gilbert. How you ever got to be an officer I'll never know. You don't have any idea how to behave. Your mother and father. . . .'

Gilbert's arms dropped wearily. He leered up at Ellen and pursed his lips. 'Go on, give us a feel. You know I've always fancied you.'

Ellen made to leave him and then turned back.

'Well, you've got a very funny way of showing it, Gilbert Reeve. It was a complete waste of time your parents sending you away to school. They'd weep if they could see you now.' She turned away. 'Well, you can just get on with it.'

Ellen set off for the pub and called back over her shoulder. 'I'll tell them in the bar and they can come and see to you. They were happy enough to get you into this state. They can jolly well come and sort you out.'

Despite numerous enquiries, including one to the local Member of Parliament, Kathy never heard anything further from Hoda, the nurse who had been caring for her husband, Dave. Eventually she received a missive from the RAF saying that Dave remained missing and now had to be presumed dead.

After a brief period of depression at the end of the war Kathy was rarely without male company. All of her *affaires-de-coeur* were discreet and conducted with decorum. With Philip away at school and then in London it could have been a lonely life. During the sixties she took up with Bryan, a brewery representative. He'd been visiting the Lord Nelson for years. He was older than Kathy, a quiet, retiring, self-effacing man, and perhaps a surprising soul for Kathy to find so attractive. Bryan was one of those ruddy-faced, sandy-haired men destined always to look much younger than his age.

He was married, but his wife had been in a home for the mentally ill for many years. There were no children. He continued to live in the bungalow that he had shared with his wife but he often stayed until late in the night at the Lord Nelson. It was a way of life that seemed to suit them all.

Kathy had worked in some guise in the hotel from the time she was four-teen. First taken on as a part-time scullery maid, she had also worked as chambermaid, waitress, barmaid and cook. Over a period of forty years she succeeded in making herself indispensable to a succession of landlords. When the incumbent retired in 1975 she successfully applied for the job herself. There was little that she didn't know about the hotel or the trade but by then the pub had reached a very low ebb.

Always energetic and brimming with ideas she set about rejuvenating the place. Down came the arty-farty nets, corks, floats and crab pots that festooned the walls of the public bar. She put a carpenter to work repairing and refinishing the original wooden tables and chairs that had been stored out in the garages. To much acclaim they gradually replaced the unloved red vinyl, chrome and glass that had been brought in only months earlier. She also introduced a menu for bar food with the intention of eventually reopening the dining-room if things took off.

Kathy and Philip were sitting companionably at the breakfast table when the phone rang. Philip was poring over the local newspaper and eating toast and honey. His mother was drinking tea and flicking through a magazine while she waited for her toenails to dry. The sun shone in through the window and the radio quacked in the corner. Through the open door in the utility room the washing machine was in the middle of a spin cycle and the budgerigars were twittering and tweeting in the background.

'Get that will you, Phil? I'm just going to bring in those cloths.' After a cursory glance at her toenails Kathy pushed her feet into her slippers and stood up. 'If it's the brewery tell them we need two but tomorrow will be fine.' Kathy was still in her dressing-gown, her hair was wrapped in a towel and she was without the benefit of make-up.

'Righty-ho.' Philip finished his mouthful and put down the paper. He wiped his mouth carefully on his napkin and leaned across to pick up the phone on the dresser behind him.

'Hello?' He paused a moment.

'No. This is her son. Can I. . . ?' He listened intently.

'Oh, yes. Of course . . . yes.' The caller spoke at some length.

'Oh?' Frowning, Philip stood up. 'Oh.' He sat down again, suddenly. 'Oh, I see.'

The caller continued.

'Right, well, thank you for letting . . . Yes. Yes. Thank you again.'

The caller rang off. Philip stood up to replace the telephone but then sat down suddenly on the table edge. He remained motionless for some minutes. Eventually he leaned over to the dresser and replaced the phone.

'Who was that?' Kathy bustled in with a wicker basket of dried washing. 'Was it the brewery?'

'No.' Philip paused a moment. 'It was Cavell House . . . the . . . er . . . the convalescent home.' He got up, checked that there was water in the kettle and switched it on.

'Oh. What. . . ?' Kathy began folding up tea towels. 'What did they want? Everything all—' She turned suddenly and looked at Philip. He had his back to her. With his arms braced on the draining board he was staring out of the kitchen window. Kathy saw his shoulders begin to shake. He gasped once and then turned to face her, his face crumpled into a mask of shock and grief.

'Ellen's dead,' he whispered. He gasped again. 'She died . . . early this morning.'

Kathy stopped what she was doing and stared at her son.

'She was dead when they went to see her this morning.'

'But. . . .'

'Brain haemorrhage, they think.'

Kathy sat down hard just as the kettle came to the boil.

Peter and Margaret managed to clamber down the cliffs at a point not far from the safe path that Nick and Ellen had used during the war.

'If you're a very good girl I'll show you how to catch a crab with your bare hands,' Peter said.

'And I'll do the water into wine bit, shall I? Would sir prefer red, white or rosé?'

'No, seriously. We can have crab for tea. There's absolutely nothing quite so fine as a fresh crab, a little vinegar and bread and butter. Except two fresh crabs, of course.'

'Of course, what?'

'Better than one.'

'Don't they catch them in pots?'

'They do, but Mum showed me where to look when the tide's out. The crabs hide up under the clay sills at the edge of the lows. If you feel along carefully you can find them. You have to watch your fingers, but it's pretty straightforward. I'm not sure but I think it was Harry who showed her how to do it. I suppose it might have been her brother John. It's one of those things, if you didn't know about it, it would never occur to you.'

They spent an enjoyable time on the beach but found absolutely no sign of any crabs. By the time they reached the cliff tops again they were both exhausted and very wet. But they were laughing. They'd had a good time.

'You'll have to show me that trick with the crabs again another time,' laughed Margaret.

'I'd rather show you another little trick I can do, when we get back.'

'Mm, that sounds promising.'

Arm in arm they hurried back to Cowper's Cottage.

At four o'clock in the afternoon Philip and Kathy drove to Cavell House to collect Ellen's personal effects. They were both dressed very smartly but sombrely. Ellen's suitcase and a plastic bag were waiting in the office for collection. A nursing auxiliary got Philip to sign for them. Of Margaret there was no sign. Kathy wanted to go to Ellen's room and became upset when Philip said that Ellen wouldn't be there and that there was nothing more that Kathy could do for her. Kathy stopped and stared at her son. Tears welled in her eyes.

'Do you think I don't know that?' she screeched. 'Do you think I'm stupid?' She took a few steps and then turned again and looked at her son. 'I just wanted to do it for me.' She pounded her hand on her chest and burst into tears. 'I just wanted . . . to see . . . where she was . . . for me.' Bent double, Kathy was overcome by racking sobs. 'It was just . . . for me.'

Philip put his arm round his mother.

'I'm sorry, Mum. It's just I thought that Ellen's bed was probably already in use by someone else.' He wiped his eyes. 'Come on.'

Eventually Kathy straightened. She sniffed, dabbed at her eyes and nodded. 'I expect so.'

Philip led her back to the car. As he put the case into the boot Kathy removed Ellen's book from the plastic bag. Once they were under way she opened the envelope that had served as a bookmark.

'There's nothing here. Where's the letter, and the photo?'

'Ellen gave them to me a day or two ago.'

'Well, you might have mentioned it.'

'I'd forgotten it, to tell you the truth. She had started to reply but couldn't write properly. My guess is that she was in trouble then. She asked me if I would finish the letter and post it to the woman in California. I remember thinking that she seemed rather odd. Certainly not herself. Best thing we can do is give it all to Peter. He can decide what he wants to do with it. Isn't it odd that no one's seen Nick since 1953 though?'

'Yes.' After a moment Kathy resumed. 'I remember him turning up at the pub, out of nowhere. He was going to see someone about a job, I think. He dropped in for pint and a sandwich, for old times' sake he said. I have to say he wasn't looking great. He looked rough. When I told him Ellen was up Back Lane he couldn't finish up his drink and leave fast enough.'

'Yes. We saw him up at Peter's.' Philip laughed suddenly. 'Maybe Ellen did for him. I bet she went for him after we left and she's put him under the patio. Wasn't it about then that she had a bit of landscaping done?'

'No, that was years later. . . .' Kathy snorted with suppressed laughter. 'That's a terrible thing. . . .'

'I know, I'm only joking.' Philip patted his mother's hand. 'We saw him later outside the pub. He was trying to hitch a lift down to the depot. We'd just come back from the cliffs.'

'Makes you wonder what happened to him though, doesn't it?'

'We'll probably never know. A surprising number of people disappear every year. You read about them in the paper occasionally. It happens more than you'd think. Maybe he was fed up, going to start a new life somewhere else, with someone else. People do.'

'Wasn't that when we had the floods? January 1953? You know, the real bad floods when—'

'Oh. Yes. I think you're right.'

TWENTY

Early in October Peter packed a bag, took a taxi to Cromer and caught the train to Norwich and then on down to London. After checking in at the Soho office he went to see Abigail. He hoped that they might spend some time together at the flat to sort out the last knockings of what had been their marriage. They had barely spoken since Ellen's funeral. In truth he realized that they had hardly exchanged a dozen words in over a year.

To Peter's irritation Abigail continued to work and then she spent much of each evening on the phone. Finally she packed a bag and hurried off next morning on a buying trip to Italy. She telephoned Peter from the airport to say that she had decided to take some holiday. After Italy she was going on to Thailand. She didn't expect to be back for several weeks.

So with a quick exchange of 'goodbyes, see you's' and 'take care's' on the telephone it was all over. Peter could see no point in hanging around Abigail's flat on his own so the same day he collected a van and packed his belongings. After leaving his keys on the hall table next morning he drove up to North Norfolk. After he had moved Ellen's car and parked it in front of the cottage there was plenty of room to store his stuff in the garage. Much of it would go when he got around to sorting it out properly.

It had been a lonely and frustrating few days but he had had time to make a decision or two. Ellen had left him the cottage and he had decided that he would live there. His job required a degree of itineracy and Cowper's Cottage would make an ideal base. Not living in London would also be an advantage. He had never really liked the place. Even as a student he had been glad to leave the capital.

And then there was Margaret. They had been enjoying each other's company enormously since they met at Ellen's funeral. Peter had been sufficiently happy that he occasionally found himself feeling guilty, it being so soon after his mother's death. Margaret had given herself so enthusiastically and so often that he felt that there could hardly be much in the way of a workable marriage between her and her husband. They hadn't discussed any future together but he was hopeful despite Kathy's scepticism. Sitting in the bar one lunchtime the subject had come up. It was Kathy's view that Margaret seemed rather nervy and brittle.

'I should be a bit careful, if I were you,' she said.

Several weeks passed. Peter was on his usual lunchtime stool leafing through the paper and carrying on a desultory conversation with Kathy as she polished glasses. It was early and they were alone.

'Robert was in yesterday evening,' Kathy said. 'Reeve,' she elaborated unnecessarily.

'Oh, yes.'

'He arrived the day before. I had to tell him about your mum.'

Peter looked up from the sports pages.

'Oh yes. I meant to tell you. He put a note through the door. You know, condolences.'

'He was terribly upset. After I told him he went and sat in the corner by himself. He spent ages looking out of the window. He said last night that he went down to the churchyard to see the grave.'

Kathy tutted and busied herself with raffle tickets and money for a moment. 'I do wish they'd put these in the proper place . . . He's bought Clyffesyde, the Popes' old place. Says it needs a lot of work.'

'I bet.' Peter wrinkled his brow. 'The house must be fairly close to the cliff edge these days, surely? Much of the back garden went down the cliff years ago. There can't be much left behind the house.'

'No. You can see it from the upstairs windows here.' Kathy gestured at the ceiling. 'It must be less than a hundred feet from the back door to the edge.'

'Doesn't that bother him?'

'He says it won't come any closer, not appreciably, or not for years anyway. Not since they've put in the revetments and breakwaters on the beach. He says it'll stabilize the cliffs. He's had it surveyed and all properly looked into.'

'Ha!' Peter chuckled. 'Have you seen that cliff fall just the other side of the plantation? It's punched a bloody great hole through the revetment. There must be fifty feet or more that's been buried. Once the sea gets to work. . . .' He looked sceptical. 'I'm not sure I'd be quite so confident.'

'The house is standing on marl apparently.'

'Oh, well. I suppose that might help.'

'Anyway,' Kathy continued brightly, 'he's going to change the name back to Cliff House. That's what it used to be years ago.'

'Well, that'll make all the difference,' Peter laughed. 'That'll certainly keep the cliffs from falling down.'

'No. You know what I mean.' Kathy took a mock swipe at Peter's head across the bar with a tea towel. He swayed back on his stool and grinned.

'He's got his son with him. Nice lad, Richard, or Richie as he calls him.'

'How old is he?'

'Six or seven. He's just started school so he's going to be here for the foreseeable future.'

'Hmm.' Peter turned over his paper. 'Where are they staying? Here?'

'No. They're in the house, in that annexe where Mrs Pope's sister lived for a while.'

'It'll be good to have someone in there again. It's amazing how quickly a place goes to rack and ruin if it's left. And Cliff House is certainly an improvement on Clyffesyde. I always thought it was a dreadful name. Hardly anyone could spell it.' Peter drained his pint and nodded as Kathy picked up the glass.

'Yes. Please. And whatever you're...' He stretched, scratched his stomach and yawned.

'Oh, dear. All this relaxing and sea air. It's terrible. I could get used to this.'

He laughed. 'It's alarming just how quickly a nice comfortable routine sneaks up on you. Get up late, couple of rashers in the pan, wander down to the shop, back, coffee, read the paper, tidy up a bit, down here for a pint and a sandwich, wander along the cliff tops, bit of fresh air, home, mug of tea and a piece of your excellent fruit cake, a page or two of the book, dinner, watch a little bit of TV, etc, etc, and so to bed.'

'Yes.' Kathy studied Peter for a moment. 'I shouldn't get too cosy if I were you. You'll have to go back to work soon, surely.'

'Well, not for a bit. I don't need to start again until the New Year.'

'That long? What on earth are you going to do with yourself until then?'

'Oh, I'll manage. I'm enjoying it. It's a long time since I've had a proper holiday, a real change of pace. Three years. You forget I spend most of my time away, in hotels and motels. Living away from home, or else I'm travelling. I'm sick to death of motels, hotels, airports and airlines. This,' he spread his hands and looked about the bar, 'this is really nice. It's a treat.'

Kathy nodded and returned to the raffle tickets which were still causing her some disquiet.

'Have you heard from Abigail at all?'

'No. Well, nothing of interest. We shuffle bits of paper back and forth for signature. Nothing to say to each other these days. We're almost done now though.'

'What about Margaret?' Kathy caught Peter's eye. 'We haven't seen much of her recently.'

'No, she's been busy. She was supposed to be coming over at the weekend but I haven't heard from her for a day or two. I'll give her a call if she doesn't ring.'

The week before Christmas Robert was finding it difficult dividing his time between the builders, the plumber, the electrician, the architect and Richie, his son. It hadn't been difficult while the boy was at school all day but now the holidays were upon them Richie needed entertaining. He had some friends in the village and was pretty good at keeping himself occupied but Robert appreciated that his son needed and deserved time with him.

They'd taken to going fishing together on the beach. Other than for the need to secure lugworms for bait it took little preparation. Robert had bought them each a rod and tackle and found a man just outside Cromer who sold worms at the roadside. The cost of buying the bait seemed entirely reasonable set against the labour and sheer unreliability of trying to dig the worms themselves.

At the bottom of the garden at Cliff House the cliff face had slumped to form three quite gentle inclines all the way down to the beach. Robert was particularly thankful for this. While Richie ran up and down the cliff with some abandon he found the descent easy enough but felt every one of his sixty-two years as he tried to struggle up the cliff face on the way home.

Today he was standing out on a sandbank. The tide had turned and he was aware that he would need to keep an eye on the lows filling up behind him. Their rods were propped side by side in metal stands stuck vertically in the sand. Robert stood between them staring out to sea. Every once in a while he cast a glance up at the rod tips but they did no more than quiver predictably with each wave that swashed gently towards him on the beach. Richie had tired of fishing and was building a dam at the foot of the cliff where a trickle of groundwater flowed out to form a wet fan on the sands.

Robert was sad. That Ellen had died was devastating. He'd looked forward to returning to the village with much impatience after that evening with her in the Lord Nelson. Then Kathy dropped the bombshell. He had heard the words and understood but it had taken some time for the awful truth to sink in. She was gone. He would never ever set eyes on her again. And he'd missed her funeral. Missed her funeral? Ha! He'd missed her for the best part of a lifetime.

She'd put him straight when they'd met at the Lord Nelson. Her face had burned with indignation. She'd blinked back angry tears. How could he have been so stupid, believing Gilbert all those years ago? All that time wasted. Well, perhaps not wasted, just Ellen-less. And his father, how could he have believed it of him? Yet another waste.

Robert had felt really down since arriving back. Every once in a while he found himself staring at nothing. Sometimes he wept. Now he could no longer see the horizon. It was a blur through his tears.

Hearing Richie splashing through the low behind him, he quickly wiped his eyes. He felt for his handkerchief and blew his nose.

'Dad! Have you got any sweets? Is there any drink left?'

Richie puffed up alongside him.

'Have you caught anything?'

'No.' Robert looked up again at the rod tips. 'I'll give it a little bit longer, if you're OK, then we'll call it a day.' The boy nodded and wiped his nose on his sleeve. Robert took a Mars Bar from his pocket and handed it to his son.

'There's still some squash in the bag if you want some.'

'Oh, Dad. It's got a tear and it's starting to melt.'

'It'll be fine.' Robert's fingers had been working away at the Mars Bar in his pocket in his anguish. 'Are you all right for a bit longer?'

'Yes.' The boy nodded his dark head and eyed his father as he bit off a piece of the Mars Bar. He had the same tanned complexion and blue eyes as Robert.

'Do you want a bit?' He proffered the chocolate bar. Robert shook his head.

'It would be good if we could get a cod again.'

'Yes. I don't really know but I think it's a bit early for cod. They're not usually about yet, or not in any numbers. Someone told me that, one of the workmen. I think that one we caught was probably just a fluke.'

'Perhaps it was lost.'

'Yes, sadly for it.'

Richie cavorted about on the sandbank for a moment and then stopped abruptly. He rooted in his jacket pocket.

'Look what I found.'

He pulled out a tangle of string, several small shells and a piece of iron pyrites before finding the item he sought.

From the cliff top Peter watched the two figures below on the otherwise deserted beach. They were too far away for him to be certain but he thought that it was probably Robert and his son. He wondered where they had been able to get down the cliff. They looked happy and animated. The boy was capering about energetically. Peter watched for a moment before turning away to skirt a new bite out of the cliff top. The pair below disappeared from his view behind a headland.

Christmas was only days away. It looked as though he would be spending it with Kathy and Phil. He hadn't seen or heard from Margaret for some time, but he no longer expected to. Unable to contact her he had gone in desperation to Cavell House and caught her as she was leaving one evening. They'd sat side by side in the front of the Mini and she'd told him that she was pregnant. Convinced that the child was her husband's she had decided that she couldn't possibly see Peter again. She apologized for not letting him know but she said she hadn't really known what she wanted to do and wasn't sure that she could trust herself with him. Peter wondered whether he could have fathered the child but Margaret was adamant that it could only have been her husband.

So there it was. He had lost Margaret, with whom he thought there was some possibility of a future, although to be fair, nothing was ever promised. What passed for his marriage to Abigail was over. The last time he'd phoned her someone called Gianfranco answered and told him in broken English that Abigail was in the shower. He'd heard whispering and had convinced himself that he'd caught Abigail hissing at the Italian to say that she was out. There had been a moment of stifled laughter before the Latin put the phone down.

His mother was dead. He had lost her after not having seen her for an age. Now he was living alone in her cottage. He never knew his father, apart from that brief meeting in January 1953, over twenty-five years ago. In view of the fact that no one had seen his father in all that time and no one knew anything of his whereabouts it seemed a remote chance that he would ever materialize. Peter wondered whether Nick knew that he was his son. He had wondered the same thing many times. The conclusion that he kept returning to was that his father hadn't liked him for some reason or was disappointed in him in some way. Ah well, he thought. That was his loss. Frankly he didn't care much one way or the other now, but it rankled.

It also irked him to learn that Nick had a daughter who had known him, at least until his great disappearing act of 1953. Peter had pored over the photograph that had been enclosed with Louise Stark's letter to Ellen and had been jealous. He thought he might go to see Louise in Ventura next time he was in California. It was only a short distance up the road from LA and she obviously knew their father whereas he did not.

Peter stepped over a sagging loop of rusty barbed wire and nearly turned his ankle on something beneath the rough grass. He kicked at it and then stooped to lever up the rotting remains of a red painted signboard. DANGE MINES KEEP OU it said in white capitals. A piece of rotten edging that had obviously been home to numerous woodlice and a worm came away in his hand. He let the edging and board drop back to their resting place.

Wiping his hands on his handkerchief he wandered over to the edge of the cliffs. Below him Robert and his son were visible again. They were huddled together over something. Glancing away to his right Peter could just make out a couple of arc lamps twinkling in the fading light at the depot.

Richie held out his find, a rectangle of metal, corroded, dented and newly scratched where he had tried to clean it. Minus its lid, it was quite clearly a cigarette lighter.

Robert took it and examined it. He rubbed it between his fingers and then on the leg of his jeans.

'That's interesting. Where did you find it?'

'It was in the stones at the bottom of the cliff, where I was playing.'

'Here. Hang on to it for a minute. Let me. . . .' Robert gave it back to his son. He felt in his inside pocket for his reading glasses and put them on.

'That's better. Now we can have a proper look.' He took the lighter from his son and after a moment went to the edge of the low behind them. Crouching at the waters edge he swished the lighter about and then rubbed it vigorously. As he stood up and dried it on his sleeve he glanced quickly at the sea that was now edging over the sandbank to their left and into the low.

'We've only got a few more minutes here and then we'll have to get back on the other side of this low. We don't want to get cut off.' He held the lighter up in the fading light.

'It's an old Zippo. It's American. There's something written on it.' Robert peered closely at the lighter. 'I can't make it out.'

'Let's have a look,' Richie took the lighter and studied it intently.

'Can you read it? What does it say?' Robert took down his rod and began to reel in his line. 'I must say it looks remarkably well preserved. It must be thirty, no, nearer forty years old, I'd guess. If it is that old it must have been buried in clay or something of that sort.'

'There's a number and some bigger letters.'

'Yes. Can you make out any of the inscription?'

'It looks like a capital 'I' and an 'O.' No, it's a 'C.' There's something else.

It's the same on the other side. Oh, with an 'N.' So it would be 'N-I-C'
something. Nice! It could be nice.'

'I suppose so. Shall I bring your line in?'

'Yes, please.'

'What about the number? Can you make it out?'

'Yes. It says something 'AT' and little numbers.'

'That will be the patent number, I expect.'

'Oh, yes. Pat.'

Robert finished reeling in Richie's line and began gathering up the rest of
the fishing gear.

'There was a fellow here during the war had a Zippo lighter. He was in
the Lord Nelson some evenings. He used to call it something. What on earth
was it?'

'Do you want it?'

'What?

'Do you want it? The lighter. Do you want to keep it?'

'No. I don't think so.' Robert straightened up and put his hands to the
small of his back. He peered up at the cliff tops.

'Someone up top.'

Richie turned to look and immediately waved at the lone figure silhouet-
ted against the fading light. The figure eventually waved back.

'Windproof Beauty.'

'What?'

'Windproof Beauty. That's what the fellow called his lighter.'

'That's a funny thing to call it.'

'I think it was marketed as that. It was actually known as the Windproof
Beauty. Presumably it would spark up and stay alight in the wind.'

'Did you have one, Dad?'

'No, I've never had a lighter. I never smoked. Never needed one.'

'Do you want it, then?'

Robert shook his head and bent to pick up his fishing bag.

'We'd better get going. If we stay any longer we're going to have to take
our boots off and frankly I don't much fancy putting my feet in ice-cold
seawater.'

Richie held the lighter in front of his face and peered at it intently. He
gave it a brief kiss.

'Bye-bye then, you Windproof Beauty,' he whispered. He drew back his
arm and hurled the lighter far out into the sea.

Robert paused and both he and his son watched to see where it came
down. Peter was too far away to see the splash.